STIENBOEK

Hope you enjoy!

Dan Powers

A NOVEL

DAN POWERS

outskirts press

Stienboek
A Novel

v5.0

Outskirts Press, Inc.
http://www.outskirtspress.com

ISBN: 978-1-9772-7285-0

PRINTED IN THE UNITED STATES OF AMERICA

Dedicated to all the teachers, administrators, and school staff with whom I've had the honor to work.

In 1951, the year after I was born, John Steinbeck was working on a new novel. He began each day's work by writing a rambling mix of domestic and personal minutiae interlaced with thoughts, plans, comments, and fears about the book. Addressed to his editor and good friend Pascal "Pat" Covici, the letters were published in 1969, a year after the author's death, as *Journal of a Novel: The East of Eden Letters.*

In the early 1970s, as a twenty-something, I stumbled across the publication. For the first time, I saw the creative process as something human and messy rather than inspired from on high. Most importantly, it felt possible for the first time, and I wanted to try my hand at the work. In that trying, I have found much enjoyment over the years in my various attempts to give shape to my own minutiae, thoughts, plans, and fears.

So, with my gratitude to Mr. Steinbeck and his abundant talent, *Stienboek* is my belated thank you.

Dan Powers
June, 2024

EDENTON AREA SCHOOL DISTRICT

The Fox Valley watershed in Northeast Wisconsin is drained by the Fox River and its major tributary, the Wolf River. The Fox River consists of an upper and lower section which, because of the common misperception that rivers in the northern hemisphere always run south, often confuses area students studying local geography. The misunderstanding occurs because when referring to a river, the terms "upper" and "lower" relate to elevation, not direction. In the case of the Fox River, the upper or higher elevated branch is south of its lower branch. This feature gives the river the uncommon distinction of flowing north. Between the two branches lies shallow Lake Winnebago, the state's largest inland lake. The Fox enters the lake from the west, emerges from its northwest corner where it enters Little Lake Butte des Morts before heading northeast and finally flowing into Green Bay and eventually Lake Michigan.

After the glaciers, but well before the common era began, the area was home to thousands of Native Americans from multiple cultures. For millennia, the Fox River carried these ancient travelers along two hundred miles of pristine prairie, grasslands, and stretches of thick woods and forested areas. With only a minor two-mile portage between it and the Wisconsin River, it served as a continuous water route between the Great Lakes and the Mississippi River.

Of course, time brings change. And the nature of change causes stress for humans in the form of perceived and real threats to the status quo and to what they hold dear. For the indigenous cultures, the valley, and the river itself, change came in the form of French explorers followed by the trappers and traders who plied their paddles along these same river routes. Beginning in 1634, explorer Jean Nicolet arrived and was followed forty years later by Marquette and Joliet who gave the ancient waterway its current name, Rivière aux Renards (River of the Foxes), a reference to one of the doomed indigenous cultures.

Then came the settlers and farmers who plowed the grasslands and cut the trees to supply the timber to build the houses, towns, and cities along the river leading eventually to a thriving lumber and paper industry. By the late 17th century, an ever-growing trickle of European farmers began flowing into the area. Among them, in the early 1830s, a group of like-minded Germans – which included members of the Stienboek family – headed west from the denser southeast urban centers of what would, in 1848, become the state of Wisconsin. Arriving in the Fox River Valley, they took up their plows around what became the farming village of Westen (German for west), which in time, and as more English-speaking people took up residency, became Westown.

Meanwhile, on the opposite bank of the Fox River, a logging operation and a new flour mill began to flourish and attract various associated riverfront businesses, all of which needed employees. This, in turn, drew more residents who eventually organized into the town and later the city of Edenton.

Westown managed to remain an agrarian unincorporated hamlet on the east side of the river until the mid-twentieth century, at which time, the state government deemed it necessary to construct a bridge across the Fox, creating a narrow but inextricable link between Edenton and Westown. As anticipated, traffic increased, requiring major improvements to the nearby state and county highways.

In the eyes of some, this was progress. For others, it further irritated a long insistent itch under the collars of those on both sides of the river who tended to distrust, even disdain, change or variation of any sort. A few years later, Edenton, Westown, and some other area small schools were prodded by multiple factors and pressures to consolidate into the Edenton Area School District.

Predictably, local frictions again bubbled like hoar frost from the ground, causing even more previously unquestioned common values to be questioned. What could be more human than that?

STIENBOEK V. STEINBECK

As a teacher and high school principal, John Stienboek was a highly respected fellow, as was his father who had established and run a successful plumbing business and been a longtime supervisor on the city council, as well as a multi-term school board member.

When appointed as the first Edenton Area School District administrator in 1958, John was also known to be a steady man who believed in the educational importance of tradition and religion and not coddling unruly students, or for that matter, teachers. Nor was he likely to get sucked into all the national controversies caused by the 1954 Brown v. Board of Education ruling which forced the desegregation of schools. The community appreciated and approved of John's glacial approach to the social, political, and educational fads foisted on schools by the government and the trickle of newcomers moving into the district.

In 1990, when John Stienboek had his name posthumously placed on the newly renovated Edenton High School building, he, even in death, ignited another revival of a long-running family controversy. This was the second time John had caused the debate to spontaneously combust. The first was in 1961 when the area towns reluctantly and grudgingly merged their schools into a single new district, and John was named its first superintendent.

The point of contention was that the branch of the family to which John belonged, who mainly lived on the west side of the Fox River in and around the small city of Edenton, pronounced their surname the same as the Nobel Prize-winning author John Steinbeck. In 1963, an aunt even claimed that the Steinbecks and Stienboeks were originally one clan back in the Prussian maritime province of Pomerania, from which both the novelist's and the Stienboek families had emigrated. The claim, however, remained but a theory. No documentation was ever provided.

By contrast, the more rural-oriented side of the Stienboek clan, many of whom owned tracts of land on the east side of the Fox River around Westown and Cooper, adamantly stuck to what they claimed to be the original family pronunciation of Steen–bach. They considered John's family version of the pronunciation to be an existential threat to family, identity, and tradition. They could not fathom how or why such a thing had been allowed to take root. After all, a name was sacred. Like long-held religious, social, or political beliefs, it was not an either-or proposition.

They were quick to correct anyone: neighbor, stranger, clerk, or solicitor, as to the proper pronunciation. Neither would they abide the wishy-washy who tried to thread the needle by alternating the pronunciation depending upon whom they were talking to. To their way of thinking, one could not have a foot in both camps. Being of two minds was not an option. You needed to choose. And your choice would place you firmly on one side or the other.

But now, with John's family pronunciation firmly attached to the high school for twenty-two years, and with the Edenton population and community having exponentially exploded, most current residents were no longer aware that the one-hundred-and-sixty-year controversy had ever existed. Unless they should happen to notice both clans spelled their name the same, they naturally assumed these were two separate families. Even among most longtime locals, it had been accepted that the "Steinbeck" faction had, so to speak, won the day.

Nonetheless, there are still those, when asked about the high school, take considerable delight in responding, "Never heard of it. You must mean John *Steen-bach* High School."

2012

1

Dominic had been there since 6:15 a.m., and the day wasn't over yet. Yesterday's long twelve hours tugged at him. He was tired, and his attention had wandered. He stared blindly out his open office door, hoping to marshal a second wind when Ryan Davvis appeared across the cafeteria and stopped in his line of sight.

Dominic felt unease, as if he were spying from one chamber of an hourglass, covertly peering through the narrow neck toward the other chamber. It was a curious and disquieting perspective, but it did embody the separate realities the two men lived. It also increased Dominic's concern for the man.

Ryan rubbed at the damp November cold clinging to his jacketless arms. Dominic noted a look of concern – or was it more – on the handsome but often unreadable countenance. Maybe the look suggested the preliminary budget meeting over in the district office had not gone well. Dominic knew he'd hear about it soon enough.

Not for the first time, Dominic felt grateful his job focused on visible and tangible, objective concerns like buildings, maintenance, supplies, buses, fuel, and schedules. By contrast, Ryan, who was beginning his second year as principal at Stienboek High School, walked an invisible and subjective daily tightrope. Being relatively new to the Fox Valley meant he was walking it partially blindfolded, facing a daily balancing act between staff and students, needs and expectations, urgent vs. important, and change vs. status quo.

Ryan's shoulders sagged, and he twisted his neck side to side.

The movements reminded Dominic of the other tension Ryan was trying to balance. There were lingering, deep resentments carried over from last year when the new governor and the state legislature fanned flames of outright anger and angst among teachers and other unionized public employees, including those under his own supervision. Act 10, The Wisconsin Budget Repair Bill, had stripped away most bargaining rights for teachers and had led to 100,000 people filling the streets and Capitol building in Madison last February. The protests had lasted into the spring. Bitterness and acrimony were still palpable in the mood and demeanor of most teachers and support staff, especially here at the high school. It was a hell of a time to be a new principal.

Dominic was keenly aware the traditional sentiments of support and respect for schools and teachers had been shifting for some time. Also, like everywhere, the Fox Valley had been slammed by, and not yet recovered from, the national economic crisis and recession of two years ago. Many of his neighbors looked at the still bleak jobs market, projected multi-billion-dollar deficits, and their property taxes and believed the governor had taken the right steps. A plurality of the public sentiment was that for the good of all, the teachers and union needed to be taken down a peg. But that wasn't happening without a fight. The nightly news still carried related stories of lawsuits and recalls. With each move and countermove, the sides became more divided and less willing to compromise. With most public unions having been neutered, Dominic knew if the school board played hardball this year, you might as well toss what was left of teacher and staff morale into the toilet and flush twice. He now kept antacid tablets in his desk.

Ryan wiped the fog and mist from the reading glasses he held in his hand. He'd just started using them over the summer. The small act seemed symbolic, but Dominic wasn't sure if that was for positive or negative reasons. There was much he didn't know about the man.

Ryan had come from Minneapolis, a city kid who had attended the University of Minnesota for both his undergrad and master's degrees. He had been one of two assistant principals in a large city high school before applying at Stienboek. His only previous connection to the Edenton area was his marriage to Lisa Kames, the only child of a local couple. Lisa had been a year behind Dominic in school. They had even dated for several months before abruptly breaking up after prom. Dominic was very conscious of never having mentioned this to Ryan.

At the time of Lisa's tragic death, caused by, of all things, a bullet that ricocheted off a parking meter and nicked the artery in her inner thigh during a botched drive-by, she had only been thirty-seven years old and married to Ryan for barely three years.

The news had been a major topic of local gossip and debate for the better part of a year afterward. People mostly expressed honest condolences and sympathy to the Kames family. Some saw the incident as a reminder of why they stayed away from, or had fled, the big city. Some, particularly those who chose to see peoples' destiny as tied to the Old Testament's sense of justice and righteousness, couldn't help but whisper among themselves that perhaps Lisa's fate was a matter of her chickens coming home to roost.

Two springs after Lisa's death, when Stienboek's long-time principal Walter Hannig announced his retirement, Ryan applied for the job. Many wondered out loud why he would want to make such a move since his only tie to the area was dead.

When they were dating, Ryan had sometimes accompanied Lisa on her rare trips back home to visit friends and family. She'd first introduced him to Mr. Hannig, her former principal, when they attended a volleyball game to watch Lisa's former team play their fiercest county rival. The two men had hit it off, and while

Lisa watched from the stands with a younger cousin and a sullen-looking uncle, they had spent much of the game talking shop while standing in the gym doorway from where Principal Hannig could maintain his supervisory vigil over the proceedings.

Local scuttlebutt surfaced, along with some hard feelings, when the seventy-year-old principal was rumored to champion Ryan's candidacy as his replacement. Hannig made no secret of his contact with Ryan that had started back when the younger man had reached out to him while working on his administrative license and then afterward when he'd become an assistant principal. Not public, however, was Principal Hannig's belief that the district, and especially the high school, needed new blood and leadership from the outside world.

Dominic had been on the interview committee for the final three candidates. He had favored Barb Nickels, the current principal of the two elementary schools. The third candidate was the principal of the high school from an adjacent district who wanted to move closer to home. Many speculated he'd get the job because his wife was a Stienboek.

The school board hired Ryan. However, the usual coming together to present a unanimous showing did not occur, and the board vote had been a 5-2 split decision. Several theories circulated as to the message being sent by the two opposition votes. Dominic knew Ryan was aware of the split. Last winter in the middle of the Act 10 turmoil, he'd talked with him after a faculty meeting. Ryan was feeling frustrated and referred to the 5-2 ratio, doubting he'd ever get anywhere near that level of support for his instructional initiatives.

Ryan disappeared beyond the door portal. Uncharacteristically, Dominic Samilton continued to stare into the vacated space. He wasn't a man to waste time in his day. As head of maintenance and transportation, his usual task-at-hand approach to life didn't tend toward either aimlessly staring out his door or philosophic musings. He wasn't a man who considered whether a glass was half full or half empty rather only if it needed to be topped off or drained as the situation warranted. He leaned heavily on a practical approach to life, but he also considered himself a perceptive man. Along with his easy, friendly demeanor, these traits made him good at his job and allowed him to manage his crew effectively and efficiently, which in turn made him both valuable and well-liked.

But now, his mind wasn't ready to reengage with work. Without shifting a muscle, Dominic slid his focus upward to the red digital clock numbers above the door and then back to the door opening. He tried to capture the exact point at which his attention shifted from the world inside his office to what lay outside. The impromptu frivolous exercise seemed to align with his forever fascination with paired opposites. Heads-tails, in-out, day-night, north-south. The list was never-ending. That they were so ubiquitous seemed to hint at some deep hidden aspect of human psychology. He considered such speculation beyond his pay grade and expertise, so he didn't waste time trying to figure it out. They just were. Being aware of that fact was sufficient.

A few moments later he shook off his reverie. Glancing at his bus roster and sticky notes, he reached for his two-way radio. He needed to notify a few drivers that either some students they had brought to school this morning would not be riding the same bus home or an additional kid had permission to be on their bus and where they should be deposited along the route. He'd also let them know he'd be driving Karl's route tonight. His senior driver was at the emergency room in town getting stitches in his hand caused by a hurried and careless reach into the blades of some farm implement.

He called the office to see if any last-minute changes had come in. "Sharon, this is Dom. Over."

While he waited for her to respond, he wondered, as he had more than once, why Mr. Hannig had backed Ryan for principal. An outgoing administrator didn't typically do that. Surely, Hannig wouldn't hold some sentimental notion that being among the people who knew Lisa best would help or be good for Ryan. He had been Lisa's principal; he knew all the rumors – maybe better than most.

The two-way radio crackled to life. "Hey, Dom. This is Sharon. I was just going to call you. We have one change on bus 6. Over."

2

Ryan paused in the hallway to glance through the front office windows. It was a habit that afforded him a moment to prepare for what he might encounter upon entry. Sharon Edmonds, the office receptionist who handled visitors, the phone, attendance, and a myriad of other details, including at times acting as his first line of defense, was speaking with a mother whose firm grip on her toddler's hand kept the child from escaping through the outside door. He recognized the woman. Her oldest daughter, Zoey was a freshman. That put a dozen years between her and her little sister. Ryan wondered if the woman viewed that as a blessing or a curse. Either way, a simple, polite "hello" should suffice and allow him to escape to his small back office.

He needed a couple of aspirin and a few minutes to close his eyes. The long budget prep meeting had been more ominous than he had anticipated and left him feeling anxious. Superintendent Demian and the district business manager had walked the rest of the administrative team through the numbers and implications. The takeaway message was not good. Per-pupil state funding would again fall well short of actual needs. Payroll, the lion's share of any school budget, would need to be addressed.

Then beyond all the usual costs and equipment, they needed to address the additional capital expenses of a boiler in the middle school, roofing repairs at the oldest of the two elementary buildings, and a replacement bus for the one they'd already towed twice this fall. These couldn't be put off any longer. On top of that, district technology for students and staff needed updating and, in some cases, replacement. In the current environment of cross-district open enrollment, schools lost students and funding to their surrounding competitors for less significant reasons.

The bottom line was they'd need another district referendum to exceed state spending caps. That would mean another long, exhausting, and stressful campaign if it were to have any chance of passing.

The team was completely aware of the depressing realities. They all knew the school board would undoubtedly split on the idea as they did on almost everything nowadays. There was no assurance a second referendum in four years would even get off the ground. And if it did, it was probable that one or more of the board members would actively work against it in the community.

They also knew what the real elephant in the room would be. Local unemployment had still not recovered from the recession and global financial crash four years ago. The economy was still struggling. Voters would be understandably reluctant to raise their property tax and allow the district to exceed the revenue caps imposed by the state legislature back in 1993. The meeting ended with each of them assigned the task of beginning to prioritize possible program cuts. They'd also need to consider the possibility of personnel layoffs. Since Act 10 had become law last June, layoffs were no longer strictly governed by seniority and the contract with the union. They'd need to develop new criteria and that would open the principals to allegations of favoritism.

Ryan's stiff neck and forehead throbbed. He focused on Sharon and the woman while he squeezed the back of his neck and then rubbed his right temple. Knowing he was running late, he pulled the door open and entered. He only had thirty minutes to gather himself, return a phone call, and finalize his notes and slides for the faculty meeting after school. Physically, mentally, and emotionally preoccupied, he failed to notice the boy sitting off to the side as he entered.

"Hello, Mrs. Ackerly." Ryan greeted the woman as he slipped around the counter. "Nasty day out there, isn't it?" He kept moving toward his office.

The woman looked his way. "Hello, Mr. Davvis." As she spoke, her attention shifted toward the seated boy, followed by a disapproving glance over her glasses which distorted her features. Sharon caught Ryan's eye while reaching for her radio which had just crackled to life. She inclined her head and cocked her eyebrows toward the boy. Ryan followed their gaze. As soon as he recognized the young man, he knew his prep time was gone. He'd be lucky if he got to use the faculty bathroom before leaving for the meeting in the library.

3

With a small sweep of his hand, Ryan Davvis motioned toward his office before the boy, who was already on his feet, could say anything. The source of the immediate problem was evident as soon as he stepped in front of Ryan. It was written in white letters across the back of his dark blue tee shirt – the school colors. He was glad the boy was in front of him and couldn't see his amused grin and shake of his head. He closed the door behind them and gestured to the chairs around the circular table where he often worked. One was his old wheeled swivel desk chair of imitation brown suede. The others were common blue office furniture with curved metal frames rather than legs.

Ryan set his budget files and notes at his workstation next to his computer. Rather than sitting at his official desk, he'd sit at the table with the boy. Years before, he'd absorbed Walt Hannig's advice about sitting behind his desk while dealing with discipline issues. It only added to the likelihood of an escalating confrontation.

The boy had claimed the swivel chair, as he always did. It allowed him to keep his body in motion while talking. His slender arms splayed out, each hand gripping an edge of the round table. He alternately pushed and pulled, making the chair move back and forth. The motion made Ryan think of a child pretending to be steering the family car. It also reminded him of how hard it could be for the boy to keep a grip on his thoughts and impulses. The fidgeting didn't bother Ryan. Besides, demanding him to sit still would be less than productive or wise.

"How are you, Ayden? And how may I help you today?"

"Mr. Davvis, I'm pissed, and you can fire Mrs. Z. You're the principal; you can do that, right?"

"I assume you mean you're upset. And I'm quite sure firing Mrs. Zowak would not resolve the issue... for either of us." The fantasy of dismissing the staff's senior and most influential "yeah, but-er," trickled across his mind.

"Now, I'm going to go out on a limb, Ayden, and guess your story has something to do with your shirt?"

"Limb? Anyhow, there's nothing wrong with my shirt. It ain't got no swear words or bad pictures or ads for beer or stuff. It's part of my new business I'm starting."

Genuinely curious, Ryan asked, "Business?"

"Yeah! You know my friend, Allan. He showed me this book from the library of things people said."

Ryan indeed knew Allan Sparks well. Like Ayden, he had qualified for special education support back in third grade, which was about as young as a student with behavioral issues could usually be eligible for services. Even before then, it had been abundantly clear the two boys should always be scheduled into different classes. Each was capable of self-ignition into defiant behavior. Together they were a match in an oxygen tent.

Unfortunately, Allan derived amusement from daring or provoking Ayden's lack of impulse control, occasionally leading to an in-school and an occasional out-of-school suspension. For his part, Ayden considered Allan to be his best friend and refused to implicate him other than to say, "I got dared by somebody."

Ryan knew Mrs. Berry, his special-ed teacher and case manager, was helping Ayden begin to realize that real friends do not dare friends to do stupid things that get them in trouble. But Allan seemed to hold some magical sway over the boy. He was one of the few who hung with him both in and out of school, and as Ayden often pointed out, "Besides, Allan's funny."

The boy raced on, earnestly defending his business plan. "A book can't be bad if it's in the library, right? Allan showed me some funny sayings. Some even made me think to figure out what they meant. Ain't that what books are for? To make you think?"

Without a noticeable breath, he continued. "And you know how my mom has the craft and stencil store? My business is gonna let kids pick out sayings, and I'll put them on a tee shirt for them. See?" He jerked his thumb up, pointing to his back with pride, and kept talking. "Everybody thinks it's funny. A couple kids already want to look at the book. I mean, if the sayings are from famous people, they can't be bad. So, I don't know why Mrs. Z got a bug up her butt and told me I couldn't wear this in her class...which I didn't mean to do anyhow."

Ayden abruptly halted his soliloquy and again began to steer the table.

Ryan asked, "Did you have the shirt on all day? Did anyone else ask you to change or turn it inside out?" The thought that other staff avoided addressing Ayden about the shirt would be a concern.

"I had my sweatshirt over it. But you know how hot Mrs. Z's room can get sometimes. You should fix that."

"Did your mom stencil the quote for you?"

Every teacher, counselor, and principal who worked with Ayden knew Mrs. Quant well. Ryan felt sure if she had, she'd probably told him not to wear it to school, even though, he assumed, schools had always rubbed Anna Quant the wrong way. She could be a handful, but he liked her, as he did Ayden.

"No! I did. But Mom helped me make it straight."

Ayden brought his chair to a halt, pushed back his curly dark hair, and stood so Ryan could see his back and how neatly the quote had been aligned and printed. It was an unfamiliar version of a common euphemistic insult. It was also definitely not school-appropriate, so he tried not to smile.

I Can't Believe That Out of 100,000 Sperm
YOU
Were the Quickest

"And that quote is in the book?"

"Yep."

"Who said it?"

"A guy named Pearl. You know like on a necklace."

"Who is he?" Ryan began to feel like he was being outmaneuvered.

"No clue. But he's in the book, just like I wrote it. I can show you."

Ryan twisted his lips before asking, "What do you think the quote means?"

Ayden enthusiastically explained how he knew it was a funny insult right away, and how the word "sperm" made it funny. He added, "It's a good idea, ain't it? I mean, if everyone was wearing one of my shirts, then even in boring classes, kids would be learning 'cause they'd be seeing all these famous sayings everywhere."

"That's very entrepreneurial," Ryan conceded. "And you're right; there are no *'bad'* words on it. But we've talked about age and place appropriateness before, right?"

Ayden tried to counter Mr. Davvis' point. "But guys insult each other all the time."

Ryan trod softly. "I realize some students sometimes do. But I'm sure you can see why a school doesn't want to promote that behavior. Plus, what happens when the younger kids see you on the bus? They'll go home and ask their parents about the quote. Then the parents will be calling and yelling at me. You understand how that causes a problem, right?"

"Well, yeah, but..."

Ryan could see Ayden was again working himself up to defend his idea, so he preemptively said, "Let me think about your idea, and we'll try to work something out. We can't do it now though. I have to get to a meeting. But in the meantime, you leave your shirt at home." He glanced up at the clock on the wall. "It's 2:30. You're not in Mrs. Zowak's class now, are you?"

"No. I'm in ESL with Mrs. Berry."

"Then you head to her room. But I'm going to ask you to turn the shirt inside out, and then go to your locker and put your sweat-shirt back on. Okay?"

"I guess."

"I think that's a fair compromise. How about you?"

"I guess."

"Now, last thing before you go, did you yell or speak inappropriately to Mrs. Zowak?"

"I might a swore a little, but I didn't yell and run away like I used to do. And I came here when she told me to."

"I'm glad you did. But, what do you mean 'you swore a little?'"

"I might a said 'dang.'"

"Dang?"

"Maybe 'damn.'"

Ryan let his breath out, grateful the mild expletive wouldn't require him to escalate the matter or impose consequences. "You know what you need to do, don't you?"

"Switch the shirt."

"And?"

"Apologize?"

"I think you're man enough to do that. What do you think?"

"I guess."

Ayden turned his tee shirt inside out.

"Thanks, Ayden, for following the rules."

"I guess." The boy headed out of the office toward the hall which would be full of students moving between classes. He stopped and asked, "Hey, Mr. Davvis? What's that 'on-tray-thing' you said about me? Does that mean stupid? My dad is always telling me I'm lazy or stupid when he's home."

Ryan looked up from where he'd just sat at his desk. "Is your dad home now?"

"No. But he said it last time he texted me."

Ryan kept his face blank and went back to Ayden's question. "On-tray-thing? I'm not sure what you mean?" Then it hit him. "You mean an *entrepreneur*? That's a person who starts a business. It takes guts to do that, and you have to work hard to make it a success. If it works out, entrepreneurs might make a lot of money. If it doesn't work, they can lose a lot of money, but they learn from their mistakes and try something else."

"Yeah, but what if they lose their money again?" Ayden asked.

Ryan read the concern on his face and was sure he was thinking about his mom.

Ryan smiled. He stood and walked to the door. He would have liked to squeeze the boy's shoulders as a show of support but thought better of it. Mrs. Berry had mentioned Ayden said his family never hugged. "True entrepreneurs learn from those new mistakes, too, and try again. They are willing to take risks until they succeed. They have lots of resilience. It can take lots of tries before things work out. That's what makes them special people. Just like your mom. They won't give up. They keep trying."

Ayden's face scrunched like he was thinking hard. "That sounds okay, I guess." Then he added, "Yeah. That's just like my mom."

The boy didn't wait for a response. He headed off to his class. Ryan looked back to the clock, realizing his prep time was almost gone, but so was his headache. He turned to the blinking light on his phone, knowing in his gut it would be a third "urgent" message from Thynie Marsh, the one school board member he would thoroughly enjoy being honest with and telling her to fuck off. He deleted the message as soon as he heard her voice and dialed her number. It irked him that he knew it by memory. At least he'd have the pleasure of cutting her short to get to the faculty meeting.

4

Thynie Marsh inherited her name by way of her maternal grandmother Theona Thynie, a.k.a. Grandma TT. The practice of repurposing family names as given names was a family idiosyncrasy. It reached back decades before the nineteenth century when the family came to the valley. Thynie's often shared theory was that the naming practice produced an accumulative strength in each new generation of women. As proof, she'd list the many strongly opinionated women in her lineage, reaching back to long before women were encouraged to speak up for themselves. She proudly displayed in her home a May 1919 newspaper photo of her great-grandmother protesting at the new capitol building in Madison a month before Wisconsin's passage of the 19th Amendment – though she'd always add, "Of course, great-grand-mama was an anti-war suffragist and generally against all of President Wilson's goofiness."

Thynie was not shy. She was dedicated to the proposition that everyone should know her position about everything. Whether her naming hypothesis was true or not, no one who knew her, especially her husband, Irving Marsh, would argue with the fact that in Thynie's case, the mold had been not just broken but shattered. After they'd married, Thynie installed herself in both of Irving's business ventures and proved to be such a force she had obtained the nickname T-Rex. She was aware of, and enjoyed, the moniker, though no one used it to her face.

On her paternal side, Thynie was a proud member of the

Steen-bach branch of the Stienboek family tree, and as such, referred to the high school with that pronunciation. For the most part, other board members had learned to quit being annoyed and not rise to the bait, though an occasional eye roll was not unusual. Thynie embodied and fully embraced her branch's tenacious spirit when it came to insisting on family loyalty, tradition, independence, and governmental frugality in terms of taxes and interference. She had solid backing in the Westown area and a respectable portion of Edenton proper. She was in her third three-year term on the school board.

Two other members, one being her husband's cousin, Bobby Marsh, who'd been elected last April, leaned in much the same direction and represented a growing shift toward her point of view. They tended to support her lead on most important issues. However, the Edenton Area School District had a seven-person board, and three votes had not been enough to secure the board presidency for Mrs. Thynie Marsh last spring, which again went to Charles Templeton. They rarely agreed on much and, to make matters worse, he was a FIB, a transplant from northern Illinois, a "Fucking Illinois Bastard." To Thynie's credit, she never uttered the acronym, let alone the epithet.

5

Like a pacemaker, the passing bell regulates the life rhythm of a high school. At its signal, students pulse through doorways and along hallways, their mass movement adding to the systolic pressure pushing them along to their next class.

Leaving Mr. Davvis' office, Ayden burrowed his way into and through various scrums of slow-moving students on their way to the final hurdle of their day. At Stienboek, the shortened last period of each day was ESL – Extended Support and Learning. The idea was that each teacher and aide would work with a manageable smaller group of students to help them keep up with or go beyond their class work. The goal was for each staff member to create a closer bond and relationship with their group members than they could with the one hundred or so students most high school classroom teachers encountered each day. Some staff met the challenge and turned theory into reality. For others, ESL was a typical study hall. Some students used the time effectively while others chatted or napped.

Ayden liked his group. Mrs. Berry's room was a safe place at the end of each day. He especially liked Lilly who talked with him even though she was pretty and Steven who had some kind of autism but was smart in math and really into monsters. Ayden thought sometimes the monster stuff got to be too much, and he'd lose his patience with him. His friend and nemesis, Allan Sparks, was also in Mrs. Berry's ESL group. Sometimes he would tease or pick on Steven. If Mrs. Berry had stepped out or was occupied with another student, Ayden usually intervened. When Allan referred to the group as a pod of losers, Ayden would remind him that made him a loser too.

Ayden could tell Mrs. Berry cared for him. She didn't automatically blame him when he "lost it" and acted out. She'd help him connect the dots and figure out what was going on inside his head. Sometimes, she intervened with other teachers if they forgot, or ignored, his IEP – Individualized Education Plan – which spelled out his accommodations and included having extra time when taking a test. The bad news was she pushed him because she knew he was smart, much smarter than some of his bone-headed behaviors might indicate. That made him feel good, even though on some days he wasn't completely convinced she was right.

Taking advantage of his short, thin frame, he weaved his way along through the crowd. Halfway down the hall, a familiar voice surfed over the general din as if riding the wave of moving bodies. It echoed off the metal lockers and cement block, gaining volume until it slapped hard against his ears. "Hey, Quant-ski. Been visiting your special buddy Davvis again?"

Ayden thrust his hand up above the surface of heads and extended his middle finger. "Up yours, Allan," he hollered without turning around. Once around the corner, Allan's taunt hit home and caused a stab of hurt and embarrassment. Ayden reacted by reaching out and pushing a classmate's locker shut, almost catching the boy's fingers. He immediately apologized, "Sorry," but didn't stop.

Students began disappearing into various classrooms. Just ahead, Ayden spotted Lilly reaching for something high in her locker, exposing her belly. He imagined her shirt moving higher, but the image exploded when he saw Mrs. Berry watching his approach. As usual, she was stationed outside her door, monitoring the hallway, and checking that her students brought the materials they needed.

"Hi, Ayden. Get your math homework, please. We'll check that first."

He knew Mrs. Berry wouldn't miss that his tee shirt was inside out. And even though she had never said anything out loud, Ayden knew she got frustrated when another teacher didn't address her students' dress code violations or other misbehavior and instead sent the offender back to her room while she was teaching – as if her lessons and students weren't of equal importance to their own.

As he opened his locker, Ayden – rather clumsily – turned his back to block her view. He tried to appear nonchalant as he rearranged and straightened folders to ensure the magazine he'd hidden there wasn't visible.

Ayden's furtive attention to neatness made Mrs. Berry suspicious. But having a good sense of which issues to prioritize with her students, she didn't approach. She was more concerned with any lingering angst or resentments the boy might have about the reversed tee shirt. She didn't want them resurfacing as a problem on the bus ride home.

"Ayden, would you grab your sweatshirt while you're there."

"Mr. Davvis already told me that."

His tone confirmed her concern. As she greeted other students, she saw him pull his sweatshirt over the inside-out shirt. He gently closed his locker door – which was unusual when he was upset – and then averted his eyes as he quickly entered her room. Knowing her students as she did, Mrs. Berry recognized Ayden's behaviors as signals. He needed help processing something.

The second bell sounded. Mrs. Berry looked up and down the hall. Seeing no stragglers, she took a deep breath and followed him in.

6

Instead of sitting at his regular raised desk and stool – furniture Mrs. Berry had researched and convinced the Pupil Service Director to purchase because it included a foot bar that swiveled, allowing her fidgety kids more physical movement – Ayden went to a corner study carrel and laid his head down. Apparently, her assessment had been correct. The boy was attempting to contain whatever had occurred since she'd seen him first period.

Mrs. Berry got the rest of the group settled, cleared up a few confusions about the math assignment and content and then pulled a chair next to Ayden. She sat so she could talk to him quietly yet keep an eye on the rest of the room. She leaned in. "Ayden, did something happen about your shirt? Are you upset with yourself or with someone else?"

"Both." He sat up.

"Well, one-to-ten, how upset are you?"

Within a few minutes, she had the gist of the story, which in Ayden's telling outlined how he was unfairly kicked out of Mrs. Zowak's class and sent to the office. She soon had him back at his regular perch and made sure he and the others knew how to solve the assigned homework problems, knowing that one or more would arrive tomorrow without having finished them.

When the dismissal bell signaled the charge for the busses and student parking lot, Ayden uncharacteristically dawdled. Mrs. Berry recognized his hesitation as avoidance of something. "Ayden, are you okay to ride the bus home? I can call your mom to pick you up if you want."

"I've gotta do the bus. It's dropping me in town, and Mom's taking me to another counselor. Social Services is making me go 'cause the old one retired." Vocalizing this single complaint had been enough, and he was gone before she could ask another question.

Mrs. Berry sat at her desk and looked at the empty desks. She knew she had a soft spot for Ayden. He made her think of her brother. Both had a certain charm. But while Ayden was short, slight, and unfocused, her brother had been the opposite. He was tall and strong, which ensured minimal taunting from his peers about being in special education. She'd gotten much more teasing for her orangy-auburn hair than he'd faced over his struggles to read or sit still.

Also, unlike Ayden, he had always been single-minded. From an early age, he'd been enthralled by the animals and everything mechanical on the family dairy farm they had grown up on in the Kickapoo Valley outside of LaFarge. He'd eventually took the farm over when their parents retired. So, Mrs. Kim Berry knew there could be happy endings for these kids. She also knew that wasn't always the norm. Each success was hard won, requiring lots of support – something her brother had, but was quite minimal in Ayden Quant's life.

7

Dominic backed the bus into the narrow space as if he'd done it hundreds of times, which, of course, he had. Rather than a nuisance, he enjoyed filling in when a driver was absent. He knew many of the kids on most routes and their parents. Plus, it gave him a chance to meet some of the newer students. He removed the key. The diesel motor chattered as it shut down. He closed two windows and swept out the interior, picking up two pens, a paperback copy of *The Red Badge of Courage,* a math book, and a red hooded sweatshirt. Even in his day, the novel was a staple in tenth-grade English. The math book was sixth grade, and the sweatshirt was a familiar one. The pens would go in the box on the table outside of his office that he used to display the various untraceable items found on the buses. Most were gone within a week. He grabbed the trash, added a new bag for tomorrow, and headed across the back parking lot toward his office.

Using his master key fob, he entered the door nearest the football field, then stopped to check the showerhead he'd replaced in the girls' locker room last week. From the adjacent locker room, he heard mumbled off-key singing to a classic tune.

"And good old boys were drinkin' whiskey and rye,
singin' this will be the day that I die."

Matthew Lam had his oldie station streaming through his

ever-present earbuds. From 3:00 until 8:00 p.m., this end of the high school was Matthew's cleaning assignment. If there was a basketball or volleyball game, he didn't leave until after 10:00. Dominic liked and trusted the young man. He reminded him of himself a couple dozen years ago when he'd been in his early twenties.

When Dominic got to his office, his daughter was hunched in his chair studying something she'd laid out on his desk. "Hi, honey. How was your day?" He set the lost books and hoodie on a chair by the door, then walked around his desk and lightly kissed the top of her head.

"Do you know what Mr. Schmelzing said to me in history today?"

Dominic knew this could go either way. At fifteen, Nala was at that age of uncertainty where she could find fault or insult in any comment made to her. On the other hand, she liked Mr. Schmelzing and often spoke highly of him. "What did he say?"

"Before class, I was looking at an old globe on his back shelf. He came over and pointed out how the United States, Canada, and Europe all looked bigger than Africa. "See," she pointed to the book in front of her. "This old Atlas shows the same thing. He suggested I look up their actual sizes."

"What did you find?"

Nala picked up her smartphone, tapped in a few words with her thumbs, then pointed at a chart. "Look. Africa is bigger than Europe and the United States combined. It's the second biggest continent."

Dominic took off his jacket and hung it on the back of his chair behind his daughter. He looked over her shoulder at her phone. "Hmm. I never knew that."

She continued, now sounding a tad agitated. "You know what else, Dad? Did you know Europe owned lots of African countries? Mr. Schmelzing says that even when he was a kid back in the 1960s, some countries were still European colonies."

"I guess I never thought about it," Dominic admitted.

Nala swiveled the chair around to face her father. Disbelief was evident in her face and voice. "Dad! What the heck." Her disbelief was now tinged with frustration. "How could that be?"

Dominic wasn't at all sure where this was heading. He hated seeing his daughter getting herself upset, especially by something from so long ago. He answered with the only related logic that came to mind. "Well, we were a British colony. I really don't know anything about the history of Africa. It wasn't covered when I was in high school."

His daughter continued to stare at her phone and the map. "It's still not covered, Dad. And we were a colony well over two hundred years ago. Not fifty."

Not sure where to go from here, Dominic waited a few moments before tacking in a different direction. "How was practice today?" When he got no response, he rubbed his daughter's shoulders and repeated the question.

"Huh?" Nala continued looking at her phone, but her voice indicated she was willing to move on. "It was okay. Mrs. Shimone worked us pretty hard. She thought we played sloppy last game even though we won."

"I can't say I disagree with her. If it had been a stronger team, you would have been in trouble." She gave him a variation of her "give-me-a-break-Dad" look. He winked at her.

"Honey, I'm going to do a walk-through to drop off these books left on the bus and see if anyone needs anything. Then we can head home. I'm beat." He held up the red sweatshirt. "Help me remember to drop this when we pass Ayden Quant's place. I'm sure he'll need it tomorrow."

"That's all he ever wears. What is wrong with that kid?" Nala asked as she returned her attention to the world map in front of her.

Thirty minutes later, father and daughter pulled out of the parking lot. Nala took her earphones from her backpack and asked if she could listen to her music. When they pulled into the Quant's gravel driveway, Dominic handed the well-worn hoodie to his daughter who wrinkled up her nose at the thing before making a show of a deep sigh of resignation. She removed her headphones and jogged toward the porch and door. Muffled lyrics spilled from the headphones she'd left on the seat next to him. They sounded far away and foreign as they escaped from the small device and tried to reach across the age and culture divide. Dominic picked it up to listen.

...I'm fortunate you believe in a dream
This orphanage we call a ghetto is quite a routine...

Spending so much time around kids, Dominic heard more than his share of the music his daughter and her peers enjoyed. But he wasn't a fan. Remembering his parents' struggle not to disparage his music when he was a teen, he tried to do the same. But rap was an effort. The world it came from was thankfully a million miles away from his reality. The lyrics, which usually were about things he preferred Nala not to have to deal with at her age, moved too quickly for him, and the lack of a real melody made it almost impossible to consider it music. Like most parents, he felt kids grew up too fast. Mrs. Berry once mentioned that her students swore they'd never heard of "Jack and Jill" or the "Itsy-bitsy Spider." At least his daughter knew about them.

Nala got back in the car. "Ayden's mom is as strange as he is. She didn't even say thanks. What a bitch."

"Name calling? Really?"

"Sorry. But she's not very friendly."

Dominic waited until she buckled her seatbelt and then handed her the headphones "She is quite a character. But she's had..." He decided to not finish the sentence. "Thanks for running the hoodie up." He patted her knee. "Let's go get some dinner." He backed out.

Nala asked, "Were you listening to this?"

"All I could understand was the line about a ghetto. I know all the kids love rap, but I'd bet most have no idea what the words actually mean. But, as you know, I'm more of a country music guy. Lots of melody and sad lyrics I can understand and keep up with."

"Well, I get the words."

"Yeah?"

About a half mile down the road, while looking straight ahead through the windshield, Nala added, as if she was trying the idea out for the first time, "You may not have noticed, but I'm Black."

Dominic kept his eyes forward and took in a very slow breath. Was this the first time she'd referred to her skin as a statement and not as a question? His lungs became uncomfortably tight. When the air began to finally force its way out, he said, "And, you're also half white. And you've never seen a ghetto except on TV. You've been with Mom and me since before your first birthday."

Nala held out her hands, first looking at their backside and then turning them to examine her lighter palms. "Then why did Mr. Schmelzing go out of his way to tell *me* about Africa instead of telling the whole class?" She put her headphones back on.

Dominic turned at the next intersection. His headlights stabbed and slid through the darkness but were not able to reach the far side of the fields. Her question made him uncomfortable because the answer was obvious. He wasn't sure what his daughter was announcing. He had no idea if it was something she had recently decided or if she was only now clueing him in. But into what? He wanted to ask her, but those words would be hard to find and even harder to get right.

From the beginning, he and Kate had let Nala know she was

adopted. They'd fill in a little more whenever she had asked for more details. By fifth grade, they'd told her most of what they knew. Her father was a Somali immigrant, and her Polish mother was from Chicago where Nala had been born. They explained they'd been told that her biological parents were not together and that she had been put up for adoption in Minnesota where they'd been living.

Dominic replayed in his mind his and Kate's conversations before adopting a Black baby and bringing her into white rural northeast Wisconsin. They knew there'd be issues. But at the time they, or maybe just he, didn't fully process them or consider the questions they raised. They'd just thought it the right thing to do.

The adoption agency had listed some of the likely pitfalls. But everyone's main concern was centered on having the child become one of the lucky ones who got adopted and not just moved along a conveyor of foster homes. At the time, he just didn't know what he didn't know. That wasn't like him. Dominic now realized he had blindsided himself by assuming any possible issues would come from how neighbors and future classmates reacted to their daughter and not how she might perceive herself.

He pulled into their garage and turned off the truck. "Honey. You know you can be purple or anything you choose, but you'll always be my daughter."

Nala rolled her eyes. She wordlessly kissed his cheek before hopping out and disappearing into the house. A moment later, with his tail in full gear and scampering as quickly as his stiff arthritic legs allowed, their old lab Moses greeted him with a single woof as he stepped out of his truck.

8

Ryan sat at his desk, rerunning the faculty meeting in his head. He slumped, stretching his legs, hooking one foot over the other, tapping his dark brown loafers in time with his heartbeat. His mood and spirit felt as heavy as the premature night pressing against the window.

He slowly raked his fingers through his thick hair, which for now was mostly the same color as his shoes. At forty-four, he assumed that wouldn't last much longer. He laced his knuckles behind his head and pointed his toes to add another inch to his five-foot-eight frame. Just below average. For the last several years, it had felt more than *just* below.

At the meeting, the Language Arts teachers, along with the literacy specialist, had presented the committee's latest draft of grading rubrics for both informational and persuasive/argumentative writing. They were based on the recently adopted Common Core Standards. The staff gave their colleagues a fair hearing until it was proposed some writing standards could best be addressed outside of English and Literature classes. That quickly sparked responses from other content area teachers.

"What am I supposed to skip to find time for that?"

"I don't get it. Why would you think writing fits with Algebra?" The major "Yeah, but" rationale that was raised more than once was: "I'm not an English teacher, how am I supposed to teach writing?"

Ryan kept his face expressionless, while he pondered the implications of certified high school teachers saying they would not be able to assess student writing against a rubric. To him, it made perfect sense that writing and reading be a part of most classes.

After several minutes of protest, Mrs. Zowak surprisingly quieted the waters when she suggested there might be some sense in the idea of others "occasionally" requiring students to do some writing – though perhaps the Language Arts teachers could come back next month with ideas of how this might work "in reality." Ryan was grateful for her tentative support. If she had added to the chorus of nay-sayers, implementing the committee's work would require more political capital from Ryan than he thought he had.

The second half of the meeting was his to carry. He presented his prepared PowerPoint, introducing what was called "formative assessment." Even as he prepared for the meeting, he knew it might be a bridge too far for many. The concept was to have teachers adopt informal procedures for assessing student learning on an ongoing basis and, if need be, modify their teaching and activities before testing and grading. A few leaned forward and showed some interest. Most sat expressionless. Some sat back as if trying to distance themselves from the idea. Implementing it would mean still another thing added onto their plates. Others interpreted it as being asked to test their teaching rather than the students' learning.

He'd anticipated the reactions and to a degree empathized with them. He knew he was pushing the envelope. But that was his job. They'd have to get used to it. There were too many D and F grades. The fault couldn't all be placed on the kids. He ended the meeting by assuring them this was just something he'd like them to think about for future discussion.

As the staff filed out, amidst the general chatter, he'd heard the mumbles. "... administrators... more changes... like everything we do is wrong ..." He'd felt his defenses rising. Then Mrs. Zowak had appeared in front of him, saying she'd like to talk to him in the morning. He agreed without asking what the topic was. As she turned to leave, she added, "Interesting presentation, Mr. Davvis."

He wasn't sure how to interpret her intonation but took advantage of the moment. "Bernadette, I want to thank you for helping to move the idea of writing in the content areas along. They value your opinion."

Mrs. Zowak turned back to him. "I'm not sure I'd label what I said as 'moving the idea along.' It might be more accurate to say I called a time-out. Good night, Mr. Davvis." She gave him a half smile and left.

Ryan sat up, stiffening his back against the chair, both feet on the floor. He thought about the overheard comments as the staff left the meeting. He couldn't help but sense some personal antipathy there. He shifted in his chair to keep the feeling from gaining momentum.

Damn it! Why can't they... the thought was too jumbled to take shape. He blew out a long breath to clear his frustration. *I'm not the bad guy here.* But he also didn't want to fall into the trap of seeing them as the bad guys. They were still being hammered in the media by the governor as greedy and whiny. They'd heard the talk about making Wisconsin what was being called a "right-to-work" state, basically doing away with unions. He wanted to believe the political fault lines were temporary. He knew they weren't.

He glanced at the table Ayden Quant had been steering during their discussion just two hours ago. *We all know too many kids are falling through the cracks.* That thought disjointedly made him think about Lisa. Had she, like Ayden, spent time here, at this table back when it was Walt Hannig's office? He decided he'd have to ask him sometime.

The wind gusted loudly, rubbing cold, wet darkness against his window and mood. He put his hands on his knees to push himself up, intending to go home. Instead, his eyes were drawn to his bottom desk drawer, the only one he kept locked.

DON'T. It won't help. The thought was so loud he may have let the words escape his mouth. The photo, the last one he'd taken moments before she'd hurried outside to respond to a text, a moment before he heard the shooting, was at the bottom of the drawer, face down, purposely buried deep beneath schedules, staff directories, and class rosters. To reach it, to touch it, would require reaching through the living, the names of those whose daily lives physically interacted with his, the students and adults who made up his life now, those to whom he now felt a responsibility.

But, damn it, don't I have a responsibility to myself too? What about what I need? He didn't list them again. He'd chewed on each item so often that they existed as a single masticated ache sitting permanently undigested in his gut. An existential torment that might only dissolve and pass if he found answers and explanations or at least memories, anything that could hint at why Lisa had done what she'd done... was who she was. Maybe even something to help understand why he continued to flirt with disaster by dealing with his anger and pain the way he had been.

The photo wasn't interred deep enough – never was, probably never could be. It was many things for him, but now it was a reminder of why he'd needed to apply for the seat he now occupied and why he might lose it in disgrace if his hypocrisy and unfitness to run or lead a school were exposed.

He forced himself to stand, reached for his coat, and turned off the lights. Even in the dark, every pixel that made up the photograph stared at him, challenging his manhood and ability to engage with the living or dead. He knew that would continue for as long as his pain and inability to forgive continued to breed equal portions of hate and love that coursed through him with every heartbeat.

9

Ayden typically fell asleep right away. His mother thought it was the meds that tended to knock him out early. But not tonight. He rolled from his left side to his right then back again before sitting up. He had counselors on his mind.

His mother had reluctantly ushered him through the in-door of the mental health system after that day back in sixth grade when he'd jumped from resistance to total non-compliance. He'd flipped over desks before running from the building, ending up wandering around a small mall before walking out of town toward his house, five miles away. A county sheriff's deputy found him about halfway there.

Later that same evening, his mother found him missing from his room. His father hadn't let her call the sheriff this time or look for him beyond the yard. He came back on his own when he got cold and scared. The following week, Anna Quant went against both her instincts and her husband's attempted veto and sought the advice of the school psychologist. She was advised to seek counseling on her own. Luckily, social services picked up the cost.

Ayden saw his first therapist, an older woman, for almost two years. He'd thought she was okay. He learned some strategies for coping when he felt like he was losing it, though he rarely remembered them in real time. In the spring of Ayden's seventh-grade year, the woman retired and he was transferred to a new person. That didn't go well.

Ayden thought this new woman talked too much and asked stupid questions. "Why did you do that? You knew that wasn't a smart thing to do, right?" He intuitively fell back on his tried-and-true, rope-a-dope strategy, answering with an uninvolved, "yes, no," or "I don't know." When necessary, he'd promise not to do it – whatever it was – again, or that he would change his ways and not be so defiant. How stupid.

But the part that galled him the most was the woman insisted on referring to his mom as his stepmother. When he tried to get her to stop, she said, "It's fine and dandy for you to call her your mother, but I think it's important for our sessions that I refer to her as she is – your stepmom. Why does that bother you?"

Ayden could only say, "Because she *is* my mom. If anyone is a step-anything, it's my dad."

Ayden's memory of being brought to Wisconsin and meeting his stepmom was sketchy. He remembered a few fractured details. But much of what he retained were impressions of the experience and what he'd been told later, mostly by his stepmother. He'd been not quite four years old and living in West Virginia. He remembered being hungry. He remembered not being able to wake his mother up, then living with his aunt who said his mom was dead. He was with his aunt for a few months. He was alternately ignored and yelled at. She didn't like him.

He vividly remembered meeting the man he was told was his father. He just showed up one day. His aunt said he had to go with him because she couldn't afford to keep him. He rode in the man's truck for a long time. He had the impression the man was mad at him. The man also blamed his mother over and over again for using oxy-something and now ruining *his* life by having to take Ayden. Ayden remembered being confused when they got to the man's house and was told, "This is your new mom." But he also remembered hers were the first kind words he'd heard in a very long time.

The following month, when he had the same argument with the therapist, he got called from his room that night and bawled out by his father who repeated much of what he'd said about his birth mother on their drive from West Virginia. He then added Ayden better stop arguing with the woman. Ayden got angry and summoned the courage to ask his dad if he was his *real* father.

"Don't be an idiot. Of course, I am. You think you'd be here if I wasn't?"

With no more conversation, and against his mom's objection, Ayden was sent back to his room. To this very bed.

The rest of that year was a disaster with multiple suspensions and failures. He rallied somewhat for the first half of eighth grade, before backsliding again the second half of the year. Then early that summer between eighth and ninth grade, Ayden was elated when his mother told him the woman had moved, and there'd be no more sessions. Then a shop-lifting incident involving a National Inquirer with a cover that implied there'd be nude pictures inside brought him into contact with the juvenile criminal system. The family was required to resume counseling.

But this new counselor, this Mr. Powells, whom he'd seen after school today for the first time seemed better. They'd sat in comfortable chairs. There was a couch, but it was against the far wall. Powells had a wooden desk, some book shelves, and not much else except a few framed pictures and posters on the wall. Ayden recalled the small poster on the inside of the closed door. *"Don't believe everything you think."* He'd asked what it was supposed to mean, but Powells said it was a reminder to himself, and maybe they'd talk about it sometime. The office reminded him of Mr. Davvis', except there was no round table to hold on to. Plus, it was bigger and the desk and furniture were better quality.

After introducing himself, Powells surprisingly started the

conversation by revealing how, before Ayden came in, he'd been thinking about when he was a little kid. He told Ayden when the doorbell rang, his older sister would tell him they'd come to take him away. "For years after that, I was afraid of doorbells." They both laughed. Then Ayden got the typical questions about school, home life, and himself. But sometimes Mr. Powells added something about himself, and he even let Ayden ask a few questions. It felt more like talking rather than a test.

Toward the end, Powells asked Ayden a strange question. "You've played hide and seek, right?"

Ayden felt leery but also relaxed. He answered. "I guess. Sometimes. When my cousins were over by us."

"Did you have a favorite hiding place?"

"If I really didn't want to be found, I hid under the front porch." He turned his head, picturing himself in the safety of the darkness beneath the porch, so he elaborated. "Under the porch is covered by this crisscross fencelike stuff. I guess to keep out skunks or raccoons. But the end part is loose. I'm kinda small, so I could just squeeze through. My cousins didn't know about it. No one did, 'cept me. There's bushes all around, so nobody could see in 'cause it's dark under there. But I see out, and I hear 'em running all around looking for me and calling my name."

Powells noted the slip into present tense. "They never find you there?" he asked.

Ayden didn't hear. His stare and attention were on a small, framed picture on the desk. It looked like an old farmhouse but with an extra section on top, like for a bell. It was set just over the top of a hill. An American flag was on a pole. It made him think it might be an old-fashioned schoolhouse. The red roof and white front were lit by the sun, but the surrounding sky, which took up half the picture, was a dark menacing gray like a bad storm was coming. Two little, weirdly shaped buildings were stuck into the bottom of the hill. *Houses?* Even though they were supposed to be closer, the houses were smaller than the school. They didn't have any doors or windows. A narrow red path led from the bottom edge past the houses, up to the top of the hill, and over the crest to the school or whatever it was.

While Ayden's eyes were occupied by the picture, another part of his brain was back hiding under his porch listening to his parents calling his name. His mom's voice sounded worried. She smooshed his first and middle name together – "A-Lee." She only did that when no one, especially Dad, was around, or if he was sick. His dad just sounded pissed.

Giving Ayden a few moments, Powells gently interrupted. "Is that where you hid when you'd run away?"

Ayden was startled, like he'd been found and dragged out of his safe place. His eyes and attention whipped back to the man who sat at an angle to him rather than face to face which always made him uncomfortable. But the therapist's expression was calm and understanding, not at all threatening. Ayden's heart decelerated.

"Come on, Ayden," he said gently. "You know how this works. Of course, your mom filled me in on some of this stuff, like when you ran away. And you're pretty sharp, so you know the last counselor you were seeing sent me her files. After all, believe it or not, we're all on your side." Ayden's face made it plain he did not believe all the adults were on his side.

"If it's okay, I'm going to ask you just one more question before we end here." He waited.

Ayden looked back at the picture before replying. He wondered why the small houses had no openings, thinking what if there were kids in them... or in the school? "You want to know why I used to run away, don't 'ya?"

"Maybe another time we could talk about that. What I'd like to know is how it felt when you were hiding, and no one could find you?"

He looked at Mr. Powell's face to make sure it wasn't a trick question. Then he looked at his knees. "Like a superpower, like I was invisible and safe."

"How about when your parents were looking for you? Did it feel safe then?"

"I..." The boy's voice ended like it had run into a period – as if he meant it to be a one-word sentence.

Powells didn't prod. After a few moments, Ayden added, "Kinda. But not always. Sometimes it was like I both wanted and didn't want them to find me – but they couldn't. But the last time, about a year ago I think, I got kinda scared. So, when they went back into the house, I got out and ran down the road, further away. I went down to this culvert that runs under the road. That time they did call the cops, and that's where they found me."

"That must have been scary?"

"He was a guy my dad knew, so I seen him before."

"Still," Powells said, "I would have been scared. I assume you thought you were in trouble."

They both went quiet. Ayden's legs began to bounce. He slipped his fingers beneath his thighs with his thumbs on top, unsuccessfully trying to keep his legs still, trying to hold himself in place. He moved his eyes across the carpet from left to right and back again. Suddenly he asked, "What's the story with that picture? Is that a school?" He tilted his head toward the small frame.

"It might be." Powells leaned back in his chair and raised his right foot onto his left knee. "Why do you think it's a school?"

"I don't know. The flag, I guess. It's bigger than the houses, which are weird shaped and go right inside the hill. Shouldn't the houses be bigger in the picture, you know 'cause they're closer? And why don't they have any doors or windows? The school has a small window up high, and it looks like there's a door."

"That's a good observation. I wonder if the artist thought about all that or just saw things differently."

"I guess. Do you think he wanted them to be different?"

"Maybe... You're a pretty smart young man."

"Not really." Then as if a page in his head had turned, Ayden added, "Are you still afraid of anything?"

"You mean besides doorbells?" They laughed again. "Yeah, I get uncomfortable about some things. I was a little afraid to meet you. I didn't know if you'd like me or not. But I'm okay now we've talked a bit."

The boy didn't know what to say to that, so he asked, "Do you ask adults about what they're afraid of?"

"Sometimes."

"Why?"

"This is what I think." Powells dropped his notes and file on the floor. "I think the things that make us afraid – even if we don't know why or want to admit they scare us – they sometimes make us say or act in ways we don't even understand. Do you ever do that? I know I do. Sometimes it gets me in trouble with my wife."

Ayden laughed again. "I guess."

"Yeah. You get it better than most adults do."

As this last memory faded, Ayden's eyes drooped. He slid down beneath his covers; he was still smiling at the thought of Mr. Powells getting in trouble with his wife.

10

Exhausted, Ryan arrived at school at 6:45 a.m., his regular time. Sharon was already going through phone messages and recording absences. She smiled and gave him a wink. Mrs. Zowak was also waiting. She didn't wink. He'd forgotten she'd asked to talk after yesterday's faculty meeting.

His night had not been good. It was a mistake to have gone to bed early. For most of an hour, he'd been unable to stop his mind from perseverating, caught in a loop of budget cuts, referenda, and tense faculty meetings. He woke multiple times. Each time the red digits on his alarm clock mockingly glared at him through the darkness.

He distinctly remembered seeing 3:37 a.m. That was when the strobe-like images he'd hoped were repressed and buried escaped: Lisa coming home late looking disheveled; he, thinking her tired, helping slip off her coat, kissing her neck; her scent carrying the gut-stabbing certitude she'd been having sex. The sequence repeated, then again and again. Each time the clues, the certainty more obvious, until he jerked to consciousness. His heart racing, soaked in sweat, his alarm screaming.

He knew why it had all come crashing back. The faculty meeting had left him frustrated and doubting his aspirations and abilities. Tired and feeling impotent, he'd been easy prey for the old memories and indecisions. Maybe he should have opened the drawer and smashed the damn photo. Instead, like he always had, he'd frozen, capitulated, wanting to believe, needing to believe her words that night. *"Don't ask. I can't explain. I don't know why. I don't want to lie to you. Please, just believe me. I love you."*

That was four years ago. Since then, he'd continued to tell himself he'd acted rationally, and reasonably, wanting to be understanding and forgiving. *For better or worse.* That was the vow, wasn't it? It was one slip. Beautiful women were constantly being hit on and tempted. Anybody could slip. He'd thought about it himself and had had opportunities. He'd come close once. But didn't.

She had closed the bathroom door and showered. Came out and kissed him. Repeated, "I love you." Adding, "I'm ..." then hesitating, not finishing. No apology. No explanation. She kissed his cheek and went to bed. He'd wanted to scream. *Tell me what's going on*. Make her explain. But how? He would not allow himself to become emotional, or lose control. That might lead anywhere. He stayed reasonable and rational. He'd not say anything he couldn't take back, that he couldn't live with.

He walked the neighborhood after she'd gone to bed, repeatedly finishing her aborted phrase in his head: *"I'm...what... leaving you. I'm... bored, not happy, unsatisfied..."* If she had finished, and filled in the blank, would she have added still more? *"You're always too tired, always at school, always so predictable, so conventional, so incompetent."*

Each possible line inflicted a fresh cut, an accusation it would be hard to defend against. He wanted to believe she might have said, "I'm sorry." But if that was true, why would she have stopped herself?

He'd found himself standing in front of Doody's Pub where they often went for food and drinks. It was busier than normal, but nothing like it would be next week for St. Patrick's Day. He began to shiver, not knowing if it was the chilly, spring, night air or the shock of what he'd just learned. He couldn't bring himself to go in, sure they'd see the humiliation on his face. Or worse, maybe they all knew already, had been regaled by some stud bragging about having just been fucking his wife.

He returned to the apartment to sit in the dark, his brain circling the drain, desperately trying to hold back a gauntlet of emotions. Eventually, he'd clambered into the lifeboat of her "Please" and "I love you." He clung to his thin, hastily built craft through vertiginous waves and troughs of fear and nausea; until finally the humiliation and his violated dignity shamed and blackjacked him into vowing never to ask "Why." He could ride this out, stay rational and understanding. What he couldn't bring himself to ask himself, to contemplate, was whether he could ever forgive.

When, within a month, he found it wasn't just one slip, he doubled down, persisting and clutching to his decision, to his lifeboat and vow, functioning but living on the impossibly thin edge between pain and suffering.

"Good morning, Bernadette. Come on in." He tried to sound focused and receptive but knew he didn't quite pull it off. Motion sensors flickered the ceiling lights to life along the passageway as he led her back to his small office beyond which were a small conference room and the offices of the two high school counselors and social worker. He unlocked his door and hit the light switch. The artificial florescent light highlighted the still dark cold morning framed in the window.

"Please. Have a seat." He gestured to the chairs around the round conference table as he hung his coat in the tiny alcove.

Mrs. Zowak declined the offer to sit. "I've only got a few minutes. I've got to get a lab set up." She continued to stand, her red-sweatered arms crossed.

Ryan stepped back around her, taking his seat behind his

desktop monitor and keyboard. He pressed the power button starting the soft hum of the cooling fan and the warming of the unfathomable digital circuitry. Usually, while he waited for the screen to present his calendar for the day, he'd go brew a cup of dark roast from the Keurig machine Sharon kept filled for him in the adjacent mailroom, but that wasn't going to be an option this morning. Instead, he faced his visitor. The bluish light appeared to enlarge her eyes behind her glasses. For a second, Ryan had the sensation of a mouse caught in the stare of a hungry owl. He was sure she was aware that by standing, she held the metaphorical high ground.

Without prelude or context, she asked in a pitched but not unempathetic voice, "What are we going to do with that boy?"

This wasn't what Ryan had expected to hear. "Pardon? I thought you wanted to talk about yesterday's faculty meeting. What boy?"

"Ayden Quant. Who else?"

Bernadette Zowak was an acquired taste. It had taken much of Ryan's first year as principal to realize this. Since then, he'd made progress toward the acquisition but wasn't all there yet. He thought it foolish to trust the relationship, but he had come to respect her and sometimes felt she reciprocated. They'd gotten to a place where if they didn't see eye to eye on something they mutually deemed important, they'd attempt to listen and discuss the matter until they understood the other's perspective. Sometimes they found common ground. Sometimes, not.

Ryan was especially grateful for her support and surprisingly calming effect last winter during all the unending political turmoil. More than half his staff had attended the mass protest demonstrations at the capital in Madison – after which two teachers announced early retirement and one aide quit at the end of the year. His spring and summer had been stressful, trying to fill positions from a dwindling number of applicants. He'd replaced one teacher in late June but only managed to sign a new graduate social studies teacher and an aide in late August, just in time for the beginning of school in September.

Ally would be too strong a word, but Ryan knew having Bernadette Zowak generally on his side, or at least not working against him, had been a huge help. He knew, in his tenuous position, she could have been the wave to capsize his career at Stienboek. It had been a hard year to be a new principal trying to build a relationship with a new staff. It was a hard year to be in education at any level.

Mrs. Zowak's longevity and personality had made her a force in the community, as well as at the school. Many of the local parents had themselves been her students. She was one of two current district staff – the other worked in the cafeteria – who had worked under John Stienboek back when he was the high school principal before becoming superintendent. She had been at the football game when he'd had his stroke. She had even been asked by John's widow to deliver one of the eulogies at the funeral. Although Mrs. John Stienboek had been aware of the clashes between her deceased husband and Mrs. Zowak, she also knew of the respect he held for her, that they had had for each other. She had sometimes wished she was as strong-willed as the then-young Bernadette Zowak.

Not all the Stienboek relatives agreed with the choice. But the new widow insisted. In her eulogy, the young teacher modulated her acerbic wit and managed to capture John's humanity and strengths, as well as a few infamous foibles. She had family, friends, and faculty laughing and nodding along, especially as she recounted their "dispute" over salaries back in the days when superintendents were not required to offer female teachers equal pay with their male colleagues.

Ryan needed a few seconds to shift his thinking and respond. "Ayden told me he'd taken off his sweatshirt before your class because it gets warm in your room. He said he forgot about his shirt. And that he might" – Ryan used air quotes to emphasize the boy's words – "have said damn, when you rightfully called him on his choice of quotes for the shirt."

"Well, I have to say it's ironic that he, of all people, chose that particular quote – if it was actually a quote." Ryan cringed slightly. Zowak's sarcasm was well known and usually tolerated by students and most parents, especially those she'd taught. It seemed as if her gray hair and heirloom status gave her immunity. Any other teacher who let similar lines slip out in their classrooms might well find themselves called out by the student or their parents. At least once last year Ryan had to get involved in a situation.

Zowak continued, either not noticing or choosing to ignore Ryan's wince. "He wanted to go back to his locker and get his sweatshirt. I told him to just reverse the shirt. We were starting the chapter test, and he was going to need all the available time and probably more. Going to his locker wasn't a good option."

"Do you think," Ryan wondered out loud, "he purposely left it in his locker?"

"God knows what that boy thinks. Some days I think he's a master manipulator, and then other times I'm not sure he has any idea what's going to come out of his mouth. You know, I had both his parents in class. Anna, his mom, hated school but worked hard. The father was pretty useless. Skated by on his looks. He was a mediocre jock and a party boy. I sincerely hope, in the end, the boy is an apple that rolls as far as possible from that tree. I know Ayden didn't get to choose his parents, but until he learns to quit defying any reasonable request we make of him..." Mrs. Zowak left the unspoken implications speak for themselves.

"Which, of course," Ryan felt obliged to say, "is why he's been in special-ed since third grade." He wasn't sure if he said it to remind himself or her. "By the way, Kim Berry told me he was seeing a new therapist last night. From what I hear, hopefully, this one is better than the last one."

Zowak looked at the clock on the wall. "What am I supposed to do about his test and grade? Did you suspend him? I didn't ask last night. You looked a bit worn out after the meeting."

"If I suspend him every time he acts up, he'll miss more days than he's here. Besides, with his mom at her shop, and his dad always on the road, he'd be home alone. He's better off here. He can come here to take the test. Would that help?"

"He'd miss a lab, but it would give his partner a break. Actually, she does quite well with him. She gets him involved and doesn't put up with any of his nonsense. He seems to respond well to her."

"Who's his lab partner?"

"Zoey Ackerly."

"I saw her mother in here yesterday. She was just leaving when I came in and found Ayden waiting for me. I wonder what Zoey says at home. Her mom gave the boy a bit of a look as she was leaving."

"I don't think that girl would say anything bad about Satan. But she expects everyone to be as interested in science as she is. She's probably one of the most talented science students I've had."

"Is Ayden ready for the test?"

"I doubt it. He hates to read or study, but he listens and has a good memory, so I'm sure he'll manage his usual C, maybe even a B." Zowak checked her watch against the wall clock and said, "I've got to go get ready."

"Drop off a copy of the test with Sharon up front. One of us will proctor it with him."

"Okay, but my question still stands. What are we going to do with that boy?"

When she was gone, Ryan glanced at the bottom desk drawer as if it contained a loaded gun rather than a photograph. It was like storing gasoline next to a burning candle, a scab aching to be picked at. What was he trying to prove? That someday he might stand up to his, to their, past? He wished he had never taken the damn picture, immediately knowing that was a lie. Still exhausted, he felt his mind slipping back to last night's dreams when a soft knock broke the spell, and he looked up.

Sharon came in and placed his filled coffee cup on his desk. "I thought you might need this after going one-on-one with Mrs. Z so early in the morning."

Ryan managed a grin. "She keeps me on my toes, that's for sure. Thanks for the coffee." The brief exchange helped his mood. He clicked on his calendar. Wednesday, November 21st. "Alleluia. Last day before a four-day weekend." He asked Sharon, "Do you guys have a big Thanksgiving get-together going on?"

Sharon and her husband both had family nearby, but Ryan couldn't remember what they'd done last year. She looked at the floor. "No... Not big." Then quickly reciprocated. "Are you still planning on leaving right after school to drive back to the Twin Cities to see your folks?"

"I am. But I'll come back over the weekend. Beat the traffic and catch up on some stuff. Maybe go see Walt Hannig."

The office phone rang. Sharon turned to go. "Deer season. Lots of parents excusing their kids so they can get a head start on heading up north to go hunting. If you make it up to Sturgeon Bay, give my love to Walt."

With a smile and a little wave, she turned and left. Watching her lifted Ryan's frame of mind. He cocked his head, but no single thought came into focus. He checked emails while the coffee finally woke him up. Then he headed out to be by the doors as the busses began to drop off students.

11

Dominic heard the thump. He spun his chair around as he continued his phone conversation. "Thanks, Miller. I appreciate you getting the new starter so quickly. You know better than anyone, that we're living on borrowed time with Bus 8. I only hope it lasts through the winter, and we can get a replacement next year."

Glancing at the *Playboy* magazine that had just landed on his desk and then up at Mike, he added a silent hand gesture meant to say, "What the hell is this about?" Mike just grinned at him.

Dominic finished the call. "So, if someone drops the bus off tomorrow by 8:30, you'll be able to get it installed before the afternoon run? Great. Thanks. I really appreciate it, Miller. Bye."

He hung up and turned the magazine on his desk face down in case someone else should walk in. "I assume there's a story here, and you're not just bringing me this because there's an interesting article I should read?"

"Took it from the Quant kid on the bus last night. I'd just stopped to let off the Bostrand twins. Someone hollers out 'Ayden's got a dirty magazine.' So, I walk back to see what's going on. Said I couldn't take it because it wasn't his. You know how he gets, all up in your face. Then he says he found it under the seat."

Dominic's lips twisted. He liked Ayden Quant and felt bad about him and his mother having to put up with his dad, who Dominic had known as a loudmouth and bully since their elementary school days. He thought it mostly a good thing the man was always on the road driving cross-country. He wasn't much of a father or husband when he was home. "Okay, fill out a bus discipline referral and put it in Ryan's mailbox with this." He enclosed the magazine inside an intra-district-mail envelope and handed it to Mike. Feeling a prickly irritation that the kid was in trouble again he added, "Mike, remember Mrs. Berry asked that Ayden sit up front so you can keep an eye on him?"

"I try, but you know how it is. I can't always watch him and the road at the same time. And it's not like Quant always does what he's told. Besides, that was way back in September, and he'd been behaving pretty good."

Dominic knew his driver was right. "I know. All right. But put a note on your dash or something. I promised Kim we'd do our best to help keep the kid from getting in trouble."

Mike sat down to write up the bus referral. "You know, Dom. Quant is in high school now. Isn't it about time the kid started to take care of himself? We can't keep babysitting him like he's in the third grade."

"I hear you. He's one of them kids who saps up a lot of everyone's energy." Dominic emailed Kim Berry a brief heads-up about the magazine and referral. Taking his jacket from the back of his chair, he headed out the door. "I got to go over to the middle school and check that boiler before I meet with Ryan later. He pulled on the coat, then turned back to say, "Thanks, Mike. You do a good job with the kids. Some days that's harder to do than most people realize."

Up - Down.

On - Off.

Light - Dark.

Dominic flicked the switch on and then off for a third time, remembering how this simple act had started his fascination with paired opposites when he was just a kid. Moving the little lever back to the up–on position, he added "Opened - Closed" to his list since that's how electric circuits work.

To make up for the few seconds he'd dawdled away, he stepped quickly to the pressure gauges along the back wall of the boiler room. Within those few steps, his conscious mind recalled and categorized yesterday's conversation with his daughter as "Black - White" and his thoughts about Ryan as "Known - Unknown." Over-simplifications. But handles to hold on to. Both conversations reminded him of the old saying about putting toothpaste back in the tube.

Tapping a knuckle against the gauge brought him back to the task at hand. The pressure was down a couple of psi since he'd called Falcone HVAC out in October to check the system. Dominic went to school with Robbie Falcone, had always liked him, and trusted him for these small routine jobs that didn't require a bid. After testing, Robbie had been 85% confident the boiler would make it through the school year but probably not two. He'd suggested praying for a mild winter.

Dominic hadn't been surprised by the news. He'd been telling the board for almost three years the system was ancient and needed to be replaced. They finally gave him the go-ahead to get an estimate and start putting together an RFP – Request for Proposal. Hopefully, it would make it into the capital budget this time.

He locked the boiler room door and headed back to the high school. He hoped Ryan was in a better mood than yesterday when he had appeared anything but upbeat. Upbeat - Downbeat. He checked his watch and quickened his step.

12

Ryan recognized Dominic's voice followed by Sharon's laugh. Their easy banter and familiarity tapped his "outsider" button, which he tried hard to ignore. Still, a jolt of isolation hijacked his heartbeat and collided with a touch of jealousy. He took a moment to exhale slowly, letting his gratefulness replace his sense of hollowness.

Both were locals who had welcomed him early on. Additionally, between the two of them, they seemed to know nearly everyone in the district. On several occasions, one or the other had shared some context about a student or a family that helped him prepare or better deal with a situation. Each had family roots going back at least three generations in the area. Sometimes Ryan could overhear them talking and even teasing each other like siblings. He knew Dominic's Nala babysat for Sharon's kids when they were small. It was a sharp reminder he hadn't had that kind of friendly bantering relationship with anyone for too long.

"Who you two gossiping about now?" Ryan asked when he stepped from the hallway.

Sharon swung her chair around. "Dom was just saying how he ran into this old couple..." She turned back to Dominic and asked, "They have to both be in their nineties, aren't they?" He nodded and she turned back to Ryan. "Anyhow, they were at Culver's in town, and they started quizzing him about what's going on here at the school, which they, of course, still call '*Steen–Bach*.'"

Dominic checked, "Walt Hannig told you about the old pronunciation battles, didn't he?" Ryan nodded.

Sharon looked to the doors to make sure no one was about to enter. "The couple had heard from Thynie Marsh's mother how their property taxes were sure to be going way up again, and they needed to keep an eye on the shenanigans going on here at the high school."

Dominic added, "Never underestimate the Marsh network."

Even with these two, whom he considered allies, maybe even friends, Ryan still refrained from saying anything more than, "Just what we need." One of the first pieces of advice he'd received upon arrival in Edenton was that everyone was somehow related, and whatever you said about someone, would get back to them.

The old couple's comments confirmed the uphill struggle a referendum would face. He'd already assumed Thynie would sniff him out as a weak link in her efforts to counterattack and derail a referendum. Dominic interrupted the thought. "You ready?" Ryan held up his ever-present yellow notepad.

They headed toward the varsity gym to check out a list of facility issues the gym teachers and coaches hoped would make it into the budget. Classes were in session, and the halls were empty except for the usual classroom sounds leaking from opened doors as they passed. With a year under his belt and having been in all the classes at least a couple of times, Ryan could visualize the unfolding scene in each room.

Just outside the band room, Dominic said, "Saw you coming back after the meeting yesterday. You weren't exactly clicking your heels."

The men stopped. Enthusiastic strains of "Have A Holly Jolly Christmas" penetrated the block wall into the hallway. Mr. Karin was trying out arrangements for the annual Christmas Concert coming up in a few weeks. They listened for a few seconds before Ryan replied. "It's not looking rosy or jolly." Reminding himself Walt had said Dominic's instincts about the community were usually good, Ryan added, "How do you think the idea of another referendum would fly?" His eyes indicated he didn't expect a positive reply.

"Like a pig wearing a lead cape. Lots of folks, even those with kids in school here, seem to like the governor's promise of lowered property taxes. They're not going to jump at the chance to give it back right away." They began to walk again.

"Even if it meant program or staff cuts?"

Dominic stopped. "It's that tight?"

"Not sure yet, but Superintendent Demian sees it as a possibility."

Rounding the corner and seeing the hall still empty, Ryan continued. "I'm scared it will get even worse."

Dominic put his hand on the gym door handle but didn't pull it open. "Worse?" He looked at Ryan. "Worse, how?"

"It wasn't discussed at the meeting, but everyone knows the staff contract agreement ends in the spring. With the union losing its ability to negotiate, and jobs and the economy still stagnant, I'm concerned all last year's shit will get thrown into the fan again. Dom, you know them all better than I do. You think the board will play hardball now that it has all the leverage?"

"They're going to be under a lot of pressure to do just that," Dominic answered. "Not to mention you can count on T-Rex to make sure the fan is turned on high."

"T-Rex?"

"It's a nickname Thynie picked up years ago from her husband's employees. It may fit her attitude, but the short-arm thing doesn't fit. If anything, she has quite a long reach around here."

Ryan's shoulders visibly slumped. "Great, a T-Rex with long arms." Dominic pulled the gym door open, releasing the sounds of thirty high school kids playing hoops.

When Ryan got back to his office, his mail-cubby was full. With a sigh, he grabbed everything and went back to his desk to work his way through the pile. First up was an intra-office envelope from one of the bus drivers. He opened it. His laugh reached Sharon. She'd never heard him laugh that loud before. Despite her somber mood, she walked back to see what was up and stuck her head around the corner. "What's so funny?"

He held up the *Playboy* magazine between his thumb and first finger. She raised her eyebrows in mock horror, then said. "That's how you're spending your time now? You've got to get yourself a girlfriend."

Still chuckling to himself, Ryan shook his head. "Would you please tell Mr. Quant to visit me before he goes to lunch? I suspect he's been waiting to hear from me all morning."

Sharon turned as she left and asked, "What month is that?"

Ryan checked the cover. "October, last year. Why?"

"Oh, just want to make sure it wasn't the issue my picture was in." She left. He stared at her fleeting backside and told himself not to say anything stupid. But he couldn't censor his imagination.

13

Dominic recognized the click of heels. Sharon appeared in his doorway. Other than the boys' basketball practice in the gym, and his cleaning crew, everyone else had headed home to prepare for their Thanksgiving feast tomorrow. Even Ryan had taken off for his long ride across the state as soon as the busses had cleared the parking lot.

They made eye contact, yet Sharon still knocked on the door frame before entering. "Hey, Dom. You got a few minutes?" Her tone indicated this wasn't just a quick "Have a good holiday" visit. She looked like a different person – like she'd been carrying a weight on her shoulders for days. He hadn't noticed that this morning.

He rolled his hand open. "You bet. What's up?"

She stepped in, hesitated, then reached back and closed the door. Again hesitating, she reopened it halfway before pulling a chair up to his desk. Dominic felt his stomach tighten.

"I wanted to tell you this personally, so you'd know, but please keep it to yourself for now." More hesitation. "I'm leaving Dave." Her eyes pleaded with his. "You know I've put up with the drinking for years. And I know he keeps the place going, but it's gotten worse. I could deal with it when he just blamed me whenever something went wrong, but now he's doing it with the kids." Mentioning the kids made her reach for the tissue box on his desk and wipe her eyes.

"I'm so sorry, Sharon. But I'm not surprised. I don't know many who would be surprised. Hell, most of Dave's family wouldn't blame you."

Sharon gave him a weak smile. "Thanks. He always used to do his drinking at home and pick his fights with me mostly after the kids were in bed. But for the last year or so, he's been going down to Sophie's. I'm sure half the folks around here know that by now. Some days he's gone by the time the twins get home from school. Says they're old enough to be home alone. They're in fifth grade, Dom. What the hell's he thinking? Sometimes he doesn't come home for dinner. I've spent the last year worrying about him killing himself or someone else on the road. I can't go on like this."

He knew she needed a hug. Stuck behind his desk, he instead handed her the tissue box. "Do the kids know?"

"No, not yet. And when I told Dave, he just sneered and dared me to leave. Said I didn't have the guts, and even if I did, he'd never agree to a divorce." She covered her face and used the tissue to wipe her eyes. Glancing at the door, she looked back up and whispered just loud enough for him to hear. "Dom, he said he'd tell people I've been screwing around with 'that new principal I work for'. Said I probably was anyhow. Even worse was when he said, really soft and mean-like, 'Remember how that worked out for Lisa?'"

"What the hell?" Dominic looked away, remembering last spring when he and a few of his buddies were at Sophie's for a burger and a few beers. He'd gone to the restroom and Dave was at one of the urinals with his head resting on the wall. Dominic had stepped to the other, asking if he was okay. Dave grunted, then slurred, "You trust this Davvis guy? I mean, have you seen him being maybe too friendly with Sharon? These good-lookin' fucks think they can get anything they want. You know, what the fuck, the guy married Lisa... I mean, we all know her story, don't we?" Dominic looked over to see the man smirking as he gave himself an exaggerated shake and fumbled with his zipper.

Feeling a flush of anger, Dominic had turned away and zipped himself up, then decided to be reasonable. He forced a chuckle and said, "You gotta be kidding, Dave. For one thing, Sharon wouldn't ever put up with that from anyone. And two, Ryan is not only not that kind of a guy, but I think he's still in shock about Lisa being killed. Besides, he's got so much on his plate, he wouldn't have the time or energy to flirt, not to mention that'd be a surefire way to get his ass fired. Especially around here."

Without flushing or washing his hands, Sharon's husband had just stood there staring at the door. "Well, you make sure Davvis knows about those two teachers old man Stienboek chased out of here real quick back when we was kids, and he found out they were doodling each other. Remember? The guy's wife divorced him. Took him to the cleaners real good."

Dominic flushed and stepped to the sink. In the mirror, he saw the door closing and Dave Edmonds' back disappearing. He remembered thinking Sharon deserved better. On the drive home, he had dismissed the man's question as ludicrous.

Dominic turned back to face Sharon, hoping he'd only drifted off for a second. She had composed her face. "Nuts, huh? I think he's pickled his brain. Anyhow, I just wanted you to know before it gets out. You've always been a good friend, someone I could trust in a jam."

"You know you can always talk to me, Sharon. Just let me and Kate know what we can do to help. You can drop the kids at the house if you ever need to. You know Nala thinks of them two as her little brother and sister."

Sharon blew her nose into the tissues she still held, stood, and dropped them in the waste basket. She glanced at the partially closed door. "I'd better get home before people start a rumor about us. I'm not looking forward to tomorrow. We're going over to

Dave's parents, and I'm scared to death he'll say something in front of everyone or make some kind of a scene...especially before I can find a way to tell the kids."

After she left, Dominic had trouble remembering what he'd been about to do before Sharon stopped by. He pulled his "to do" notes from his pocket, wondering if he should add warning Ryan about Dave Edmonds to the list. His heart ached for Sharon, but there was nothing practical he could do at this point. Maybe he'd go hunt awhile on Friday morning and give himself a chance to think it over.

14

Taking County Highway S out of town, Ryan avoided most of the Sunday after Thanksgiving traffic heading south on State Hwy 42-57. He'd left right after breakfast so he'd have enough time to stop at school before going back to his apartment on the eastern edge of Edenton. He'd spent the night in Walt Hannig's spare bedroom.

After his retirement, Walt and his wife Betty had moved back home to Door County. Deciding a house would eat up too much of their time and energy, they had rented a second-floor, two-bedroom apartment in the newly converted 1921 historic Sturgeon Bay Westside School building which sits atop a hill overlooking the bay and equally historic shipyard. Walt had once told Ryan how much he loved the idea of having come full circle. This was the very building where Walt had attended, taught, and been principal until 1980 when John Stienboek had hired him as Edenton's middle school principal. Two years later he was tapped to take over at what was then called Edenton High School – until John died and his name went on the building.

Ten months after the move, Betty had died of pancreatic cancer. She had refused any surgeries, chemo, or radiation, saying at seventy-five she wasn't going to go through all that and make both their lives miserable just for an extra month or two of suffering. From diagnosis to burial was three months.

Watching the old couple manage their ordeal, Ryan had been

struck with how their love and acceptance brought the couple together as opposed to how he had struggled with those same factors in the last year of Lisa's life. Betty's death bonded Ryan even closer with his mentor and friend. He'd visit every few weeks. They'd do some fishing, take hikes, and talk shop. As his predecessor, Walt was the one person who understood and whose advice he could trust. As protégé, Ryan helped Walt stay connected to the school he loved.

By 9:30 that morning, Ryan had reached the outskirts of Manitowoc and headed west on Hwy 10. As the sun-sparkled waters of Lake Michigan faded from his rearview mirror, his thoughts lingered on last evening's conversation. They'd bundled up and hiked the Cove Estuary trail at Crossroads before getting take-out lasagna and then a bottle of Pinot Noir from the Madison Avenue Wine Shop just down the hill from Walt's loft. Both establishments enthusiastically welcomed Walt as a friend and a regular.

Ryan reflected on how he'd selfishly dominated the visit with a conversation about his frustrations at school. He'd needed to vent. On their walk, he'd updated Walt about the prospects for another referendum and his painfully, plodding progress in sparking enthusiasm for instructional changes. Then over dinner and wine, he surprised himself when, for the first time, he shared his growing doubts about his ability to win over and hold the staff together through what he saw coming.

"Patience and relationships," Walt reminded him. "There's a lot of good people there. But all of you were under a lot of stress last year. Trust takes time to build."

"I only see it getting worse this year." Ryan shoved his last bite of garlic bread into his mouth. Still chewing he added, "Dominic thinks the board will be under a lot of pressure to take advantage of the staff's weakened position now that the legislature has castrated them. I'm feeling anxious about how that's going to play out."

Walt pushed his plate away. As if it held significance for him, he unhurriedly poured equal measures of the remaining wine into their glasses. "I don't think Superintendent Demian will go for that. On the other hand, after last April's election, I'd guess her influence with the board has waned some. Good thing Templeton is still the board president. I think he'll be a fair broker. But with their new advantages, it might be a tight thing. It could turn into a brawl, and it's going to put you principals in an awkward position."

Ryan felt a surge of frustration. He'd been hoping for more than simply stating the obvious. He read his mentor's expression for more but only saw the fatigue that had set in after Betty's death.

Walt rubbed both hands over his face. "And that's where being honest with the staff will be crucial for building trust. They're not going to blame you for all that's happening if they feel you're being upfront and honest... and trust them."

Ryan countered more tersely than he'd intended, "Unfortunately, any trust I inherited through your backing didn't last long in last year's political bloodbath. So, I'm not sure that's all that comforting."

He had almost added, "And then there's Lisa." The thought worried him. Since the dream had returned the other night, he feared his school and private life were colliding. His inability to pump the brakes and alter the trajectory on at least one of them was becoming palpable and dangerous.

Walt said, "I was a lot luckier. I had Betty with me." He moved the empty wine bottle on the table only to replace it in the original spot before continuing. "I apologize. That came out callous. I only meant to say your situation is...harder... lonelier."

"No apology needed. I'm..." Ryan stopped, unsure why. Memories, embarrassment, shame, fear? All possible candidates. Glancing out the window into the dark, he remembered walking the streets that first night, wracked in isolation and disbelief as if he'd suddenly been ripped out of his own life. He'd stared at his own truncated shadow, a legless, castrated, prostrate torso on the sidewalk, cast by a light from the pub he knew he could never again enter, torturing himself because Lisa hadn't finished her own unfinished "I'm ..." sentence. He looked across the table and saw the concern on the old man's face. "I'm grateful for your friendship, Walt."

They broke the maudlin mood by moving the dishes to the sink. Ryan started to put them in the dishwasher, but Walt insisted he'd take care of them in the morning. "Let's finish our wine and enjoy the view."

They carried their glasses to more comfortable chairs and contemplated the shipyard lights across the narrow bay. For Ryan, each singular, stark reflection dotting the dark water emphasized the cold and coming ice. After a few minutes, Ryan thought Walt might be falling asleep, so he raised the question that had been on his mind while driving up the peninsula.

"Say, Walt. Last Tuesday after the faculty meeting, I was in my office – sometimes I still think of it as your office." He adjusted his voice to sound as casual as possible. "Anyhow, I found myself wondering if you had many occasions to call Lisa in. You know, for some issue or concern? She'd never talk about her high school days, but I'm guessing she may have been a bit on the wild side."

Walt finished the last sip in his glass, setting it down on the small table between their chairs. His motion was slow, almost as if he was stalling.

Ryan knew Walt's longevity as Stienboek's principal meant he knew things: backgrounds, histories, details underlying the rumors and innuendos, probably even those undoubtedly whispered behind his back, labeling him as laughable and pathetic for coming to Edenton. Walt knew the people. Ryan was convinced he must know many of the secrets that might help him.

He'd been willing to gamble everything. If he hadn't been hired, his backup plan was to apply for a Social Studies position Walt had said would be posted once the new principal was in place. If necessary, he'd consider leaving education, the career to which he and his parents had committed their lives, the only career he'd ever wanted, to move here. If there was something to learn, anything that might help him understand and stop the black hole metastasizing in his gut from completely swallowing his dignity, his manhood, his dreams. Walt must at least hold some clues.

But then Walt had moved back to Door County, and that had been followed by Betty's illness. Ryan had not been aware the couple had been planning the move. Out of respect, and despite his sense of urgency and desperation for answers, he'd put off trying to mine Walt's memory. On top of that, all the difficulties of his first year had consumed him, leaving him too exhausted to do anything else. But now the moment finally felt right, and he'd asked the question.

Walt leaned back in his chair, taking a few additional seconds before responding. "I've been a little worried you'd begin to see ghosts in that building."

"No ghosts... at least so far," Ryan said. He swirled the last swallow in his glass, drank, then placed it on the table. "I'm not sure why that popped into my head," he lied.

"Like you," Walt began, "I made a point of talking with all my students. Of course, a principal ends up spending more time with some students than with others."

Ryan surprised himself when he chuckled. "My current 'frequent flyer' is a freshman named Ayden."

"Is that the Quant's boy?"

Ryan cursed himself for getting Walt off track.

The older man continued. "I never met the lad but did get a few warnings my last year: 'Wait till he gets to high school'. I do remember his dad and his stepmom, Anna. The dad tended to be full of himself and a bit of a bully. I didn't think it was any loss to the community when he moved away sometime after graduating. He went somewhere east... West Virginia or maybe East Tennessee. Then he's back and marries Anna. She was a serious no-nonsense kid who couldn't wait to get out of school. Rumor had it she didn't know anything about a child until they'd been married about a year, and he came home from a road trip with Ayden. The boy was maybe three or four at the time."

Ryan filed away the information but wanted to get Walt back to his question. "So was Lisa a frequent flyer with you?"

Three more long seconds of silence. "Like several of the girls, she'd stretch the dress code now and again. Mostly...she was like lots of the kids. You know. Hormones bouncing off every surface in the building – actually, sometimes not just from the kids. Lisa wasn't a discipline problem. But..." Walt looked over to a cabinet above a sideboard as if he'd forgotten it was there. When he turned back to Ryan, he rephrased his comment. "I think it was her junior year. She got real interested in little kids and started volunteering to work with the primary grades, especially the kindergarten. After that, she took school more seriously and ended up teaching 4-K in Green Bay where you met her, right? At a wedding?"

"Yeah." Then he surprised himself by revealing, "Well, actually, we'd met briefly before at a conference." Not wanting to elaborate, he probed a bit further. "Why do you think she changed back then? I mean about little kids, then going into teaching?"

From the look on Walt's face, Ryan thought he was going to backtrack and ask about the conference. Instead, he stood up. "I'm going to need to climb into bed pretty soon, but let me get us a quick nightcap." He got a bottle of brandy from the cabinet and poured a bit into two glasses before sitting back down.

"You know... I think humans are the only creatures on this planet that ponder 'Why' questions." He tasted the brandy and contemplated the glass for a moment. "I used to ask Betty 'why' she married me. She'd dated guys who had money and prospects. But she'd just smile and say, 'You figure it out'. I guess women need to keep some mystery in their lives."

Ryan tested his drink. "And did you? Figure it out?"

"What I figured out was that the question was my way of telling myself I wasn't worthy. How do we learn to believe all that negative stuff? I had to learn to cut that crap out. But in the end, do we ever know why we, or anyone, does anything?"

With a turn of his head to face Ryan, Walt asked, "I never told you the story of the burning monk, did I?"

Ryan knew Walt well enough to realize pushing him any harder for an answer, or even a theory about Lisa, wasn't going to get him anywhere. Besides, he was suddenly very tired and a bit drunk and needed to head home early the next morning. "Burning monk?"

"June 11, 1963," Walt shifted to better see Ryan. "A couple of buddies and me were off duty, having some beers in Saigon just a few blocks from the Presidential Palace. Of course, now it's called Ho Chi Minh City." Ryan knew Walt had been in Vietnam early on before it began to preoccupy and divide the country, but he'd never talked about his experiences there.

"We see a group of young Buddhist monks all in yellow robes gathering at the corner. Then a blue car pulls up and this older monk gets out and sits – you know, in that cross-legged position they do, right in the middle of the intersection. So, we're curious and walk over to see what's up. Still had our beer in our hands. We squeeze our way up close when we see another monk suddenly empty a five-gallon can of gas all over this guy who just sits there motionless, except he's fingering these beads – you know, like a rosary or prayer beads. Well, we turned and looked at each other. You know, wondering if we should do something. Then the old guy strikes a match and drops it on his robe... doesn't utter a sound, just sits there straight back with his head high and burns to death."

Ryan wasn't sure what to make of the story. Walt stood and swallowed the last of his brandy. Almost to himself, he said, "Now there's one hell-of-a-*Why*-question." He took a step toward his bedroom before turning back. "Thanks for coming, Ryan. Your friendship is a real blessing for an old guy. I put a towel and washcloth on your bed, and I'll make some eggs before you take off in the morning. Good night."

The sky had clouded over by the time Ryan pulled into his spot behind the school. He wasn't surprised to see Dominic's truck and detoured to his friend's office. "Mr. Samilton, are you living here now? Did you get any hunting in?"

"Feels like it sometimes. Could say the same to you. I went out in the woods behind the house Friday morning. Saw a few small ones but didn't take any shots. The ladies in my life aren't much on venison anyhow. How was your trip back to the Twin Cities? Are your folks, okay?" Dominic asked.

"Yeah, they're fine. Mom filled me up then loaded me up with leftovers to bring home."

"So, you're just getting home?" Dom asked.

"Yeah, but not from there. I came back early Saturday and drove up to Sturgeon Bay and saw Walt. Spent the night there."

Dominic sat back and ran his fingers over his tightly buzz-cut hair before clasping them behind his neck. "You're a good man, Mr. Davvis." His voice conveyed sincerity.

"Well, we widowers have to stick together."

"How's Mr. Hannig doing? That sure was such a raw deal about Betty."

"Well, he sure appreciated you and everyone who drove up for the funeral and sent all the cards and flowers. He's hanging in. Seems the hometown restaurants and wine shops all love him. And he still has friends there."

"I'm happy to hear he's doing okay and didn't turn into a monk after Mrs. Hannig passed."

Ryan pulled up a chair and sat. "Funny you should say that. Do you know anything about his time in Vietnam? Some tale about a monk setting himself on fire?"

Dominic scratched his ear. "Nope. As kids, we all knew he was a vet. He always made sure the students participated respectfully in a ceremony in the gym every Veteran's Day. But I never heard him talk about his service experiences. Why?"

"Nothing really. Just a weird story he told me over too much wine. Probably made the whole thing up. You know how he sometimes likes to pull your leg to make a point." Ryan stood. "I'll let you finish up and get home to Kate and Nala. I'm just going to check my phone messages, see what excitement awaits me tomorrow, and if Mrs. Thynie Marsh left me any words of wisdom before the next board meeting. Then I'm headed home and have a beer with mom's leftovers. See you in the morning."

After Ryan left, Dominic typed "burning monk" into his computer. He found himself staring at the images. He tried to picture a young Mr. Hannig seeing the whole thing from somewhere in the crowd. He read the Wikipedia description of the event. It was the kind of thing that might change a man who saw it. He thought about how little students really know about their teachers or the other adults in their lives.

When his thoughts turned to Ryan, Dominic decided it was time to get out of there. He put Ryan's chair back along the wall, remembering how just before the holiday last Wednesday Sharon had sat there telling him her news. He locked his door and headed to his truck, wishing he could find a safe way to warn Ryan about her husband.

15

Ryan finished toweling off, his naked body more awake than his mind. He rubbed his hand across the steamy mirror revealing a Monday morning blurry echo, a reminder of himself but not the real thing. He lathered his face. His hand raised but refused to begin to the task of scraping his features from beneath the soapy foam. The eyes staring at him from the misty silvery surface seemed intent on strip-searching his mind. They probed toward the incongruent, alien part of him that had materialized not long after Lisa had admitted she was cheating on him.

He thought about how the hurt had gradually become manageable, how he'd talked himself into accepting the situation. She'd told him it wasn't about him, he wasn't the reason, that he'd never been mentioned let alone discussed. It was like she was saying he didn't exist. Maybe at the time he didn't. Maybe his need for her to be discreet, to protect him from humiliation, had erased his real self, allowing him to convince himself that not reacting would somehow help. That saving the marriage was reason enough to stay. Even a month later, when she came home late carrying a different scent on her, he had pretended he could handle it.

It was then he'd begun to wonder if *not existing* offered certain freedoms. And shortly after that, he'd been startled and alarmed to find an emerging fantasy, a desire rising among the ashes of his soul, a need to have another man's wife. The thought became a demand. It replaced his self-pity. Suddenly, although the pain remained, the suffering faded. He rationalized it as an understandable reaction born of jealousy and revenge... possibly more. He fought against the possibility it was something that might have been in him all along, a cancer consuming the person he'd always thought he was. Uninvited thoughts and images ebbed and flowed for the next couple of months. He had battled back by taking on more responsibilities at school. But as he expanded the length of his workday, he'd obsessed about how Lisa might be filling her extra free time.

Despite the fantasies, he'd refused to accept the possibility he might be susceptible to adultery right up until the day the volunteer library assistant pressed her breasts into his back. He'd been working in a back corner of the library as he sometimes did to get out of the office and away from the phone. She'd smiled and pointed to a reference book a student had failed to return to its proper place. Rather than walking around the wooden table to retrieve it, she'd stretched over his back to reach for it.

Ryan's razor finally began to remove whiskers and foam. He rinsed the blade and looked back to his reflection. The eyes in the mirror asked how he'd been so reckless as to over-rule his usually reliable instincts and filters. He could hear his voice. "Mrs. Rupert..." He'd hesitated only a second to acknowledge to himself that completing the sentence could be an embarrassing miscalculation and, considering her husband's position on the board, a distinct possibility of costing him his job. "Are you being provocative?" When she didn't move, he added, "Or are you suggesting something?"

Her reply crumbled his willpower and previous self-denial about his susceptibility to adultery. "And if I was, Mr. Ryan Davvis, what might you do about it?"

Ryan had spent a good portion of his evening pondering that

and other questions. The thought of illicit sex was exciting but had never been more than a momentary pleasure. As soon as he asked himself why now, the answer was obvious. Revenge. As Lisa slept next to him, he was amazed and appalled to discover how satisfying, how pleasurable parts of his brain found the concept.

Two days later, when Mrs. Rupert met him at a St. Paul motel, he found himself indulging that very pleasure and embracing the role of dominant – teaching her "what he might do about it." It was a side of himself he hadn't known existed before he'd bent her over the bed. Her willing submission, the opposite of Lisa's controlling sexual instincts, was immediately addicting despite the realization that each demand he made of her felt like a betrayal of himself and all he thought he stood for.

The memory – further reinforced just last Friday afternoon in another motel with her – triggered arousal, making it difficult to concentrate on shaving until the distorting effect of the moisture on the mirror cleared, and he could again see clearly. Unlike his motivations, he feared her lust and compliance would eventually be about more than sex. Even though she was a willing player in their game, it didn't lessen his culpability in the possible destruction of her family, or his self-image and reputation.

The continued reckless desire and behavior – so much the opposite of who he thought he was – felt suicidal. It was dissolving his ability to believe or trust anyone, including himself. Ryan was aware of the real possibility at some point his cancerous behavior could metastasize. But he also knew he'd return over Christmas. The reason didn't matter anymore, only the need.

He wiped his face clean and then brushed his teeth. He needed to dress and get to school. He took a deep, slow, controlled breath to distance his conscious mind from dwelling on the nightmare vision of Superintendent Demian and Mr. Templeton, the board president, barging into his office, ordering him to leave the premises immediately, announcing his two lives had collided, and there would be no survivors.

16

Kim Berry wasn't the only one to think Bernadette Zowak's approach could at times feel like an incoming heat-seeking missile. Even now, more than an hour after students and most staff had gone home, the woman's unannounced entry had seemed disrespectful. Her sensitivity came from years of interruption by other staff who felt justified in barging in whenever they became exasperated with one of her students. Even having the door closed didn't discourage them. "Can I see you for a minute, Mrs. Berry?" Or, "Are you busy, Mrs. Berry?" as if they couldn't see her students sitting there, as if her teaching was of little or no consequence or value when measured against their frustration or need to inform her that one of her students had interrupted *their* class. Early on in her career, it had happened on a regular basis. Eventually, Kim called out the major offenders, first in private and then occasionally during faculty meetings. Now it occurred much less frequently. But still enough to be aggravating.

Nonetheless, she managed to be polite. "Hello, Bernadette. You're here late."

Notwithstanding the woman's uninhibited personality, the two were friendly, if not close. They were longtime colleagues and two of the few remaining clandestine smokers on staff. Kim's wit could be sharp, but she didn't come close to matching Zowak's overt sardonic nature. Kim had what she called the "special ed chip" which, along with her background and brother's struggles in school, gave her the patience and empathy to effectively work with the kids she did. Bernadette Zowak, who was ten years older, freely admitted she did not. What they did share was a vehement passion for teaching and public education. They'd had their differences – some would say arguments – over the years. But to the surprise of many, they'd never had a serious clash. In fact, they liked and respected each other. And they could be formidable when they teamed up.

"I was called from on high to meet with the superintendent and board president." Despite the sarcasm, Kim knew Bernadette respected both. "They proposed we have some informal chats about where we go after our current contract terminates at the end of this year. I was a bit surprised. They won't have to negotiate with us since our *'beloved'* governor and legislature did such a good job of selling the fiction of deficit reductions as their cover for breaking the unions." Zowak placed her coat on one of the raised desks and sat at another.

Kim was interested. "How'd that go? Anything hopeful?"

"Well, no promises, but they want to have some dialogue. They suggested that since I was the lead negotiator, I recruit a rep from each of the buildings to sit in. That's why I stopped. To see if you're interested?"

"Isn't that something that should be voted on by the membership?"

"Membership? Since Act 10 eliminated mandatory membership, a number of members have decided to discontinue paying union dues. They don't see what they'd get for their money, since we can't bargain anymore. Plus, since our salary rates have been historically near the bottom in the area, and we've constantly lost experienced teachers – which, mark my words, is going to get worse – there are only a few of us left who have taught and been here long enough to know the history. We'll keep everyone updated and informed." Zowak stopped, then added, "God! I need a smoke. Well, how about it."

"Which?" Kim asked. "A smoke or joining these little chats? When will they start?"

"In early February, after the second semester gets going."

Kim shut down her computer and straightened some papers. "Who'll be involved on the board's side?"

"Both Superintendent Demian and President Templeton. But they'll need to include Thynie or one of her minions." Switching into sarcasm mode, Zowak added, "If nothing else, it will give you a chance to test how far your legendary patience can be stretched. And I need you to keep me from getting too out-of-line. Besides, I think most of the rest of the staff would be intimidated to be in the room."

Kim placed her elbows on her desk and aligned her fingers prayer-like while resting her chin on her thumbs and covering her mouth with her fingers. She stared at the back wall for a few seconds. "Okay." She straightened herself and added, "What do you think will happen with health insurance? With Scott's diabetes, that's my biggest worry."

Bernadette Zowak watched her feet swing the desk's swivel foot bar several times. "Don't these things drive you crazy?" She looked over to Kim. "Our portion of the premium is going up. Some districts are already switching to cheaper and more restrictive policies. We won't have any say in what they decide."

"That's not very reassuring. We've always traded salary for good insurance, and now that's going away. We've been going backward since the state put revenue caps on tax levies in the early 90s." Kim reached for her coat behind her desk and stood.

Mrs. Zowak continued. "I can't blame folks, especially the young ones, for jumping ship. But by dropping out of the union, we're giving away the only way we'll ever get the right to negotiate back. I'm going on the record, Mrs. Berry. Wisconsin is going to suffer a serious teacher shortage very shortly, and you know darn well, they'll find a way to blame us for that too."

Showing her own sarcastic side, Kim said as she put her coat on, "You sound optimistic."

"Kim, you've been around here a long time. Do you see anything to be optimistic about?" Mrs. Zowak also grabbed her coat and started toward the door. "Have a good evening, Mrs. Berry. I suggest we both go home and have a smoke and a glass or two or three of wine."

Kim brought her plate in and sat. Her husband Scott poured her a half glass of red wine. On weekdays, the couple enjoyed the PBS Newshour while they ate. The program shifted from the national and world news summary to an interview with a congressman who ignored each posed question, preferring to pivot and pontificate on why Obama's recent reelection was a danger to the country. He particularly singled out the billions he saw as being wasted by the president's education department trying to bribe states into adopting Common Core state standards.

Scott hit the mute button. "You're pretty quiet. Rough day?"

"Bernadette stopped after school. She asked if I'd join some talks with Superintendent Demian and the board about where we go after this year's contract ends. I told her I would. She also thinks they'll play around with our health insurance." Kim downed her wine. "But for now...," she held out her glass for a refill, "all I want is to get to the holidays without any more shitty school-related things happening."

17

Regular school board meetings were held on the third Wednesday of each month. However, with Thanksgiving and the opening of deer hunting, it had been moved up to Monday the 26th. Because board president Charles Templeton was a stickler for starting promptly at 7:00 p.m. and following all open-meeting rules, members could usually expect to be home no later than 10:00. Tonight, with alternating spits of snow and frozen rain in the air, most were grateful the agenda had moved along in an orderly manner. They'd wrapped up regular business before 9:00. At that point, Templeton adjourned the public meeting for a five-minute break before reconvening in the superintendent's conference room for a closed executive session.

Thynie and Bobby Marsh were the last to rejoin the group. It was obvious they'd been talking, and Thynie started in as soon as they took their seats. "What's this about meeting with teachers to talk about salaries?" She managed to capture both Templeton and Demian in her cold gaze. "They can't negotiate anymore."

Superintendent Demian responded calmly. "This is not negotiations. It's a simple conversation to head off future problems and unrest down the road. When the contract ends this school year, the salary schedules that have been in place for years also end. We're going to need to figure out a way to fix salaries and increases for current and future staff. It has to be clear and not arbitrary. Not to get input from the staff would be asking for trouble."

Bobby Marsh jumped in. "That's no way to run a business. We need to be firm."

Templeton's response was terse. "Let's keep in mind this is a school and not a factory or a ..." He didn't finish, but it was clear he was about to refer to Bobby's house painting business. "The posted agenda says we were convening to executive session to discuss insurance and a possible referendum, not this stuff. We need to move on."

Everyone resettled, and the superintendent briefed them about the alternative health insurance inquiries she'd been making. After several questions and clarifications on how to proceed, Templeton launched into the second topic – a referendum to allow the district to go beyond the revenue caps. His position was clear. "We knew these expenses were coming, and we know they're much needed. We can't keep kicking this can down the road if we're going to keep our kids safe and give them what they need to compete. We just heard again from Dominic in the open session about anticipated, and in many cases, dire repairs and replacements that can't be put off any longer." Templeton took a deep breath. "So, let's hear what everyone's thinking."

Two hours later, he noted it was now almost 11:00, and most of them had to be up early for work in the morning. He tried to keep his tone even as he repeated himself. "Thynie, we agree about a less costly health insurer when the contract ends, but if we did what you're recommending and moved money from the general fund to cover a replacement bus and the needed repairs rather than go to referendum, we'd still be limping along with outdated technology, have a dangerously low fund balance which could risk our credit status, and we'd need to cut some programming and probably some staff."

Thynie appeared to enjoy the sound of exasperation that had

crept into his voice. She made eye contact with her two allies before responding. "But isn't that why the governor and legislature gave us Act 10, so we would have more room to maneuver without having to ask taxpayers to cough up even more to pay teachers a nine-month wage that's more than many of us make in a full year?" Several around the table exchanged glances. Her husband owned a very busy food franchise in town and a successful insurance business for which she worked part-time as the bookkeeper.

Templeton responded. "You know the referendum would have nothing to do with wages or benefits for staff. We're talking capital costs only."

Thynie pounced. "We need to take advantage of this. That's what people voted for. Need I remind you; the governor handily won our county? Elections have consequences, and people expect us to now use our ability to save money and make some cuts if needed. Besides, we'd all certainly agree, wouldn't we, you can't please everyone or meet every need. Everyone knows we offer too many programs already. It wouldn't hurt to cut back some of the fat."

Mrs. Kanzlin, whose son excelled in the arts and drama, fought back. "So, where would we cut? Maybe in the athletic programs? After all, sports are by far our most expensive extra-curricular programs." Thynie's son, Jake, was the junior quarterback on the varsity team and a starter on the basketball team, just as his oldest brother had been. She also knew the community would never support that, so she didn't respond. Sports were, and always had been, a major point of pride for the Edenton community. Last year, two of the varsity teams, boys' football, and girls' basketball, had made it to the state playoffs.

Another voice weighed in. "I'm not at all sure we agree there are too many offerings, either in academics or in extracurriculars. Lots of parents moved here because of those programs. If they were cut, they wouldn't hesitate to pull their kids. If parents use their school choice option, we lose the student and the state funding."

"Well, some of us," Thynie spoke confidently to her two allies, "and many in the community at large think we've grown too big, too fast. It's not sustainable. We're going to end up with the same problems as city schools, and you certainly don't want that to happen here. If some kids went elsewhere, we'd lose some money, but in the long run, we'd save because we wouldn't have to always be making changes and adding on, always asking for more. We already know from demographic projections that if developers keep buying up land for more houses, we're going to need another elementary school and eventually a larger high school. Who's going to pay for that?"

Unable to resist herself, Mrs. Kanzlin interrupted. "Maybe at that point, we'd be ready to build a new modern high school. A building able to handle all the new technology we're going to need to compete with surrounding districts."

The "if looks could kill" stare she got from Thynie indicated the remark had struck home. Her response started two whole tones higher and louder than normal. "Well." She adjusted her voice. "For those of us who actually grew up here and love it the way it is, or at least how it *was*," Thynie paused for extra emphasis, "and don't want to be part of the urban sprawl that's ruining the place, I don't see that happening. We're already seeing more families turning to home-schooling. Others are looking into online schools to get away from all these state standards and stuff. People are getting fed up that we keep raising their taxes and turning Edenton into something they don't recognize as the school they went to."

Templeton exerted his prerogative as board president. "Okay, it's now ten after, and we're all tired. We've agreed Superintendent Demian will talk with surrounding districts and get projections about healthcare costs from other providers. As far as the referendum, it appears four of us are in favor of moving forward, so I'm going to put it on the December agenda for public discussion.

"Remember, none of us should be out and about in the public talking about it – pro or con." He swept the table with his glance, making eye contact with each of them. "If we go forward, there's a lot of work to be done before next April. And..." Templeton paused until he had everyone's attention. "I'm sure we're all aware that discussions in this room are not to be discussed elsewhere. Outside discussions between board members are considered a walking quorum and a violation of open meeting laws." Another pause. "Let's reconvene and formally adjourn and get home before the sun rises."

18

Dominic's desk phone rang just as he was finishing work on the monthly order for paper products. The school district went through mountains of toilet paper and paper towels. To run out was not an option.

"Dom. It's Ryan. Can you come to my office for a minute?"

"Sure. What's up?"

"Best to wait until you get here."

When he got to the office, Sharon wasn't at the front counter. Since their conversation a couple of weeks ago, he'd tried to check in with her at least once a day. Lately, she'd been visibly frustrated because her husband Dave was avoiding any further discussion. She didn't want to tell the twins or make it public until they'd sorted out the stalemate. He went back to Ryan's office.

When he entered, he was surprised to see Nala sitting at the round table. Her hands were on the surface clenched hard into fists, and Ayden Quant sullenly sat near the window, staring at his feet. The boy was the first to speak. "I said I'm sorry!" His words were aimed at the floor and came out aggressively. He looked up to Dominic and softened his tone. "I told her I was sorry, Mr. Samilton." Dominic looked at Ryan.

"We had an altercation in the hall during passing. Nala says Ayden called her the 'N' word. She slapped him and then almost knocked over a girl."

"That was an accident when I turned around. If I didn't get out of there, I would have beaten the crap out of him." She looked to her father with a pleading in her eyes he'd never seen before. "Daddy, he called me *that* word." Tears filled her eyes.

Dominic felt instant fear and his gut tightened as he stared at the raw pain on his little girl's face. But this wasn't unexpected. He wasn't surprised. Edenton was like everywhere else; the word hadn't disappeared from everyone's vocabulary. But he'd only heard its ugly sound in his presence a handful of times since the adoption and never aimed directly at his daughter. He recalled the incident from early fifth grade. The teacher had told him a student had used the word but not to Nala's face. She didn't think Nala had heard, but she hadn't asked her. She'd just wanted Dom to know, in case he heard about it later – "You know how people talk."

She said she had reprimanded the student. Had explained it was a bad word, and that she never wanted to hear it again. Dominic had accepted she'd done her duty and handled the incident the best she knew how. Maybe the best he himself knew how. She had enforced school policy – *Bullying or name-calling will not be tolerated.* "The boy said he was sorry," she told him. "He didn't think he'd done anything wrong," then adding, "He said, 'That's what my parents called them at home.'"

All Dominic had heard at the time, as if it had been shouted in capital letters and underlined, was the word THEM. *Called THEM at home.* His face must have contorted because the young teacher had suddenly looked alarmed and quickly added, "Can you imagine?"

He and Kate had feared such incidents ever since the adoption, knowing that at some point it could happen, would eventually happen. The episode had moved the possibility of his daughter facing such hostility to reality. Still, he wasn't prepared and had no idea what to say to the teacher at the time. He had thanked her for letting him know. He'd empathized with her embarrassment for having to face an unpleasant duty. He'd said he understood when she told him she'd rather not say who the boy was and thought that should be confidential to protect him. They'd agreed the kid was just parroting what he'd heard at home and probably didn't understand the impact. At the time, he had accepted the excuse. Only later had he realized the implication of who deserved protection and who didn't.

Dominic started to ask a question. Ayden interrupted. "I didn't call her that. I just asked if it bothered her to be, you know... You know, like it bothers me to be picked on by some teachers and other kids at school 'cause I'm in special ed. I thought it must be harder for her 'cause anyone can see she's..." He stopped talking, realizing what he almost said again.

Dominic thought of Nala's words on their way home last week. *"You may not have noticed, but I'm Black."* She'd even held her hands out as evidence, as if to accuse him of being that naïve, or maybe even trying to force him to accept the fact. But his reaction had been to point out she was also half-white, point out the positive, assure her that her glass was half full, suggest that would be enough. She was smart and involved. She had friends and talents. He realized he'd been clinging to the idea that she'd been and would continue to seamlessly adjust, to fit in.

He gently asked her, "Honey, is that what he said? Do you think maybe that's what he meant?"

"All I heard was THAT WORD."

Her dark eyes brimmed with anger. Dominic wanted to hug and protect her but simultaneously, and despite his flashback a moment ago, to help her understand it was just a word after all and not worth reacting so emotionally, so out of control.

"I said I was sorry," Ayden pleaded. "I didn't mean you were one of those. I just wondered..." his words faded. In frustration, he smothered his face in his hands and dropped his elbows to his knees.

Nala stood. “I want to go home.”

Seeing a way to de-escalate, Ryan agreed. “Dom, why don’t you take Nala home for the rest of the day? She’s still obviously quite angry and upset.”

Like the word Ayden had used, Mr. Davvis’ words touched a raw nerve. Instead of her hand, this time Nala hit back with unchecked sarcasm. “You mean uppity?” She suddenly spoke in dialect, something Dominic had never heard her use. “Like, ya’ll don’t need no uppity, angry Black girls with attitude ‘round here?”

The words and tone stunned Dominic. “Natalia! Stop that. Where did that come from? You apologize to Mr. Davvis right now. You know he’s always been on your side, and he didn’t mean that.”

Nala turned her back. Her shoulders heaved as she let out a single sob. Ryan and Dominic looked at each other, trying to make sense of what had just happened. Ayden remained staring at his own feet, wishing he was safely under his porch.

Surprised to hear her father’s use of her legal “Natalia” name, Nala took a long, sighing breath, not to calm herself but in resignation that her father and her principal just didn’t get it. She reached for a tissue from the box on the table. She blew her nose, and while still holding the tissue in her fist, she picked up her books from the table and clutched them to her chest. “I’m sorry for being rude Mr. Davvis. And maybe Ayden didn’t mean it. Okay?” Then in a disheartened voice, “I shouldn’t have overreacted.”

“Technically, I should suspend you both, at least for a day. But if you both are saying it was a misunderstanding...”

Through tight lips Nala softly but firmly injected. “I didn’t misunderstand the word, just that he didn’t mean it the way he said it.”

Her dad said, “Nala, let Mr. Davvis finish.”

“That’s more than fair, Nala,” her principal said. “Go home until tomorrow. I’ll let your teachers know you have an excused absence.”

Dominic and Nala left the office and headed down the long

hallway toward her locker. She walked quickly, several steps ahead of her father. The sight of her bent back and bowed head made her father feel sick. He'd somehow terribly bungled the whole thing. But all he'd done was react honestly. Making it worse was the realization he still hadn't been prepared and didn't know how to handle the situation. It was a feeling he wasn't used to having.

19

On the drive back to school, Dominic's mind was like a stuck phonograph needle on an old vinyl record. Bump...I don't understand...bump...I don't understand...bump. All the way home after he'd left Ryan's office with Nala, he kept telling her, "It's okay, honey. It wasn't your fault. I'm not mad at you." He knew he was trying to apologize as well as ease her distress. But the only response he'd get was, "I know, Dad."

"I understand you getting mad at Ayden, though it would have been better if you didn't smack him."

"I know, Dad."

"You know I love you, don't you?"

"I know, Dad."

"Why would you say something like, 'uppity Black girl'? You don't talk like that." Dominic was surprised with how troubled, almost betrayed, he felt by her reaction. "You know Mr. Davvis didn't mean any of that stuff you said."

"I know, Dad."

"He is on your side. You know that, right?"

Her response to this question was the only time she offered any elaboration. "I know, Dad. It's just ... I'm just not sure which side that is." Dominic had no idea what to say to that. He wanted to ask her what she meant but didn't. Not until he had time to think about it himself.

He turned back into the parking lot behind the school. As he came to a stop, he muttered. "I don't get it." He put the truck in park, then closed his eyes. *Why would she purposely misinterpret Ryan's comment about her going home? She'd just said she wanted to go home.* His daughter's words echoed loudly in his ear. *"...don't need no uppity, angry Black girls with attitude 'round here?" Why would she lash out in some ghetto dialect like some inner-city kid?* Hadn't they rescued Nala from all that when they adopted her?

For a moment, his brain went blank. Then it doubled back to the thought. *Jesus!* His eyes opened. *Did I really think that? Did I think we were saving her from that life, from being Black?* He didn't remember. Didn't want to remember. He supposed it was possible, at least to some extent. And, *if I had, would that have been so wrong?*

Dominic often conjured up the first time he saw her. She toddled across the playroom at the agency, clutching the ends of a small white baby blanket over her head, shading her eyes. She'd stopped directly in front of him and Kate. Looking up at them, she'd fallen back onto her diapered bottom as if she had meant to sit. Her almond, dark eyes, eyes almost too wide for her face, focused on his like she could see and absorb more than most eyes could. She had tugged her blanket from her head and held it out to them. He could still see it all in his mind's eye as clearly as if they were all back there now. He saw her cropped hair. Cut short, as if to hide its true nature. He knelt to accept her blanket and fell into those dark eyes and face.

His hand was on the door handle, yet he continued to sit, staring at the back of the building. He was trying to take hold of what was gnawing at him. Across the school's ball field, at the Edenton Elementary School playground, kids were out for recess running and hollering. He watched them for a full minute not knowing what he was looking for, until he saw a girl playing four-square with a group of other girls. It took several seconds before he spotted her brother shooting hoops with some friend. The Genefers. He knew their names, but not the names of the kids they played with. He couldn't remember ever having them on a bus route he'd covered. Yet somehow, he knew where they lived. He knew they were the oldest of the four Black children in the school, along with maybe a half dozen Hispanic kids. Westown Elementary had one light-skinned mulatto girl. He wondered if he was using that term correctly.

Realizing he was thinking of them as different and separate made him embarrassed. Separate from what? The answer was obvious, from the rest of us. Them - Us? Paired opposites. Two Black kids at the middle school but only Nala here at the high school. A student population of just over a thousand. And not one Black teacher or staff person. He wondered if that had ever crossed anyone's mind. It was the first time it had ever crossed his. He tried to imagine slipping it into his report at the next board meeting. *"The estimate for the new bus is $100,000 and, oh by the way, has anyone else noticed we don't have any Black or even Asian or Hispanic teachers in the entire district?"*

That night, Dominic anxiously tapped on Nala's bedroom door. "Good night, sweetheart. I love you." He stood still, holding his breath, worried he might not hear a reply.

"Love you too, Dad."

The response eased but didn't erase the unsettling apprehension he'd felt since the incident in Ryan's office.

Kate was already in bed, reading. She devoured a novel a week. He crawled in, kissed her goodnight, fluffed his pillow, and rolled onto his side away from her reading light. Three minutes later, he was sitting up, needing to go over the incident again.

"Can't let it go?" Kate asked.

"I get her reaction to the Quant boy's stupid comment. But..." In his head, he heard his daughter's words. "Why would she blurt out that 'uppity, Black girl' stuff? I was embarrassed. I'm sure she picks it up from all that rap stuff they listen to." He knew he was looking for someone to blame. "Maybe we were wrong always calling her Nala instead of Natalia."

"I get why you're upset about the boy. My first reaction was to march back to school and demand Ayden be suspended. But neither Nala nor you believe he was using it as a racial slur. What I don't get is why you're so upset about her words and reaction. Why would calling her Natalia change anything? That's not like you, and you know it. As soon as she talked, she called herself Nala. Using your logic, if we shortened Natalia to Nat, she'd turn out to be a lesbian."

"Maybe I can't let it go because I was embarrassed for Ryan... and for her."

"You said you were embarrassed too. I think that's what you need to think about."

"Kate, I just don't want Nala to think she has to act that way. That's like putting a chain around her neck and ..." he struggled to finish the image. "I don't know, and then trying to swim across the Fox River against the current."

She looked at him. "Really, Dom? That's the simile you want to go with?"

It took him a second before the implication became clear. "You know what I mean. I told her I'd – we'd – love her even if she was purple. Maybe that would be easier. At least being purple wouldn't come with all the racial baggage."

"I think Kermit might disagree."

Dominic looked confused. "What?"

She smiled and caressed his face, trying to relax him. "You know, 'It's Not Easy Being Green.' Look. She's a teenager, Dom. There's going to be outbursts. Life gets very confusing and complicated as girls become women. You didn't have any sisters. But there's going to be times we're going to scratch our heads and try to figure out who or what our daughter is turning into."

Dominic turned so he could see his wife's eyes. He wasn't a man who raised his voice, but just to be sure he purposely whispered. "But I don't want her to turn into a ..."

He found himself again at a loss for words. "I don't know. Into something she's not or doesn't have to be, something that can get in her way or get her hurt. What I'm trying to say is, why does she have to decide to be one or the other – Black or white."

"I'm not sure how much we'll get to say about that," Kate said. "She doesn't have an on-off switch. You should talk to my folks about my sisters. It might make you feel better. They were completely convinced Cindy was going to become an alcoholic hooker and Barb an anarchist. Most girls go through an identity crisis or two. But like my sisters, Nala is going to be fine. She'll figure it out."

"And then what?" he asked.

Kate kissed him. "Then she'll tell us, just in case we somehow missed it."

Dominic sighed, then covered a sudden yawn. "I know she will. It just scares me. I thought when she wanted her hair straightened, she was fitting in. I'm ashamed to admit that but even more so about how I felt when she stopped. I should have seen that as a good thing, that she was being herself, but to be honest, it bothered me. I felt that way because I was worried for her, but you know, I think you may be right. It's more about me than her."

He rolled onto his back, lacing his hands behind his head. "Pretty shitty, huh? Nala has a nightmare of a day, and I'm here whining about my own feelings. I don't know how to fix this for her."

His wife leaned over and kissed him. "The first thing you're going have to do, that *we're* going to have to do, is realize we can't fix this or most of what she'll face. At the time we adopted her, we needed to think, to believe, it couldn't be that bad. We grew up here and believed people are mostly good. We had faith we'd be able to handle it.

"We need to have faith Nala will find her own way to not just survive but to thrive. I'm glad we were too naïve to think too deeply about all the implications or to doubt whether Nala, *our daughter*, could handle it."

Dominic sat up. "Why would you say that?"

"The way I figure it," Kate said, "is most parents think the way we did; that they'll be able to protect their kids, no matter what. If parents worried beforehand about their children being able to handle all the shit that comes with life, nobody would have kids. But we chose Nala. She wasn't an accident – which is how more than a couple of our friends became parents. And sure, now Nala's life is getting more complicated and scarier. But I have no doubt you, we, would choose her all over again. We'll support her and love her, while she works and even suffers her way through this. And you, my dear, are a very good man when it comes to support and love."

Dominic laid back down. The tension in his face and body eased. "Well, there's no harm in mixing in a bit of advice with the love and support. After all, I'm pretty darn good at fixing things."

He closed his eyes. Kate caressed his face. "You're her father, Dominic Samilton. She'd expect no less."

He rolled over again and was quickly asleep.

Kate finished her chapter before turning off her light. In the dark, she said a prayer for her daughter and her husband. She found sleep didn't come as easily for her.

20

From his usual post, just inside the main door to the gym, Ryan watched Nala drive the lane for a layup. He applauded when the ball dropped through the net just feet from where he stood. As both teams moved toward the other end of the court, Ryan, out of habit, absent-mindedly scanned the bleachers on both sides of the court. His gaze came to rest on a section of bleachers above the Edenton bench. A memory from years ago materialized. He'd been standing in this same spot talking with Walt Hannig after Lisa had introduced him to her former principal.

At the time, Ryan had been working on his administrative license in Minneapolis, and the two men had talked through much of the game while Walt kept one eye on the game and his other on the crowd. Ryan's attention tracked to the exact spot along the top of the stands where Lisa had sat with her cousin just behind their uncle that night. His memory dredged up a previously unnoticed detail – Walt's periodic glance at the Kames trio. At the time, it seemed natural since Lisa had just introduced them, and Walt hadn't seen her in several years. Ryan wondered what ever became of the uncle. He tried to remember the cousin. She had driven Lisa's parents to Minneapolis for their wedding. Their only visit. *Does she still live around Edenton? Probably not, or I'd have run into her by now.*

The teams rushed back toward him. A shrill whistle stopped the action, sending the Stienboek 5'10" sophomore center to the free-throw line. The girl took a deep breath to calm herself before clunking the shot off the front rim. She got her own rebound and passed it out to Nala in the corner, who sank a twenty-foot shot. He and the Stienboek fans all cheered as the teams headed back upcourt.

Nala was the best shooter on the team and one of the only two with notable ball-handling skills. Her basketball abilities suddenly associated themselves in Ryan's consciousness with Nala's skin color. Another part of his brain tried to compensate for the stereotype connection: *Aren't most of the top players, men and women, in the NBA and college teams Black?* He remembered the incident in his office the other day. Even though he didn't think she'd specifically meant to, Nala had all but accused him of being racist. *Shocked wasn't the right word. I was embarrassed. Could she have seen that somehow?*

She'd apologized. The next day she did so again, explaining she'd been upset by Ayden's use of the N-word. Still, he'd felt "called out." *Why?* Growing up, he'd always attended public school with African Americans. Then working in the Minneapolis school system several of his colleagues were Black and Hispanic. But he realized none were *close friend*s. True, he'd always been angered by anyone tossing around racial slurs, genuinely thought they were bigoted assholes. However, he also knew, he'd never confronted any of them...*which would undoubtedly have led to a fight I'd have lost.*

Cheering fans brought him back to the game. He looked to see Nala dribbling down the sideline and hitting a teammate under the basket with a bounce pass for an easy layup. *She's good.* He could see her being pulled up to varsity next year as a sophomore. She was a team player. She'd fit in well. He spotted Dominic and Kate in the stands. He wondered how they'd feel about that. Most parents reveled in the affirmation of their kid's skills. Some balked for various reasons.

While the action moved back to the other end of the court, Ryan's recall returned to Minnesota. He'd sometimes counseled rambunctious Black students, telling them they could make their life easier if they'd learn how to "fit in" better.

The buzzer sounded at the end of the first quarter. Ryan's previous unexamined assumption that "fitting in" should be a simple option, simply a matter of choosing to do so, lingered and bothered him. He wondered what he'd actually been asking his former students to "give up," by telling them to "fit in." How did they internalize his remarks?

The home crowd stood and applauded as the team walked to the bench for water and Mrs. Shimone's second-quarter instructions. Ryan wondered if he and Dominic had become close enough to ask his thoughts on the matter.

He stepped out to get a drink from the bubbler and check the adjacent halls. It would be a long night. This game would be followed by the varsity game. He generally enjoyed attending evening student events. The games, concerts, plays, and other competitions gave him something to do and a way to meet and talk with parents and community members outside of formal meetings. It was part of the job, but since he had no one at home, it was a welcomed distraction and better than just watching television and thinking too much. Especially lately. He was keenly aware he'd been slipping back into the habit of letting his mind get trapped in that damn loop, the same thoughts conjuring the same accusations and feelings, always leading nowhere, yet always ending up in the same place.

He took a long drink then straightened and wiped his wet lips with his fingers. The simple act raced his mind ahead to the upcoming winter break, which he and everyone else considered a "Christmas" break. But knowing he'd be seeing Mrs. Rupert made it difficult to think of it as a religious holiday.

He heard the buzzer for the start of the second quarter and became aware of someone queued uncomfortably close behind him. He stepped sidewards to avoid backing into the figure. He glanced behind him. At first, he didn't recognize the face, but then realized it was Sharon Edmonds' husband, though his first name wasn't coming to mind. He'd only been formally introduced once at last year's staff holiday party. He hadn't even had a conversation with the man. Mr. Edmonds hadn't yet bent to drink. The name came to Ryan. "Oh, Hey, David. Good game huh?"

He didn't wait for an answer and turned to go back into the gym. The voice, louder than needed in the nearly deserted hallway, took him completely off guard. "Yeah, that little dark Samilton girl can really shoot. Guess that shouldn't be a big surprise, huh?"

Ryan paused, trying to decide if he should turn and confront the remark. It felt like a personal challenge. The comment echoed the thoughts he'd been having only minutes ago, making the words sting like a slap to his face. It was a challenge. But it was also a chance for a small bit of redemption.

However, an altercation in school with his secretary's husband would not increase his job security and would estrange his relationship with Sharon. Frustrated, because once again a rational decision, and an avoidance of public confrontation, made him feel like a coward.

Thinking he'd made the right decision for the wrong reason, Ryan entered the gym just as the ball was in-bounded.

21

Ryan hit "Save" and glanced at the time in the corner of his laptop screen. 9:50 a.m., well ahead of his 10:30 estimate and the 1:00 p.m. meeting with the rest of the administrative team. Friday meetings were unusual, but Superintendent Demian wanted everyone's updated projections and to discuss the referendum before going into the week before Christmas when things always got a little crazy.

Completing the report, however, didn't make Ryan feel any better about it. He looked back at his list of potential changes to class offerings along with the associated shifts in staffing assignments and hours they would entail. He'd been working on it off and on for the last three weeks, ever since the November budget meeting where they'd been tasked with looking for any "fat that could be cut." That was the irritating phrase Thynie Marsh had used in a phone conversation just yesterday.

The principals all saw it differently, knowing any substantial changes would be cutting into muscle and tendons, not fat. If it happened, Walt Hannig's observation about putting the principals in a tough spot would be an understatement. Ryan knew for him, it could easily destroy any chance he had of gaining the trust of the staff or implementing the instructional changes he was promoting – which, after all, was the reason Walt had championed his application. *Toast.* That's how he'd end up. Like Walt's burning monk.

He was rubbing his face to stop his mind from going down that path when a faint pleasant scent followed by a sniffle made him look up. Sharon stood in the doorway; eyes brimmed with tears. A jolt of concern and alarm instantly traversed his spine, searing his gut. He stood. "What's wrong, what's happened?"

He wanted to go and hug her but stopped himself after stepping around his desk. Sharon's lower lip quivered as she visibly struggled to find words and then get them to leave her mouth. "The babies... somewhere in Connecticut." She stopped, blinked the tears into freefall down her cheeks, and took a slow deep breath. "It's on the radio and online. Some school named Sandy Hook Elementary. Someone shot their way in. They're saying lots of first graders and staff are dead. Those poor babies...the parents ...I can't image...trying to get there, not knowing and..." Her voice stopped working.

She looked toward the front office where the phone lines were sounding. The phone on Ryan's desk buzzed. He turned and stared at it. Then his cell phone, lying on his desk, vibrated a second before the ringtone sounded.

Sharon wiped her sleeve across her eyes. "I've got to get the phones." She hurried back to the front. Ryan typed "breaking news" into his search box then picked up his cellphone, letting his desk phone go to voicemail.

The others sat around Liz Demian's conference room. Ryan and Board President Charles Templeton entered at the same time, closing the door behind them. As soon as they were seated, Templeton took the lead. "Look, this isn't like 9/11. Back then, no one knew what was going on and any place might realistically get attacked." He looked around the room. A few heads nodded in agreement.

Demian jumped in. "All of the buildings are getting some panicked calls, especially the two elementary schools. I've contacted the sheriff who has squads circling the county schools. But they don't want them parked in front of school buildings. That might cause more alarm than calm. Besides, they can't cover all the buildings in every district in the county at the same time. Dominic has his staff double-checking that all doors are closed and locked."

Templeton said, half to himself, "It sounds like this crazy S.O.B. in Connecticut shot his way in." He looked around the table again. "If this is as bad as they're saying, with all those little kids shot, this is going to cause more outrage than Columbine or the other shootings before. We need to be on the same page in terms of what to say to parents and students. We need to ease their fears. Then we can figure out where to go from there."

Ryan respected Templeton's straightforward demeanor. He'd gotten to know and appreciate the board president over the last year through informal discussions at various high school events, school board, and other meetings. Templeton was a retired fire chief and EMT. Ryan assumed images of mangled children would be more vivid for him than for the rest of them. Ryan pictured Lisa bleeding on the sidewalk outside the ice cream shop. That had been a handgun. He refused to imagine her being shot by a rifle, in the chest or face rather than the leg. The picture was just too horrible to take shape in his imagination. Beneath this gruesome thought, Ryan was also aware of the clear impression Templeton wouldn't hesitate to demand his firing if... He stopped himself from finishing the thought.

The middle school principal wondered out loud about having a lockdown drill next week. Barb Nickels, the elementary principal, was immediately against the idea. "With this all over the news, the little ones couldn't handle that so soon. Parents would be in an uproar."

Superintendent Demian interrupted. "Let's take one step at a time." She passed out a sheet of paper. "This is the message I've drafted to go out by email and phone message to all parents before school ends today. I've already sent an email and voicemail to all staff letting them know that if students ask, they should assure them our buildings are safe and the sheriff is keeping an eye on things and to remind them this happened a thousand miles away.

"I'll follow up with another message after this meeting that if they're asked, they should tell people the board will be reviewing all safety measures and take any necessary steps to assure the safety of all Edenton students and staff."

They reviewed the draft, making minor word changes. Demian said, "I want to be sure we all appreciate the staff, as well as kids and parents, are going to be spooked by this. Hell, I'm spooked. So, pay extra attention to your people in case anyone is having difficulties. Especially as more news and details come out." Ryan saw Demian looking at him when she added, "That goes for yourselves, too. Let me know what requests you get, so we handle everyone the same. We don't want to open that can of worms. So, keep me in the loop.

"You should all be back in your buildings, so I'm cutting our planned meeting short. One last thing though. If you haven't already emailed your reports to me, do so before leaving today. I can work with them and get back to you if I have any questions."

As they gathered their things, the superintendent added, "Ryan, would you stay a few minutes? Mr. Templeton and I have something to discuss with you." All eyes turned toward Ryan. He sat back down. As the others filed out, his mind swirled like water going down a drain with him caught in the vortex. His eyes blinked, trying to clear themselves, but all he saw was his job disappearing.

"Ryan?" He heard his name.

Then a second time, now in a female voice. "Ryan?"

He blinked once more. Turning his attention to the voices, he rubbed one eye. "Sorry..." he rubbed a little harder. "I must have a loose eyelash."

Demian spoke. "Like the last referendum, there will be a community group doing outreach to promote the referendum. Walt Hannig oversaw that, so I'd like you to do it this time."

The superintendent explained. "You're the newest to our team, so it will be an excellent opportunity to expand your profile in the community. While, by law, the school district can't promote a 'Yes' vote, we can provide the data and make sure everyone knows the issues – the whys and what ifs."

Ryan realized this wasn't his nightmare coming true. Blood and oxygen returned to his brain, and he gratefully accepted the assignment. Demian and Templeton briefed him on the details, contacts, and timeline, after which he left.

By the time he reached Stienboek, the brief spurt of relief had worn off, replaced with a feeling of being rebuked, given a veiled hint about expanding his community activity. He knew he might be reading too much into the assignment, but his mind still ran on.

Are they hinting the community still has questions about me and why I'm here? What someone who married Lisa was really like? Are they saying I need to get out there and show them who I am, show them I'm a leader, even though I can't convince my own faculty to make the changes I was hired to get done? How easily he could fall back into a loop of paranoia startled him.

Students had filled the halls during passing time. He received some "Hi, Mr. Davvis, or "Hey, Mr. D" greetings. He noted the lack of concern on their faces about what had happened in Connecticut that morning. Surely, with all the cell phones, some had seen the breaking news. The holiday break had them looking forward, not backward. That was as it should be. They were too young to put themselves in the shoes of parents whose six-year-olds would never have another Christmas.

By the time he reached the front office, he'd almost cleared his head. Almost convinced himself his morose feelings and obsessions were just unwarranted games his mind was playing on him, fears he needed to better control. Sharon turned and weakly smiled. Her eyes showed more tears lurking.

Back in his office, he hung his coat up, dropped his notes on the table and sat. That's when he started to see himself as the fall guy if the referendum failed. His hands took hold of the curved table edges, and he began pushing and tugging, swiveling the chair. The movement brought to mind Ayden Quant's attempt to steer the table through his anxieties and troubles. Ryan felt a sudden deep kinship with the boy.

22

When he woke on Saturday morning, Ayden saw the truck in the driveway. Actually, because his bedroom was in the basement, he saw only the wheels. There was a trailer still attached, so his dad was likely only home for a few hours. His excitement to see his dad remained for less than a minute before a chill of apprehension bubbled up his spine. He pulled on his pants, then rummaged through his closet to find the tee shirt with the quote that had gotten him in trouble with Mrs. Zowak. He headed upstairs. His mom was sitting at the table with his cereal already in the bowl.

"Your father showed up last night after a stopover at Sophie's. I want you to eat and then disappear for a while until I can see what's what. I'll tell him you'll be back in an hour to visit before he takes off for the Upper Peninsula." Without pause she added, "And why are you wearing that stupid shirt Dad gave you? You shouldn't have shown your dad that book or the quote."

"Yeah, but it's funny." He hadn't told his mom how it had gotten him in trouble at school, or his idea about getting other kids to pick quotes that she could put on shirts at her store, and they'd split the profits. He still felt a little bad about lying to Mr. Davvis about him making the shirt himself.

"Why do I gotta leave?" he weakly protested, knowing the answer to his question. It made him mad, but arguing would only make his mom more anxious than she already was. He finished eating, clattering his dishes into the sink before grabbing his hooded sweatshirt and stepping outside. He immediately backed up, ran down to his room, then reappeared wearing a second hoodie, a stocking cap pulled down over his ears, and some gloves. He'd intended to let the door bang as he left but realized startling his dad awake wouldn't help anything. He caught it with his foot at the last second.

The wind was light and out of the southwest so it didn't bite. Like yesterday, the temperature hovered a bit above freezing. He grabbed his bike from the open garage and started down the road, putting his anger and confused feelings into pumping his legs and driving each pedal stoke as hard as he could. He had no destination in mind.

A quarter mile up the road his legs began to ache. He backed off trying to maintain top speed and looked ahead for the first time. Three hundred yards further along, the road crossed over a small gulley and culvert. It was a favorite spot for Ayden. In the spring, a low wooded swampy area on the opposite side of the road collected water that ran off under the road, moving swiftly toward some unknown place and attracting all kinds of wildlife. Being mid-December, the gully should be dry and frozen, but with the warmer temperatures, Ayden slowed to see if there might be a trickle and maybe a fox or something. A vaguely familiar car was parked just off the road in ruts leading through a low thicket of mixed trees to the next field at the top of a rise.

He slammed on the brakes and let his rear tire skid up and turn him around. Still straddling the bar, he awkwardly walked the bike to the side of the road and looked down along the gulley which traversed a forty-acre field before disappearing into another wooded area. He dismounted, taking some pleasure in watching the sedges, rushes, and grasses of varying shades of brown stiffly swaying, waiting for the first heavy snow to lay them down until next spring's sun came. He sidestepped a few paces down the steep slope to peer into the culvert. He jumped and almost lost his balance when he heard, "What the fuck, Ayden! You scared the shit out of me." Allan Sparks' head stuck out from beneath the road.

Not having arranged to meet here, Ayden was startled and confused by his friend's sudden appearance. "What you doing under here?"

"Get your fucking bike off the road." Allan's head disappeared back under the culvert like a turtle retreating into its shell.

Ayden walked his bike down the slope, laying it down out of sight of any traffic. He peered into the shadowy tunnel. Allan was squatting above a small trickle of water, which, devoid of sun, had formed a small pool skimmed with ice. The boy had poked a few holes in the thin film with a stick and seemed mesmerized watching the trapped water trying to escape onto the surface. As Ayden squatted, Allan brought a lit match to the partially smoked cigarette he stuck between his lips. He took a deep inhale while urgently waving Ayden into the culvert.

Ayden bent and moved in next to Allan. "Where'd you get the cigarettes?"

Allan exhaled the warm pungent smoke from his lungs into the cold air. "It's not a cigarette, stupid." He held it out to Ayden. "Here, try it."

"Where'd you get pot? Is it safe here?" Ayden nervously glanced past Allan to the opposite end of the culvert under the road. "There's a car parked over there in the trees."

"It's my mom's."

"WHAT! No way, dude. You don't have a license."

Allan took another hit and again waved the joint toward Ayden. "I just took it. My parents took my dad's truck to Appleton. I didn't want to go, so they said, 'Fine. Stay home.' They won't be home for hours."

"So, you stole your mom's car?" Ayden asked incredulously.

"Don't be such a pussy, *A-Lee*." Allan emphasized the name he'd once heard Ayden's mom call him, something he only did if he really wanted to get a reaction.

Ayden backhanded Allan hard in his shoulder. His hand slipped up and caught Allan partially across the side of his face, almost causing him to drop the joint. "Hey, watch it numb-nuts," Allan said.

"I told you to never call me that!" Ayden said, not caring if the situation escalated.

Uncharacteristically, Allan didn't respond at all. He just looked at the far end of the culvert for a long moment before almost apologetically asking, "Do you want some or not? It's pretty good stuff." He took a hit, held it out to Ayden, and released the warm sweet smell into the still air, further deescalating the moment. The thin line of smoke from the end of the joint drifted into Ayden's eyes.

He squinted at the tightly wrapped paper. The remainder barely extended beyond his friend's fingers. Allan had already smoked most of it. Multiple thoughts ran through Ayden's mind in a confused rush, smothering any warning signal or impulse. He reached for the joint and imitated his friend's action, immediately coughing the smoke back out of his lungs and throat.

"Don't waste it, damn it." Allan took the joint back and again inhaled deeply. He handed it back to Ayden who burned his fingers on the exchange but managed not to drop it. This time he was prepared and was able to hold the smoke in. He took another hit, then passed it back. Allan took a last hit, then crushed the lit end and swallowed the tiny remainder.

"You ate it?" Ayden asked in surprise.

"Not gonna waste it." He smiled and asked, "Do you feel the buzz, dude?"

Ayden leaned back and closed his eyes. He felt a little dizzy, not sure if it was from the smoke or pot. "I think so."

Allan smirked and sat back against the corrugated metal. "Sometimes, it doesn't hit you right away, when it's your first time."

Ayden quickly defended himself. "I've had it before."

"You're lying. You always lie. You'd have told me if you'd tried it."

"I think I'm starting to feel it," Ayden countered.

The boys lay back, temporarily hidden and secure under the road. After a couple of minutes, the cold of the ground and lack of any sun began to cool the sweat Ayden had worked up on his bike. He sat up. "Shit, it's cold under here." He pulled his second hood higher up over his head. He hadn't been planning on stopping. He edged his body out of the shade, seeking whatever little warmth the sun might be putting out over the tree line to the east. Looking back, he asked, "Hey, Allan. What you think about all them little kids getting killed in that school yesterday? That's really fucked up, don't ya think? I mean... what if that shit happened here? What would you do? I'd run, I wouldn't just hide like they say, you know, waiting for some crazy asshole to come and blow me away."

Allan shifted, but only enough to stretch his legs. For a few moments, he again seemed mesmerized by the narrow band of cold water now barely moving past his feet. "I should bring my dad's pistol to school. Then shoot the son-of-a bitch so he'd know what it feels like."

Ayden thought Allan's voice lacked enthusiasm or any sense of heroism, so he tried to escalate the idea. "Yeah. My dad's got a couple of hunting rifles. Maybe we should have a secret gun locker at school. That way if some idiot breaks in, we can blow him away before he hurts anyone. We'd be like heroes or something in the newspaper. Maybe even on TV."

Allan glanced at him but didn't respond. He stared down again. Ayden considered repeating the idea, making it even funnier by adding machine guns and hand grenades to the locker, when Allen, without looking up asked, "Do you think maybe water feels sad or scared as it's freezing into ice?"

Ayden was on his back with his arms huddled across his chest for warmth. He thought for a moment. "I don't know. I guess. Maybe."

Suddenly changing moods, Allan sat up and enthusiastically almost shouted, "Dude. Did you *really* call your girlfriend the N-word?"

Ayden also sat up, confused by the sudden shift. He'd anticipated getting some shit from Allan back when it happened, but he hadn't said a thing back then. "She ain't my girlfriend. I don't even like her. Besides, you said it first."

"Yeah," Allan admitted, "but I didn't say it *to her*. I was just wondering what that must be like. I didn't think you'd say it. No wonder she clobbered you."

"I mostly ducked. She barely touched me."

"Liar. I heard she got you good. What did Davvis do? Why didn't you get suspended?"

"He sent Nala home."

Allan scrambled out of the culvert and kneeled by Ayden. "What! How did you not get suspended?"

"I apologized and explained I didn't mean it in a bad way... that I was just curious like you said, that I didn't even mean to use that word; that it just slipped out. Nala said it was okay and that she believed me. So, Mr. Davvis let me go."

"*She* said it was *okay*?" Allan sounded incredulous.

"Not that way, dickhead. She didn't say it was okay to call her that, just that she knew I didn't mean it that way."

"So, why did she get sent home?"

"She wanted to. She was pretty upset. Her dad was there. When Mr. Davvis said she should go home, she got pissed again and said some Black-sounding stuff that got her dad mad. I ain't never heard Mr. Samilton mad about anything before. Even when kids puke or write shit on a wall. Anyhow, I think she just had to go home because she was so upset, not 'cause she was suspended or nothing. I gotta admit, I felt bad about the whole thing."

"That's 'cause you're a pussy. I think it's pretty funny."

Ayden threw a handful of lifeless grass at Allan's head. "You're the pussy. At least I had the guts to ask her."

They fell silent until Ayden shivered. "I gotta get going. My dad came home last night, but he's taking a load up north this morning." He stood and brushed his backside off. "What are you doing out here so early, anyway? And what if a cop stops you driving your mom's car?"

Instead of answering, Allan pulled his cap down over his ears, gave Ayden the finger, and disappeared back into the culvert under the road. "I ain't ready to leave yet."

Ayden shrugged. "Don't freeze out here, dummy." He pushed his bike back up onto the road and began pedaling back toward his house. He hollered over his shoulder and repeated himself. "Hey, Allan. See you Monday." As his legs began to pump and thaw, he wasn't sure if he was hoping his dad was still there...or not.

23

When her math book hit the carpet, Nala thought of the muffled thud as a period to a difficult day. She turned off her reading lamp, sliding beneath the white sheet and comforter and tugging them up to her chin. She leaned back against the headboard, working her frizzy ponytail across the fluffed pillow, searching for the perfect position, and finally let herself remember. A friend, Jason, a nice boy she liked, had always felt comfortable with, had touched her hair while they were bunched up in the hall waiting for other kids to clear out of Algebra class before they could fill it up again. He asked, "Do you like it like this? Why don't you just make it normal?" Her friend Zoey punched him in the shoulder. Told him to quit being a rude ass.

But Nala knew he wasn't being rude on purpose; he just didn't know. Had no way of knowing; had never been around Black people. Still, his words twisted in her gut, in her mind, announcing to her, to the world, that she was defective, a fraud. Maybe he was right, maybe he wasn't, but she didn't have anyone she could talk to about it. Not her friends or even her parents... only with Lang.

She closed her eyes and pulled in a slow, full, deep breath. The darkness funneled in and filled her, freeing her mind to seek the comfort of her brother's voice. She couldn't remember exactly when her parents first told her she had been a twin. All they knew was that her sibling had died in infancy.

What Nala did remember was that in Mrs. Holman's

second-grade class, a classmate saying – not in a mean way – "I wish I had dark skin like Nala, so I wouldn't have to take a bath every night." That evening before bed, she had asked her mom about Langston. That was the name her parents had told her about.

They didn't know she thought of him as Lang, and they didn't know how much she now needed him. Back then, she had just wanted to make sure she remembered his name correctly and assure herself that he would have looked like her. Her mom confirmed his name, then explained that even though they hadn't been identical twins, she was sure they probably had lots of similarities. Nala remembered specifically asking, "What about his skin and hair?"

"Most likely a lot like yours, honey," kissing her arms and hair. "Why?"

Nala answered, "I don't know, just wondering." She hoped she was telling the truth but wasn't sure. After that, she hadn't felt a need to ask again. She mostly thought about Lang when she heard the word "twin" For the most part, he was tucked away in the back of her mind. Buried but not forgotten.

Then, sometime in fifth grade when puberty started to mess with her body, the feelings of being alone and different started to reappear. Not long afterward, after hearing a boy – but pretending not to have heard – use the actual word "nigger" about some Green Bay Packers player who had dropped a ball or something, feelings exploded and became insistent and assertive.

Scared to bring it up to her parents, fearing they might be ashamed or regret adopting her, she was pleased and surprised that night to discover Lang – not just in the back of her head but deep down inside her. And he wasn't just a dead infant anymore. Like her, he'd grown up. But unlike her, he was very talkative and had an opinion on almost everything. She'd been sitting on her bed in the dark with her confusion and fears swirling in the air, upset by that word she'd heard. Trying to calm herself, she'd taken and held a deep breath and found him waiting there as if her breath and troubles had brought him back to life, back to her.

Centered on the breath she now held, Nala slowly, through pursed lips, began to release the collected air, letting it carry her cloistered silent conversation and thoughts into the open darkness of the room.

Lang? It's me...

Me?

She paused to consider. Her given name was Natalia. Once, out of curiosity, she'd looked up the name: "Birth of the Lord" – once commonly given to girls born around Christmas. Her birthday was December 4th, just a few weeks ago. Mom had made her favorite cake.

But is that who I really am?... What if I'd been born a few days earlier in November? Would I have been given a different name? Would I have turned out to be somebody else; maybe somebody less confused? More like... like what, like who?

No answer came.

Perhaps her birth mother called her Natalia because she had had a best friend with that name, a Natalia whose grandmother willingly emigrated from some European country.

I'll never know.

She had no idea if the woman who had made and carried her was even alive, or how to find her...wasn't sure she would even want to know – or ask.

Two, three... Which is me?

The rhyming couplet often looped in her head, fusing her sense of self with the intangible notion of two-ness or three-ness, what her math teacher called "concept of numbers." Lang had first raised the question – *Which is me?* The question had taken a long time to settle in, but since then it had grown from a nagging sensation to an existential preoccupation, from a slight breeze into a category five hurricane.

She accepted her Natalia name as "real." It was on her birth certificate which her adoptive parents had tenaciously jumped through multiple hoops to obtain after the records had been opened, knowing she would need it to anchor her existence to her legal self, her nativity, her Natalia-ness.

But is that my "real" self? Is there ever a real self? After all, there are unreal numbers in math.

The questions made her curious. She could remember how before she was old enough to read, her dad would hold her on his lap, writing and pointing to each letter. "N-A-T-A-L-I-A. That's your real name, sweetie." But for as long as she could remember, she thought of herself as Nala. Not many people even called her Natalia. And for a few years now, 'Natalia' – as a name, as a person, as a way-down-deep-inside-sense of self – was shrinking, little by little hardening like a chrysalis, beginning to crack and split.

Even now, eyes closed, she felt Natalia, the adopted and embraced part of her being, ebbing, giving way. She refocused on the slow, long breath leaving her body. She thought of it as Lang exhaling. She'd breathe in formless feelings, and he'd breathe out focused thoughts and new questions.

Last Saturday, while her parents were out, she'd been channel surfing and came across a news station showing pictures of the little kids killed in that horrible school shooting just a week ago. She couldn't watch. They'd never have another birthday, their favorite cake, or even a Christmas. Propelled by the pictures and Lang's existential push for her to verify life, including her own life, she found herself in her parents' room, opening the safety box and checking their copy of her adoption papers.

She'd been born in Chicago and then moved to Minneapolis. She'd been with a foster family before being adopted by her new parents and brought to live, grow up, and go to school in Edenton, Wisconsin. No one ever asked her how that felt or explained how to absorb it all. She thought she'd been doing a good job for the most part, fitting in... mostly...*until stupid Ayden Quant asked me that horrible question, and today Jason asked about my hair.*

Dad and Mom never hid the fact she was adopted. They never hid how much they loved her and how special she was to them. They'd always told her she was the little girl they had always wanted but couldn't have. But for some time now, Nala understood it had always been obvious to the rest of the world, as she grew up enfolded in dad's and mom's lives and world – she wasn't really theirs.

But. that's all I wanted to be, still want to be, who I always thought I was, until...

What now came to mind was that Black boy on the news last February, with the hoodie sweatshirt who got shot in Florida; and President Obama saying if he had a son he would have looked like the dead boy; some TV people saying he shouldn't say that kind of thing.

Some sixth-grade memories came loose. Three years ago. Back when the confusing feelings became confusing experiences with memories still itchy and jabbing, still vivid and clear as the pale scar near her left eye from when she'd crashed her bicycle into a tree because her BFF dared her to ride with her eyes closed.

That was when she began to question if her Natalia-self really existed. Two friends – girls she'd known since kindergarten – began acting standoffish, and one of the substitute teachers seemed not ever to see her at all. But one memory, one pain, never went away and still hurt like she was again running into that tree. It was when the bicycle friend "accidentally forgot" to invite her to a sleepover. Dad and Mom commiserated; told her it was normal. Kids get older.

People change. Groups break into smaller cliques and hang more with others who share their likes and dislikes. It was confusing. *I thought I shared those same things too. Lang, what's wrong with me?*

She listened as hard as she could for his answer inside the controlled breath she was releasing into her darkness. Nala was one-hundred percent certain Lang would have been like her, played with her, and taken care of her; would have helped her to know what she needed to know, and helped her to find and be her real self. But instead, he died, long before he even knew his own name.

Recently, she had become convinced he had been named for a famous poet, the one she discovered on a small poster in the back of her English class. She'd looked him up. Mrs. Turley, her teacher, had seemed embarrassed, regrettably couldn't tell her much about him, or his poems, or if he might have had a younger sibling who called him Lang. Nala wished she'd been named after some famous author or poet, someone whose words and ideas could help her to understand who she was, who she was supposed to become. *Was that in February too? Back when school was sticking some Black History into the shortest month of the year, back when that Black boy was shot and killed walking back from a convenience store.*

For a moment, Nala stopped her slow exhale. Just long enough to wonder if she might have been next to Lang in the same crib when he quit breathing. Maybe it had been a mistake, and she was the one who was supposed to sleep forever instead of him. Was she a mistake? Did his death make her less convenient, less visible, someone who could be given away? There were no pictures of Lang. She didn't remember his sounds, his baby laugh, his cry, or the day and the moment it all stopped forever. Yet, on nights like tonight, she could hear his voice, a voice now cracking and changing with puberty. She was sure she would recognize it even in a crowd of strangers.

When she restarted her exhalation, Lang had a new thought ready for her. *Foster home, Nala. Your papers said you were a foster kid after I left.*

Her brain, getting low on oxygen, flashed a fantasy scene: a family with skin and hair like hers, a young girl maybe eight or nine, holding her on her lap, talking to her, calling her Nala because she so loved *The Lion King* movie and especially the young lioness named Nala. Watching the movie over and over, explaining the story as it unfolded, she sang the songs to the transitory baby girl who enjoyed hearing and feeling the stream of words, enjoyed the melodious breath and sounds flowing over her, making her forget to fuss or cry. The girl would kiss Nala's head, letting the tiny hands grab hold of her fingers, telling the infant she loved her as much as she loved the real Nala.

Was that where my name came from? Has it traveled with me from the beginning?

Her breath was gone. She opened her eyes. She probed the blackness now thinned to grey, finally settling on a sliver of reflection glinting off the glass protecting last spring's eighth-grade graduation photo. It hung above her beanbag chair. The image wasn't visible. It doesn't matter. She knows she isn't, can't be, that girl anymore.

A light tapping and soft voice filtered through her closed door. "Good night, Nala. I love you." The voice came every night. Whether she was awake to hear it or not.

"Love you too, Dad. Good night." The light in the hall went out, and his footsteps faded toward her parents' room. She stared at her side of the door, which separates her two worlds, wonders for how much longer.

"Langston?" She silently whispers. *"I feel horrible...like a traitor."*

Now, she clearly hears Lang. *"You're tired, girl. Go to sleep.*

You've got a math test in the morning – the last day before Christmas break, before a whole new year."

She yawned to refill her lungs and surrendered to her bed, to her need to trust everything will all work out... she will work out... Mom and Dad and Lang will all work out. Her heavy eyes close and her tired mind sees a cartoon-like, un-equivalent equation chasing its tail around the dark room until it dives down and slips within the pages of her algebra book. She turns onto her side.

Good night, Lang...

24

In a school, the last day before an extended break requires patience and flexibility. Last night's holiday concert was packed and successful. The experienced choir and band director always produced a high-quality and entertaining program. They worked well together and attracted a lot of students to the music department.

With Christmas Eve not until Monday, teachers had done their best to get in a full week's work. Some managed to squeeze in a chapter or unit test before the long eleven-day break. When they returned, there would be less than three weeks to finish up the semester and give and grade finals.

Ryan kept his schedule as open as possible so he could spend time in the hallways. His only calendar reminder to himself was to check in with the new staff and lend any needed assistance in tamping down enthusiasm that might be getting out of hand. He'd hang mostly around the underclass halls. Freshmen were mostly larger middle schoolers and susceptible to the holiday spirits. He also was aware the word "sophomore" literally meant "wise fool," and for some, the "wise" part didn't show up until the end of the year.

His first stop after lunch would be to sixth-period sophomore English. It would be an informal drop-in. He'd never conduct a formal evaluation so close before a holiday. Evelyn Snede, an attractive, single, first-year teacher, was having some trouble establishing boundaries with her students. The girls wanted to be her friend, and the boys wanted to flirt or act out to gain her attention. Striking the balance between professional and behavioral expectations without squashing young egos and becoming an unfriendly hard-ass can take time but must be done as quickly as possible.

Evelyn Snede was one of seven hires in the last two years. This represented almost ten percent of the teaching staff. Three teachers had retired when Walt left; one was planned, but two were last-minute early retirements, saying they saw the writing on the wall when the new governor was elected the previous fall. They'd heard the talk about attacks on the state pension fund, rising contribution rates, and the governor's thoughts about changing to a 401K fund tied to the stock markets.

In his first year, Ryan needed to hire a long-term substitute to replace the Algebra teacher who had been on maternity leave and decided not to return after her baby was born with a serious health issue. He'd had to replace two teachers and one aide last spring when they'd left for other districts that paid better. Their combined experience had been nineteen years. One replacement had two years of experience. Evelyn Snede was just out of UW-Oshkosh. The aide was a transfer from nursing home care where her back was giving out, and she needed better benefits and a predictable schedule. Superintendent Demian saw the turnover in Edenton in general as a problem but was ham-strung by current fiscal and political conditions. She worried out loud about how to get the board to see it as a problem.

Ryan headed toward the hallway. "Sharon, I'm going down to the cafeteria and scout things out. I'll be back in a while."

"Okay. When you get back.... Never mind."

He was about to ask her what she was going to say, but the office door opened, and he heard, "Hey, Ryan. Glad I caught you. You got a minute?"

"Sure. Walk with me. I was just headed to the cafeteria."

The one-minute question took ten. Afterward, Ryan roamed the cafeteria greeting students, congratulating others for last night's concert, asking how things were going, and following up on a few previous conversations. He made a point never to stay too long with any student or group. He didn't want to intrude on their free time. In general, he just wanted to see and be seen, be a non-threatening reminder they were in a school.

He spotted Ayden and Allan at a table along the far wall and moved in that direction. As he got closer, he heard their give and take: "No way. Yes, way. You're stupid. Well, you're..."

Ryan interrupted the last comment when he perched on the bench across from them. "No way, yes way, what? And nobody here is stupid." He looked both boys in the eyes to emphasize the point but lingered on Allan. The boy was hard to like at times, especially the way he held sway over Ayden. He was the kind of kid who seemed to relish causing trouble but too often managed to avoid consequences. Allan didn't blink. Then he feigned a sarcastic grin and explained. "Ayden thinks the Packers are going to the Super Bowl. No way! They've got two more games to screw it up. And if they make the playoffs, they'll never get past the 49ers."

Ryan took a middle stance. "Well, I think they're good enough to win it all, but it always takes a lot of luck to go all the way." Three loud beeps signaled the end of freshman lunch. The boys stood quickly. "Have a good holiday, guys. And I know you'll keep a lid on things this afternoon. The holiday doesn't start for a few hours yet." Ryan reminded them to take their trays. As they turned to leave, he remembered something. "Ayden, things got busy, and I forgot to get back to you about your tee shirt idea like I said I would. Do you still have the book of quotes?"

The boy seemed evasive. "I think maybe I returned it already. I'll have to check." He kept walking. Ryan heard Allan ask him, "What book?"

The cafeteria emptied in much the same way water drains from a pool when the plug is pulled – seemingly no movement at first, followed by a sudden rush and backup. Ryan picked up a few forgotten trays and scraps from the tables. He positioned himself to keep the next wave of students from pushing and rushing in. Once things calmed down to the usual clamor of teen voices trying to say everything all at once, he loaded a tray with a slice of cheese pizza, a small salad, an apple, and a carton of chocolate milk. He chatted with the lunch crew, complimenting their patience as he went through the line. He thought about taking his tray to the lounge. He ate there once or twice a week. Sometimes he felt like he was intruding on their space. Other times, like now, he simply wanted to avoid questions that he wasn't at liberty to discuss, or for which he didn't have answers – at least ones they'd like.

Back in Minnesota, as a vice principal, he usually had his lunch in the teachers' lounge. He felt, and was seen as, an integral part of the teaching staff and students' daily lives – not an administrator. He was comfortable with them and they with him. He missed that feeling. But that was then, back before his life seemed to crumble, and he constantly felt as if the ground beneath his feet was unstable. He opted to go back to his office to eat.

Sharon was off to lunch. One of the two designated aides who filled in for her at the front counter was on the phone. He sat at his round table and started on the salad.

After the busses left, Ryan returned to his office to write up a note for Evelyn Snede telling her how impressed he'd been. Instead of the usual last-class-before-break fluff, she had her students working in pairs and searching through different sections of *A Christmas Carol* to discover how Charles Dickens' words created mood and tone. The kids seemed into it, and even though this had been an informal drop-in on his part, Ryan wanted to support and recognize her work.

He was tidying his desktop, ready to head out when Sharon stopped in. He greeted her. "Well, Sharon, we made it. Merry Christmas to all of us and a relaxing break." Her lack of response made him stop what he was doing, "What's up?"

"Do you have a minute, Ryan? I have something I need to tell you, but I didn't know when the right time was. I know how busy you are. But I think you need to know sooner rather than later."

Not what he was expecting. Ryan's stomach knotted.

Ten minutes later, Sharon slid her hands, palms down, across the table, and with tears in her eyes said, "That's not the worst part."

Ryan was still trying to digest what she'd told him. He felt stupid, guilty of having been so wrapped up in his own issues that he hadn't seen how unhappy and stressed she'd been. She'd explained that she was leaving David; how last summer she'd finally gotten him to agree to see a marriage counselor. They had driven up to Green Bay to avoid prying eyes. It was a one-and-done. David refused to go back, saying the woman was obviously biased, probably a dyke, only wanted to talk about his drinking, and ignored his side and all the things she wasn't helping with around the farm.

Ryan recalled the last time he'd seen her husband. How he'd been rude and made a racial remark about Dominic's daughter. His distaste for the man grew to out-and-out disdain and anger as Sharon related how he had refused to take her seriously at first, blaming her for all their problems. How he warned her that he'd contest everything, including the kids, would make sure she got nothing out of the farm, out of their savings, even though much of it was hers. He'd even researched and informed her he'd be entitled to a portion of her pension. If she walked away from their fifteen years of marriage, he promised it would be with only her clothes and nothing more, not even her reputation.

Ryan tried to offer some help. "What's that supposed to mean? From the little I know, he's the one whose reputation is in free fall."

Sharon turned her palms up, and the tears brimmed over again. Instinctively, Ryan reached out and covered her hands with his. Her watery, scared, blue eyes locked onto his. He wondered if he'd crossed a line and was about to pull back when her fingers squeezed around his. "Ryan..." her grasp tightened. "Dave said if I left, he'd tell everyone, especially the kids, that we're... that I'm having an affair with you. That I was a slut and was just as bad as..." She stopped herself and blushed. Her hands and eyes retreated to her lap. "I'm sorry. But he'll do it. I know he will. His drinking makes him always angry and looking for others to blame for everything." She sniffled and took a tissue to wipe her eyes and nose.

"I feel so stuck. I don't know what to do. I've talked to a lawyer. David doesn't know that." She blew her nose. "I don't care about the farm or the money. I just need to get out. But if I do, he'll do everything to get the kids on his side, and he'll try his best to drag you into this. I know he'll come after you."

Her hands were back on the tabletop. Ryan leaned across and took them again, the wet tissue making the connection more intimate. This time, his eyes dove deep into hers. "Look, you can't, you know you can't give into his threats. I'm sure your lawyer told you his threats are empty. And as far as being involved with me, no one is going to believe that, especially about you."

They sat looking at each other for several moments, aware Ryan's hands were still on top of hers. He asked, "What were you going to say a moment ago? About what Dave said. That you were as bad as who?" In his gut, he knew the answer but had to ask.

Sharon squeezed his hands. More tears came, but she never

looked away. "I'm sorry, Ryan. I'm so sorry. I didn't mean to let..." Her eyes pleaded for forgiveness.

He nodded, letting his eyes convey his understanding. He pulled her hands slightly toward him and held them as tenderly as he could. "You know, maybe a rumor like that would enhance my reputation around here."

She laughed. Looked at him. Ryan tried but couldn't read her eyes. He'd never been good at reading women. Lisa had once told him, "Any pretty woman could have you eating out of her hand."

The thought was painful. It reminded him she had said this to him barely a week before he realized she was cheating. Sharon's head turned. His eyes followed. Dominic was standing at the door with his eyes on their coupled hands.

25

"Mr. Schmelzing, can I talk to you for a minute?"

Her U.S. History teacher looked up from the article he was reading and swiveled his chair to face the doorway. He swallowed the bite of the sandwich he was chewing and enthusiastically waved her in. "Of course, Nala. Come on in. What's up?"

His classroom was one of her favorites. It was what she imagined a college classroom would be like, a place for learning but also questioning. From day one back in early September, Mr. Schmelzing started his classes with what often seemed like a random question. "*How* do you think people would react if..., *What* kind of person would it take to ..., *Why would* it make sense for someone to...." The question was always intentionally vague and never hinted at a correct answer.

By early October, Schmelzing rarely asked questions about specific factual knowledge. Instead, he'd ask *why* questions which required students to support their answers with the facts. Throughout the class, individuals would eventually see the connection to his opening questions. It was as if lightbulbs were being switched on at different times. Nala loved the feeling of her brain lighting up. She thought Mr. Schmelzing had a way to get them inside the minds of whatever person or group they were studying.

At some point, someone would always ask, "Well, why didn't they just do 'such-or-such'?" Mr. Schmelzing would always praise the inquiry. "That's a really insightful question." He'd encourage them to explore the idea within the context of the times, or when necessary, he'd point out that "such-or-such" wouldn't be invented, discovered, or possible for another century. In the end, the students themselves usually had created a deeper understanding of how and why things happened the way they did.

Yesterday, Mr. Schmelzing had ended class by announcing after the holiday break they'd use the last few weeks of the semester looking through what he called a "cause-and-effect lens." The goal would be to discover the links between the events they'd been studying and, as he'd described it, "...how they affected the early twentieth century, back when your grandparents and great-grandparents were your age."

Before falling asleep last night, Nala had thought about "cause and effect" for a good while. She thought about how her real grandparents' lives would probably have been quite different from the Samilton family history. By the time she fell asleep, she'd decided to ask Mr. Schmelzing a question she knew she'd never bring up during class.

Nala walked up to his desk. He took a sip from his coffee mug to wash down his sandwich and wiped his mouth with a paper towel. "How can I help you, Nala?"

She started by asking, "Why don't you eat in the teachers' lounge?"

"Well, I mix it up. Sometimes I eat there to catch up with some of the others and check out what gossip is trending. But sometimes," he held up the magazine he was reading, "I just need some quiet time."

Nala smiled. "It sounds like the cafeteria. Except there's no place to go eat in quiet."

"So, what's up?" he asked taking another sip from his mug. "I hope you don't mind if I keep eating. The next period starts soon."

"No that's fine. I'm sorry to bother you during lunch."

"No problem."

His smile made it easier to begin. "You probably don't remember, but a little while ago..." Nala was struck by how much her world had changed in that short time span. How she had told her dad she was Black without really knowing exactly what she was trying to tell him; how she'd got so upset in Mr. Davvis' office after Ayden had used the N-word; and how all those little kids could be massacred in a school, and all adults did was argue about guns. Her "little while" suddenly seemed like a year ago.

She got back to what she was saying. "...a little while ago, I was looking at that globe in back, and you pointed out Africa's size compared to the other continents and suggested I look up their actual size."

Mr. Schmelzing put the last of his sandwich in his mouth. "Uh-huh." He swallowed. "Did you?"

"I did. That same day. After practice, in my dad's office. I showed him and told him it made me mad."

Schmelzing sat quietly. A hint of a satisfied glint was in his eyes.

"My question is..." Nala took a deep breath through her nose. "Why did you tell me that? I mean, yesterday you said we were going to start to look at cause and effect. So, I got to wondering what caused you to suggest I look that up. It wasn't part of a class lesson or anything." She stopped as if she'd suddenly just come upon a traffic light turning red. She waited, sure that she knew the answer. There was no anger, only curiosity on her face.

"And the effect was it got you upset?" Schmelzing said. He scratched at the back of his neck. "I guess the way you were looking at the globe made me think you'd be interested."

"Would you have suggested that to anyone else? I mean, to look up the actual sizes?"

"Maybe. If I thought the student might be interested. But, probably not. It's unlikely."

"So, you thought I'd be interested in Africa because..." She held up the backs of her hands.

"I guess I did. Was I being insensitive?"

"No," she said quickly. "No. I didn't mean it that way. I was just wondering. You know, about cause and effect."

"Well, I probably was being insensitive, or at least tactless," Mr. Schmelzing admitted. "I'm sorry. But now I've got a question. What caused you to wait so long to ask me this?"

Nala saw he wasn't offended by her question, but she didn't have an easy answer to his. There were too many moving parts. "I guess... I guess, I'm just starting to wonder about some things." She smiled and added, "You know, more cause and effect. That's your fault. You're always pushing us to look at things in different ways."

"That's a high compliment coming from you."

She blushed. "After I calmed down some – I mean about the size of Africa on the maps – I started thinking it was probably because they wanted to make Africa look small on purpose, unimportant... only good for getting slaves." She hadn't intended to add the slave part.

Mr. Schmelzing said, "That would be an accurate and reasonable conclusion considering the history. But so you have the whole picture, you may also want to look up something called the Mercator Projection. We cover it in World Geography if you take that class later."

Mr. Schmelzing looked at the clock. "I need to get ready for class. And so do you." He wrapped the remains of his lunch in the brown bag it came in and tossed it at the trash basket by the door. "Don't do that in the cafeteria."

She started to leave. "Merry Christmas, Mr. Schmelzing."

He stopped her. "Nala..." She turned. "It was brave of you to come and ask your question. It was a great question."

She stood quiet for a moment. Instead of thanking him, she asked, "Why aren't there more Black people, or even more women, in the history books?"

"Wow, that's a question that would require a lot more time than we have. But the simple answer is that so far, most history has been written by white men, and we, I'm embarrassed to say, have been avoiding your question for too long. So, keep asking."

Nala swallowed her next question. "Thank you, Mr. Schmelzing."

"Merry Christmas, Nala. And happy New Year."

26

Ryan sat in his dark apartment with his packed bag already by the door for an early departure in the morning. He looked forward to Christmas with his folks, a night out with his former colleagues to catch up on things, and at least one, maybe two, hook-ups with Mrs. Rupert. He'd booked a room at a Hampton near the university and far enough away from his old school and parents' home to assure anonymity. He needed a release. Living in Edenton as a bachelor principal didn't leave much space for letting his hair down, not that he'd had the time.

Closing his eyes, he sank into himself enjoying the feel of the worn leather beneath his fingers and palms. For a few moments, his mind cradled the prospect of multiple days off before his hands moved, first caressing, then vigorously rubbing and squeezing the armrest. He recognized the warning sign but couldn't summon enough will to stop. It took less than a minute to wring the past into the present; the memories of sitting in this same chair, doing the same thing when Lisa didn't come home until late in the evening. He knew he should get up and go do something but knew he wouldn't. His mind sank back even further.

He'd met Lisa Kames in Madison at a conference about the academic and social-emotional needs of gifted and talented students. He'd been having lunch at a linen-covered round table in the conference center with some Minneapolis colleagues – a couple of principals and resource teachers. She'd approached to chat with one of the resource teachers. They'd sat together in a session during the morning round of lectures. The woman introduced Lisa to the others, moving counterclockwise around the table. When she got around to Ryan, who was sitting just to her left, Lisa reached over and squeezed his shoulder and without hesitation announced, "Oh, I know Ryan quite well. We had an affair some years ago."

The table went silent. Ryan almost spit up the soda he was sipping. Lisa let it sit for only a moment. "Just kidding. Nice to meet you, Ryan, everybody." She glanced at her watch. I better go. Enjoy the afternoon sessions."

When she'd gone, one of the women said, "It seems those good looks of yours work even in Wisconsin." Embarrassed, he'd mumbled something about the poor girl needing glasses or counseling.

His hands again began to struggle against the arm of the chair as the memory skipped to the next day, to Lisa's room after dinner. She'd lifted her skirt and urged his mouth to her panties, after which she'd generously reciprocated. He struggled to keep his mind's eye on that part of the scene, blocking what he knew was coming later. But old familiar lines, like spring-shot pinballs began looping and crashing unimpeded around his mind.

I've seen the way men look at you
When they think I don't see
And it hurts to have them think that you're that kind

An old tune and lyric still sometimes heard on the oldies channel, from the 60s long before he had any idea what such words meant or how they would feel...

A woman wears a certain look
When she is on the move

...or how much pain they could evoke.

But it's knowing that you're looking back
That's really killing me...

His hands stopped grappling with the chair. However, his exhausted mind continued careening in reverse until it collided with the shock of their last moments together as he knelt beside a terrified Lisa on the sidewalk. Then the rewinding reel of his thoughts took him inside the ice cream parlor to the booth where they'd been sitting. Next, always next, he relived the taking of the photo just as her phone's tango rhythm announced an incoming text. Although the photo was locked in a drawer inside his locked office, over two miles away within the brick and mortar of Stienboek High School, his closed eyes saw it as clearly as if it was in his hand.

As he began to succumb to sleep, other details of their last day returned. He'd left that Saturday morning before she was up and spent much of the day at school to avoid any discussion of the previous night. She had gone out but was back early. Something seemed to have changed, but nothing was said.

When he got home, she kissed him and begged him to go for ice cream. "Please, like the old days, back before..." She kissed him again. "I want to explain. I can do that now; I promise so you'll understand and maybe forgive me. Please, Ryan. I need to tell you everything."

He remembered wanting so much to believe her. But he also wanted to push her away and scream – at her and at himself. But mostly he needed to hear her explain. He showered, and they had left.

When Ryan opened his eyes to the darkness of his apartment, lit only by the glow of the night light in the bathroom, he was surprised to find his cheeks were dry. For the first time, the memories had come and gone without a single tear. He wondered why.

27

The five men met for dinner at the same place they used to meet up after school on the second Friday of each month. It had been eighteen months since Ryan had moved to Wisconsin, and they'd all been here together to give him a send-off party. If they had asked Ryan, he'd have said it felt like eighteen years. That farewell evening had been subdued and more touchy-feely than any of them had anticipated. For the previous two years, their get-togethers were the only way the other men had gotten to talk with Ryan outside of school. Since Lisa's death, it had become almost impossible to coax him out. He'd attended a Timberwolves game with Trent, but that had been about it.

Tonight, when they'd all arrived, they'd gotten a table and ordered a round of drinks. Ryan assured them he was fine, although Stienboek High and Wisconsin's constant political battles had left him little time for anything but work. He gave them a summary of the referendum and its dubious chances of passing. He had to promise them he wasn't making up this Thynie Marsh character and that she indeed seemed hell-bent on making him miserable. He was noncommittal and vague in answering questions about Lisa's parents and appreciated that they didn't probe very deeply. When the drinks arrived, he filled them in on his parents whom they'd all met at one time or another. He then insisted and urged the men to share what was going on with their wives and kids.

Like Ryan, Jim Black had taken a job as principal in a smaller rural district. The school was thirty or so miles northwest of Minneapolis. He and his wife had wanted to get out of the city to raise their three kids. More than once he gleefully commented that his current commute was less than fifteen minutes rather than the forty-five minutes in city traffic his old job had taken. The other three still worked together at the high school where they'd all been on staff and become friends. Trent, the youngest among them, was one of the three school counselors. Bill Hoen, the choir director, and Bob Suzi who worked with special education seniors, especially those with behavior disorders, were both in their late forties. They shared a love of travel, a bawdy sense of humor, and being very good at what they did. Hoen and his wife, who taught choreography, put on award-winning musicals year after year, and Suzi worked magic coaxing those who needed it to the finish line and a high school diploma.

A second round of drinks arrived. Suddenly, out of an urgency to tell Ryan some news he'd just remembered, Suzi almost spilled his. "Hey! You're not going to believe this. Do you remember Doug Rupert, from the school board? He's a financial mucky-muck at one of the medical centers?"

Ryan almost choked on the beer he'd just swallowed. Wiping his mouth with a napkin, he cautiously responded. "Yeah? Why?"

"Well, he resigned from the board. It seems his wife – remember her, tall, pretty girl, short dark stylish hair, and a great ass? She worked for a year as a volunteer in the library."

Ryan sensed whatever was about to be said wasn't going to include him or his secret rendezvous with her at his motel tomorrow. He relaxed and showed some concern. "What about her? Is she all right?"

Suzi took a long drink while making eye contact with the other men, all of whom already knew what was coming. He set his drink down and continued. "Well, I'm going to guess she's probably not okay. Word is, she filed for divorce. Claims old Dougy has been dipping his financial wand around the hospital with more than one assistant or other. There's even a rumor he'd been screwing someone connected with the high school."

Back at his motel, Ryan couldn't sleep. He spent much of the night trying to reign in his suspicions and apprehension and speculating about the Ruperts. Why had she suddenly filed for divorce? Had she only recently found out about her husband's affairs? It had never crossed his mind that Doug Rupert may have also been cheating. Then again, he had never considered why she had. He'd never asked himself why she had leaned across him in the library. The truth was – he hadn't wanted to know. Now he had to contemplate the disastrous consequences if he was the reason for her decision.

His mind replayed what had happened that first time in the room just down the hall from where he now sat. Before she'd arrived, he'd decided he'd just apologize and back out of the whole game. But the words hadn't come, not when she'd stood at the door in that short, tight black skirt, not that he'd tried hard to find them. She had repeated her dare. A moment later he had her over his knee, panties around her ankles, her squirming and laughing pleas as pleasurable as the feel each time his hand came down on her bottom. When she promised to do anything he wanted, every part of his mind and body swelled with excitement and power. Taking her had been an act of revenge. At the time, he'd assumed it was aimed at Lisa. Now he knew his high-minded sense of being above adultery had also been a target.

In the dark of his room, Ryan weighed the anticipated pleasure and release of Mrs. Rupert's arrival against his sordid motivations and his recurrent fears of being revealed as an adulterer. He should run before she got here, escape back to Edenton, to at least trying to do the right thing. But the desire to stay was strong; to force her to explain the divorce, to beg forgiveness for not telling him about Doug, to submit again and allow him to exorcise his fear and anger, leaving only the shame to deal with.

It was after 2:00 a.m. before he undressed and climbed into the bed and under the covers hoping sleep was within reach. Behind closed eyes and semi-consciousness, his unbridled libido taunted his sense of self-preservation and rationality. It was still easy to pretend Mrs. Rupert was his due, a justifiable way to fortify himself against the encircling clouds he faced in Edenton.

28

Nala, Zoey and two other friends stood in line, the smell of hot popcorn adding to the excitement of a Saturday night together at the movies. They weren't alone. Several dozen more teen girls were there to see *Breaking Dawn* – Part 2 of the Twilight saga. From the chatter, it was clear many were there for a second and even third time. Some were with boyfriends. The girls had all been surprised to see Allan Sparks there with Lilly McKnight. No one was aware they'd been dating. Since about sixth grade, they'd all wished they were as pretty as she was. Zoey had always admired Lilly's drive and desire to work hard. Still, they had whispered to each other, wondering if her learning disability extended to her choices in boys.

Christmas break was almost over. Tuesday would be New Year's Day, and Wednesday they'd be back in classes. Unlike most of their friends, Nala and Zoey looked forward to going back to school. Since second grade, when they had first met in Mrs. Holman's room, they enjoyed each other's company. They were two of the best readers, liked math, and were consistent 'A' students. They both excelled in sports. Even as ninth-graders, Nala was a standout on the basketball court, and Zoey was assured a starting position on the softball team next spring. Academically, they each had their sights on excelling, but Nala knew that Zoey's academic drive was stronger than hers, especially in science, which was Zoey's passion. Language Arts was more Nala's thing. She couldn't remember a time when she wasn't reading well above grade level. She could read and comprehend anything she'd come across. In middle school, she'd realized she particularly loved the power of fiction and storytelling.

For as long as she could remember, especially over the summer, she'd have one of her parents drop her at the library in town to browse and get a new pile of books. Last summer, she'd moved into the adult stacks, looking for new more challenging material. She'd spotted Alice Walker's *The Color Purple* and remembered hearing somewhere it was controversial but also a prize-winning book about a young Black girl. She sheepishly put it between two other books when checking out. The librarian had hesitated for what felt like a full minute, looking like she was going to refuse to let her check it out, but then, without a word, let her have it. Forewarned, she kept it between the other books in her book bag when her mom picked her up.

It was challenging in more ways than Nala could have imagined. Mostly written as a bunch of letters, the style reminded her of Beverly Cleary's *Dear Mr. Henshaw*, which she'd read in fourth grade. She quickly realized Walker's story was about a lot more serious stuff than divorce. She had to admit it was sad and scary, and there were parts where she was, for the first time, just plain lost and confused. She processed what she could by explaining it to Langston each night. When that became too difficult to do, especially in parts that were too horrible and embarrassing to think about even with Lang, she returned it – depositing it in the book drop rather than bringing it into the library.

Nala assumed Zoey would become the valedictorian in four years. Nala wanted to come as close to a 4.0 average as possible, but being on top wasn't what she wanted. She didn't want to stand out any more than she already felt she did. In a way, she was like Bella Swan in the movie, a bit of a misfit, moved to a strange place, who finds being a teen and coming of age has brought challenges she'd not anticipated.

The girls inched closer to the snack counter when Zoey gave a small wave over Nala's head. Nala turned to see Ayden Quant waving enthusiastically. He and his classmate Steven were among the younger crowd exiting *Monsters Inc.* from Theater 2. "Really, Zoey? Ayden Quant?"

"I know, but he's not so bad. Mrs. Zowak usually pairs him with me in science labs. He's a lot smarter than most people give him credit for. He asks some good questions I'd never think of. Believe it or not, he even makes some insightful observations. He just has trouble staying focused and following directions. But I keep him on task pretty well."

"I hope Mrs. Zowak pays you to do that. She'd have to pay me a lot. You remember what he said to me that day, don't you? He almost got me suspended."

"Yeah," Zoey said as they moved up to second in line. "Who doesn't remember? You almost took his head off. And none of us would have blamed you if you did. But remember, you also said you forgave him when you realized he was just being Ayden and not some racist asshole."

"I'm not sure I forgave him, just ..." Nala stopped. She'd glanced back and saw Ayden's face suddenly become angry. He was intently staring across the lobby to the game room area. She followed his gaze, seeing Allan playing some shooting game with Lilly standing beside him. She turned back to Zoey. "Does he like Lilly? I think he just spotted her with Allan, and he has one of those if-looks-could-kill faces."

"All the boys like Lilly. What's not to like? Why?" Zoey looked toward Ayden. "Uh, Oh." Nala felt a couple of bills being jammed into her hand, just as the guy behind the counter asked, "What will you have girls?" Zoey said, "Here's for the popcorn. Get me a medium soda. I'll be back in a minute." She headed over toward Ayden and Steven.

The girls settled into their seats with a few minutes to spare before the lights dimmed off, and the reminders to turn off cell phones, clean up your trash, and trailers of upcoming movies began. While their two friends discussed Bella's human-to-vampire transformation back at the end of Part 1, Nala turned to Zoey who was sitting on the aisle. "What was that all about with Ayden?" She handed her friend some napkins and the popcorn they were sharing.

"I guess I feel a bit protective of him. He's like a puppy dog. I know he and Allan can be best buddies one minute and then at each other's throats the next. Anyhow, he's mad Lilly is out with Allan. He thinks he'll get her in trouble."

"So, he likes her?" Nala asked.

"Like I said, who doesn't like her? She's so pretty and nice. I'm sure he has a crush on her too. But I got a feeling maybe it was more about Allan than Lilly. Who knows. Boys are so weird."

Zoey picked some of the buttered kernels off the top. Nala pulled her coat around her shoulders. It was always chilly in the theater, winter or summer. As she made herself comfortable, she considered Ayden Quant. If Zoey liked him, even thought he had occasional good insights when he wasn't getting in trouble, maybe she'd been hasty in her judgments. Maybe there was more to him than an immature goof. But *Monsters Inc.*? It was probably Steven's idea. Everyone knew he was fixated on monsters.

Like a stone skipping across water, her mind touched on several fleeting thoughts. She wondered what Ayden's home life was like. She was sure it was not as secure as her own and realized she might have always thought less of him because of it. He acted different than most, and she wondered if that might be like looking different. Wasn't that what had led him to ask his stupid question that day? Her thought train ran out of steam and faded as the theater went dark, and the camera led them into the world of teenage romance and vampires.

2013

29

The small conference room felt cramped. Ryan took the only remaining seat. He'd just come from seeing the busses off. Shedding his coat in his office next door, he carried the crisp fresh smell of a cold January day with him into the room. "Sorry, I'm late. I had to sort out a bus matter."

He was attending Ayden's IEP – Individual Educational Plan meeting as the school's Local Educational Agent. Usually, Jillian Crik the school psychologist filled the required role, but she'd received a call that morning from her father in Antigo telling her the Hospice nurse didn't think her mother was going to make it through the day.

Annual IEPs for every special education student are required and spelled out by federal and state law. They are legal documents. By statute, an IEP is written by a team that includes the parents. The law and the entire process are meant to protect the child's rights to needed services in the least restrictive manner possible.

For students like Ayden, moving into and through high school, the IEP requires the inclusion of a Postsecondary Transition Plan. The PTP identifies the measurable steps and support services related to each student's post-high school goals.

Mrs. Berry began the proceedings by introducing herself to William Powells, whom, with Anna Quandt's approval, she had invited to the meeting. She noted that Powells was a licensed psychologist and therapist and his input could be valuable. She asked the others to do the same, then thanked Powells again for coming. Ayden's previous therapist had never made an appearance.

After the introductions, she quickly and efficiently explained the process for reviewing and revising the IEP. None of this was new to anyone in the room. Mrs. Berry sat, as always, closest to the Smartboard so she could see everyone's face as they looked up at the screen. As most students did, Ayden had plopped himself and his backpack down on the seat at the far end of the table. His mom sat next to him. From previous records, Mrs. Berry had noted that Mr. Quant hadn't attended an IEP since Ayden's original one in third grade. Just to be sure, she asked, "Will your husband be joining us?"

"No."

Mrs. Berry didn't probe. But Ayden's father never appearing in school was a red flag that could not be explained solely because he was a long-haul trucker, spending more time on the road than at home.

Representing Ayden's classroom teachers, Bernadette Zowak and his English teacher, Mrs. Eiker, sat along one side of the narrow room with William Powells, Jennifer Bradley the freshmen counselor, and Ryan across from them.

Mrs. Berry walked the group through a review of Ayden's goals and accommodations from last year. His academic modifications were typical. He was allowed extra time to take tests and could retake them if needed. Because of his ADHD and other diagnoses, teachers were asked to modify classroom assignments and tests to focus on the essential information and skills. In reality, this usually fell to Mrs. Berry.

Zowak and Eiker reported that so far this semester, the consensus was Ayden's inconsistent grades were not due to a lack of intelligence but to spotty effort and missing assignments. When asked, Ayden signaled his agreement with his usual, "I guess."

Mrs. Eiker said, "I hope you know, Ayden, we're all on your side. All your teachers like you and know you can do better."

"No way Mr. Pattone likes me, and I hate him," Adyen rebutted. "He..." A sharp look from his mom stopped further comment.

Mrs. Zowak said, "In high school, it's not about liking or not liking a teacher. More is expected of everyone, and you need to step up and be more personally responsible."

Mrs. Eiker asked if assignments and expectations were too hard.

"No!"

"Can you get your grade up with a little more effort?"

"I guess."

"Will you let me know when you need help, so you don't fall too far behind?"

"I guess. Okay."

Ryan made a suggestion. "I wonder if Mr. Powells has anything he might share that could help guide our thinking." The group turned their attention to the psychologist. He'd been sitting throughout with his hands folded on the table. He smiled at Ayden before speaking.

"I should probably first explain my clinical work is trauma-focused, meaning the impact trauma experiences have on all parts of a child's development. Instead of starting with the idea that something is *wrong* that needs fixing, we begin by asking *what happened to* them. That's crucial. We then help connect those experiences to the person's emotional and behavioral responses. Ayden and I are working on that part, his ability to recognize and cope with emotions that get triggered." He looked at the boy again, adding a wink.

Mrs. Zowak said, "No disrespect, Mr. Powells," but doesn't everyone have bad things happen to them at some point growing up?"

"True enough. But I'm not referring to normal experiences that can be considered traumatic. We're talking about sustained chronic events. When this occurs at an age when children have no say or control over what's happening to them, or even the ability to speak up, or maybe before they have any understanding of how things should be, it becomes what we call developmental trauma. This is especially problematic when it occurs at the hands of those who should be loving and protecting you. And, as the name implies, it can affect development in a variety of ways. The only defenses a young child has is learning not to trust anyone and to hit the 'flight or fight' button ASAP. Such traumas don't disappear just because the child grows up, or we adults want it to."

Ryan leaned in, making eye contact. "I know this isn't the time or place, but can you quickly fill us in on how we as a school might use what you're telling us?"

"Well...the place to start might be to be aware of what we call ACEs – Adverse Childhood Experiences. Research has identified ten of these that are closely associated with potentially severe impacts on a person's life. As you'd expect, poverty and divorce are two more common ones. About twenty-five percent of kids in America experience at least one of them. But the longer the duration and severity of the experience, and the more ACEs experienced by a young person, the more the likelihood of a big problem down the road."

"So, to my point," Mrs. Zowak added, "lots of kids experience ACEs."

"On average, about 80% of kids experience zero or one ACE between birth and age seventeen. Another 10% experience two over that period. That means the other 10% in that age group experience between three to ten.

"Anyhow," Powells said, "Schools are in a difficult position with lots of different challenges and privacy issues, especially nowadays, but you have some data you can draw on; like those who qualify for free and reduced lunch and maybe other areas that correlate with

ACEs like homelessness. That data might give you a better picture of what your students here at Stienboek, or in the district at large, are facing. In time, it might help change the common perception and default question of 'What's wrong with that kid' to 'What's happened to them'. I truly believe even that change in attitude can make a big difference over time."

Mrs. Berry cleared her throat. "Thank you, Mr. Powells. If you have more information on the topic you could send us, I'd appreciate it."

Over the next forty-five minutes, she facilitated the group to a consensus on needed revisions, deletions, and additions to Ayden's goals, making a few changes to his modifications along the way. At each step, she made a point of making sure Ayden and Mrs. Quant were clear about each requirement for him and the school.

After everyone had left, she sat reflecting on the meeting and the situation with Ayden and his non-participating father. She found she admired Anna Quant. Rather than obstructive and uncooperative, the woman seemed to be like so many others in a difficult marriage and doing her best to raise a difficult child – in this case her stepson. She felt they had connected. She'd even gotten a genuine thank you from her when she and Ayden left.

Mrs. Berry gathered up the loose papers and files. She flipped off the lights and headed to her room to drop them off and head home. Next door, she could hear Ryan's voice on the phone. He was explaining something about a referendum support group. By now, everyone knew they again needed to be asking to exceed the revenue caps on next April's ballot. She was glad her professional responsibilities and headaches were centered on the nineteen special-ed students who made up her caseload. Most days, that seemed like more than enough.

She knew Ryan lived alone, tragically widowed. Back in 1993, when she was hired at Stienboek by Walt Hannig, Lisa had been a freshman. But the only times they crossed paths would have been if the girl happened to be in a class where she was supporting a student. She had no real memory of Lisa but had heard some rumors back then and, of course, more comments after she'd been killed and again after Ryan was hired.

Mrs. Berry got to her car. She started the engine and opened the window an inch. School grounds were designated non-smoking areas, but the staff lot was almost empty, so she lit a cigarette while she waited for the heater to warm the car. She slowly blew the smoke out the open window and thought about the information Powells had shared on Adverse Childhood Experiences.

As she drew in the next lung full, she pondered how Ryan seemed to have withdrawn into a world of his own after asking the therapist about their application in a school setting. She assumed he'd been contemplating the possibilities. Again, blowing smoke out the window, she wondered how many ACEs Lisa must have faced if what she had heard was even half true. She took one last drag, opened the car door to exhale and stamped out the half-smoked butt. She put the remains in her unfinished morning coffee mug to dispose of when she got home.

30

The next morning, Ryan stood at one of the hallway intersections during passing period. Whenever his schedule allowed, he liked to be in the halls at different vantage points to greet and monitor students. He enjoyed the interactions, and it was a reminder to staff that they also should have a presence in the halls. They were generally pretty good about it. Only once in his eighteen months as principal did he feel it necessary to privately remind a teacher of the expectation and its importance.

He had chosen this particular spot today on purpose. He spotted Ayden in the crowd. "Hey, Ayden. Can you hold up a minute, I wanted to ask you something?" Seeing the look on the boy's face, he quickly added, "You're not in any trouble." They stepped to the side to avoid causing a backup. Ryan made sure he looked casual so others wouldn't assume Ayden was in any trouble. "I thought the meeting last night went well. I hope you felt good about the positive things said about you."

"I guess."

"Well, as Mrs. Berry said, just push a little harder, and you'll pass everything and won't have to make up any courses. We're all rooting for you. You know that don't you?"

"Yeah."

"Okay. Well, you go on so you're not tardy. Let me know if I can help in any way."

"Thanks."

As Ayden turned to go, Ryan asked, "You seem to like and get along with Mr. Powells."

"Yeah. He's fine."

"You think he's helping you?"

"I guess. I mean he's a lot better than the last lady. I've only met with him a few times." Ayden looked around to notice the halls were almost empty. "I better go."

Ryan took a pass from his pocket and signed it, adding the date and time. Here, give this to your teacher if you get there a little late. But don't dawdle, okay?"

Ayden laughed. "Don't what?"

"Dawdle. Don't take your time or go slow on purpose."

"That's a funny word. Mr. Powells is funny too. He told me how his sister made him afraid of people coming to their door when he was a little kid."

Ayden hurried off at a slow jog. Ryan refrained from telling him not to run. Instead, he headed back to his office thinking about all the things that made him afraid.

31

Dominic chose the far back booth for the same reason he'd suggested Sunday night. It was the quietest spot on the quietest night of the week, a brief respite between Friday's fish fry crowd and Saturday's drinkers and diners and then Monday's dart league. On his way in, he'd asked Tammi, who was behind the bar, to tell Ryan he was in the back.

"Sure thing, Dom. You want menus?" Tammi's warm smile and friendly greeting were an attraction on its own. She made everyone, locals and newcomers, feel welcome. Her good looks also made many of the local men choose seats where they could keep an inconspicuous eye on her as she moved around the bar and tables.

Tammi's mother, Holly, had been a few years ahead of Dominic in school. She and Tammi's Grandma Sophie owned Sophie's Choice. The grandparents had bought the place in the mid-70s and rechristened it simply as Sophie's because the purchase had been her idea. Sadly, after they had turned the business around, Sophie's husband had died. Some years later, Sophie was courted by a real estate guy from north of Green Bay. Eventually, he wanted her to sell the establishment, get married, and invest the profits in his business. She felt tempted, but, as she says, "I came to my senses." No further explanation was ever given. The real estate guy quit coming around, and the name on the sign was changed to Sophie's Choice with posters from the 1982 movie prominently displayed.

Dominic thanked Tammi and took the menus. He'd just taken

off his jacket and got seated when Ryan arrived. He tossed his coat into the booth and slid in after it. "Damn, that wind is cold. I appreciate you coming. Since the holidays, it seems any time I try to get down to your office, I either get sidetracked or you're out."

Dominic handed over a menu. "It works out well. Kate and Natalia got a veggie pizza and a video. Kate said Natalia ironically picked out, of all things, the old Meryl Streep movie of..."

"*Sophie's Choice*." Ryan interrupted, noticing Dominic had referred to his daughter as Natalia instead of Nala. "What fifteen-year-old picks out stuff like that? Does she know the storyline? That's heady stuff."

"Yeah. God help me. They'll both be in tears when I get home." Without opening his menu, Dominic said, "So, I'm going to fortify myself with a Sophie Burger with cheese, fries, and all the works."

Ryan stood. "Sounds like a plan, I'll go order. What do you want to drink?"

"I'll have a tap Leinenkugel's. Thanks."

While Ryan went up to order at the bar, Dominic thought about the awkward incident just before the Christmas break when he'd walked into Ryan's office and saw him and a tearful Sharon holding hands. He'd assumed she'd just told him she was leaving Dave and that Ryan was consoling her. Still, it made him feel uneasy. What if someone else had walked in? What if some parent, or Liz Demian, or worse, what if Thynie or Sharon's husband had stopped by? He was still trying to erase the last two images from his imagination when Ryan returned.

He set down a pitcher and two glasses. "I took the liberty of getting a pitcher." As he poured them each a glass, Dominic wondered if Sharon had mentioned her husband's threat. Ryan lifted his glass and offered a toast. "Here's to a new and better year for all of us."

Dominic used the opportunity. "Last year could have ended a

lot worse if someone like Thynie had walked into your office that last day instead of me."

Ryan remembered flushing when he'd turned and saw Dominic in the doorway. His mind had gone blank almost to the point of panic. Luckily, Sharon had said, "I just told him, Dom. About me and David splitting." She'd moved her hands to her lap. After a few awkward moments, she'd left, followed a minute later by Dominic. After they'd gone, Ryan felt guilty, aware that beneath the deep empathy and concern he'd felt for Sharon, had been another feeling. It had startled him.

Ryan replied to Dominic's question. "You're right, that would have been a nightmare. Undoubtedly, half of the town would have heard Thynie's version of what she saw even before Santa started dropping gifts down our chimneys." His light-hearted response contrasted with the twist in his gut at the thought. He swallowed a portion of his beer to counter the burn.

Shifting the focus, Ryan asked, "Has Sharon told you any more of where she's at? I don't feel like it's my place to ask her about details, or if she wants some time off, or..." The weight of the inadequacy of his offerings caused the sentence and his voice to trail off.

Dominic said. "I don't know all of what she told you, but Dave is still in denial and unwilling to talk and drinking more. He's making it real hard on her."

Ryan told Dominic about the encounter with Sharon's husband at the basketball game back in early December. "Maybe their deteriorating marriage had something to do with the man's weird behavior?" No way was he going to mention the asshole's slur about Nala. "I'd heard he was a drinker. But it wasn't something I was going to ask Sharon about. He wouldn't hurt her, would he? He's never abused her or the kids, has he?"

"No. She said he hasn't and besides, I'd have heard about it. But

Dave is the kind of guy who blames everyone else for his problems. Anything that goes wrong is proof the world is out to get him. He doesn't deal well with change. So, when the kids got to be school age and Sharon started working at Stienboek a half-dozen years ago, he acted like they were all abandoning him – like it was a plot against him. He hired some part-time help, but they'd always leave because of his micro-managing and always finding fault. Of course, his drinking didn't help.

"Anyhow, it's common knowledge they haven't been good for some time, so the split isn't a big surprise. Dave's reaction isn't a surprise either. He's old school. Believes wives don't leave their husbands." He paused for a moment. "I'm no counselor, but I'd guess in his mind, it's logical to blame her for the whole shebang."

Dominic took a sip of his beer while keeping his eyes on Ryan who was staring into his glass. Then, having decided to take the plunge, he continued. "Even though it's his own damn fault, it also seems a good bet he might want to find some way to shame her, find someone else to blame, to point a finger at, so he can be the martyr. He's believing his own crap, and he won't think twice about hurting someone else. He'll think he's justified in doing it."

Both men fell silent. Dominic tried to remember how long ago it had been that Dave Edmonds had quizzed him about Ryan in the men's room right down the hall. Maybe he should have mentioned it at the time, but it seemed too crazy, and it was before Sharon had shared her plans with him. His eyes drifted across the booth. For some reason, he sensed Ryan was somehow blaming himself. He didn't know what to make of that.

Ryan said, "Sharon told you about his threat, didn't she?"

Dominic nodded. "Yeah."

Ryan said, "I told her not to worry about it, that in a way it was flattering. But Dom, you know as well as I do, that's the last thing any of us needs."

"Anyhow, I'm glad she warned you," Dominic said. "So, you may not want to make a habit of holding Sharon's hands at school or anywhere else. People around here are mostly fair. They won't be hard on Sharon for leaving. They know the history. But that probably won't extend to you. You haven't been here very long. And..." he stopped.

"Go on," Ryan urged.

Dominic took another drink of beer. He hadn't thought through how this conversation might go, let alone planned on going this far. This was way beyond his comfort zone. He took a long moment until the words arranged themselves.

"Look, Ryan. You must know some of this, that some still wonder why you came here. You know how some people can be. How they can add two plus two and come up with five, particularly if it fits what they already think or believe." Dominic hoped he could stop there, that Ryan would just accept the vagueness and not ask any questions.

However, after glancing toward the bar area, Ryan did ask. "And what do they think?"

Dominic said, "I feel real shitty telling you this stuff." He sighed and took a deep breath.

"Lisa's first two years of high school were rough for her. Both academically and socially. She was getting hit on by a lot of older guys. Eventually, she'd got a bit of a reputation because she started dating some of the sleaze-balls. She'd go with someone for a few weeks and then dump them. Most of these guys were the type who bragged about their conquests and... well, word spread. Later, even though she became a good student and quit going out with the jerks, lots of people remembered her for those early years, and they were glad when she left for college and seldom came back. Then she showed up engaged to you, and they all wonder if she's got herself another sucker and how long you're going to last." It was obvious this was hard for Dominic to recount.

"Well, when word came back about what happened to her and..."

Ryan consciously kept his voice low. "You mean, there are people who actually think..."

Dominic quickly interrupted him. "No, not that *you* did anything. But they wonder why you'd want to come here. I have to admit, I did too."

"Here you go, guys." Tammi was suddenly standing at the table with two burger platters and her usual smile. "I don't know what serious school stuff you all are yapping about, but it's time to stop and eat your dinners. Mom said 'hi' and added some extra fries for both of you. Is there anything else you guys need?"

Dominic glanced at Ryan and then said, "We're good. Thanks, Tammi, and thank your mom."

She started to turn, then added. "By the way, Dave Edmonds came in and is at the bar. He asked if those were your car and truck out front. Since Sharon works with you guys, I told him you were back here, but he just sat at the bar and ordered his usual Jack Daniels."

The men turned to look toward the bar, which was mostly screened off by a partial wall, hanging signs, and other miscellaneous paraphernalia. Ryan said, "Thanks. The burgers look great." Tammi walked away. Ryan picked up a fry and studied it.

"Dom, I appreciate you telling me all this." He stuck the potato in his mouth and chewed. "I guess on some level I knew, or at least assumed a lot of it, but thanks for saying it out loud."

As they worked on their food, both men occasionally glanced toward the bar area. After a few minutes, Ryan shifted to the topic he had wanted to discuss and explore with Dominic.

"I've got – the whole admin team has – some real concerns about the referendum. You said before you think it's going to be a hard sell." Ryan pulled a list from his pocket and handed it across the table. "These are people Liz Demian has contacted about being on the community support group she's put me in charge of. Are there any others that might be worth asking? Are there many who might be against it initially but might be convinced to change their minds? Do you think if we run the same campaign as a few years ago, it'll be enough?"

Dominic looked over the list. "Last time Thynie was the only opposition on the board, and the referendum only passed by a couple of percentage points. She has two allies now, and the timing is a lot worse." Dominic shared a few thoughts on Ryan's other questions. He touched on some possibilities, but, in the end, urged Ryan not to bet his life on it.

They paid their bill and said good night to Tammi and her mother. Neither Dominic nor Ryan attempted eye contact with Dave Edmonds who was lecturing someone sitting next to him at the far end of the bar. When they got outside, Ryan remembered something. "Hey, Dominic. That night I mentioned running into...," he pointed back toward the bar with his thumb, "It was at the freshman girls' basketball game against Menasha. Anyhow, while watching Nala dominate the floor, I somehow started connecting that crazy incident with Ayden Quant and my old assistant principal job back in Minneapolis and, well..." Ryan tried to recapture what he wanted to ask. At the time, it had seemed so clear, but now it seemed confused and tangled up in his head.

Dominic zipped his coat against the wind. Into Ryan's pause, he said, "I'm still embarrassed about that and all I can say is I'm sorry again about her, Nala's, Natalia's outburst. She had no right to take that out on you."

"That's not what I meant." Ryan turned up his collar. "She had every right to be upset. That's kind of what I was trying to get at," but he shifted to a different question. "Doesn't she want to be called Nala anymore? I notice you've been using Natalia. Around school, everyone still calls her Nala. I can always let the teachers know she wants to be called by her given name."

They'd been slow walking as they talked and reached Dominic's truck. "No, she's still Nala. Maybe more so now than ever. It's just me having trouble with… I don't know, having a teenage girl who is growing up faster than I want her to, faster than I can change to catch up with her. I think I'm just worried about who she may want to be, you know?" Dominic opened his truck door and stepped up into the seat. "Anyhow, Nala will always be Nala, so I guess I shouldn't get bent out of shape. Kate's right. She'll figure it out."

Ryan extended his hand. Dominic removed his glove and shook it. "I don't think you have much to worry about. If they all were like her, we'd have fifty applicants for every teacher listing. You're a lucky man, and you and Kate have done a wonderful job raising her. You should be proud. See you tomorrow." Ryan headed to his car.

Dominic closed his door and started his engine. He adjusted the heat to blow across the windshield. While he waited, he felt grateful to Ryan for picking up on the Natalia vs. Nala thing. *I'm being an ass,* he thought. Then he thought about how much he'd come to like Ryan and was relieved that he knew about Dave Edmonds' threat. He hoped that situation would resolve soon and not get any uglier.

He slipped the truck into gear. Before touching the gas pedal, he realized he'd interrupted whatever Ryan was trying to say about Nala's basketball game. He glanced over at Ryan's car and for a moment was confused. Ryan was opening his trunk and pulling out his spare tire. *What the hell?*

Dominic pulled over next to where the car was parked and rolled down his window. "Flat? Let me give you a hand." On a hunch, he said "I've got a pump here that works off the cigarette lighter. Let's try that before you change it." He reached behind his seat to get the pump, confident there wasn't a puncture in Ryan's tire. He wondered if Ryan had figured it out too.

32

"Why does he always do that?"

Ayden's frustration, was apparent in his voice. Mrs. Berry swallowed the bite of apple she'd been chewing and looked up from her emails. She was trying to catch up on the daily in-house onslaught and respond to a parent's question. She'd also been hoping to enjoy a brief bit of privacy while she ate her half sandwich and honey crisp apple slices. Too frequently, she sabotaged her lunchtime by requiring one or more of her students to bring their lunch to her room and make up some missed assignment or finish a test.

"Good afternoon to you too, Ayden," Mrs. Berry said, trying not to sound irked by the intrusion. "Why does who do what?"

"Mr. Murphy. He always just puts math problems on the board and says what to do and thinks everyone can follow what he's saying. If he ever turned around and looked, he'd see half the kids are lost or not paying attention. I mean, it doesn't matter to me. I'm pretty good at math, but a lot of the other kids are just lost."

"Well, have you, or anyone else asked him to explain?" Mrs. Berry asked.

"When you do, he just says the same thing over again, only slower. Like you're an idiot. But you know what's going to be awesome?"

"What might that be?" She deleted several emails, wishing people wouldn't always hit "Reply All' to everything.

"I heard that pretty soon robots will be doing most of the teaching anyway."

She finally gave Ayden her full attention. "And you think that would be awesome?"

"Well, yeah! Just think you could just learn when you wanted, and it would never yell or act like you're dumb. You could turn it off when you wanted to."

"You do know I'm a teacher, don't you? I'm not sure I like the idea of being replaced by a robot."

"Not you. I just mean the ones that don't like kids and don't answer questions. Most teachers are okay, I guess."

"Well, I'll take that as a compliment then," Mrs. Berry said. She wasn't about to get into a conversation with a student about another teacher. "How's your mom doing? I enjoyed getting to meet her at the IEP meeting."

Ayden scoffed. "Well, don't get *her* goin' on about teachers and school."

"She seemed concerned but very nice at the meeting. I thought we got on pretty well."

"She said you were okay."

"Well, that was nice of her. I'm sorry I didn't get to meet your dad," she added, hoping to gain a little insight into the family dynamics.

"He was driving somewhere. But he never comes anyhow. He doesn't like school even more than mom." Ayden hesitated a moment then asked a question. "Did you know she's a stepmom, not a real mom? Did you know that?"

Mrs. Berry wasn't sure why he'd ask but replied in the affirmative. "Yes. Of course, I did," adding, "Ayden, you know that just because she wasn't pregnant with you, your mom can be both a stepmom and a 'real' mom at the same time. Sometimes, stepmoms make the best moms."

Ayden's lips tightened, and he looked up like he was thinking hard. Mrs. Berry still wasn't sure what to make of his question and reaction. She took another bite of apple and gave him a few moments. He finally replied. "Yeah. I guess so. I just wish she was my birth mom and had me as a baby. I was already four years old when I met her, but she seemed to like me, so it was all right. It was just weird because I didn't know my dad either until he came and got me after my real mom died. He didn't like my real mom. He blamed her for having me."

Mrs. Berry swallowed and said, "That must have been a very confusing time for you." She wasn't sure why Ayden had chosen to tell her all this now. She was glad the boy felt safe with his stepmom, but it didn't do anything to alleviate her concerns about his father. She decided to focus on the positive. "Well, it sounds like your stepmom loves and cares about you. That's the main job for a mom."

"That's what Mr. Powells said too," Ayden said.

Mrs. Berry tacked. "Speaking of Mr. Powells, it was nice of him to come. He seems nice. I know you just started with him. Is he helping you?"

"Mr. Davvis asked me the same thing. Yeah, he's fine. Can I stay in here?"

"Ayden, this is my lunch period, and I have some things to do. Why do you want to stay in here?"

"Allan's being a jerk. He's been in my face telling me how he's... he's going out with Lilly."

"He is?"

"Yeah, and he knows I liked her first."

"You know, Ayden, it's really up to Lilly who she goes out with. It's not based on who liked her first."

"I know. But he keeps telling me stuff. I'm sure he's lying, but it's like he's trying to make me mad or something and get me in trouble. You told me to be careful about that and not let him trick me into doing stuff."

Mrs. Berry made a mental note to talk with Allan. "Okay. You can stay, but you have to sit quietly back over there and work on something so I can finish my lunch and emails."

33

On their way to speak at the Westown Town Council meeting, Ryan and Superintendent Liz Demian approached the bridge that partitioned the Edenton Area School District into two sections. The structure often reminded Ryan that some residents of the City of Edenton side, where the high school, middle school, and one of the two elementary schools stood, had on occasion expressed befuddlement about the thinking, politics, and worldview over there, across the bridge they were now crossing.

Because Demian was driving, Ryan was staring at the not-quite-frozen current below. Growing up in Minneapolis, he knew the Mississippi River ran south. He had assumed all rivers in this part of the country did the same. As the car reached the halfway point on the bridge, he realized the river, illuminated by lights from the bridge and along the bank, was moving north.

"Wow, that's embarrassing," he admitted. "How could I *not* have noticed that the Fox runs north!"

"Luckily," Demian said with a slight grin, "I hired you as a principal and not a geography teacher."

Mildly amused but also aggrieved by his ignorance, Ryan complained, "When I first moved here, people seemed to enjoy telling me that Westown is *east* of Edenton, but I don't remember anyone commenting on the Fox River running north. I'm pretty sure that's unusual."

A second later, he repeated himself. "How could I not have noticed that? I've been here a year and a half plus a few times before getting married." He was conscious of omitting Lisa's name. "I've crossed this bridge a hundred times. I swear I think my mind is going."

That was all Ryan planned on saying, so he was surprised when an unplanned question left his mouth. "Why *did* you hire me?"

Liz Demian didn't answer right away, so Ryan added, "You must have had lots of applicants with more experience. I know you had at least one good internal candidate."

She gave him a glance that was hard to read in the dimness of the car. With her eyes back on the road she replied, "Why? Did I make a mistake?"

Having not anticipated his own question, Ryan was not ready for hers. He wondered what would happen if he said yes. But, before he could say anything, she continued, "To be honest, we didn't get as many candidates as we might have before all the political machinations and fighting that year. Plus, as I'm sure you're aware, we're not the highest-paying district in the area. Which raised the question in my mind about why you'd be willing to take a pay cut to come to rural Wisconsin and take on even more work and hours."

Ryan knew it wasn't a question. She'd heard his "I don't want to be an assistant principal all my life" answer to the same basic inquiry during his interviews. He waited for her to continue.

"As you may or may not know, Walt came to me after your application came in. I was surprised by that." She grinned and slightly shook her head. "He played me like a fiddle." She went quiet for a quarter mile before continuing. "I told Walt that you being from a big city school concerned me. He countered, saying your combined positions as assistant principal and your high school's curriculum coordinator meant you were current on standards and instruction as well as leadership and student behavior.

"I..." she glanced at Ryan then back to the road. "I hope this doesn't offend you or sound insensitive. But I was also concerned because being a widower made you a young, single man. I didn't think that was a good idea, thought that you'd get bored and lonely around here and leave, or worse, get into mischief. But of course, Walt had an answer. He told me how he'd been a kind of mentor while you were working on your admin license even before you were married. He went on to say that his years in the service, especially in Vietnam, had made him a good judge of character, and he was confident if you got this opportunity, you wouldn't be giving it up any time soon."

A moment later, she added, "I hope he was right."

Hearing about Walt's belief in his character and ability, Ryan turned his head to stare out the window into the darkness. Demian registered his movement as she slowed and turned onto School Road.

Wanting to bolster Ryan's confidence, she added a bit more. "Walt thought you had a good grasp of how to implement and balance the federal No Child Left Behind high stakes testing and accountability issues and the new Common Core standards. He thought you had vision. The kind of vision and energy we were looking for. That's high praise coming from Walt Hannig."

Ryan turned to face Liz but didn't respond.

"He also said you were ambitious. Not for yourself, but for being somewhere you could make a difference. He kept reminding me we needed new blood in leadership. Which, by the way, was the only reason why Barb Nickels wasn't chosen. That, plus she does an excellent job right where she is. She's great with young kids and with their parents."

Ryan said, "You know you didn't need to tell me all that."

"Yes, I did. Nine years ago, I was the outsider here. I remember the stress and near panic of being in my second year of a two-year contract."

They pulled onto the crushed gravel that made up the parking lot surrounding the old three-room school building that now served as the Westown Town Hall. It was one of two such buildings in which area students had attended until the 1958 school merger. Because the City of Edenton had about sixty percent of the population, a much larger tax base, and had recently updated buildings, the district was named the Edenton Area School District. In exchange, a new Westown Elementary School for kindergarten through fifth grade was built, after which students were bussed across the bridge to meet up with the other district sixth graders and mingle together through their middle and high school years. Eventually, the other older Westown schoolhouse was burnt as a training exercise by the local fire departments.

The lot was nearly full. As they looked for a parking spot, Ryan thought the crunching sound of their tires on the cold packed surface had a forlorn quality to it. After shutting off her engine, Demian turned to Ryan. Before she could remind him, he said, "I know. We're not exactly going to be welcomed with open arms by the good men of the Westown Town Council."

Liz added, "And they are all men – including Thynie Marsh's brother."

That caught Ryan's attention. "You've got to be kidding me. Are they everywhere?"

"Fortunately, he's not as – how should I say it – in-your-face vehement as his sister. But these are practical and conservative folks, mostly current and retired farmers, and they're going to have a lot of questions about why we want another referendum. They're going to want to know about every additional penny in taxes we're proposing and how it will benefit their elementary school, not just those on the Edenton side of the river. My guess is they voted for our new governor by a wide margin, and they like that he's promised lower property tax. They're not going to take kindly to us asking for some of that back."

A white SUV parked next to them. "Good, Barb is here," Liz said. "I'm glad I'm not going into this without her. She knows all these folks because she spends a good portion of her time on this side of the Fox River. They know and trust her."

Ryan wasn't sure Liz Demian could say the same about him on his side of the river.

34

The spotlight and strobe lights suddenly broke through the 3:00 a.m. darkness illuminating the interior of the car. The reflection in the rearview mirror blinded the young driver. It caused instant panic. He took his foot off the gas pedal, and his speed quickly began to descend from... he wasn't sure. He remembered seeing 75 mph, maybe a bit more.

The last he'd looked, only blackness filled the rear window. But then he'd got caught up in thoughts about finding his aunt's house once he'd reached Mequon and how much trouble he was going to be in when his parents found Mom's car gone. Surely, his aunt would make him call home to let them know he was okay. He was thinking maybe he should keep on going into Milwaukee or even all the way to Chicago. He'd been smart enough to grab a credit card and cash from his dad's wallet for gas and food. He glanced at his coat on the passenger seat which hid the funds and his dad's pistol, which he'd taken just in case. If he ended up in a city, he might need it to scare some creeps away.

Allan looked again into the mirror, but the lights were so bright he couldn't see anything. He twisted the mirror down and saw the terror in his own eyes and the tears beginning to flow from them.

"PULL THE CAR OVER, NOW!" The amplified command from the squad car felt like a physical blow to his body and now numbed mind. Without ever touching the gas again, Allan steered onto the shoulder and braked to a stop. Far out in the dark field on the side of the road, he stared at the farthest reaches of the flashing lights and remembered the trickles of water turning to ice under the culvert that last time with Ayden. He heard the squad car door slam and glanced at the backlit figure, hand on holster, approaching in the side view mirror.

Ayden's dream was weird. His leg was in the mouth of a toothless dog. He was wondering how a dog could lose all its teeth when he finally became conscious enough to know he was in his bed. His mother was shaking him, trying to wake him up.

"A-Lee, wake up. Wake up. A-Lee." Her voice was insistent – he must be late for school.

When his eyes opened and focused, she asked, "Do you know where Allan went? His dad is on the phone looking for him. Did he say anything yesterday to you about going anywhere? Ayden. Wake up."

"He's home. Is it time for school?"

"No, he isn't. It's 4:30 in the morning. His parents are looking for him. They said he might have his mother's car. Did you know where he was going or anything about it?"

"Mom, no! We haven't even been talking much. He's been a jerk, and I've been staying away from him. He was saying lies about Lilly in our class, and I didn't want to get in a fight with him."

"Lilly? Lilly McKnight? The one that lives in Westown?"

"Yeah. But I'm pretty sure she broke up with him." Before he'd finished his sentence, his mother was gone. He wanted to go back to sleep, but he kept picturing Allan's mom's car parked in the trees by the culvert where he tried his first joint and they talked about being a hero if anyone started shooting at school.

Superintendent Demian's urgent text sounded on Ryan's phone just as he pulled into the parking lot. She asked him to come to her office immediately. Before the front office door closed behind him, Sharon said, "Liz Demian called and wants to see you right away. What's up?" she asked, adding the tease, "Have you been bad again?"

The remark may have sparked his default fear and caused a skipped heartbeat, except that Demian's text had also said she was calling a Crisis Team meeting at 8:00 a.m. Never a good thing, but an indication this wasn't about him. "Not sure, but I better go find out." He dropped his stuff in his office and headed over to the district office with a sarcastic mumble to Sharon. "Happy second semester."

Demian's secretary waved him right in as she intently listened to someone on her phone while scrolling on her computer screen. The superintendent also motioned him in, pointing to the conference table, indicating he should take a seat while she finished the call she was on. "Ryan just got here." Ryan recognized the board president's voice on the other end of the call. "The rest of the team will be here by 8:00. We'll go over the protocol and work out the details, and I'll get back to you by 9:00."

She looked over to Ryan as she listened. "Right. All calls or questions come to me, through my secretary. Please make sure the rest of the board knows that and they don't speculate or offer comments. Especially, you know who." She listened for a few seconds. "I know she's the one the parents contacted, but do the best you can please. I'll get back to you ASAP. Thanks, Charles. Yeah, you too."

Demian hung up the phone and turned to Ryan who immediately asked, "Which parents contacted whom, about what?"

"You know a freshman named Allan Sparks?"

Ryan nodded. "Of course. He's EBD with Kim Berry."

"His parents called Thynie this morning. About 6:00. I understand they live near each other." Ryan raised his eyebrows in question. "The parents were notified this morning by the state police that Allan shot himself in the mother's car after being pulled over somewhere down in Ozaukee County."

Ryan felt his chest collapse, leaving barely enough air to gasp, "What? Is he dead?"

"According to Thynie, the police think it was an impulsive suicide, but the dad insists it must have been accidental, or the cops were covering up something. Do you know Mr. and Mrs. Sparks?"

"Only a little. But that sounds like the dad. Though I sure can't blame him for reacting with disbelief and anger. Christ! How does a parent deal with something like this?"

Both were silent for a few moments. Ryan tried to remember his last interaction with Allan. He vaguely recalled refereeing a debate and name-calling between him and Ayden sometime just before the holidays. He wished Allan's parents had called anyone but Thynie Marsh.

Ryan asked, "Did Thynie call you? What did she say?"

"No, of course not. She called Charles instead of calling me directly as she should have so I could activate the crisis plan. He said she was on the warpath, but he calmed her down. And, Ryan, so you know..."

The ominous pause lasted only two seconds but felt much longer. "According to Charles, Thynie said the boy's parents blame you. You and the Special Education Department. Since I didn't talk directly with her, I'm not sure how much of that is Thynie's interpretation, or was said by the Sparks."

The accusation hurt. It was human nature for Allan's folks to want to lay blame on someone when such devastating news fell on them. He knew Thynie wasn't going to stand up for him, but he hoped she had at least defended the others. Someday, he was going to have to dig into her seemingly unconditional dislike for him. But for now, the personal accusation had to take a back seat. He needed to consider his staff, especially Kim Berry and the kids. How was he going to help them? He hadn't even begun to absorb the news about Allan yet, let alone process it. He'd never been in a school that had had an adult suicide, let alone one by a student. Death in a high school due to accidents or drugs was not uncommon, but suicide was something different.

"Thanks for the heads-up, Liz. How do you want me to handle this? We'll have kids starting to show up in a few minutes. I assume rumors will be floating in the halls before the first bell. I'd like to go talk with Kim Berry, so she isn't caught totally off guard. I'll tell Sharon all calls are to be funneled here. I'll be back before 8:00 for the Crisis Team meeting."

35

Despite his muddled and numb mind, Dominic's nose still worked fine. He followed the smell of slow-cooking pot roast into the kitchen. Kate was sitting at the table. She looked up, scared. "How horrible. Do you know what happened to the Sparks boy?"

"All I've heard is that sometime last night he took his mother's car and was going south on 43. It's unclear where he was headed, though I guess there's an aunt who lives somewhere around Mequon or Reedsville."

He pulled a chair and sat facing his wife. "Sometime around 3:00 a.m., he was pulled over by a state trooper. As the guy approached the car, a shot went off. By the time backup got there and they approached the car, they found him dead. Shot in the chest. They assume it was suicide and not that he was planning to shoot at the cop."

"God! Those poor parents."

"It seems he took his dad's pistol when he left. I don't know the details, but his mom found him and her car gone when she got up sometime in the night. Her husband drove around looking for him. They got a phone call from the state police about 5:00 this morning."

Kate shook her head in disbelief, her eyes closed in empathy. "I can't imagine. How can anybody deal with that?"

Dominic gave a concerned glance down the hall. "Is Nala in her room? What did she say when she got home?"

"Just that everyone was talking about it. At first, that he'd stolen his mother's car. Later rumors started about the shooting. Her friends wanted her to ask you about it. She told them you wouldn't be able to say anything."

"Hmm. Smart girl."

"I don't think she or her friends knew or liked Allan much. Still, she's pretty shook up. They've all been together in the same grade with him forever. She feels guilty. She asked twice how you can be around someone for so long and not know them, or even try to know them." Kate caught Dominic's eyes and added in a quieter voice, "Remember her asking almost the same question when some of her friends were backing off, not so long ago?"

Dominic's eyes and nod showed he remembered. He stood and kissed Kate. "I need to check on her."

He tapped on her door. "Nala? It's dad. Can I come in?" In the few seconds before she responded, he found himself thinking about that very question. She was veering in a direction he'd naïvely never considered, didn't understand, and wasn't sure he'd ever be able to. Recently, he feared his practical advice and suggestions may have made him persona non grata, at least to some extent. He thought about her twice-asked question. *How can you be around someone for so long and not know them?*

Nala opened her door. "Dad, did Allan really shoot himself?" With wide vulnerable eyes, she stared directly into his eyes, hoping it was somehow not real. He hugged her closely and was grateful when he felt her hug him back. When he finally let go, she sat on the edge of her bed. Dominic moved her school backpack from her desk chair. As he turned it around to face her, her eighth-grade graduation picture hanging on the wall caught his eye. He looked from its surface to his daughter's face. From past to present, then to now, smile to tears.

He sat slowly. "Honey, we, I don't know what happened or why. But yes. It appears he did."

He saw bigger tears forming in her eyes. Feeling helpless to protect her from the ugly truth, he wanted to hug her again. He remembered a similar look on her face, in Ryan's office with Ayden Quant when she'd pleaded, "Daddy, he called me that word."

"Why? Why would he do that?"

For a second, Dominic was confused. Was she asking why Ayden had used that word or about Allan?

"I don't know, honey. Maybe..." His hands went up in a feeble gesture of not knowing. He rested his elbows on his knees and slowly shook his head. "Maybe he was feeling overwhelmed or scared or hurt about something. All I can guess is that after he took his mom's car and got pulled over, he panicked."

"Why would he have a gun with him?"

Dominic again shook his head and gave another unknowing shrug. "I don't know his parents very well. I mostly know Allan because I'd see him with Ayden all the time."

Nala suddenly sat up straighter. Something on her mind. "I think Ayden might have been mad at Allan. At the movies, over Christmas, we saw Allan there with a girl from his class. Ayden was upset they were together. He said Allan just gets people in trouble."

Dominic was surprised. "You were at the movies with Ayden?"

"No, Dad. Zoey and I and some other girls were there to see the *Twilight* movie. Ayden was with another boy from his class. They were there for that *Monsters Inc.* animated movie. Anyhow, Ayden is sometimes Zoey's science partner. She feels, I don't know, kind of protective of him. She went over to talk to him and that's what he said. I wonder if he's feeling bad about Allan?"

"I'm sure he's upset."

"Frienemies," Nala suggested, almost to herself.

"Huh?"

"You know, like being a friend and an enemy at the same time."

"Did you make that up?"

Jumbled crisscrossing feelings of certainty and uncertainty ran through Nala's body. She folded her hands on her lap and answered the first part. "No. I just heard the word before." She looked up. "Dad, he won't ... I mean, Ayden wouldn't do anything like that, would he? I know he can be impulsive. Remember that whole thing last fall when he called me, you know... when he didn't really mean it that way."

"How could I forget? And I have to say I'm very proud of you for forgiving him that day in Mr. Davvis' office and being concerned for him now."

Both dad and daughter knew they were purposely skipping over and didn't want to mention what else had been said in the room that day. "You could always ask Ayden how he's feeling. I mean if you were comfortable doing it. Maybe you and Zoey could ask together."

Nala tried to picture the scene. "Maybe. I just wouldn't want him to think I was being mean or trying to get even for hurting my feelings." She had another thought. "Dad, do you think people who kill themselves go to heaven?"

"I don't know, honey. I think if a person is so mixed up or scared or miserable that they do that, I sure hope God wouldn't hold it against them. Plus, I want to think it was kind of an accident. Why do you ask?"

Nala hesitated, not wanting to give too much away. But the moment and conversation had her feeling close to her dad and safe enough, so she decided to be honest. "I was just thinking about Lang bumping into Allan in heaven and discovering that they both knew me."

Dominic's surprise was evident on his face so Nala explained. "Langston, Dad. My brother."

"Oh, yeah." The reference had thrown him. He had no idea why she would have made that connection. He couldn't decide if, or what, he should ask. He was acutely aware she was the only person who could make him feel this unsure of himself. Not wanting the silence to get awkward, Dominic said, "Well, I'm sure they'd agree you were an amazing person." He knew it came off as a typical lame, dad comment. He wished he knew what she was thinking. Instead of asking he stood. "Mom almost has dinner up. I'll go set the table."

Back in the kitchen, Kate asked, "How is she?"

"She asked if Allan could go to heaven and then wondered if he might run into Lang."

Kate looked puzzled. "Langston, her brother?"

"Yeah. I didn't even know who she was referring to at first. Has she mentioned anything about him to you lately?"

"No. At least not for a very long time. Did she say why?"

"No. And, as usual, I was caught too flat-footed to ask. It seems like ever since high school started, she always catches me off guard and I never feel like I'm on the same page with her. Nothing seems just black and white anymore."

Kate cocked her head and gave him a look.

"You know what I mean."

He went to the sink, washed his hands, and began to set the table.

36

Nala stood in the darkness outside the garage staring at the light snow in the air and covering the ground. The cold was already penetrating her winter jogging outfit. While she stretched, she questioned her purpose and felt her motivation slipping. She'd told her mother she needed a short run to work off dinner, which she had barely touched, and clear her head about the whole Allan thing, adding the exercise would help her concentrate on her homework, which was minimal and already done. She rarely stretched the truth, let alone lied. She also didn't usually run during basketball season – practices and games kept her in shape. But she did it often enough that her mom hadn't questioned her, just reminded her to be careful on the roads, keep to her usual route, and wear her reflective vest.

During dinner, her dad had received a call from Anna Quant. From what Nala could overhear, the woman was asking if Ayden had boarded the bus after school because he wasn't home when she arrived after closing her shop. With the news about Allan today, Nala detected stress in their voices. He said he'd check with the driver to make sure and get right back to her. Once he'd confirmed Ayden was on the bus and had gotten off at his house, he decided to drive over and tell Mrs. Quant in person and see if he could help.

Nala had started to worry. Zoey once mentioned Ayden telling her about this spot he liked to go. It was a pipe or something under the road somewhere on County R along her regular jogging route, which intersected with the road between their houses. At the time she'd laughed, thinking it weird and typical Ayden. Now she felt compelled to check it. She started slowly to warm up, but as the thought of Ayden's impulsivity grew in her mind, so did her speed. With it came the thought: *If I slip or twist my ankle and can't play basketball, I'm going to kill that boy.*

"Ayden, it's Nala...from school." No response. "Ayden, I know you're down there. I can see your tracks in the snow."

A thin, muffled voice responded. "What do you want? Go away and don't tell anyone I'm here."

"Ayden, your mom's worried about you. We're all upset about Allan, but you can't hide down there forever. Come on up. We can talk about it."

"You come down here."

"Are you nuts? It's dark, and I've got running shoes on. I'm not coming into some hole under the road." She didn't add *with a boy* or *especially you*. She got no response. "Besides, it's too cold. Please. Come up here. We can go to my house and talk if you want."

"Go away."

A moment later, Nala crouched in the opening. Her sudden appearance made Ayden remember when he'd found Allan hiding here. "Why are *you* here?" It was a half-hearted attempt to sound angry. "Are you going to get me in trouble again or hit me like at school?"

"No, I'm over that. I'm sorry." She couldn't believe she was apologizing to him. "I know you didn't mean it the way I thought you did. You've got to admit, it came out of nowhere, and I had a right to be angry." No response. "Your mom called my dad and said you were missing. I remembered Zoey said you came here sometimes." That got his attention. "Anyway, I don't live too far from here you know."

"I know where you live. I'm not stupid." Ayden turned away from her and stared into the dark on the opposite end of the culvert.

"I know you're not." She tried to sound empathetic, but her frozen breath and uncomfortable position, made it hard. "Matter of fact, Zoey says you're pretty smart and have good ideas in science class on projects and experiments and stuff."

"Really?" He looked back toward her. At ten feet apart in the darkness, each was mostly a silhouette to the other. But his posture and voice let Nala know she'd connected with him.

"Yeah. Really. I know you must be pretty sad about Allan. I can't believe it either. I didn't really know him very well, and I'm shook up." She couldn't help adding, "Even though he was kind of... I don't know, rude and kind of an ass to me and my friends at times. But I know he was your friend, at least most of the time. I mean, at the movies last month Zoey said you were upset because Allan was with Lilly." She knew she was rambling, so she stopped.

"He was saying bad things about her."

Nala squatted on the frozen ground at the edge of the opening, the same spot Ayden had occupied not long ago. She asked, "Do you like Lilly? I got the feeling you did. She's pretty and nice."

Instead of answering, Ayden began telling his story. "My mom woke me up early. She said Allan's mom was on the phone asking if I knew where he was or if I knew anything about him taking her car. I was asleep and said no. Meaning I didn't know where he was. We were kind of pissed off at each other, and he never told me anything. I was staying away from him. After Mom left, I remembered finding Allan right here," his arm gesture indicated the space they now occupied. "Back before Christmas." His head moved as if he was scanning their surroundings. "He had his mom's car parked over in the trees across the road. He said sometimes he took it when they were gone. I wasn't lying. I didn't remember until I woke up more."

"Did you tell your mom later?" Nala inquired.

"No," he admitted. "I didn't want to get Allan in trouble. Now, I think it might have helped or stopped him from..."

"You were just trying to be a good friend." She didn't know what else to say except what her dad had told her. "Nobody knows what happened for sure." She added, "But whatever it was, even if you told your mom this morning when she woke you up, it wouldn't have made any difference. You shouldn't feel guilty about that."

"I guess...but I do."

"Maybe we all should," Nala said.

Her legs were cramping in the cold. She shifted but didn't want to sit on the icy ground. "Come on, Ayden. Let's go home. Your mom's worried, and I'm freezing."

It took a few seconds, but he said, "I guess."

Nala stood and took a step up the bank. When she didn't hear any noise behind her, she looked back and asked, "What's the matter?"

"Did you know my mom's not my mom? I mean, she didn't have me, but she acts like a real mom and all that."

"What?" Nala's mind jumped to her own situation. She forgot she was cold and crouched at the opening again.

"My real mom died of an overdose when I was a baby. My dad wasn't even around then. I didn't know him until he came and brought me here."

"Wow! That's harsh." Nala hoped her birthmother hadn't suffered the same fate. She wasn't sure she'd want to know. "That was crappy. My mom and dad were always honest with me about being adopted. Not that they had a choice."

Nala couldn't make out Ayden's face, especially with his hoody pulled tight. His voice, however, betrayed some confusion. "What do you mean they didn't have a choice?"

"Ayden. I just told you I know you're good in science." She heard the sarcasm in her voice. The boy could be so exasperating. "You know what genetics are, right? I know you've noticed I'm Black. You asked me how it felt, remember? White parents don't have Black kids."

"I know that." Nala was actually glad he didn't sound insulted. "It's just, I sometimes feel like I don't belong here or anywhere else. I thought you might feel the same way sometimes."

Zoey's words came back to Nala. "You know, Zoey was right. You do have some good insights." She suddenly, shivered. "Come on, before I freeze."

They climbed back to the road and walked together. Instead of talking, they each studied the stars in the cold sky as if looking for something. When they got back to the crossroad, Nala said, "Thanks for telling me that stuff, Ayden. I'm real sorry about Allan. I hear the student council is meeting with Mr. Davvis tomorrow about maybe having Allan's picture hung by his locker or something."

"That would be..." Ayden wasn't sure how he felt, and he couldn't find the word to finish. "I'll see you tomorrow, Nala." He turned and headed home.

Nala was glad she'd found him. She bounced a few times to warm herself then took off running in the opposite direction toward her house. Along the way she communed with Lang, silently talking through all she had just learned about herself and the boy who up until today, she'd always tried to avoid.

37

As she listened to the parent on the other end of her headset, Sharon noticed the attractive tall woman standing at the entry door waiting to be admitted. She pushed the release button below the countertop and buzzed her in. As she continued to listen to the caller, she mouthed, "I'll be with you in a minute," noting the woman was no one she'd ever seen before, and her coat looked very expensive. "Okay. She knows you're picking her up at 2:30 for her appointment?" Sharon asked into the mouthpiece." A moment later saying, "Fine. I'll check her out when she gets to the office and tell her you'll be parked by the door. Bye, Angie."

Sharon added the sticky note reminder next to the others and looked at the visitor, now aware of her meticulous makeup and stylish, short dark hair. "Hi. Can I help you?"

"Is Mr. Davvis in?"

Sharon wasn't sure why, but she instinctively felt a bit wary. Ryan usually let her know if he was expecting someone. "I know he's in the building, but I'm not sure if he's in his office at the moment. Do you have an appointment?"

"No, I don't. It's kind of a spontaneous visit. I'm a friend of his from Minnesota. I was in the area and wanted to stop and say hello. I'm sure he's busy, but..." She replaced the end of her sentence with a smile, finally adding, "You know, before I head back."

Sharon weighed the alternatives. Knowing perfectly well that

Ryan was in his office she stood. "I'll see if he's back there. May I ask your name?"

"*Mrs*. Beverly Rupert."

Sharon thought the emphasis odd.

Sharon tapped on Ryan's door frame to get his attention. Leaning in and keeping her voice down so as not to be heard up front, she announced, "You have a rather attractive woman friend from Minnesota here to see you, Mr. Davvis."

The fact that she'd used his last name, something she never did in private, caught Ryan's attention before the rest of the message sank in. "Mr. Davvis? Really? Who did you say was here?"

"A *Mrs*. Beverly Rupert." She leaned into the *Mrs.* just as the woman had. "She said she was...." Sharon stopped talking when it appeared all the blood had drained from Ryan's face. "Are you okay?" His reaction affirmed her instinct about the woman. "I can tell her you're out or not available?"

Ryan recovered. "No," he hesitated. "Just tell her I'm on the phone and will be with her in a few minutes."

"Are you sure? I don't mind..."

"No, thanks. Just tell her I'll be a few minutes." His abruptness made Sharon feel both concerned and dismissed.

Sharon passed along the message, inviting Mrs. Rupert to have a seat. Wondering what caused Ryan's reaction, she couldn't help but steal a glance as the attractive woman stepped away from the counter. It was disquieting. Ryan was often inscrutable. But he'd never had a friend from his past stop at school. Especially one with Mrs. Rupert's obvious physical assets. When she looked up again, she found Mrs. Rupert's eyes were studying her. She said, "I'm sure, *Ryan* will be with you in just a minute or two." She took some satisfaction in using his first name.

When he appeared, Ryan greeted his guest with a hard-to-read, "Well what a surprise. Please, come in." He allowed her to step ahead of him. "First door on the left." Sharon noticed he'd almost exaggerated making no physical contact with the woman.

Ryan closed his office door and pulled out the chair across from his workspace for her before sitting on his side. She unbuttoned her overcoat, revealing a tight skirt and low-cut blouse more appropriate for a romantic evening on the town than a school visit. Once she settled, she asked, "No hug?"

"Bev, why are you here? Why would you come here to school?"

"Don't you think you owe me an explanation for ditching me over the holidays? Just a lousy text, 'Need to go back.' No other explanation or anything. That was a shitty thing to do, don't you think?"

When he'd tapped out the text, Ryan remembered wondering what "back" even meant at that point. Which way, which place was "back" for him? And "back" when? "Back" before Lisa, or during, or after her? His text was short because at the time he was confused and trapped, incapable of separating the past and future from the present. The feelings had finally overcome his lust and anger. He'd checked out and left just as the rising sun eased the darkness outside and in his mind.

Ryan knew he should concede and explain his panic and anger at learning from his friends over dinner she was going to divorce her husband. But her sudden appearance in his school was a violation of the murky, unspoken rules of their affair. It poked a hole in the wall he'd erected to separate the two parts of himself. He was in no mood to concede anything. Instead, he countered. "I don't understand. Suddenly you're accusing *him* of infidelity? Why didn't you let me know about that?"

She didn't seem surprised that he knew. "Well, you weren't at the hotel when I got there, were you? Anyhow, I got tired of his affairs. I decided I wanted out. Besides, you never seemed interested in talking about spouses before, or for that matter, any personal discussions or questions."

"Did you know about him, were you thinking about getting divorced before we...while we..." He kept his voice even, though he wished he could have shouted the words.

"Doug cheated on his first wife. I know because it was with me, and I'm sure I hadn't been the first. When he asked me to marry him, I knew he was just looking for a trophy wife, but I didn't care. But I was surprised how quickly I started seeing signs he was at it again. Men are so pathetically obvious. So yeah, I knew. Of course, the good news was it made it, I mean *us*, easy. You had to feel the same way."

Ryan suddenly felt like a man hearing cracking sounds racing through the thin ice beneath his feet. "What is that supposed to mean?"

She crossed her legs. "Come on, Ryan. You had to know." The shock on Ryan's face was evident. She reconsidered. "You didn't, did you? My God! You really didn't know about him and Lisa? Wasn't that why you were so... eager? I assumed we both relished the irony of us hooking up. Otherwise, why did you..." Her voice trailed off before adding, "If you didn't know Lisa was..." Again, she didn't finish her sentence.

Ryan's inner voice shouted her missing words. They reverberated in his skull. All he could think to say was, "That's not true."

"I'm not the only one who knew, Ryan. You can ask around back home if you don't believe me."

Ryan felt humiliation explode over and through his entire being as if he'd just been doused in gasoline and set on fire. He immediately wondered whether his buddy's comment at the bar about Doug Rupert "screwing someone connected with the high school" had, as he thought at the time, been a sign they didn't know who it was or actually their way of letting Ryan know they knew it was Lisa. He tried to concentrate.

"Does Doug know about us?"

"Not yet. I haven't mentioned it, and his ego wouldn't let him believe it if someone else told him. I've come close a few times; I'd love to see his face. But weirdly, while Minnesota has no-fault divorce, it also, rather surprisingly, still criminalizes adultery. All he knows is his indiscretions won't come up as long as he isn't an asshole about a generous divorce settlement. Besides, I like him thinking he's the only 'bad guy' here."

The revelation that adultery was a crime back home had never occurred to Ryan. It added to his disgrace. He didn't know where to put any of this information.

"Why are you here, Bev? Why don't you just tell me I'm an asshole and be done with it."

"Why? Because we both know we're two sides of the same coin, and a rare coin at that. We can continue what we both obviously enjoy."

Ryan almost winced at the metaphor. Yet, he knew he'd be lying to deny he'd enjoyed the sex.

Rupert continued. "Sure, in the beginning, it was about revenge sex. At least it was for me. I naturally assumed it was for you too, that you knew about them and that was why you... well, you know. You knew I was attracted to you. Still am. You'd be surprised how many of the gals around that school felt the same way about you. Good looking, caring, likable – and you so much need to be liked, don't you?" Her tone shifted with the last part of her comment.

As Rupert paused to see if he'd respond, Ryan's mind amended her assertions. It wasn't a need to be liked, or even simple revenge that had driven him. It had been an overpowering need to prove his manhood and to feel some control – things he'd never admit to her.

When Ryan didn't answer, she added, "I bet the other ladies

would be amazed to know what lurks below that nice guy image." She fixed her eyes on his, shifting and recrossing her legs. This time letting her skirt ride high up her thigh.

"Anyhow, I'm giving you a chance to make it up to me. I'm heading to Appleton to meet a college girlfriend for a couple of days, to shop and catch up and bash husbands. I'll be at the Holiday Inn until Sunday morning, but my friend thinks I'm heading home on Saturday morning. That means I'll be there all alone all-day Saturday – and all night. Surely, Appleton is a safe distance from here for you."

"I'm not coming." Lisa's admonition that good-looking women could so easily make a fool of him rang in his inner ear.

She coyly stood. "Oh? We'll see." She inclined her head toward the front office. "If you'd like to invite your secretary out there. We both know you'd enjoy that, don't we? She's pretty. But I have a better ass. If not her, I'm sure we could find someone. Who knows, maybe my friend would be interested. It seems her husband has become rather a disappointment to her."

"I'm not coming!" Ryan whispered, keeping his jaw tighten so as not to fling the words at her. "I think you need to go now. I've things to do."

"I'll bet you do?" She again inclined her head toward the front office. "It would be a real pity if you didn't show... again." Her tone softened. "I really do like you, you know. Our spouses cheated on us. We don't owe them anything. We have the right to enjoy each other in any way we want. I'll bet Lisa didn't know you the way I do, did she?"

She pulled a note from her purse and set it in front of Ryan. She'd written, "Holiday Inn – You owe me!" With that, she left.

Ryan's chest felt tight, and his palms were sweaty. He should hate her for coming here, for her last comment about knowing him in a way Lisa didn't. But it was true. So, instead, he hated himself.

He wanted to believe if their visit to the ice cream shop had gone the way Lisa had planned, and she had told him everything, even about Doug Rupert, that he'd have had the courage to do the same. But he didn't.

He could hear Bev Rupert give an overly friendly goodbye to Sharon adding a, "I hope to see you again," on her way out.

A moment later, Sharon was at his door. "What was that all about? Anyway, I was just about to buzz you. Thynie Marsh is waiting to see you. I told her you had a meeting with the student council at noon. She insisted she needed to see you. You should have seen the look she gave your friend on her way out."

38

With Thynie Marsh waiting, Ryan didn't have time to throw up or suffocate in his mortification after Mrs. Rupert's visit. He closed his eyes trying to breathe, trying not to dwell on Rupert's accusations about Lisa and her husband and, even worse, that other people knew. He'd have to find a way to see if it was true. He certainly couldn't go back to his friends and ask.

What had cut deepest was her assertion that they were two sides of the same coin. He wanted to believe she was wrong. Wrong about Lisa and her husband, and even more wrong about them being alike. He knew, however, that the margin between wanting to believe and actual belief wasn't permeable. Her comment, "I bet the other ladies would be amazed to know what lurks below that nice guy image," sat heavy on his chest. Was it a threat?

Ryan jammed and squeezed all the racing thoughts and fears into a corner of his gut where they continued to twist, smolder, and burn. Then he invited Thynie Marsh back to his office.

Luckily, the visit was brief. She hadn't come for a discussion. She'd wanted to pass on her "firsthand account" of the Sparks' accusation, quoting Mr. Sparks, "Allan always complained Mr. Davvis was never on his side." She emphatically wanted him to understand that while she was on board with the plan for having additional area counselors available in the building – "because all Allan's many friends must be traumatized" – she vehemently disagreed with the decision on how to respond to student requests for a memorial.

She said the Sparks family would see it as the school disrespecting their son and more proof that Ryan was once again "never on Allan's side." This latter part of Thynie's monologue was uppermost on his mind as he headed to Mrs. Zowak's room for a meeting with the student council.

The tables were arranged in a square. Each had two council members with the remnants of their lunches on cafeteria trays. Ryan sat next to Mrs. Zowak in the empty chair saved for him. As their advisor, she summarized the council's proposal for a memorial gathering in the gym, with parents invited and Allan's picture being hung on his locker. As he listened, knowing he was going to have to deny the request, the burning still simmering in Ryan's gut flared into his esophagus.

Mrs. Zowak ended her summary by saying, "However, I was just explaining to the council that while their instincts are good and understandable, there may be some practical and unanticipated problems with some of the suggestions." She looked at Ryan. "Perhaps, Mr. Davvis, you can talk to that?"

Ryan wanted to kiss her cheek for having prepped the kids for what he'd have to tell them. He cleared his throat. One of the boys interrupted. "Did Sparks really shoot himself? That's what the online daily news is saying, but they don't mention his name. It just says a Stienboek student." Another student added, "Why don't they say his name?"

Ryan stepped in. "Well, these are the complexities Mrs. Zowak was alluding to. This is a horrible tragedy, and everyone is still in shock. At this point, I don't even know if anyone knows for sure what happened. But we're not a news organization. We're a school community, and we need to support each other – the students and staff. That's why we have several additional counselors available for anyone who wishes to talk privately about how they're feeling or any concerns they might have."

Zoey Ackerly asked, "What about the freshman class? They'd like a memorial gathering, even if it's just for them and others who knew Allan. Then it wouldn't interrupt the entire school."

Hoping he could find the right words, Ryan said, "As Mrs. Zowak pointed out, that's a good and natural thing to want to do, to remember and honor someone who has passed. It's very human and respectful. But, here's the problem in this case. We know from other schools where a tragedy like this has occurred, that we need to be concerned about the message it might send to any other student who is struggling or upset. It's a tough call, but we can't take that chance." He paused to look around at each student.

"What I can promise is, we'll let everyone know when we hear about a service, and any student who has permission to attend will be excused."

At the bell, the council students headed off to classes. Ryan thanked Mrs. Zowak for having the foresight and having prepped the kids for what he had to tell them. Instead of, "You're welcome," she replied. "Well, I had to assume even the board would know it was a no-brainer to avoid a spectacle around a suicide." He considered hugging her. Instead, he again repeated, "Thank you, Bernadette."

Ryan headed toward his office as the last few straggling students disappeared into their classes or the cafeteria. In just over a month, they'd been forced to face the reality of twenty-six massacred primary students and teachers in Connecticut and now the suicide of one of their own. He thought back to what William Powells had called Adverse Childhood Experiences. He didn't know if any of this was consciously on their young minds or not. He was sure, however, there was a cost to be borne by every one of these kids.

He neared the high school offices. Like a rearend car collision, his concerns for his students plowed at high speed into the earlier humiliations unleashed by Mrs. Rupert and Thynie's tongue-lashing.

His chest suddenly constricted and his heart raced. He stopped and concentrated on slowing his breathing. He blindly stared out through the floor-to-ceiling windows toward the visitor's parking lot. He realized he was hoping to assure himself that neither of the women's cars were out there. Only once before had despair gripped him to this degree – the night he'd learned of Lisa's cheating.

"You expecting someone?"

The voice startled Ryan back to the moment.

Dominic could see how tired Ryan appeared. "You looked kind of lost in space. Are you okay?"

"Just a lot going on." He took a deep breath.

"That's an understatement. I don't know how you hold it together. Anyway, I was just on my way down to the library to work. Sharon put one of the emergency counselors in my office."

"Oh, yeah. Sorry about that." Ryan felt his focus returning. "I asked her to put Mr. Powells in there because it's just around the corner from Kim Berry's room. Her kids were the closest to Allan, and they don't all have the best support system at home. Powells is part of our Employee Assistance Plan contract. I met him a bit ago at an IEP meeting. So, I called, and he was able to free up some time to help out. Seems like a nice and smart guy. I'm hoping her kids might be more likely to go talk with him if they didn't have to go far. I was planning to ask you this morning and then got sidetracked. Sorry."

"No problem. I think Ayden was just going to meet with him," Dominic said. "Oh, just so you know, last night I got a call from his mom. She was worried when he wasn't at home when she got there. Wanted to know if he'd taken the bus. They live out by us, so I stopped over to talk with her. While I was there, Nala went for a run and found him. She got him to go home, but I guess he was feeling kind of guilty about Allan because they were on the outs with each other about something or other."

"I'll touch base with him later too. That kid has enough on his plate without feeling guilty about this. Your Nala is quite a special kid. You think she's ever forgiven me for that thing with Ayden in my office a while back?"

Dominic quickly reassured him. "You didn't say anything wrong."

As soon as the words were out of his mouth, Dominic sensed he was still putting the blame on his daughter and that wasn't his intention. The incident was two months ago, and he still felt guilt about how he'd reacted. He wanted Ryan to know that, so he tried to sort out his thoughts. "It was just a traumatic thing for Nala. I didn't realize at the time how sensitive she was... about the whole... thing. I was caught off guard. I think I wanted to believe it was something she never thought about... would never have to think about. I'm the one who did something wrong. I should have been prepared to support her, not jump on her. I knew sooner or later something like this would happen. I'm still trying to sort it all out. Anyways, she tells me she and Ayden worked it out."

"You know, Dom," Ryan said. "I think I started to mention this at Sophie's, about how I was giving that kind of stuff some thought a while ago. How back in my Minneapolis school, I sometimes would tell kids, especially Black or Hispanic kids, they had to try harder to fit in. Now I'm wondering how they took that and maybe even what I meant by it. Anyhow, I'd like to talk with you sometime, if you're willing?"

"Maybe you should talk with Kate. She's a lot smarter about this stuff than me. But sure, we can talk."

39

When Ayden rounded the corner, Mr. Samilton was just leaving his office. He slowed until the man was well down the hall before continuing toward the doorway. Since he'd been foolish enough to use the N-word with Nala back in December, he sometimes imagined Mr. Samilton jumping out and ambushing him.

He glanced around the open cafeteria space across from the office. A woman was wiping down the tables that divided the area into rows and aisles. Ayden knew she was Steven's aunt but couldn't remember her name. He was relieved no students were lurking about who might see him. The clanging of pots and pans mixed with the voices of other women coming from back in the kitchen area didn't concern him. Turning into Mr. Samilton's office, he was surprised to see who was sitting there. "I wasn't expecting *you*."

"Come on in, Ayden. You can close or leave the door open. Whichever you prefer." Ayden shut it. Mr. Powells indicated an open chair across from him. Just like at his office, he was not sitting behind the desk.

Ayden sat. "Are you a school counselor too?" His eyes ran across the top of Mr. Samilton's desk.

"No, but Mr. Davvis asked if I'd come and help with any students who might want to talk to someone about your friend, Allan."

"He wasn't my friend," Ayden quickly corrected. "Well, he was, I guess. Sometimes but... He wasn't a real friend. Not really." His words came out jerky like a beginner's start and stop first attempts to coordinate using a clutch while shifting gears. "Mrs. Berry told me real friends don't do things to get you in trouble." Stop... Start. "Besides, he said some bad things about Lilly. Did she come to talk to you? She broke up with Allan. Maybe that's why he did it." Stop... Start. "It wasn't her fault. But she won't even look at me since we heard... I think you should talk to Lilly."

As he talked, Ayden's eyes found a photo standing on the desk. He leaned over so he could get a better angle. "That's Nala." He pointed. "Mr. Samilton's daughter. Well, not really. You can see she's not white. She was adopted."

Powells leaned in toward Ayden. "Whoa there, Ayden. Let's back up a second. First of all, you're right. What happened with Allan was not Lilly's fault. And it's very good of you to be concerned for her. But I'm hoping you're not feeling like it was your fault in any way. Because it's not. No matter how mad you may or may not have been with him, or no matter what you might or might not have said to him, you did nothing wrong."

"I guess...but I kind of did. Back before Christmas." Pointing to the photograph he said, "Like I told Nala, I knew Allan took his mom's car, at least once. And I never told my mom. Not even when Allan's mom called yesterday morning looking for him. Maybe if I'd told, he'd have gotten grounded or something, instead of...."

"When did you tell this to Nala?"

"Last night. When I got home from school, I went down to a place where I sometimes, you know, go to think. All of a sudden Nala shows up and finds me there. We talked for a while, and then she got cold because she'd stopped jogging and said we should go home because my mom and her dad were worried about me."

"She sounds like a good friend."

"That's the weird thing. She isn't." Ayden looked over at the shut door. "I called her the N-word once, on accident, but she thought I meant it. Boy, was she mad. She even hit me. We both almost got suspended."

"Then, why do you think she came looking for you last night?"

"I don't know. I guess 'cause maybe she was worried."

"I think you're right. I think it was because she was worried, but I also think she knew you were sad and maybe upset."

"I wasn't going to do anything to hurt myself."

"Of course not. Because you're learning to make decisions that help, not hurt. Like coming here to talk even though you didn't know I would be here."

"I guess," Ayden shrugged but looked pleased with himself.

Powells doubled back. "Will you tell me about the time you knew Allan had taken his mother's car?"

After Ayden relayed the story, Powells asked, "You didn't want Allan to get in trouble, right?"

"I just told him he was a dummy and that I'd see him at school."

"And this was over a month ago?"

"Yeah."

"Ayden," Powells again leaned in to be sure he had the boy's attention. "I don't know many people, especially fifteen-year-olds, who would have done anything different than you did. Did you have any suspicions then that Allan might hurt himself?"

"NO! I mean, he was just Allan. Sometimes he was funny, and other times he seemed sad or was a jerk. But that's just the way he is."

Powells locked eyes with the boy. "You have nothing to feel guilty about."

"What if..." Ayden stopped.

"What if, what?" Powells gently prodded.

"What if we might have smoked a little pot that day?"

"You know that wasn't a good choice. But it doesn't have anything to do with yesterday." He sat back in the chair. "Next week at my office, we'll pick up this discussion – including about the pot. You're not in trouble, but I think it's worth talking about. What do you think?"

"I guess. Can I go now?"

"Of course, but before you do, I just want to ask you, are you now, or have you ever thought about hurting yourself?"

"No! I'm not crazy?"

"Ayden, suicide is not about being crazy. It's about feeling like you're in a hole and can't get out."

"That's crazy. There's always a way out," Ayden confidently said.

"I'm glad to hear that." Powells stood. "We'll talk next week unless there's anything else you want to ask or say?"

Ayden stood. "Remember that picture in your office. The one with the dark skies and the school and little houses with no doors or windows."

Cocking his head slightly, Powells waited.

It took a few seconds before Ayden finished his thought. "I think maybe that's how Allan was feeling."

40

Ryan's cell phone vibrated and played the blues riff he'd chosen to announce calls. His first thought was to let it go to voicemail. He was bone tired and his mind and body felt as if he'd gone fifteen rounds with a kickboxer. For now, he just wanted to escape.

Since dawn Monday through Friday evening, every waking hour had been a drain on his physical and emotional energy. Attending to the general shock and grief among Allan's freshman classmates and Mrs. Berry, who was having a hard time, but insisted on being in school with her students, had not been easy. Layered on top of that were the questions from the community, staff, and school board, all of whom Thynie Marsh had informed about the family blaming Ryan. Yesterday, the family had bypassed Ryan and notified the district office that Allan's wake and funeral would be held next week. He'd attend both, but the thought of the parents making a scene with him was a nightmare scenario.

Then there had been Mrs. Rupert's unexpected visit. He pictured her at the Appleton motel expecting him, confident his lust would push him to show up at her door. Even as he'd packed his overnight bag, Ryan knew it was still a possibility. The week also included two evening meetings with members of the referendum support group. They wanted to be sure they understood all the charts about mil rates and tax levies and were armed with facts and counterarguments to the expected pushback he and Superintendent Demian had heard firsthand at the recent Westown meeting. All in all, the week had been overwhelming and exhausting.

It had also been the start of the second semester. Normally by now, he'd have gone through all the semester D and F lists and touched base with those students and teachers. As an assistant principal in a large city school, he'd done this for only the junior class in his charge. Because Stienboek was much smaller, he'd taken it upon himself to meet with all struggling students. He started with seniors for whom an F could affect graduation and then skipped to freshmen to emphasize getting off on the right foot. He then worked his way through the sophomores and juniors. It wasn't the only thing he was behind on, and it all added to the accumulating weight and stress he now felt pulling at him.

He picked up the phone and glanced at the name. Relieved it wasn't Mrs. Rupert, he punched the talk button and tried to sound upbeat. "What's up, Dominic?"

"Ryan, Sharon moved out from the farm this morning. She wanted you to know but isn't up to telling you herself right now. I told her I'd fill you in. She's pretty upset as you can imagine."

Ryan looked at his ceiling wondering what else could go wrong and fighting the urge to scream, but he was glad she was away from her husband and hopefully safe. He blew all his air out and then asked, "Where are you?"

"I'm out front of your building. I just came from her place."

"Come on in." Ryan ended the call. His concern spiked. He'd been so wrapped up in his own week that he now felt obtuse and guilty about not checking with Sharon to see how things were going at home. In fact, he'd handed her a lot of additional work, from screening and redirecting inquiries that came in about Allan to coordinating the extra counselors in the building, tracking tardies and class absences of students who met with them, as well as copying and organizing handouts for the referendum group meetings. He headed to the door to meet Dominic.

Ryan's small kitchen area, like the entire two-bedroom apartment, was sparsely furnished and thinly decorated. It was clean and neat, but it didn't seem to have been added to since Dominic had last been here not long after Ryan moved in. The open-space design allowed Dominic to note the overnight bag opened on the couch. He had the sad sensation that Ryan could easily pack up all he owned and disappear overnight and not leave a trace behind.

Noticing his glance, Ryan said, "I'm driving up to see Walt. After the week we've all had, I need a scenic drive to clear my head." Gesturing to the dining table he added, "But I can put on some coffee."

"No, but thanks. I don't want to keep you. It was just Sharon made me promise I'd let you know in case she was late on Monday or in case Dave should decide to come poking around."

Hearing Sharon's husband's name reminded Ryan of his mysterious flat tire after last seeing the man. "Well, at least I'll be getting my car out of harm's way until Monday. What happened? Is Sharon, are the kids, okay?"

"They had another fight when David finally got home last night. She said he'd parked his truck halfway off the driveway and had to struggle to get out of the cab. She was reheating his dinner plate when he banged through the back door and started cussing and swearing about seeing a mouse on the porch and how he'd let the kids have an inside cat so they wouldn't have any f-ing mice in the house. The next thing she knew, he was carrying the terrified cat by the scruff and tossing him out the door. Luckily, the kids were in bed.

"I guess he kept hollering and making threats until he passed out. When he did, Sharon did some packing, then got the kids up just after dawn, and they left."

"Christ!" Picturing Sharon dealing with her six-foot-three husband fostered anger and concern for her as well as a realization of how much he cared for her. "Did the son-of-a-bitch touch her?" Ryan asked.

Dominic shook his head. "She says no. His abuse has always been verbal. David Edmonds has always relied on his size and anger to intimidate but has always stopped short of getting physical as far as I know."

"Where is she?" Ryan asked.

"She's at a place her friend Toni inherited just up the road from the grocery store in Cooper. The people who had been renting it bought a house recently. She left Dave a note but didn't say where they were going. He'll find out soon enough, but for now, she's safe and has some time to think."

Ryan sat, so Dominic did too. "Well, thank goodness for friends like this Tony guy." He was aware of feeling some jealousy.

"Toni is a girl. Wasn't she at your wedding?" Dominic asked. "I thought she drove Lisa's parents because they refused to drive in the Twin Cities."

At first, the information didn't register with Ryan. "It was Lisa's cousin who..." he stopped. "Are you saying this Toni is Lisa's cousin, Antonia?" He described what he remembered of the woman.

"Yep, that's her. She and Sharon were a few years behind Lisa in school."

Ryan flashed back to the first time he'd seen Toni. It was at the same volleyball game that Lisa had introduced him to Walt. He met her after the game. He also recalled not being introduced to the uncle the girls had sat with while he and Walt gabbed on and on about Ryan's administrative coursework. The man had left in a hurry at half-time. Ryan became aware Dominic was still talking.

"You looked surprised for some reason."

"It's just strange. It wasn't all that long ago that I found myself wondering if Lisa's cousin was still around. It never occurred to me to ask you or Sharon. I assumed she'd moved from the area. I just never saw her around, and Edenton is not exactly Minneapolis. You run into everyone at least once every few months."

"Toni lives up in Green Bay somewhere. She moved out after high school. This place was way too conservative for her. I heard some rumors back in high school, but I think she became a lesbian and is living with a woman eye doctor."

Dominic's naivete amused Ryan. "I'm not sure anyone all of a sudden becomes a lesbian. But I can imagine this might have been a tough place to grow up if you weren't straight. Lisa never said much about Antonia after the wedding."

The topic made Ryan realize something. "I can think of a few kids at school who wouldn't surprise me if they're gay, but the issue hasn't come up since I've been here. Not even a rumor of bullying. Am I missing something I shouldn't be missing?"

"Well," Dominic suggested, "You may want to have a little talk with the counselors. I'm sure a few kids take some crap, but unless someone was way-out-of-the-closet, most people around here live by the 'Don't ask, don't tell' mantra."

"You do know Obama overturned that a couple of years ago, right?"

"I think I do remember hearing that."

Noticing the time, Ryan said, "If you talk with Sharon again before Monday, tell her she has my full support, and I'm sorry. She can call or text if she needs something or if she needs Monday off. God, Dominic. That's a shitty thing for her to have to deal with."

"I'll check with her tomorrow," Dominic said. "I'll tell her I told you and give her the message. She'll appreciate it. She trusts you; you know. I don't think she would have left, at least not yet, if she didn't." Dominic stood and offered his hand.

Hearing that Sharon trusted him buoyed Ryan's spirits. "She'll be okay, right? Dave won't do anything stupid or be too big an asshole will he? Will her family support her through this?"

"Her family will, for the most part, and so will some of his. But it's going to be hard on her and the kids. Being busy at school will be good for them all. It may be the only normalcy in their lives for a bit. Give my best to Walt."

Dominic let his eyes roam around Ryan's spartan apartment thinking this might be the time to tell Ryan he'd dated Lisa, maybe even why it had ended. But instead, when he spoke, what came out was quite different. "Oh, I almost forgot. How do you feel about cats?"

41

After leaving Ryan's apartment, Dominic drove to the high school. Entering through the usual door by the gym, he heard the squeak of basketball shoes on hardwood, followed by coach Todd's whistle as he stopped practice to vociferously remind the boys where he wanted everyone positioned for the play they were practicing. Dominic ignored the urge to stop and watch as he sometimes did. It was almost 11:00 a.m., and he'd already spent close to four hours of his Saturday morning helping Sharon and then talking with Ryan. He wanted to check his emails and get home. But he also sought the quiet of his office to sort out his thoughts and feelings.

On the drive from Sharon's to Ryan's place, he'd begun to feel better about her situation. He'd helped her and the twins get settled in until Toni had arrived to acquaint them with the place. She'd gotten them organized and provided the comfort and support they'd needed with the abrupt move. But since leaving Ryan's, other concerns had opened up. Ones with which his practical and pragmatic skills weren't particularly useful.

Finding nothing in the handful of emails that required immediate attention, Dominic leaned back, fingers laced together behind his neck, and closed his eyes. He visualized Ryan's little kitchen. He became conscious of thinking Ryan looked even more haggard and tired than he had a few days ago when they'd talked at school. He'd found Ryan standing in the hall, staring out the window to the parking lot. In the five days since Allan's suicide, Ryan looked five years older.

Dominic recalled his concern before Thanksgiving when he'd spied a cold and damp Ryan returning from the district office meeting where he'd learned about the need for a referendum and possible cuts. Since then, events had cascaded making the tightrope he'd always pictured Ryan walking seem higher off the ground and shaky from the whirlwind of occurrences spinning around. The real possibility the referendum might fail seemed to weigh on Ryan's mind, as did Thynie Marsh's nitpicking harassment – and now Allan Sparks' death, and the accusation that Ryan was somehow responsible, must be causing him to wobble unsteadily. On top of everything else, there had been a mysterious visit from that woman, a friend from Minneapolis. Sharon had told him about her and how shaken Ryan had looked after she'd left. Dominic hoped the drive and dinner with Walt would help Ryan regain his balance.

When he opened his eyes, he felt tired and put his elbows on his desk to steady himself. He thought about how and when he should tell Ryan about dating Lisa back in high school. He should have mentioned at least that much when Ryan had first been hired. Having not done so then made it more awkward now. But, if he had said something, Ryan might have asked why they broke up. What would he have said back then? More to his current dilemma, what would he tell Ryan now that they'd worked together for a year and a half, now that he, and Sharon, were the ones Ryan relied upon for local knowledge about navigating the hidden currents and riptides of Edenton and Stienboek?

Dominic rubbed his hands across the stubble of not having shaved since yesterday morning. He feared becoming the one to knock Ryan off that tightrope. He had no doubt Ryan wanted to know more about Lisa's past than the usual "what was she like as a kid" anecdotes. As far as he knew, Ryan had rarely, if ever, visited

Lisa's parents who, having had her late in life, were now both eighty years old and not in great health. By way of explanation, Ryan had offered that because they lived in Minneapolis, he'd really never gotten to know them and that they'd not exactly made him feel welcome before or after he'd had Lisa cremated without a religious service. Having known the Kames from when he'd dated Lisa, the explanation rang true.

He needed to head home. Kate would want to know how Sharon and the kids were doing. Kate would have told Nala the basics. His daughter had babysat for the twins when they were younger and would be furious if they left her to find out for herself through rumors. Both Dominic and Kate knew they could trust Nala not to be the source for anything they shared with her. As he locked his door and headed back through the dim halls to his truck, this last thought about his daughter reminded him of Ryan's request to talk about something to do with his old job.

Passing the gym, the chaotic reverberations of multiple basketballs being dribbled at once seemed like appropriate background sound effects to the confused thoughts and jumbled feelings he was experiencing about Nala, Sharon, and Ryan. He checked, as always, that the door had locked behind him. Climbing into his truck, he thought about how much simpler it was to deal with boilers, buses, and schedules than people.

42

Walt had cooked up enough spaghetti for six people. There would be plenty of leftovers. Ryan knew half of them would be going home with him. By the time they sat to eat, he had updated Walt on the headwinds they were facing with the referendum. It was difficult, but he'd also shared his recent insecurity about being considered the fall guy if it failed – which seemed quite possible according to Dominic and the general public sentiment. Walt revealed he'd sometimes talk with Dominic to get his take on what the more conservative folks in the community were thinking, and he had been usually right. But he assured Ryan that Liz Demian would never blame him if it didn't pass.

Ryan had also talked about Allan's suicide, including Thynie's apparent campaign to spread the family's comment about him being part of the cause. Walt had never dealt with a student suicide in his years in education. He listened with empathy, reassuring Ryan that he'd handled it as well as anyone could. He also shared some relevant context, telling Ryan about Thynie's maternal grandfather's 1930s suicide and how the family had never come to terms with it, blaming instead the banks and government for the Great Depression that had caused his bankruptcy.

Walt asked Ryan to open and pour some wine for the two of them. The room filled with the warm aroma of garlic bread as he removed slices from beneath the broiler and set them next to the bowl of steaming pasta and sauce already on the table. Each filled their plates and dug in. Wiping his chin, Ryan said, "This is great, Walt. Where did you ever learn to make spaghetti sauce like this? It's outstanding."

Walt said, "We were married for three years before Betty shared her sauce recipe. But then one of the last things she told me after getting sick was that she was glad she had taught me how to cook so I wouldn't starve."

Walt twirled pasta around his folk and into his mouth. He sipped his wine before continuing. "You know...I'm not comparing the two things, but when Betty stopped treatment for her cancer, I stupidly and regrettably related it to suicide. I thought some would see it that way and wondered why she wouldn't keep fighting. Even though I knew she was doing it, at least in part, to spare me the pain of watching her die slowly, I argued that I would treasure whatever extra time we had together... She called it bullshit. Told me I was being selfish."

Walt stopped talking and lifted another forkful of pasta to his mouth. As he chewed, he looked at a photo of his wife and him hanging above the television – two old faces ignoring the camera and looking lovingly at each other. Ryan knew the image was from Walt's retirement party. He said, "That's a great picture. I'm sorry I didn't get to know her better. She was quite a woman." He drained his wine knowing how lame that sounded.

They finished eating, and Walt poured them each a cup of coffee then walked into his bedroom. He returned, sat down, and placed another framed photo on the table. Ryan looked at the young, beautiful woman boldly looking back at him. "God, Walt, no wonder you fell in love with her." His eyes remained glued to the photo even as Walt spoke.

"I keep it next to the bed so first thing every morning I remember what a lucky man I've been. I took this photo. It was about six months after I got home from overseas and only a week after meeting Betty. I already knew I was going to ask her to marry me before someone else could steal her away.

"When I developed it, I found something uncannily familiar about the way she stared at the camera. It was as if she was saying something to me." He reached across and rotated the picture as if to reassure himself and then turned it back toward Ryan. "Like she was telling me she was eager to face, or at least to accept, whatever I threw at her, whatever the next moment, day, and years brought her way." Walt chuckled. "It was a look I saw many times. And it was the look she had when she told me she wasn't going to do chemo. But when I first saw it, there in that photo, I remembered where I had seen it before." Walt closed his eyes, revisiting memories.

"Do you recall, when you visited at Thanksgiving? I told you about the monk in Vietnam?"

Ryan nodded even though the old man's eyes were still shut. As if he had heard the movement, Walt continued. "His name, I learned later, was Quảng Đức. And moments before he dropped that lit match into his gasoline-soaked lap, he'd slowly moved his eyes along the faces of the surrounding crowd, as if he was searching for someone. Maybe, because I had just pushed my way to the front of the crowd, his gaze came to rest directly on me." Walt's eyes opened. "That's where I had seen that same look before. That total acceptance and willingness to embrace what was coming. Of course, a moment later...he disappeared in a ball of flame."

He took a slow sip of his coffee. "That look... what I saw in Quảng Đức's eyes and in Betty's, that willingness and acceptance, that's not something you see very often."

Walt set his empty cup down and took a deep breath. "You know, you had that look when I first met you. That's why, when it was time for me to retire, I told Liz Demian you'd be the one who could bring the ideas, temperament, and energy we wanted; to infuse the new blood we both believed the district needed."

Walt placed his elbows on the table and leaned in. "I'll be honest with you, Ryan. When I heard what happened to Lisa, I was sad for her and worried about you. But I was also selfishly concerned I'd hung on too long, that we'd lost you. I mean, why would you want to leave the support of your friends, family, your hometown and come to Edenton? Betty made me promise not to intrude beyond sending condolences. Then when I didn't hear from you again..." Walt's gesture indicated his acceptance of the situation.

"So, it was a real surprise when I got your email saying you'd applied. I had questions about the gap in our correspondence, but I was also excited. I told Liz that even though we hadn't talked in some time, I remained confident you were what Stienboek needed. Unlike the other two top candidates, you'd be coming in with a fresh eye.

"During the interview process, Liz saw your promise and vision, that you were likable and sincere, and adamant you wanted to be here, but she had concerns. Not about your ideas, but about you, in your ability to lead, especially during such a turbulent time. I believe the words she used were 'tentative' and 'uncertain.'

"That didn't match with the *you* I remembered. So, when she asked me if I was still sure about you, I told her you'd have the staff on board in two years. And she trusted me. She got a majority on the board to trust her which, as you know, made you, and her, some... I don't want to say enemies, so let's just say detractors.

"Now the two years will be up in June, after next semester. And Liz is still waiting to see if she made a mistake trusting me about you."

The turn in the conversation made Ryan's world tilt sidewards. Only the caring honesty in Walt's voice kept him from despairing.

Walt continued, "I've come to understand trust doesn't come

easy for you anymore. I don't know what happened to cause that. But I do know that once upon a time you trusted yourself, and you trusted in your ability to lead. Now it seems to me that if you're going to convince Liz Demian the flame is still there, you're going to have to find a way to get that look back in your eye.

"Please forgive an old man's arrogance, but the only way I've learned to make that happen is to be willing to accept yourself. I don't know what happened after you and Lisa married, or after she died, or in any other parts of your life for that matter, that made you lose that desire. But to get it back you need to learn to trust again... in yourself and those you want to lead. Without that, I'll have to admit to Liz I was wrong. I *really* don't want to have to do that. So, tell me how I can help."

Ryan sat quietly, trying to separate his emotions from the intent behind Walt's words. He could see it had been difficult for his mentor to say what he had said. He'd taken no pleasure in delivering the message. Knowing that, however, did little to alleviate the pain and embarrassment of having his pride and competency filleted and laid bare on the table. Despite the wine and coffee, a chill gripped his spine and an empty hollowness filled his head and gut. He stared at his cold hands until the words formed.

"Walt, please... tell me what happened to Lisa in high school. It's killing me not knowing and..." He let the sentence die unfinished and hoped, trusting Walt would help.

43

Nala and Ayden didn't share the same schedule. But even back before when he wasn't on her radar, and she avoided him, she'd usually see him somewhere during the day. But not today. Not even at lunch.

Last Thursday, Zoey had told her that Ayden had gotten confrontational in science class. She'd even kicked him under the table, but he wouldn't relent. It was like he wanted Mrs. Zowak to kick him out of class. Everyone knew it was because of Allan. Then he hadn't been there at all on Friday. Nala debated with herself all the way home and over the weekend about what, if anything, she should do.

Today was Monday, six days since Allan's death. The funeral was scheduled in a few days, and again she hadn't seen Ayden all day. She decided to act after supper.

"Hi, Mrs. Quant. This is Nala, Natalia Samilton. From school." She wondered why she added the 'Natalia' and 'from school' part. Mrs. Quant knew who she was. "I'm sorry to bother you, but can I talk to Ayden? I don't know if he has a cell phone, but I didn't have his number."

Silence. Nala envisioned the woman refusing to let her talk to her son. "Nala, of course you can. Thanks for calling. I was just taken for a moment when you said Natalia. I'd almost forgotten that was your real name. I haven't heard you called that in years. I'll get Ayden for you and... Nala, I want to thank your dad and you for helping track down Ayden the other day. He's real shook up, and well, I guess we all are. Thanks for your help."

Before she could reply, Nala heard the phone being laid down, followed by footsteps and Mrs. Quant's raised voice. "A-Lee. Come up. It's Nala from school on the phone for you." Ayden's muffled voice sounded distant. Mrs. Quant replied, "Well, come up and find out." Nala assumed he had asked why she was calling. It seemed a fair question. She wasn't completely sure herself.

While she waited, Nala reconsidered her opinion of Anna Quant, thinking maybe she'd been hasty, or even unfair, in labeling her as bitchy.

"Hello?" Ayden's voice sounded unsure.

"Ayden, it's Nala. I just wanted to call and see if you were okay. Zoey said you weren't in science class on Friday, and then I didn't see you in school today."

"Yeah?"

"Well, I just wanted to check in with you." Nala wished he would quit talking in one-word replies. "You know, see how you are. Last week was tough for everybody – with Allan and all. I thought you might want to talk some more; you know, after what you told me the other night."

His "Okay," sounded like a question.

Nala decided to try another approach. "Are you sick? With the second semester starting, I'm sure Zoey would get me your work. Dad and I could drop it off if you'd like."

Still sounding tentative, Ayden asked, "Did Zoey tell you what happened in science?"

"She just said you got Mrs. Zowak pretty mad, but that you didn't get kicked out of class or anything."

"I wanted to."

Nala realized lately she sometimes felt that way too. She

wondered if his reasoning might help her figure out her own feelings.

"Why would you want to get kicked out?" There was a long pause. "Ayden? Are you still there?"

A few more seconds passed before he said, "I don't know." Then more silence before he added, "Do you remember when we were kids, and sometimes I'd run away from the teacher?"

"I remember that time you went outside, and it took a sheriff to help find you. I remember Zoey wanted to organize the class to go look for you."

"She did?" Ayden was surprised.

"Yeah. So did Lilly and a few others." She didn't mention she hadn't been one of them.

"I didn't know that," Ayden said. "Why would they do that?"

It was Nala's turn to be surprised. "What do you mean, why? Because they cared."

"Really?" he genuinely sounded mystified.

"Yeah. That's a good thing, Ayden. Right?"

"I guess."

The reaction was baffling. Nala said, "But you didn't run away from Mrs. Zowak."

"I wanted to, and I don't even know why. So, I tried to get her pissed by not answering. I just suddenly felt like I needed to be out of there and be alone. I tried to get kicked out, but she didn't do it. I don't know why. She kicked me out before for just a stupid tee shirt. I told her the assignment was frick'in stupid, but I didn't say 'frick'in. She still didn't kick me out. I started feeling..." He paused, seemingly unable to pinpoint what he'd been feeling. "I once saw a picture. It had weird little houses with no doors and a small school on a hill. You could tell a storm was coming because the sky was all dark."

Nala said, "Okay." Her concern spiked.

"That's how I was feeling. I thought if she kicked me out, I could escape that storm."

"That sounds awful like you were trapped or something," Nala said. She didn't think she was trapped, but she understood what he was talking about. Her own feeling was more like she was being shoved into a sack, but she could think it through later with Lang. For now, she wanted to make sure he wasn't considering hurting himself, but she didn't know how to ask. "Yeah. I get it. Do you think you feel that way because of Allan?"

"I talked with this guy, Mr. Powells. He said I'm not like Allan, and I didn't do anything wrong. Just like you. And Mom kind-a said the same thing."

This relieved Nala's anxiety. Without thinking, Nala asked, "What about your dad?" All she knew about Ayden's dad was that he was hardly ever around, and her own dad didn't think much of him.

"He won't be home until tomorrow night. I don't even know where he is for sure. I think he's driving out in Oregon or someplace like that. But he never liked Allan, and he'll say I'm being stupid for even thinking about it."

Ayden's matter-of-fact comment startled her. "But your mom is nice, right? I mean, she called my dad when she was worried about you not being home last week. Did I just hear her call you 'A-Lee'? That sounds like what a good mother would do. Why does she call you that?"

"Lee is my middle name. A-Lee is short for Ayden Lee."

It seemed strange. Ayden had just added a name while she was shedding one. *Two, three... Which is me?* Her companion mantra took a lap around her mind. Something else to ponder with Lang. She was sure there was no middle name on her birth certificate, but she'd double-check. There just wasn't any more room inside to absorb another 'someone' she was supposed to be. Still, it made her feel cheated.

Something else her birth mom neglected to give her. Maybe, she could become Nala Natalia Samilton? She didn't like the sound of that, but it would combine the two people she was trying to be.

"Ayden, I'm glad your mom is nice, and you can talk with her. I'm glad she said you didn't do anything wrong. You believe her, don't you?"

"Yeah. I guess. Mom and me don't really talk that much, but she cares even though she doesn't have to because she isn't my real mother."

The words reminded Nala of their previous conversation and of how much she had in common with this boy. It made her appreciate that she was luckier, at least in most ways. She wanted to tell him that he could always talk with her anytime, but wasn't sure she wanted to go that far. On the other hand, he'd just described himself in terms of a picture. Maybe he might not think she was crazy if she told him how she was trying to describe herself. Maybe even mention Lang. He just might get it.

"I have to get going, Ayden. Will you be back at school tomorrow?"

"I was there today. Mrs. Berry let me stay in her room and work, so I'm not too far behind. But she said tomorrow I have to go back to all my classes."

"She sounds like a good teacher. I'm glad you have her. I'll see you tomorrow then. I'm glad you're okay. Remember, nobody thinks any of this was your fault."

"Okay..." It seemed Ayden had something else to say. She waited until he did.

"Can I say two more things? Real quick," he asked.

"Of course you can. What is it?"

"Don't tell nobody my mom calls me A-Lee. Not even Zoey."

"No problem. I won't. I get it. I know how tricky names can be. What's the other thing?"

"I'm glad your parents adopted you and you go to my school. But I think sometimes you might feel like you're alone too, and there aren't any doors. So, I'm glad you have good friends like Zoey who don't make fun of you. I guess that's three things. Sorry."

Nala felt her eyes tear up. She just wasn't ready to explain who Lang was or why he was the only one who could truly understand her. She was also thinking that this boy might be in second place. "That's very nice of you to say, Ayden. Good night."

44

"I'm heading home, Ryan. Thanks again for all..." Sharon caught up to her voice and stepped into Ryan's office. "Thank you for all your support." Her kids were waiting in the outer office. She looked over her shoulder to make sure they weren't close enough to hear. "I feel so bad David tried to drag you into our breakup. I really don't think he'll say or do anything, but I just don't trust him anymore. Anyhow, I'm glad Dom told you what happened. He said you were heading up to see Walt?"

Looking at her reminded Ryan that the main reason he'd driven to Walt's on Saturday was to avoid the powerful temptation of Mrs. Rupert waiting in an Appleton motel. Trying to ignore that thought, he said, "I appreciated Dom stopping by. It must have been an extremely difficult weekend for you and the kids."

Ryan was surprised when she suddenly looked like she was going to tear up; like she had that morning when they'd talked. He'd come in early to be here when she arrived or if she called in at the last minute. His feelings had become complicated. Rupert's comments about Sharon had put images in his head he couldn't forget. He promised himself no hugs. He couldn't be sure any hug would be solely meant as comfort for her. Besides, he still remembered Dominic's look when he saw them momentarily holding hands. Hugging would give public credence to any accusations her husband might start to make. Things were awkward and dicey enough as they were.

Sharon had been composed when she arrived. They talked for only a few minutes before the school phone began to ring. She'd given him an abbreviated summary of what had happened. He expressed his genuine empathy, concern, and support. When he asked, she told him that Dominic had notified the school bus driver on that route to pick her twins up, and, gratefully, her friend had stayed the night to make sure they ate and got on the bus. That gave the kids an extra half-hour of sleep, and she got to be alone to settle and calm herself on the drive to school. Sharon's tears had appeared while talking about the kids. Not while talking about moving out. Then she'd suddenly hugged him, thanked him, and was off to answer the phone. He was thankful it had been so quick. His body didn't have time to react and embarrass him.

"How's Walt doing?" Sharon asked. "It has to be hard on him since Betty passed. You're really sweet to get up there to visit. I'm sure he appreciates it, and I'm sure you guys have a lot to talk about."

"He's doing fine." Ryan didn't want to get into any details. He still hadn't processed what Walt had shared about Lisa.

Sharon sensed Ryan's hesitation. "Well, we better go. Dom said you'd be open to maybe taking the kid's cat, at least for a while. The landlord where we're staying is severely allergic to them."

"Dominic said you're living at Lisa's cousin Toni's place. He said she inherited and rents it out because she lives in Green Bay now. I met her a few times. But, back then, Lisa always called her Antonia, not Toni. She drove Lisa's parents to Minneapolis for the wedding. Otherwise, I don't think they would have come."

"That sounds like them. Yeah, it's Toni's house. I didn't know if you knew her or not. We've been close since middle school. We were a couple of years behind Lisa in school. I know everything about her, including..." Sharon stopped, quizzically studying Ryan's sudden Mona Lisa grin. She tilted her head, looking over her shoulder again to make sure the twins were out of earshot. Lowering her voice, she said. "Dom told you Toni is a lesbian, didn't he? And you're wondering..." Another unfinished sentence.

Ryan's first instinct was to feign shock – plausible deniability. But instead, with a slight opening of his hands and raising of his eyebrows, he admitted his culpability.

Her hands moved to her hips. Maintaining her lowered voice, she said. "Well, the answer is no," adding a moment later with a coy half smile, "I love her, but she isn't my type." From behind her, a voice asked, "Who's not your type, Mom? Dad? Can we go now?"

Sharon reddened slightly, and she turned her head. "I'm not talking about your dad. We can go in a minute. Go, wait with your brother."

When her daughter walked back to the front office, she continued. "What I was going to say... was because we are close, I know Toni can't be around cats. And Hamilton is an indoor cat. When we were leaving, the kids found him outside, and they were afraid David wouldn't take care of him. We didn't have time for a big discussion, so for now, he's quarantined on Toni's back porch. Are you sure you don't mind?"

After Sharon left, Ryan closed and locked his office door. Sitting back down, he slid the center desk drawer open and shuffled some pens and pencils around exposing the key that would unlock the one drawer he kept locked. At first, he just studied the shape and teeth on the small key. His mind wouldn't focus or decide. Instead, he replayed Sharon's suggestive "...isn't my type" comment about Toni. He remembered some time ago she'd joked about being in a *Playboy* magazine. He couldn't let his mind go there.

To detract himself, he returned to his notes from last week's school board agenda that he'd been trying to concentrate on when

Sharon stopped in. Below the Call to Order, Pledge of Allegiance, Adoption of the Agenda, and Approval of the December Minutes came the Public Comments. It was this item that had, as expected, packed the room. Usually, there might be two or three requests to speak. Last Wednesday, eighteen had signed up. All except one had focused on the referendum. Ryan had kept a tally of the comments.

Board President Templeton had suggested that, due to the number of requests to speak, it would be appreciated if each person tried to keep their comment to one minute instead of the official allotted three minutes. He also reminded the audience that because the referendum was not actually on the open meeting agenda, by rule the board could not publicly discuss it. Accordingly, board members were not to respond to or answer any questions posed. His point of order was greeted with some grumbles throughout the room. Templeton had asked the secretary to take notes of any questions, saying the board would try to provide answers at a later date.

Fifty-three minutes later, the last speaker finished. President Templeton thanked all for their comments, after which Thynie Marsh broke protocol, announcing that folks with concerns should urge others to let their opinions be known. Templeton's anger at Marsh was written across his face for all to see. But he let it go with a reminder to board members of his earlier statement.

When no fireworks commenced, and having said what they came to say, most of the audience left. Ryan's count showed ten comments were either openly hostile to or leaning heavily against the referendum. Of the seven supporting speakers, three had tellingly added real concerns about the timing, noting the effects of the recent recession were still being felt.

Along with the discouraging tally, Ryan had written some of the opposition arguments around the agenda margins. Now, as at the board meeting, he felt frustration, some anger, and minimal optimism. Important as this was to the district and possibly his own future at Stienboek, he found his thoughts and emotions sliding back to his conversation with Walt on Saturday. He realized he'd unconsciously picked up the key. Closing his fingers around it, he raised his fist to his ear as if it might speak to him, maybe add to what Walt had shared.

Rather than discipline problems, Lisa had been involved with social services. At one point the criminal justice system had also been involved. While the details weren't shared with the school, it was clear allegations of sexual abuse were involved. Walt had hesitantly shared with Ryan that at one point the school had been notified of a restraining order being issued against a family member. Despite Ryan's desire to know who, his old mentor had rightfully said, "You know I can't tell you that, Ryan."

After some silence, Walt added, "I can only guess why Lisa never shared any of this with you. I assume she must have been afraid it would lessen her in your eyes, would cause you to quit loving her. I think that was a mistake on her part. And I imagine it caused her, and maybe you, a lot of pain. But as we see in the news all the time, abuse victims often don't come forward until years later, if at all. We can only try to understand what it did to them and their lives in the meantime."

Ryan didn't have to guess. He knew. He'd lived it.

Walt had continued. "That must be a hell of a secret for anyone to carry. But not sharing it..."

"What was the local gossip?" Ryan asked. "For my first year in Edenton, I always got the feeling whenever I left a room everyone was speculating or judging me or my marriage. It's gotten better but still happens from time to time."

Walt took his time, considering how and what to say. He knew the pain of losing a wife but also realized Ryan's situation was different, in many ways exponentially worse. He'd violently lost his young wife only a few years into their marriage.

"Lisa was a beautiful girl and attracted a lot of attention from the boys, and, of course, some animosity from the girls. Obviously, this wasn't the kind of stuff kids shared with their principal. But from the bits I heard from time to time, it seemed Lisa had a habit of going through boyfriends rather quickly. She never stayed with one for very long. That invariably led to rumors about her. And, of course, some of the adults couldn't help but whisper and make connections to her family issues."

Ryan's tightened fist squeezed the key producing a cramp in his forearm. He placed the key in the lock, turning it but not opening the drawer. If he looked at her picture now, after what Walt had shared, what might he see and feel? Would he now see a hint of the abuse in her eyes? Or why she had cheated even though she swore she loved him. He wanted to find forgiveness but wasn't sure for whom – Lisa or himself. For the thousandth time since he'd taken the picture, he relived what she'd told him before they'd headed out for ice cream that day.

She'd wanted to explain, could finally explain, needed his forgiveness but wanted to do it over ice cream, back at the place where they began, before... She'd left the sentence unfinished. He now wondered if she'd meant before her cheating as he had assumed at the time, or if she'd meant before they'd met, or even way back before the things that Walt had told him about.

He wanted to exhume the picture and look but knew he wasn't ready. A significant part of himself was locked in the bottom of that drawer entangled among the pixels that made up the photo. Was it that or Lisa's image that scared him?

Walt had said, "I hope knowing this can somehow help. Doesn't make it harder. You know, Betty always had the feeling you were haunted by something. Said she was worried for you. That concerned me. I felt maybe I'd put you in that situation."

Ryan shook his head, no, but let Walt continue.

"You know Ryan, Lisa was a good person. I know she loved you and was so happy that you were marrying her. She told me that way back when I first met you, back at that volleyball game, when you two were just engaged. I believed her then, and I still do. I don't know if she escaped her past or not. I pray she did."

Ryan had thought Walt finished. They'd sat in silence for a few moments before the old man added a coda. "The relative in the restraining order is dead. Digging for a name isn't going to help you or Lisa. I suggest you focus on memories of the person you fell in love with and married, not her life before she met you. If we only dwell on the negatives, we negate the parts of the person that made us fall in love to begin with. It's a sure way to sabotage yourself and kill any chance of rekindling that spark in your eye and gut. Look to the good and consider yourself a lucky man that you ever got a chance with Lisa. I was sure when Dominic and Lisa dated, they'd be hitched as soon as they were both out of high school."

Ryan reached for the key dangling from the drawer's lock. He turned it counterclockwise and replaced it in the pencil tray. He headed home again wondering why Dominic had never mentioned he'd dated Lisa. In light of what he now knew about her, he tried not to imagine the two of them together and naked.

45

The meeting was in the amphitheater-style band room. As the staff filed in, gym teachers tended to fill in the chairs along the top level where the percussion and brass sections lived. The more involved or vocal members moved down to the woodwind chairs closer to the table behind which Bernadette Zowak and Kim Berry sat. Most, but not all, of the Stienboek teaching staff were in attendance for the informational meeting.

Promptly at 3:30 p.m., Zowak called the meeting to order, while a few late arrivals squeezed their way over others to reach the scattered saved seats near their friends.

"Mrs. Berry and I want to catch you all up on our first – I'll just call them conversations – with Superintendent Demian and two board members. As you know, these are informal since they are no longer required to negotiate with our union."

"What union?" a voice grumbled from the back of the clarinet section. "Seems to me the governor and his legislative cronies pretty much stomped the association's butt. We should have given in on the extra insurance and pension costs. Now we've lost over forty years of bargaining rights."

Zowak responded. "It wasn't WEACs fault. The Senate found a way to advance the bill even while the dozen or so Democrats fled to Illinois to keep a quorum from forming. Their amendment to strip out collective bargaining rights was added at the last minute. Personally, I was most appalled by how easily the public bought their crap – excuse my French – about greedy teachers and public unions."

One of the math teachers weighed in. "I was there in Madison marching. Lots of us were." A brief round of applause followed. "That second Saturday in March we had 100,000 marchers there, and did you see the picture of the packed galleries? We should still be down there."

"Okay, we all feel the same way, but enough venting or we'll be here all night."

The first-year English teacher Evelyn Snede raised her hand. "What happened to that lawsuit filed against Act 10?"

Mr. Schmelzing, the Social Studies chairperson, answered. "That was a federal appeals court ruling, and it said ACT 10 is constitutional. State suits are pending, but the conservative Wisconsin Supreme Court is not going to overturn their darling governor's big political win."

Zowak interjected. "And that brings us back to why we're here. Mrs. Berry and I met after school with..."

"I heard Bobby Marsh was there too, so he can report back to Thynie and make sure we don't get a raise." The interruption came from the art teacher.

Mrs. Berry answered. "He was, and so was the Board President Chuck Templeton."

"And let's keep our facts straight," Zowak added. "There are no more discussions about raises. The new law says a district only has to offer a wage increase based on the consumer price index, and that's even limited by a cap unless approved by referendum."

Mrs. Berry took over. "This scares me for several reasons, but the board is looking to change our Wisconsin Educational Association-sponsored health insurance to a cheaper plan next year."

This caused some angry and emotional outcries. For years, teachers had accepted lower wages in negotiations to have top-line health insurance. Younger teachers voiced fears about coverage for current and future kids while older staff concerns centered on pre-existing conditions and potential, more serious conditions. The two women let the staff briefly vent. "All we know at this point is they've been talking with the other county districts and plan to band together to get the best insurance at an 'affordable' cost," Mrs. Berry exaggerated her use of air quotes. "We were told we'll hear the results in the early spring."

Mrs. Zowak took over quickly to keep things moving. "Act 10, you may remember, also now requires annual recertification votes for all public unions, including our local Edenton Area School District union. Superintendent Demian said if it worked for us, they'd be okay with using the same process as this year. The law also disallows schools from automatically withdrawing union dues for members, which is why we each had to designate in writing if we agree to have that done this year."

Someone stated the obvious. "They're just hoping we'll give up and not fund the union."

Another asked, "Is it working?"

Zowak exchanged a glance with Mrs. Berry before saying, "We were told a few didn't agree." Several began to look around the room. "That, of course, is their right. But we certainly can't start turning on each other, which is exactly what the governor would love to see happen."

Mrs. Berry took up the final point. "Superintendent Demian asked us to think about salary schedules. With our previous contract ending this year, the old schedules become void. She would like our feedback on what they're drafting. She says they want to be as fair as possible to both new and senior teachers. They don't want to create an exodus of teachers to the bigger surrounding cities."

Schmelzing asked, "Did you get a sense the board will actually consider anything we suggest?"

Mrs. Berry nodded to Zowak, suggesting she respond. "I think Demian and Templeton will give it serious consideration. But in the end, it will have to be adopted by the entire board."

There was silence as teachers tried to wrap their heads around this new reality and what a non-negotiated salary schedule might look like. A twenty-plus-year Stienboek veteran, infamous with students and peers for his verbal affectations, asked a question. "You said they want to be fair and retain teachers and..." there was a slight dramatic pause for effect... "and you said before they can exceed the salary cap through a referendum" ... another pause... "then why isn't that a part of the current referendum? Couldn't Ryan have brought that up with the referendum support group he's in charge of?"

Zowak reminded everyone that with the Supreme Court ruling, and with the governor having handily won the recall election last June, they had to be realistic and realize such a thing would never fly at this time. As she began to point out that a second operational referendum would have been required, she was distracted by someone's comment. "Maybe Ryan was too busy with Sharon Edmonds."

In a tone usually reserved for recalcitrant students, Mrs. Zowak loudly said, "I beg your pardon! What did you say?"

The voice replied but in a more subdued manner. "It's just that yesterday, one of the cooks coming in early for the free breakfast kids saw them hugging in the office."

46

The kitchen clock hands finally reached 7:00 p.m. While eating his dinner, he'd unsuccessfully tried not to notice how slowly they'd been crawling. The sound of the doorbell made Ryan aware of a lingering garlic smell from the stir-fry he'd made. He'd turned the exhaust fan off after the chicken and veggies were ready. Turning the fan back on low, he headed to the door.

Sharon stood waiting, her frozen breath escaping into the darkness beyond the light, cat carrier in one hand, litter box in the other, her purse hanging from her shoulder. He quickly opened the door and relieved her of both items. He set the litter box on the floor behind the door and the carrier on a chair. He peeked into the plastic blue on top and dark gray bottomed structure. Two wide eyes stared back. The nose twitched as it unflinchingly stretched its face forward, curious about the face staring in. "I've got some litter in the car. I'll be right back."

Before Ryan could offer to go get it, the storm door closed behind her. He reopened it and waited half in, half out for her to return. When she stepped past him, the clean crisp smell of cold air clung to her hair and coat. He closed both doors, took the bag from her, and set it in the litter box. Turning back, her coat was already off and in her hand, as she glanced around for a place to set it. He hadn't considered her staying. He'd pictured her handing him the cat and box through the door, while the kids waited in the running car.

She handed him her coat. "I've got to introduce you to Hamilton. I promised the kids I'd make sure you two guys were getting along before I left."

Ryan took her coat and stepped over to the living area. "Are the kids in the car?"

"No," she simply said. "They're at the house doing their homework. They're fine together for an hour. Besides, the place has cable, and all we had at the farm is dial-up. They're in heaven."

Ryan laid her coat across the arm of the sofa, detecting the faint scent she wore at school. Sharon had moved the carrier to the floor next to where she'd set her purse, then sat on the chair and bent to release the carrier door. By the time Ryan stepped back and pulled out another chair, the cat was already perched on the jeans she'd changed into, stretching his white paws up toward the neckline of her red oversized sweatshirt.

Thinking to himself, *lucky cat*, Ryan instead quipped, "I hope Hamilton is declawed."

"I couldn't have asked you to babysit our little boy here," she rubbed her chin on Hamilton's head, "if he wasn't declawed and neutered." She ran her fingers up Hamilton's arched spine and over his ears. Ryan could hear the cat's rumbling purr. Without looking at him, Sharon said, "Aren't you glad you're not a cat?"

Two thoughts collided in Ryan's head. He thought he knew what it felt like to be neutered and declawed, but he also knew the feeling of loving hands running the length of his spine. "I don't know, Hamilton doesn't seem to mind."

Sharon repositioned the cat so he faced Ryan. "Hamilton, this is my friend Mr. Ryan Davvis. He's going to take care of you for a while. He's also my boss, so you have to do what he tells you, okay?"

Ryan reminded himself she had no idea what a tease those words were for him. The cat again checked him out, then leaped the short distance to his lap, curled, and sat waiting to be petted.

"Well," Sharon said, "that didn't take very long." She leaned over and scratched both sides of Hamilton's jaw. "Well, Hammy, seems you trust and like my friend Ryan." The purring started again. "You're going to be just fine here, aren't you? You two handsome bachelors are going to look after each other, right?"

Ryan looked at the top of Sharon's head and the ring on her left hand. He considered warning her and the cat that he might not be the trustworthy guy they seemed to believe him to be. Instead, he said, "Can I ask a question?"

"Of course." She continued to caress Hamilton's head.

He asked quickly, so he wouldn't change his mind. "Did Dominic date Lisa back in high school?"

Sharon neither answered nor raised her head to him. After a moment she asked, "Is there any wine in that bottle on the counter over there?"

They'd moved to the living room. She sat on the sofa, a glass of red wine in hand. Ryan chose his recliner. It kept a distance between them and allowed him to see her face as they talked. He'd opened a bottle of beer for himself, but it sat untasted on the end table next to him. He didn't let himself lean forward. He didn't want to appear like he was interrogating her.

"It's probably unfair to ask you rather than asking Dominic directly. I haven't had a chance to talk to him yet this week, and it isn't the type of question I wanted to march into his office and ask. And, well, it just occurred to me, I figured with you guys all overlapping in school, and you and Toni being friends ...?" He told himself to stop talking and let the sentence trail off.

Sharon took a sip of wine and looked around. The lack of pictures on the wall and personal items on any surface made her feel sad and protective of Ryan. She began her answer before she returned her gaze to his face.

"When Dom was a senior, Lisa was a junior. Me and Toni were just freshmen, so we didn't move in the same circles. I do remember being at Toni's once or twice when Dom was there with Lisa. I think they'd been together for a few months at that point."

Ryan said, "Walt was under the impression they'd end up married when they were both out of school?"

Sharon seemed surprised. "Walt said that?" Now her eyes were fully on Ryan's face.

"It just came up in passing conversation. He was saying how lucky I was to have even met Lisa because he had thought she and Dominic would end up together."

"Really?" She sipped her wine. "Did Walt say what made him think that?"

Ryan veered away from the heart of their conversation. "Just that Lisa had matured by then, and Dominic was a no-frills, traditional kind of kid and wasn't the type to take relationships lightly." He picked up the bottle of beer but set it back down without drinking. "Why do you think Dominic never told me he'd dated Lisa? It seems like it would have been logical enough to mention."

Sharon looked across the open space and then back to him. "You know, Dom would go out of his way to help anyone. If you're lucky enough to be someone he cares about, he'd do almost anything for you. But for Dom, it's *things* that have logic, not people so much, particularly people he doesn't know. When you were hired, he didn't know you. He didn't see the logic of you wanting to come here. Most didn't." She paused, picking her words carefully. "So, if he never told you... I'm sure it was because he didn't know how you'd react, and he worried it might bother you to find out he'd dated Lisa, even though it was almost twenty years ago."

"Why should he think it would bother me? They were in high school."

Sharon looked at her glass and finished it off. She then stood and walked it over, rinsed it before setting it on the counter adjacent to the sink, and returned to stand in front of him.

"I don't know, Ryan. Why does anything bother anyone?" Then more softly she added, "Why do any of us feel or do the things we do?"

Sharon put her hands on the arms of his chair, leaned in, and lightly kissed him on the forehead. "I can all but guarantee you that he's still worried about it but feels now like he's waited too long. And that, Mr. Davvis, is another example of what happens when men are too chickenshit to talk about their feelings."

Hamilton appeared from Ryan's bedroom which he'd been inspecting. He rubbed against Sharon's leg and then hopped onto Ryan's lap. Sharon laughed. "I guess I can tell the kids Hammy is comfortable and in safe hands." She picked up her coat. "Ryan, you should know, I'm not going back to David. I can't do that anymore."

Ryan nodded. "Good." When she bent and picked up her purse. He thought about Rupert's comment.

Sharon put on her coat. "Thank you, Ryan, for everything, especially taking care of Hammy. Since he's already claimed your lap, don't get up. I'll see you in the morning."

She was out the door before he could make a fool of himself with some stupid retort. He scratched the cat's head. The purring started again. "Hamilton, it's been a while since I've made that sound." He warned himself not to interpret Sharon's sisterly kiss or off-the-cuff jests as serious flirting. Time was, he'd often get such comments from women. He'd often reciprocated. But he'd never taken them seriously. Now, since Lisa and Rupert, he shouldn't trust himself to do that again. Yet, he'd just come very close.

"Don't!" he said. Hamilton twisted his neck to look at him. He slid his hand along the cat's tail. "I mean, that would be stupid. Professional suicide. I won't make that mistake again." He couldn't let his mind enter the roundabout he'd never discovered how to exit. Sharon's marriage was in tatters. He was glad she was comfortable enough with him to joke, to remind herself she was still alive, an attractive woman. End of story.

Noticing the untouched beer, he took a drink. Bottle in one hand, cat in the other, his thoughts moved on to what Dominic would be willing to share about Lisa, and how he needed to get Liz Demian – and himself – to believe he was capable of getting that look back in his eye and doing what Walt had convinced her he could do.

His nose started to tickle. He blinked to find his left eye was watery. He set the beer down just in time to catch the sneeze with his arm. He'd been anticipating this and was glad Sharon was gone before it started. "Okay, Hammy. I've got some bad news for you. We're not going to be as buddy-buddy as I may have led you to believe."

47

When Ryan pulled into Sophie's parking lot, he was glad to see only a handful of cars. However, he wasn't pleased to see Dave Edmonds in his usual seat at the corner of the bar. He nodded at the man just enough to acknowledge his presence. Ryan continued into the back room, taking the booth he and Dominic had occupied last time but sitting on the opposite bench so he wouldn't be visible from the bar.

Tammi stuck her head around the corner. "You want a menu, Mr. Davvis? Are you waiting for someone?"

Ryan was conscious of still being called Mr. Davvis and not just Ryan. Even here. Not that he was here all that often. "I'm meeting Dominic. But I'll take a tap Spotted Cow when you get a chance."

He was concerned about how Dominic might react if he pushed too hard about his and Lisa's relationship and how she was perceived by their peers back then. He stood back up and removed his coat. Tossing it on the bench next to him. When he sat again he was startled to feel more than see Dave Edmonds hulk next to him. The man placed his phone on the table, screen side up. "Well, Mr. Principal-man. Look what I got here." He tapped his stiff middle finger loudly on the table next to the phone.

Ryan looked up at the man trapping him in the booth. He simultaneously noted the jukebox come to life with an oldie he liked. Rather than feeling intimidated, he found himself irritated because the man's appearance and taping finger were covering up the introductory acoustic guitar solo and opening lyrics. He looked up at the man. "What do you want, Dave?" The song reached the first chorus.

Amie, what you wanna do...

Dave Edmonds smacked the table with the side of his fist. "Look. Recognize this!"

For a while, maybe longer if I do...

Ryan looked at the photo on the phone. It was a car he didn't recognize. "What are you on about? What is this supposed to be?"

Don't you think the time is right for us to find
All the things we thought weren't proper could be right in time...

Edmonds took the phone, enlarged the photo, and put it back on the table. "Recognize that?" His voice was louder. "That's Sharon's car. And look where it's parked."

Ryan saw his building in the background. His irritation ratcheted up. "You followed Sharon?"

"She's my wife. I can do anything I want." His voice was even louder now. "And now I got proof she's been out fucking you at your place."

The song was no longer registering in Ryan's ear. "You've got to be kidding me. That's crazy. She dropped off the kids' cat."

Edmonds slurred. "What fucking cat you talking about?"

Ryan ignored the question. "She asked if I could take care of it for a bit. Until..." He knew it would only antagonize the guy, so he didn't finish the thought. "That picture isn't proof of anything."

Dave snatched his phone and stuck it in his jacket pocket.

"Bullshit. You've been fucking my wife and made her leave me. Now everyone is gonna know you're just like that whore of a wife of yours."

Before Ryan could push him and get to his feet, Dominic's voice came from behind the man. "That's enough, Edmonds. Enough of your loudmouth bullshit." Dominic pulled the man away from the table. Ryan could see Tammi was standing behind Dominic and three more faces filled the archway between the bar and seating area.

Dominic continued. "You're as full of shit as you were back in high school." Ryan was surprised at the vehemence in his voice. He'd never even heard Dominic raise his voice before.

Tammi set the two beers she'd been holding on the adjacent table and said, "Dave, you get out of here. You're not welcome here anymore tonight. And if you..."

Dave Edmonds ignored her and faced Dominic. "Well, well, look who's here. You okay with this son-of-a-bitch screw'in Sharon? Did you know she's going out to his place, leaving the kids alone? Or maybe you've been comparing notes about Lisa?"

Dominic looked as if the man had just sucker-punched him in the gut.

"What's the matter, Dominic? Doesn't he know you and Lisa were quite the item? Everyone knew you was screwing her. Hell, most of the guys did. I remember she gave a good blow job."

Dominic reached for Edmonds' jacket collar. Ryan was out of his seat and found himself trying to keep his friend from punching the man, even though he wanted to take his head off himself. David Edmonds had a couple of inches on Dominic and several on Ryan, but he had no fight in him. He backed off and headed out of the room, pushing past the group in the doorway. Dominic followed with Tammi right behind them.

Ryan sat down heavily. For a moment he thought Edmonds had

kneed him in the testicles before retreating. He was aware of the surrounding silence and a loud buzzing in his head and of the faces in the archway staring at him, pitying and mocking him at the same time, then quickly disappearing. He still wasn't sure if he could breathe.

He put his face in his hands, Edmonds' words pounding in his head. He once again envisioned himself standing outside the pub in Minneapolis, a similar numbing electric humiliation and fear jamming all the circuits connecting his body and brain. This time he entered. Like in the sitcom *Cheers*, the patrons called out. But instead of "Norm" – the TV character's name – they chanted "Cuckold, cuckold, cuckold..." Above the bar a neon electric sign flashed the word in time with the chants. He pressed his hands harder against his face to keep the anger, fear, and humiliation in his eyes from dribbling out.

"Hey, Mr. Davvis! What are you doin' here?"

The voice didn't make any sense.

Mr. Davvis, you okay? I seen Nala's dad in the front talking with the owner lady."

He could breathe now, so he did and then removed his hands.

"I seen Mr. Samilton when we came in. I didn't know you were here too."

Ryan looked. Ayden's face seemed genuinely glad to see him before turning concerned.

"You upset, Mr. D.?"

Ryan's first instinct was embarrassment. He didn't want the boy to see him like this. It was immediately replaced with a need to protect him from the site of his principal melting down in public.

"No, Ayden I'm okay. I just banged my knee when I sat down." He rubbed his knee for effect. "Brought tears to my eyes. It really hurt, but I think it's okay now. Thanks for asking. Why are you here?"

Ayden stepped aside and pointed to the booth against the wall nearest the archway. "Me and my mom and dad came for pizza. It's my birthday. Well, not my real birthday. That's on Sunday. But Dad's gotta leave again and drive a load to Arkansas in the morning and won't be back by then. So, we came for my birthday pizza tonight."

As Ayden explained, six guys came in and slid two tables together on the other end of the room.

"Ayden, quit bothering Mr. Davvis and come pick what you want on your pizza," Anna Quant said. Ryan was grateful all these people, especially Ayden, and his parents, hadn't been there a few...he realized he didn't know exactly how long it had been.

"When we pulled in, some nut job in a truck was speeding out and almost hit Mom's car. My dad wanted to go after him, but mom said no."

"Ayden!" a loud male voice cut through the other table's conversations. "Get your butt over here. You heard your mother." Ryan looked, but Mr. Quant was barely visible.

"I better go," said Ayden.

Dominic reappeared. Before sitting, he picked up the two beers Tammi had placed on the adjacent table. Sliding one to Ryan, he said, "Hi, Ayden. Come for some pizza?"

Ayden said, "Yeah. I was just telling Mr. Davvis it's almost my birthday. He hit his knee hard when he sat down. Even had tears in his eyes, but he's okay now."

Dominic looked at Ryan, quietly asking, "Are you okay?"

Ryan picked up his beer and didn't answer.

"Ayden! Now!" His father's voice was louder than before. Some of the guys from the other table turned to stare.

"Bye. See ya tomorrow." Ayden moved quickly to his parent's booth. The glances moved to Ryan before returning to their own conversation.

Dominic took a sip of his beer, waiting until Ayden was out of earshot before addressing what had just happened. "Edmonds is gone. I wanted to make sure he didn't go after your car again, or my truck. Tammi's mom apologized and said she might just ban him from the place." He set his beer to the side.

"Ryan, that's not the way it was with Lisa." He lowered his voice and sought to make eye contact with Ryan who was staring at a neon beer sign in the window. "Everything he said was crap. He's just pissed off at Sharon leaving and everyone on her side."

Ryan locked eyes with Dominic but kept his true feelings out of his voice. "Not everything. Not everything," he repeated. "I'm not that blind, Dominic. Ever since I got here, I could feel people looking and judging. I figured it was partially because of Lisa getting shot. But I also knew something happened with Lisa growing up here, and I wanted to… no, I *have* to find out what it was, why she…" Ryan lifted his beer glass to stop himself. He drank. When he glanced up and across the room, he saw Ayden looking at him. He put the beer down.

"Can you look me in the eye, Dominic, and swear you never…" He couldn't bring himself to say the word. Looking over again to the Quant's booth, he saw a waitress blocking Ayden's view. "…that you never had sex with Lisa?"

Truth – Lie. Was there an in-between? Holding Ryan's stare, Dominic quickly decided and said, "Once."

Ryan reached for his jacket. Dominic said, "What Dave said about himself and Lisa was bull. He and a lot of other guys at school wanted to date her. They'd get mad and pass around stories and were all too willing to believe each other."

"How did all that start? Why would they tell and believe those stories about her if there was no truth behind them?"

Dominic's face showed the same pain Ryan had seen when Dave Edmonds blurted out about him and Lisa. He held Ryan's gaze.

"Because they all wanted to believe and revel in the rumors about her and her uncle."

Ryan put his coat aside, no longer ready to get up and leave. "Walt told me about social services being involved, about possible sexual abuse and a restraining order against someone in the family, but he wouldn't say who. Just that the person was dead."

Dominic drank from his now room-temperature beer. "It was Lisa's mother's brother. He died when his car hit a tree out on the highway about a mile outside of Westown. It was never determined if it was an accident or not. He'd been drinking but didn't have enough in him to be drunk. And it was on a straight-away with dry weather."

Ryan asked, "When was that?"

Dominic had to think. "I'm going to say early March of '09. Maybe around two years after you and Lisa married." He watched Ryan's face change as he absorbed the information. All his worst fears when Ryan first applied for the job had come true. He felt sick at the thought of being part of the cause for Ryan's pain.

He watched Ryan's face. His features seemed to be losing their battle against... what? It seemed as if he was being chewed on by his past, present, and future, and there weren't many more ways a man can be eaten. Why did God engineer people in a way nobody could figure them out? He didn't know what else to say. Kate had reminded him before he came tonight that listening didn't require always knowing what to say. But he felt he had to say something anyhow.

"When you asked me to meet you tonight, I assumed it was about what you asked me a bit ago about Nala and your Black students back in your Minneapolis school. I even talked some with Kate about it... you know trying to wrap my own head around the idea."

Ryan stood and put his coat on. "Maybe another time, Dom. Funny," He zipped the coat. "Walt and I were just talking about being able to accept whatever comes next. Well, I'm not sure I am. I sure wasn't ready for tonight. Thanks for being honest. I'm sorry I ruined your night. I'll see you tomorrow. I'll pay on the way out. After all, this was my idea."

Ayden caught Ryan's eye as he walked past. "See you tomorrow, Mr. D. I hope your knee gets better."

Ryan paused for a second before he remembered his lie. "Thank you, Ayden. See you tomorrow. Good night, Anna." He was about to walk away but instead turned to Ayden's father. "You've got a real good boy there, Mr. Quant. And he's smart too. You should be proud of him."

48

Dominic heard the usual crackle of static as his two-way radio came to life.

"Are you in your office, Dom? Over."

"I'm here, Sharon. What's up? Over."

"Are you alone, I've got something to tell you before the morning busses arrive. Over."

"No one's here. I'm just looking over the additional bus assignments for next week. I've got something for you too. Over."

No response came. Dominic checked to make sure he hadn't accidentally turned off his device. "Sharon, are you there? Over." He was repeating the question when Sharon came through the door and quickly sat on the chair in front of his desk.

"Ryan knows you dated Lisa." Her breathing was rapid from dashing from the front office and the urgency she felt about her message. She raced on. "He said Walt had innocently mentioned it when he was up there last weekend. He asked me why you'd never told him. I told him the truth, that if you hadn't, it was because you didn't want to make things awkward between you two about something from that long ago. He didn't seem upset, so I kind of forgot about it and then felt guilty I hadn't called you right away... and then I felt like I'd be betraying him if I did."

She stopped. Dominic could see the concern, guilt, and "I'm sorry" written across her face. Having confessed, Sharon finally took a breath. Then seeing a look of distress on his face, she started again. "I'm sorry, Dom. I should have..." Her words came to a halt when Dominic held up a hand and vigorously shook his head.

"You have nothing to apologize for. If anything, I owe you an apology for putting you in that situation. But I already know he knows. We talked last night."

The look on Dominic's face scared Sharon. "Oh my God, what happened?"

"I was going to tell you after school so you wouldn't worry about this all day."

As if he was quickly and gently as possible ripping a bandage from her body, Dominic briefly described what had happened the previous night at Sophie's. How he'd gone to meet Ryan, thinking he wanted to talk about another matter. How he'd arrived just as Dave was shouting about a picture on his phone and accusing Ryan and her of...the only word he could bring himself to use was "hooking up." Dominic jumped ahead to what her husband then told Ryan, that lots of guys had been with Lisa. He included Dave's comments about people assuming and gossiping about himself and Lisa having sex the whole time they were together. He left off the details about the brief scuffle.

"That son-of-a bitch!" Sharon's quiet words vibrated with more anger than if she'd screamed them. Her face turned ashen, and her eyes watered as she repeated, "That son-of-a bitch!"

"Sharon?" Dominic's voice carried the weight of his concern. He knew how embarrassed and vulnerable she must be feeling. They'd reassured each other that her husband wouldn't make public accusations. Being the one to tell her they'd been wrong made him feel as sick as he had last night telling Ryan what he had.

She folded her hands together on his desk but didn't say anything. In the silence, the sounds of students entering the building and flowing down the halls increased until it breached Dominic's door. "Oh my God!" Sharon leaped up. "I've got to get back to the office."

Dominic also stood. "Try not to worry. Dave was drunk and..."

She cut him off. "I've got to get back..." She hurried out the door.

Dominic could only imagine the mix of emotions coursing through her veins. He wished he had beaten the shit out of her husband last night. His rage would have more than compensated for the man's size. He stood behind his desk taking a deep breath as waves of students and their sounds flowed past his door. The opposite of rage and anxiety was calm. He knew he'd not find it today. In the last thirteen hours, he'd shared information that had the potential to shatter the lives of two people he cared about very much. He had no idea what to do. Hating the feeling, he rubbed his hands over his face, wishing he had some fixable thing to work on so he could get rid of this feeling of uselessness.

"Hi, Dad." Dominic uncovered his face. "Can I leave my books in here? I'm late, and I've got to get to gym class. I don't have time to go to my locker." Nala delivered the last words as she ran out his door. He moved his daughter's books from the corner of his desk to the chair Sharon had just abandoned a few minutes before. He sat back down and wished his meeting with Ryan last night had been to hear his questions and thoughts about Nala and his Minnesota students. He'd been curious to talk with Ryan about that, hoping maybe to get some insight and perspective. He'd even prepped some by talking with Kate. *Prepared – blindsided... Insight – confusion*. Just another day at the office lately.

49

Mrs. Berry was having her typical lunch at her desk: a small apple, carrot sticks, and half a turkey sandwich on a bagel thin. Except for food, she wasn't a half-of-anything type of person. When she took something on, she was fully in. Always had been. Even as a kid back on the family farm, she had helped out every way she could even though, unlike her brother who loved animals and farm work, she couldn't wait to leave farm life behind.

She absent-mindedly took a bite of her sandwich and reread the email she'd just composed. She diligently sent each student's parents a positive note at least once every few weeks. Stienboek High did not have the funding luxury to hire separate specialists to work with students with learning disabilities and behavioral disabilities. Like some of her colleagues, Kim Berry was cross-categorical, meaning she was licensed to work with the spectrum of issues that special education students presented.

Over her career at Stienboek, she'd seen the student mix tilt from majority Learning Disabilities to majority Behavior Disabilities. She rarely shared her hypothesis on the cause of the shift. It was what it was. The fact was, she enjoyed working with the kids with behavioral issues more. When they were able to focus and attend to their school work, they often were rather bright and quick learners. Her mission was to help them learn, assimilate, and increase their ability to make good choices. Not an easy task considering the various classroom environments they were exposed to each day.

As Kim Berry knew, most of them had had enough trauma and life events go wrong in their young lives to make appropriate reasonable choices the most ubiquitous goal in their collective IEPs.

She also believed her students' poor choices were often not actual "choices" but entrenched reactions that put the kid into a fight or flight modality. Unlike most teachers, or parents, Mrs. Berry was able to usually not take a student's behavior as a personal affront, but rather as an opportunity to understand the triggers that initiated the behavior. Incidents were an opportunity to help the student understand what was going on inside their heads. As she saw it, her job was to help them learn to cope and eventually re-wire those behaviors. This made her an empathic person and teacher. However, she was not a pushover. She made it absolutely clear to each student that, difficult as it might be, their disability would not be accepted as an excuse for bad behavior or laziness. It was both their and her responsibility to work on overcoming the obstacles. When called for, she didn't hesitate to contact parents to discuss discipline issues.

She hit SEND, picked up a slice of apple, and looked up to see Ayden Quant enter her room with his lunch tray in hand. "Ayden, why are you here this time? What is it you need?"

"I was hoping I could eat in here and start my social studies project," he said. His closed smile always made it hard for her to resist his natural charm when it surfaced.

"When is the project due?"

"In two weeks." He set his tray on one of the raised desks but didn't attempt to sit yet.

"Two weeks?" she asked. "You want to start an assignment that far ahead of schedule? Are you turning over a new leaf?"

Mrs. Berry doubted the new leaf theory and added, "Did something happen in the cafeteria or a class this morning?"

"No. I just want to get started on this."

She assumed something had happened but also didn't want to discourage his willingness to start on the assignment. "Okay, you can eat and work here, but you need to do it quietly. I need to think."

Ayden plopped himself up on the stool which, when he was standing, came to his waist. He took a bite of his sloppy joe and asked, "What are you thinking about, Mrs. B.?"

Without looking at him, she said "Remember. Work quietly, or back to the cafeteria."

Ayden's question, however, made her realize her mind had slipped back to Tuesday's staff briefing when she and Mrs. Zowak had shared their information with the teachers. While wrapping up, someone had said something about Mr. Davvis and Sharon. Her first inclination had been to call out the person, but Mrs. Zowak had beaten her to it.

She'd known Sharon since her student days. As a girl, Sharon had stood out as a friendly and kind kid. Mrs. Berry also liked Ryan and appreciated that he was even better with special education students and programs than Walt Hannig had been. He seemed to have the special-ed chip and understood the difficulties they faced. He made a point during orientation meetings to remind all classroom teachers they were required to provide the modifications called for in the IEPs.

The rumor linking the two of them was unprofessional. It was also disturbing because she knew Sharon had moved out of their house with her kids. Of course, there were also the rumors about Ryan's wife. Mrs. Berry had only had the slightest contact with Lisa in sundry freshman classes back then. Her students had always kept her mind more than occupied, and she'd never paid attention to rumors about other students.

When these memories had run their course, she looked up. The boy was staring at her. "Ayden, what's up with you?"

"Do you miss, Allan?" he asked.

"Yes. Do you?" she asked.

"I guess. I mean I've known him all my life. I know he got me in trouble on purpose a lot, like you told me, but he was funny, and I think he liked me more than anyone else here."

"More than anyone?"

"Well, maybe you like me more." The boy blushed, realizing how that might have sounded. Mrs. Berry was certainly older than his parents.

"I miss him too, Ayden. He didn't deserve what happened."

"Do you think he did it on purpose?"

"I don't know, Ayden. What I do know is that you tragically lost a friend, and you're sad. That's normal and natural. Have you talked with Mr. Powells about it some more since that day?"

"Yeah, I mean yes, we've talked more. I know now it wasn't because of me."

"That's important you know that." She reemphasized the point. "I'm very glad you realize that."

Ayden thought a moment, then asked, "You know Nala? Mr. Samilton's daughter? She said that to me too."

"That was very kind of her. I didn't know you two were friends."

"She's not a girlfriend or anything." He was thinking about Nala calling to check on him the other day and about when she had come and found him that night. "We're not going out, but we talk a little."

"Well, it sounds like she's as helpful and nice as her dad is."

"You know how she's Black?" He knew that sounded stupid, so he quickly said, "Lately it's like she's lonely, even though she has lots of friends." Then he was stuck. He had no idea what to add to that.

In a lot of ways, Mrs. Berry could read Ayden's mind better than he did. She could see he was walking around a serious idea but didn't know how to get to it. She also remembered what Ayden had said to Nala back in the fall. She was sure he hadn't meant it as a racial slur. She was also sure trying to help him unpack his thoughts now would take a lot more time than they had.

She looked at the clock. "You're a deep thinker, Ayden. And a good person. But for now, you need to take your tray back and get your stuff for sixth period. I'll see you last period, and don't forget to bring your math."

50

Sharon glanced at the time. She swiveled her chair to look down the hall toward Ryan's office. Fridays at 12:30 usually found Ryan eating lunch in the faculty lounge unless he was tied up with something or someone, as he was now. All morning, she'd had the feeling he was avoiding her. He'd been using the other hall entrance rather than passing through the front office area. After what Dominic had told her about last night, she assumed she knew why. She also knew she needed to talk with him about it, to judge how her husband's accusations had affected him. She wanted to tell him it was all bullshit.

This last point had kept her from seeking him out earlier and forcing him to talk to her. Each time she'd heard him back in his office, she froze, knowing she couldn't honestly tell him they were *all* lies. Only mostly. She'd heard some of the second and third-hand rumors back during the two years her high school career overlapped with Lisa's. Back then, Stienboek was too small not to hear at least some of that kind of gossip. And because of Lisa's close friendship with her cousin Toni, Sharon had learned some things that few others knew.

Toni loved Lisa. They had been close throughout their teens, loyal and protective. But when Toni's concerns for Lisa overwhelmed her, she'd sometimes let something slip, and Sharon picked up hints about what was happening. She'd never pried, and she never shared any of her guesses with anyone. Not with friends, or her parents, or later with her husband. Not even when other gossip seemed to confirm her guesses.

She had just refocused on her work when Kim Berry emerged from Ryan's office and headed out the door. "Bye, Kim," she said to the woman's back. At the last second, as the glass door swung shut, Mrs. Berry did turn and give her a quick wave before hurrying back toward her room. That wasn't at all like Kim's friendly demeanor. It reinforced the sense of dread already churning Sharon's stomach. She decided she needed to act. Reaching his closed door, she looked through the narrow-slit window. Ryan was staring out his window. She made up her mind, knocked, and entered.

Ryan turned his chair toward the sound while his swirling mind added up the recent onslaught of revelations. A total needed to be reached – summed up and faced. He ticked off each: Dave Edmonds' accusation, the faces in the archway at Sophie's listening to the charges of adultery Edmonds flung at him, the photo of Sharon's car with his building looming in the background. Adding in what Kim Berry had just told him, the total was considerable, possibly sufficient to cost him his job.

But it was the sum of the other things that he feared more. Beginning with his need to discover Lisa's past, find why and what had made her suddenly seek sex with other men. Added to that was Walt's comments about Dominic's and Lisa's relationship, confirmed by Sharon. And, of course, Dave Edmond's coup de grâce last night, that everyone, including both him and Dominic, had had sex of some sort with his wife back in high school. Ryan feared that when he totaled all these things and added everything together, the emotional and visceral tally might cause him to explode in a ball of flame. He pictured the monk that still lived in Walt's Vietnam memories.

His last thought before Sharon's appearance and voice brought him back to the present moment was that, unlike Quảng Đức, he knew he'd be unable to meet the eyes of those gathered to witness his conflagration with the accepting gaze of one willing to face what was going to happen.

Ryan focused on Sharon standing in front of him. He assumed the concerned look on her face, was caused by the vacant look on his. Her words seemed far away and only gradually pierced his consciousness.

"I'm so sorry, Ryan. I know about last night. Dom told me what David said. I really didn't think he would or could stoop that low. I know why he wants to hurt me, but I can't understand why he'd go after *you*."

The effort to keep the anger and exasperation evident in her eyes out of her voice strained her throat. "I should have just stayed. Not put you, not put the kids, through this. I should have stayed and prayed he drove into a tree coming home drunk or just dropped over from..." She looked stricken. "I can't believe I just said that!" She held herself rigid, feeling that if she continued or moved, she'd break.

Her rush of contrition refocused Ryan. Seeing her trying so hard to hold it together, apologizing for her asshole husband, and expressing concern for his worthless ass, shifted something somewhere inside him. He raised himself straight, which allowed him to take a full breath, maybe the first one since last night. He stood and, taking her lightly by the arm, seated her at his work table. Then, unlike the last time when Dominic had unexpectedly appeared, he seated himself facing the door. He folded his hands on the table surface and was surprised to find his body again under his control.

"There is no need to apologize for David, Sharon." He silently considered how much he cared for her. "But I also need you to know that Kim Berry just told me that someone said they saw us hugging the other morning. Kim has no idea to what extent, if any, it's been picked up by the rumor mill, but she thought I should know. I explained to her that the brief hug was a simple expression of support, and she should feel free to tell that to anyone who might bring it up." Wanting to lighten the mood, he added, "I also told her to punch out anyone who brought it up." The remark brought a subdued grin to Sharon's face.

"What are we going to do?" she asked. "What if David, or someone else, says something to the kids?" Fear was back in her eyes.

"You – we – haven't done anything wrong," Ryan reminded her. "From what I understand, most everyone knows about Dave's drinking. They know how hard you've tried to make it work, and they're not going to believe him over you. The kids are old enough to know you haven't, and wouldn't, do anything like that and that their dad is an alcoholic who hasn't been much of a father for some time."

Ryan hesitated a moment. "But there's something else you should know. Dave must have followed you the other night when you brought Hamilton to my place. He had a picture of your car in front of my building. Saying that was proof we were... you know. It doesn't mean anything, and I told him why you'd stopped by. Do you know what he said?" Her eyes widened. "He asked, 'What f-ing cat?'"

Sharon shook her head. "Sad but figures."

"Anyhow, you have absolutely nothing to be ashamed of." He left himself out of the equation. "You'll have to decide if or when to tell the kids what he's threatening. The same goes for anyone else you think needs to know."

She felt better knowing what had been said. She was grateful to Kim Berry for warning Ryan about possible rumors and would thank her herself this afternoon.

But she knew the other matter, the stuff her husband had said about Dominic and Lisa and others, would cause problems. The thought of David saying he'd had sex with Lisa nauseated her, even though she knew he was lying. But for Dom and Ryan, she feared the assertion had placed a landmine between them waiting to detonate. She didn't recall having ever heard salacious rumors about Dom and Lisa. If there'd been, she'd have gotten some inkling from Toni. It had to be just another lie David was using to lash out. If Ryan had asked about the accusation, she could only say that as far as she knew it wasn't true. Since he didn't, she hoped the two men had talked it out last night.

"Thank you. I'll have to think about that."

She was relieved the dazed despair she'd seen in his face was gone. His body seemed to have relaxed. She was aware her own had also. "I'm still sorry David has tried to drag you into this. I'm sure everyone knows you're not the kind of guy to be having affairs with secretaries."

She stood to go. "I better get back out there, and you probably haven't had your lunch yet." Ryan rubbed at some wrinkles that had suddenly appeared on his forehead. "You, okay?" she asked. Do you need some aspirin or something? I couldn't blame you after all you've been through since last night."

"No, I'm fine. Thanks though." He stood. "But we better stay away from 'thank you' hugs from now on."

Sharon gave him a real smile and left.

Ryan went back to his desk and woke up his monitor. As he waited for the screen to come back to life, he wondered if his gut had been right in telling him not to ask Sharon about Dominic and Lisa's sex. He didn't want to put her on the spot again like he had when he asked about the two of them dating.

"Mr. Davvis, do you have a minute?"

He recognized Mrs. Zowak's voice without looking up. He stopped himself from asking "What Now!" Instead, he managed a polite, "What's up, Bernadette?"

"There was a comment made about you and the referendum after school on Tuesday when Mrs. Berry and I were briefing the teaching staff about our discussion with Mrs. Demian and board members."

Ryan was about to interrupt her to explain Mrs. Berry had already informed him, but she characteristically pressed on. "Someone, I won't mention names, but you wouldn't be surprised I'm sure – seemed to think that just because you are working with the referendum support group, you should have been able to include a raise in the referendum. I'm sure the person knew better, but I reminded him and everyone else that's not the way these things work. I don't want to take up your time. I just thought you should know."

"Thank you, Bernadette, for the heads-up... and for looking out for my back. I truly appreciate it."

Zowak said, "I'm sure we agree there's been enough tension around here in the last couple of years. We don't need petty sniping or controversy. Have a good weekend, Mr. Davvis."

"And, you too, Mrs. Zowak," Ryan said as she left.

That both Mrs. Berry and Zowak had cared enough to share their concerns was heartening. But when he added their warning to his 'what-else-can-go-wrong' list, his interior voice silently yelled, "JESUS FUCKING CHRIST!"

51

Ryan pulled into the lot. He parked facing the restaurant entrance wondering if he'd recognize Toni. It had been almost six years since he'd last seen her at his wedding. Except for Lisa's parents, Toni had been the only one of Lisa's family she'd invited to the small event. She hadn't brought a plus-one. She'd stayed at the motel with Lisa's folks. He assumed they had separate rooms. He recalled Lisa visiting them the following day before they headed home to Edenton. What he remembered most about Toni was her easy quick smile, friendly round face, a tendency to talk and see humor in weird places, and, at least back then, she'd been a blond.

Last Friday in his office, he had sensed Sharon's relief not to be asked about the veracity of her estranged husband's accusations, especially about Lisa's time with Dominic. But he had questions and needed answers. So, before Sharon had headed home with her kids who had walked over from the nearby elementary school, he'd asked about contacting Toni, saying he hoped to see what she might share. Sharon had hesitated for an awkward moment before agreeing to check with Toni over the weekend.

Sharon texted him the number on Sunday. He'd called that evening. Toni was friendly but wouldn't discuss Lisa on the phone. She suggested meeting the following Sunday morning, but not at the house where Sharon and the kids were staying or at her home in Green Bay. Her wife slept in on Sundays. "How about the Perkins on

Oneida Street, 8:00 a.m.?" He readily agreed knowing his anxiety would be hard to keep in check for a full week.

As it turned out, he'd been plenty busy to keep himself from fretting – except at night. He'd told Sharon about the meeting when she asked. He and Dominic hadn't crossed paths during the week, but he was sure Sharon had told him. He couldn't think of any reason why she shouldn't. Still, it created a sense of jealousy and added to his sense of being on the outside.

Having been awake since 5:00 a.m., two hours before sunrise, Ryan was early. He left the engine and defroster running to ward off the cold and keep the snow falling from the dark gray sky from obstructing his view. There'd been slush on the highway but not much traffic. While he waited, he revisited the thoughts he'd been trying to sort out since their phone call. His mind slipped back into agonizingly familiar territory, trying to imagine what might have happened and what the truth was about Lisa back in high school. As much as it hurt, he now knew that abuse and social services had been involved. Of course, he also had the accusations Dave Edmonds had publicly thrown in his face.

Toni arrived in a Chevy Avalanche. Through the swipe of her wipers, Ryan recognized her, blond hair and all. He turned off his car and went to greet her as she stepped down. For an awkward moment, he didn't know if he should hug, offer his hand, or just thank her for coming. She smiled and gave him a quick hug then nodded toward the door. They waited to be seated without talking. After being escorted to a booth, they ordered coffee and water, agreeing they needed a few minutes to decide. Ryan used the time trying to decide where to start. Once the waitress returned with the drinks and had taken their order, Toni took the initiative. "How are you, Ryan?"

He set his cup down. "I'm fine. Busy, especially with the referendum coming up, but fine. How about ..."

She smiled and interrupted. “I don’t vote in Edenton; sorry, I can’t help there. But hey, good luck getting money out of all those folks who are still mad that the schools consolidated.” Without missing a beat, she continued. “I’m sure you’re busy, Ryan... but fine? I don’t think you’d have called me if you were fine.” Her tone wasn’t hostile or aggressive, just matter-of-fact overlaid with a dab of empathy.

“I admit I was thrown a bit when you ended up at Stienboek. From what Sharon said, I wasn’t the only one. I don’t usually read the Edenton paper anymore. Sharon is my link nowadays. Her and that old house I inherited from weird Uncle Simon. I wanted to burn or at least sell the place. No way I’d ever live there. But Ginny – Sharon said she told you I’m married to a woman, right? – Ginny talked me into renting it. Then, with all the development down there, we were going to sell, but the recession hit so we were waiting until the market turned around. Anyhow, I’m glad I had it, and that it came empty just before Sharon finally left that creep David.” She paused long enough to lock eyes, then returned to her original point. “But when you got hired, I thought I might hear from you before now.”

Ryan took advantage of the pause to apologize. “I’m sorry, Toni. I should have at least sent a thank you for your sympathy card. I was a total wreck back then, barely functioning. I didn’t know how close you and Lisa had been.” He hadn’t meant to, but he kept explaining. “I didn’t have a service because I couldn’t face our friends, colleagues, family. Plus, I didn’t know how long it would be before the police would finish their investigation before they’d release... her body, and then...” He gathered the words he needed to finish his explanation. “I had the funeral house pick her up and do the cremation. I couldn’t live with her ashes. I offered them to her parents, but they wouldn’t take them. I scattered them into the Mississippi knowing they’d float under I-94. I guess, I was thinking of it as a kind of symbolic gesture, a bridge between her old life in Wisconsin and our life in Minnesota. Pretty pathetic and stupid, huh?"

"Actually," Toni said, "she might have found it appropriate, maybe even a bit humorous." She picked up her coffee.

Ryan looked out the window at the blowing snow. When he turned back, he plunged in. "Your former principal, Walt Hannig, told me social services got involved with Lisa in high school. He mentioned abuse and a restraining order involving someone in the family. He wouldn't say who. You just called your Uncle Simon weird. Weird how? Wasn't he with you the first time we met at a volleyball game at school? Was he the one in the restraining order?" Toni didn't look surprised by the questions.

"Ryan, let me ask you this. How badly do you want to know any of this stuff? What good would it do you to know any of it?"

Ryan glanced to make sure the waitress wasn't approaching and that no one was paying them any attention. He stared at her hands wrapped around her coffee mug. Her nails were trimmed and unpolished. "Our marriage, Lisa's and mine... well, some things happened toward the end. I've been consumed ever since by two thoughts. How much was my fault? And, if there was something in her past that may have, well... if something bad had happened. Something that might mean it wasn't my fault, at least all of it. I can't ..."

Ryan stopped himself. He'd never talked about, let alone admitted, this before to anyone. Doing so now, even with the one person who probably knew Lisa best, felt like he was cheating on her – again; like he had each time he'd been with Mrs. Ruppert. He looked at the snow again without registering that it was getting heavier. If he told Toni the whole truth about their marriage, he'd have to include the truth about himself. He wasn't ready to do that, even though, despite her frank and talkative nature, he felt sure Toni had always kept and protected Lisa's secrets. Even, it seemed, from Sharon.

He was equally sure she wouldn't be judgmental or surprised by anything he told her. But he wasn't ready. He couldn't look her in the eyes, couldn't say and accept what he'd have to say and accept about himself, about who or what he had become.

He tried a different way. "I'm confused, and there are lots of things I can't face yet from our time together. Hell, I can't even look at a photo of her that I keep locked in my desk."

Toni looked quizzical and gave her head a slight tilt. "What photo?"

"I took a picture at the ice cream place just moments before she went outside and... Anyway, when I had it printed, I found I couldn't face it. I deleted it from my phone and locked the print away."

"That's understandable, Ryan. Lots of people would have that reaction."

"It's not just because the picture was the last one. It's the mix of emotions I keep seeing in her eyes. I can't explain it. It was her idea to go for ice cream, to talk and celebrate, and then suddenly she got a text, and it was like something from her past had just crashed through the wall. I need the truth if I'm going to ever be able to face that picture... or myself. I need it for me and for her."

Toni's eyes conveyed her sympathy, then lightened as the waitress arrived. "Let's eat. Then we can talk."

For several minutes, they concentrated on their food. Eventually, Ryan asked why Lisa called her Antonia and not Toni like everyone else seemed to. She laughed, pushed her plate away, and wiped her mouth with a napkin.

"Surely, you noticed our Lisa could be a bit perverse. I hated being called Antonia. But it was a game for her. When we were kids, it was her way to tease and register her annoyance about her adoring younger cousin following her around. Yet she let me hang out, almost like a sister. Later, when I got to middle school and began to realize I was 'different', Lisa was the only one I could talk with about it. You know what she said? 'No shit, Antonia'. She'd known before I did, but she'd kept it to herself and was always supportive and protective. After that, calling me Antonia became a special connection between us."

When the dishes had been cleared and the coffee cups refilled, Toni returned to Ryan's initial question. "You're right, and Mr. Hannig would have known it was Uncle Simon when the school was notified of the restraining order. But he didn't know the whole story. He'd have had no way of knowing that if social services and the judge had known the whole truth, the restraining order should have been issued against Lisa, or at least against both of them."

Ryan was stunned, and his full stomach cramped.

Toni slowly stirred her coffee, thoughtfully watching the cream swirl through the black liquid until they came into balance. "Did Lisa tell you that her father called the day after Uncle Simon's so-called accident? Did you know the old S.O.B. accused her of being the reason why his brother-in-law ran his car into a tree, telling her he'd been distraught and haunted ever since Lisa had called social services, ruining his life? Saying 'poor Uncle Simon' felt humiliated?"

"No," Ryan's subdued voice betrayed his fear about what was being implied. "She didn't tell me anything about the accident. I only first heard about it from Dominic about a week ago. At the time, I didn't think to ask which uncle. I knew there were several."

He reflexively winced thinking back to that night at Sophie's and all he'd learned. The timing of all the events started to line up in his head. Lisa's father's call would have happened only a week or so before he'd suspected, and she'd admitted, to having sex with somebody. Stuck to that memory, like dog shit embedded on his sole, was the noxious assertion by Mrs. Rupert about Lisa and her husband Doug. He closed his eyes a moment to regain his balance. Ryan said, "Dominic also seemed to think the crash may not have been an accident."

It was Toni's turn to close her eyes. Ryan knew she was debating how much to tell him. She'd been caretaking Lisa's secrets for so long that he wasn't sure she'd be able or willing to let him in. He wasn't sure, even having come this far, if he wanted to be let in.

Having decided, Toni looked across the table at him. "I'm going to guess the 'things' you mentioned happening toward the end, occured during that spring and summer right after her dad's call. It would have had nothing to do with you. It's not your fault."

For a second, Ryan mistook Toni's voice for Lisa's as she uttered similar words from that ugly night when his heart, soul, and belief in himself as a man had collapsed and nearly died, leaving him crippled and adrift, clinging to and attempting to use her *"Please, just believe me, I love you"* as his only paddle.

A clatter of dishes brought Ryan back to the present. Toni's voice became her own again. "Lisa never dealt with what happened when we were kids and what it unleashed in her. I didn't know what to call it, but I was scared of it. I knew it was only a matter of time before it showed up again."

Barely able to take in what she'd already told him, Ryan made himself listen as Toni went on.

"I was still at Stienboek when she moved here to Green Bay to go to school and eventually teach K-4. But even before leaving Edenton, we'd been drifting apart. I think I was a constant reminder to her of what had happened. When she brought you to that volleyball game, I'll bet you didn't know she'd called me a few days before. She asked me to get Uncle Simon to come, but not tell him why. I couldn't believe it, and she wouldn't say why. I wasn't going to do it, but I could never say no to her."

Ryan shook his head to confirm he hadn't known.

"Uncle Simon was confused when she showed up. She hadn't seen or talked to him since she'd moved away. She made him sit in front of us so he could hear her go on about how much she loved you and how you'd allowed her to bury the past, including him, and everyone who had ever touched her only wanting sex and ignoring who she was and wanted to be. She wouldn't let up. I don't know if it was her final humiliation of him, or she just wanted him to hear she'd survived what she believed he'd caused her to be and to do."

Ryan held up his hand. "I need to know what happened with Simon."

Toni's eyes turned sad, almost scared. "You're sure?"

Ryan nodded, but only once.

Toni drank some coffee, glanced out the window, and then at the booths that were filling up around them. Her only concession to the after-church crowd was to lean in a little closer.

"As far back as I can remember, Uncle Simon was a very, very touchy-feely guy, if you know what I mean? Even around the family. But nobody ever said anything, so I didn't think he was a total perv.

"I had always thought he was slow, and now I wonder if he wasn't also manic-depressive. But whatever it was, it didn't take much to rile him up. Anyhow, at this point, I was in eighth grade, and Lisa was a sophomore. I was aware I found girls much more interesting than guys, and I guess I'd become less discreet than I probably should have been in such a small community.

"One Saturday, Mom sends me over to his house to bring him a pie she'd made. He offered me a piece and some milk. While I ate, he starts rubbing my shoulders then suddenly starts telling me how one of his buddies told him he'd heard I was a dyke. I'd heard the word, but wasn't sure exactly what it meant so, I asked. He told me, and I still remember saying, 'Yeah, maybe I am. So what?'

"Well, Simon got agitated, grabbing my pie away before I was finished. He threw it in the garbage, saying dykes are garbage, and it was probably a phase I was going through because I didn't know anything about men.

"Being young and stupid but also mad, I told him I thought guys and their dicks were gross. Next thing I know, he's got his erection in his hand, telling me if I suck it, I'll change my mind and become a 'real girl.'

"I know I should have been scared or run away, but instead I got this image of Pinocchio – remember, he wanted to become a 'real' boy – giving him a blowjob. I couldn't help myself. I just broke out laughing. I'm not sure what that says about me, but I couldn't stop.

"Anyway, that's when Lisa showed up and came into the kitchen and saw what was going on. Uncle Simon turns and puts his thing away and Lisa starts yelling at me. 'Antonia. You get out of here. Your mom sent me to get you and said you better get home right now.' So, we jumped on our bikes and left.

"I knew she'd seen Simon, so I stopped and told her he didn't do anything. That when I laughed at him, he'd shriveled up just as she'd come in. But Lisa was so angry. At first, I thought she was mad at me for laughing. Then I thought she was scared for me. Weirdly, later, I even remember wondering if she was jealous. She started ranting about how Uncle Simon was just like the asshole guys at school and even like her father who only praised her for being pretty but never smart, never nice or good at anything she did. She kept getting more and more upset and told me about the sick comments she'd get from some of the asshole guys at school: 'Nice boobs, Kames. Or, hey, Kames, you want to make me cums?'"

Ryan blinked back tears, then stared blindly out the window.

"I think that's enough, Ryan. You don't need to hear anymore."

He didn't reply. Toni tried to mitigate what she'd already told him. "The day after your wedding, when Lisa came out to the motel, we talked for the first time in a long while. She told me how she'd woke up that morning and snuck into the bathroom to vomit because she'd dreamt about you finding all this out. She said you'd be right to call her a slut and walk out, leaving her alone forever.

"She loved you, Ryan – so much. But it wasn't in her to *not* believe you could ever love her if you knew what had happened, what she'd done. I don't know why; but for whatever reason, Lisa accepted what others told her about herself. She didn't have the room or the tools to create her own identity until she moved away, got her degree, and started to teach – and met you. You gave her that space."

A noisy family of five began squeezing into the next booth. Toni said, "Let's pay and sit in my truck."

52

The ball descended from its high arc, slipping through the net, barely moving the strings, but making that beautiful soft swooshing sound every shooter loves. "Ha! Take that, Lang," Nala announced. She pretended to pass the ball to herself by bouncing it off the backboard while she shifted identities and continued to describe the play-by-play action to the non-existent crowd she imagines is still cheering wildly for her last shot.

"Langston Samilton takes the pass. He circles and comes to a halt at the top of the key in the very spot from which his brilliant, talented sister just launched her picture-perfect jump shot. Langston keeps his dribble low, moving the ball from one hand to the other. He steps back and jumps, releasing the ball from just in front of his face. It's up and...it's a touch heavy and bounces off the back rim. The buzzer sounds. That's H.O.R.S.E., Nala Samilton wins! She defeats her brother. The crowd goes crazy."

From the far end of the gym, Mrs. Shimone's voice hushed the fictional crowd in Nala's head. "I'm glad you won, Nala. But who is Langston Samilton? Is that a cousin?"

Nala executed a quick right-handed layup to stall for time. She rebounded her shot and faced her coach walking across the court toward her. They'd had an optional Sunday practice, and she'd thought everyone, including Coach Shimone had already left. "Oh, hi. I'm just killing time. Dad's working on some budget thing I think, and he wants to do some shoveling by the doors." She hoped the explanation had shifted her coach/gym teacher's attention from Lang.

"I was just doing budget stuff too. That's why I'm still here." She walked toward Nala with her arms extended. Nala passed her the ball. Coach stepped up to the top of the key from where she (and Lang) had just let it fly.

"You still got it, Coach," Nala praised as the ball went through the net.

"You know Nala, I've been thinking. You've gotten good with your left-hand dribble. I think it's time you start using it on layups too, so you're not so predictably always moving to your right." She held her hands out, and Nala hit her with a perfect chest pass, just as she'd been taught. "Okay, guard me." Coach Shimone took two quick steps toward the right side of the hoop. Nala stepped up and planted her feet to take the charge. It never came. Suddenly the ball was in Coach's left hand, and she laid it up and in before Nala could react.

"Wow! Hashtag, I'm impressed. Show me that again," Nala said.

Coach started to repeat but stopped as she planted her left foot and bounced the ball between her legs to her left hand. She repeated that twice more before continuing in for the layup. "I've seen you practicing dribbling between your legs. So, let's combine the moves. Here, you try." She bounced the ball to Nala. "Try it slow."

Nala did. She moved the ball correctly, but her left hand lost control, and she missed the layup.

"Again."

On the third try, the ball came off the backboard at the correct angle and fell softly into the cylinder.

"Good. Now I want you to practice that, but – and I mean this. I don't want to see you use it in a game until you can do it eighteen out of twenty times, *with* someone guarding you. Got it?"

"Sure, Coach. Thanks."

"One more thing." Coach Shimone took the ball, dribbled three times in place, then tucked it under her arm. "You know Brin will graduate this year. It will make sense for Jen to move from the two-guard to point. She knows the varsity system and can run the offense, but that means they'll need a shooting guard."

Nala couldn't believe what she was hearing. She was excited but equally afraid Coach was about to ask her if she'd be willing to move to varsity next year. She was comfortable being good among her age peers, but being the youngest on the varsity would make her stick out in several new ways. Plus, she didn't have any real friends among the older girls. She knew their names but not them. They certainly did not know her. She wasn't sure anyone did anymore. She'd be an outsider. The youngest and the only ... She didn't form the word but knew exactly what the word would be.

"So, what do you think, Nala? Should I let them know you're interested? I know we'd have to talk to your mom and dad. See how they feel."

Nala realized Coach was asking her the question. "I don't know, Coach. That would be scary. I'm not sure I'm ready, and I'd be leaving my friends."

Coach Shimone dribbled a few more times. "Well, take your time, Nala. No one needs an answer right away. As far as your friends go, many of them will move up as juniors in two years; so eventually, you'll be back together. Talk to your folks. Think about it. But I want to suggest one thing for you to consider." Coach paused and dribbled the ball once before continuing.

"Be honest about what kinds of things you'll let get in the way of going after something you deserve." She bounce-passed the ball over to Nala. "The thing about success, about dreams, is that it's a lot like shooting baskets. Sometimes you get blocked by an opponent, and you have to find a way to work around her. That's one thing. But if you don't take the shot because you're afraid... Well, that's how regrets get made."

She held out her hands. Nala handed her the ball, and she shot. It hit the front rim. "Also, remember, we – and by *we*, I especially mean girls – don't always get a second shot at being who we were meant to be."

She picked up the ball and handed it to Nala. "I'll see you tomorrow. I hope your dad is done soon. It's still snowing out there." She turned and headed back across the floor. "Oh, and I hope I meet Langston sometime. Introduce me if he ever comes to a game."

Nala practiced the new move a dozen times, making four of them. When she stopped, she looked around to make sure she was alone this time before asking her question out loud. "Well, Lang. What do you think?"

She repeated the layup move, this time losing control of the ball as she went to lay it up. As she watched the ball roll toward the bleachers, a response appeared in her mind.

You mean about the cross-over?

You know what I mean. About varsity next year.

She got the ball and tried again. This time the ball bounced off her leg. She raced after it and returned to her position at the top of the arc before his answer appeared.

You wanna be A Raisin in the Sun?

Nala stood still and just dribbled, shifting the ball from her right hand to her left. She both liked and hated when Lang answered her questions with a question or reference to things she didn't get. This time, he'd done both. She knew it was the title of something but didn't know how she knew that or what the something was.

"What the heck does that mean?" she mumbled out loud; a bit frustrated.

Look it up. Then think 'bout how you gonna introduce me to Coach.

53

When they got out to Toni's truck, Ryan cleared the snow off her windshield. She got in and started the Avalanche and cranked the defroster. As soon as he was in, Ryan blew a long warm breath into his cupped cold hands and asked, "How much does Sharon know? Does Dominic know all this?"

"All Sharon knows is that Lisa and I were close back then. When we got to Stienboek, she'd sometimes hear things about Lisa and ask if she was okay. Sharon is a sweet girl who married the drunk I told her not to marry. But she can't help herself, she always sees the best in everyone." Ryan dreaded Sharon finding out how thin the best of him was.

"As for Dom, I'm not sure. I can't even remember the last time I saw him. But I know I've never talked to him about any of this." Toni redirected the heat to both the windshield and their feet.

"Dom was a senior when Sharon and I were freshmen. All I knew about him was from what Lisa shared when we did talk, which by then was less and less. He'd have heard the rumors about her before they started going out about halfway through her junior year. I don't remember how or why they started dating. But I do know Lisa thought Dom was different from the other guys. He didn't try to screw her or use her to enhance some fucked up male ego stud thing. He'd tell her she was a good person. He was excited when she made the honor roll for the first time that year and that she was a starter on the volleyball team. He came to a lot of her matches and went out of his way to treat her well, even at school." Ryan felt a little better hearing this part of the story.

"Sadly, that confused her. I think Dom upset her worldview about men which had festered and then exploded the year before with the Uncle Simon thing and led to her baiting her abusers and throwing them back like undersized fish." Toni laughed. "That wasn't necessarily meant as a double entendre."

She turned to Ryan. She saw the pain radiating from him, which his forced grin couldn't hide. She reached over and smoothed the creases on his face.

"Look. That's the main part of the story. There's no need for more details. Lisa loved you. Whatever happened between you two wasn't your fault, so quit blaming yourself. My cousin was broken. I don't know if she was born that way or got broke along the way." Toni stopped to think. "Maybe, I was to blame. Maybe she wanted to protect me from Uncle Simon and then wanted revenge for my sake and got caught up in it and ended up breaking herself. I don't know. But I'm sure she didn't want to hurt you, though I think she may have known all along that eventually she would."

"She had an affair." The words rushed out of Ryan. "Maybe some one-night stands. I don't know. She didn't try to hide it or lie. She said she loved me, and it wasn't because of me. I tried to be modern, understanding, reasonable, give it time, and make excuses for her. But it hurt too much, and I tried to get even by doing some things I'd never even considered before." He stopped. His chest was tight. He wasn't sure if he was breathing or not. He didn't care.

Toni again gently ran her palm across his features. Her thumb wiped away a tear caught in the crease next to his eye. "Ryan, we both know that particular pain, the type of pain that comes with humiliation and can overwhelm the real us. I'm sure Lisa knew it too, and it's what created and fueled her monster, and it may have killed Uncle Simon."

They sat for a full minute listening to the heater blowing the warm air. Toni took Ryan's hand, and, as kindly as she could, said, "I want to believe Lisa would have survived, would have been faithful forever with you. But Ryan, if I'm honest, I can't. If Uncle Simon hadn't sought his revenge on her by driving into that tree, I think something else would have happened."

Ryan knew he had to reject the idea. To accept it would be to accept fate over choice, revenge over love. But needing to get to the end of this, he locked the thought away for another time and forced a question through his considerable fear of hearing the answer.

"What did she do to your uncle that would have led him to do that? You said she hadn't been near him for years, except for that one volleyball game. Was he that weak-minded?"

Toni turned the fan down a notch. She wanted to say she didn't know the details. But she also didn't want to lie to him. When she didn't respond, Ryan's pain and frustration and other feelings he couldn't identify demanded an answer.

"Damn it, Toni. I've got to know it all. I don't know why, but If I don't, I'll never...." He couldn't find the words so, he pleaded with his eyes.

"Are you sure?" she gently asked.

Being this close to knowing it all, Ryan hesitated, but he knew if he didn't hear everything now, he'd never have the courage to ask again. He nodded.

"That day, after she'd found me laughing at Uncle Simon and yelled at me to leave, Lisa biked back to his place. Then later that night, she stopped at my house. We sat in the dark on an old swing set in the yard. She described what she'd done. I was shocked and scared both for her and for myself. I was sure we'd both get in trouble. I told her our parents would find out and never believe our side. I knew, even if I said something, I was only in eighth grade and was already being called a dyke, so who was going to take my side if I said anything?

"Lisa claimed Simon liked it too much and was too scared to say anything. I made her promise never to do it again. I thought it was over. At the time, I believed she had done it for me, and she'd let it go. I was wrong."

Toni then rapidly and matter-of-factly told Ryan Lisa had threatened Simon, saying she'd tell the family and everyone else what he'd done – that Toni would back her up. How she'd unbuttoned herself, telling him to expose himself again, then teased him until he'd lost control and ejaculated all over himself. She'd laughed, made him stand there with his pants around his ankles, and then, without cleaning up, drive her to town for ice cream. She'd teased him with the ice cream cone on the way home until he came in his pants again. It was sexual jiu-jitsu, using his untamed libido against him.

When the harassment at school got to be too much, she'd go back to his house. Things escalated. She'd always call him a pervert and admonish him, saying if he didn't perform better, she'd have to tell everyone he'd been molesting her.

She discovered the same thing worked on the school bullies. She eliminated the middleman, literally leaving Uncle Simon with his shorts around his shoes and scared shitless she might still accuse him. It had become a game, and she'd discovered her monster. But because she only did it to the most foul-mouthed assholes, she thought it was a monster she could control.

Toni finished by explaining that one night Lisa came home with a bad bruise on her shoulder and told her parents Uncle Simon had grabbed her and bit her. "I heard my dad that night on the phone with Lisa's dad talking about how Lisa had called social services on Simon. Uncle Simon had denied it, but that was when the restraining order was issued."

Toni asked, "Do you mind if I smoke?" She opened her window halfway and lit up. After blowing the smoke into the cold air, she continued between puffs.

"Uncle Simon lost a couple of friends. But among his crowd, others found it hilarious to tease him about doing it with his niece – though I'm sure they never knew the true story. It never went any further, and it blew over in the family, most of whom thought Lisa had been out of bounds for being over there bothering poor Uncle Simon all the time." She smoked her cigarette while Ryan tried to swallow and digest the new details. He felt as if he was being spoon-fed nails.

"But Simon was never the same. He never again looked me in the face. He stopped his touchy-feely ways, drank more than ever, and little by little crumbled. Then the so-called accident happened. Since there was no actual proof to the contrary, it was eventually ruled an accident. But I didn't buy it. I'm sure Lisa didn't either, especially when her father called and laid that guilt trip on her."

Toni took another drag, tossed the cigarette into the slush on the ground, and exhaled the smoke through the window as she closed it. She turned to Ryan. "I'm trying to quit. Ginny hates that I smoke."

Surprised that he could make his throat and voice work, Ryan thanked her.

"That had to be hard for you to relive."

"Yeah. It is. But you hearing it for the first time has to be harder. I had no intention of telling you all this. But who knows? Maybe Lisa would have wanted me to. You're either a masochist or a brave man coming here and wanting to hear all this. But I know you're also a good man because Sharon told me you were, and so did Lisa. Now that you know the story, I'd like to believe you'll be able to prove Lisa's doubts about you and your love wrong and forgive her. Maybe even still love her like I do."

Ryan watched while the snow dropped its last few flakes on the hood of the truck before softly saying, "I'd like that too. But I can't promise. It's a lot. But thank you. At least now I have all the pieces. I'll have to see how they all fit together."

Driving home, he tried to contain all he'd learned in a tight ball and hold it at arm's length to keep from crying or puking. He was only partially successful. It helped when he began to consider whether he could trust William Powells enough to help. But visiting a local therapist could add more fire to the gossip and rumor mill. That was something he certainly didn't need.

54

After the first-period bell had rung, and the late stragglers disappeared behind classroom doors, a sudden almost startling silence filled the halls. The effect was similar to a way-too-loud radio suddenly being unplugged. Ryan headed to the district office to talk with Superintendent Demian. Keeping all he'd heard yesterday from Toni Kames out of his mind was like trying to hold back water from a broken pipe. He started across the cafeteria feeling like a man with a mouth full of fillings trying not to bite down on aluminum foil.

As he passed, he glanced at Dominic's open door and the darkness within, which meant he was somewhere else in the building. He thought about all he'd learned since they'd last talked. In retrospect, the one good thing that came out of that calamity at Sophie's was that it had led to his meeting with Toni.

Stepping coatless into the icy air, he broke into a trot to cover the still slushy two hundred yards to the administrative building that housed the superintendent's office, the director of pupil services, and the business and payroll staff. He said hello to the district secretaries and refocused on what he'd come to discuss.

He'd received a phone request from the local county League of Women Voters. They wanted to provide a short presentation to the seniors next month on the importance of voting and provide voter registration materials so that current eighteen-year-olds could register before the upcoming April 2nd election. The seventeen-year-olds would have the information as a reminder when they turned eighteen later in the year. They also offered to provide an overview of the function of local non-partisan elected officials at the county, city, town, and school board levels.

Three candidates had filed last January to run for two seats on the Edenton Area School Board. Two were incumbents. The challenger owned one of the two local hardware stores and campaigned on the premise that schools should be made more efficient and run like a business. While the talking point appealed to some – probably many – Ryan bristled at the idea of schools acting like for-profit factories turning out widgets.

Charles Templeton was in conversation with Liz Demian when Ryan knocked at the open door. They were discussing the Letters to the Editor from last Friday's paper. "Have you seen these?" Templeton held the paper up for Ryan to see.

"Not yet," Ryan answered. After they'd gotten married, Ryan had suggested to Lisa they subscribe to Edenton's local paper, but she'd been adamant she didn't want it in the house. But then, before his interview at Stienboek, Ryan began to read the online version to catch up on local issues. Now he read the paper each weekend. However, last weekend his mind had been way too distracted.

Templeton set the pages down saying, "Close the door, would you."

Ryan did and sat across the conference table from them. The board president slid the pages over to Ryan. "Look. We're only in mid-February, and already the lies are coming out. Look at this one." Templeton pointed, then he pulled the pages back and read. "Once again, the Edenton Area School District wants to pick the pockets of the hard-working public to line the pockets of their administrators and teachers..." Templeton kept his voice level and free of exaggerated inflection.

He pushed the paper back to Ryan who scanned it. "See who it's from?" Superintendent Demian said. "That guy lives just down the road from Mr. and Mrs. Marsh and works at his store. I can't believe he doesn't understand the referendum is for equipment and building repairs only and not for salaries or benefits."

Of the five printed letters, Ryan noticed that four were about the referendum: two against and two in favor. One of the two supportive letters was from a member of the pro-referendum group. He didn't recognize the other name. "At least we're starting to get some outside support," he said.

"True," Demian said. "But the letters against the referendum are twice as long and a lot more passionate than the pro-letters. It's no surprise. The No Vote is always going to be more energized and vehement. We can't expect people to get passionate about spending more of their tax money on schools. Unfortunately – and we knew this going in – the recession and the battlelines around Act 10 still play against us."

Ryan pushed the paper back across the table. "Lie or misinformation, either way, I'm sure many will believe it's true."

Superintendent Demian continued. "We expected there'd be some of this. That's why we scheduled the first Community Information meeting for as soon as we did. Next Monday we'll get a better sense of the concerns people have. Then we'll update our website and mail out a Q&A district newsletter. Also, the law may say we can't do anything other than give out information, but we can respond to misinformation. I'll draft a letter pointing out the factual inaccuracies and specifically point out what capital expenses can and cannot be used for."

The board president said, "We'll have to expect more of this. On the way in this morning, I spotted two more 'Just Say No' lawn signs sticking out of the snow."

The superintendent added, "I'll be speaking at the senior center later this week. I'm hopeful those invitations continue to come in."

A few minutes later, they turned to the League of Women Voters' request. Ryan explained the ask. It was the superintendent's call. She asked Templeton's opinion. He pointed out the obvious blow-back questions she'd get from some on the board and that the league had a reputation for being left-leaning. Ryan countered and pointed out that most high schools no longer offer an official civics class. The ability to weave that important information into other classes was hit-and-miss at best. Demian knew the local league president and vouched for her ability to present voter information in a factual and nonpartisan manner. She told Ryan she wanted to see all the information, slides, and handouts two weeks ahead of time, but he could go ahead and set it up.

55

Zoey returned to the lunch table and slipped Nala one of the cookies she'd just bought. "Here, Tuesday is oatmeal-raisin day."

"Thanks." Nala took a small bite and returned her attention to Lori who was jumping topics from the upcoming social studies test to something on her Facebook feed. When she took a second bite, a thought resurfaced. "Any of you ever heard of a book called *A Raisin in the Sun*?"

Her friends looked at each other, shaking heads. "Nope," Amy said. Zoey added, "Nice title though. Why? Something you're reading?"

"No." Nala wasn't about to explain, not even to her best friend, but she summarized by saying, "I don't even know if it's a book or what. The title popped into my head the other day. It felt familiar, like I'd heard it before, but I have no idea where or when." She held up the cookie. "Zoey just reminded me."

"You have a phone," someone said. "Look it up." She was about to do just that when Mr. Schmelzing walked past with his lunch tray heading for the teacher's lounge. Lori hailed him. "Hey, Mr. S. You ever heard of *A Raisin in the Sun*?"

He stopped and looked pleasantly surprised. "Absolutely. Why?"

"Nala just asked about it. She thinks she's heard of it before but doesn't know what it is."

Mr. Schmelzing turned to the group. "It's a great movie, but definitely before your time. It starred Sydney Poitier."

Several voices simultaneously asked, "Who?"

"Sydney Poitier was maybe the first Black actor to become a mega-star. I think he was the first to have starring roles as a lead character. Back in the early 1960s that was a real breakthrough."

Nala noticed he'd directed his response to her friends. She wondered if he was hesitant to look at her because of their last private conversation. When she looked back up, however, Mr. Schmelzing was talking directly to her. "You guys should get the video and watch it. It's a good story."

As Schmelzing finished, Ms. Snede was passing. One of the girls asked, "Hey, Ms. Snede. Have you ever heard of Sydney Poitier, or was he before your time too?"

"You saying I'm old?" Mr. Schmelzing joked with the girls.

"No way," Amy said. "We know you just dye your hair gray on purpose."

"Looks good, doesn't it?" he teased back.

Ms. Snede said, "Of course, I've heard of Poitier. He's an acting icon."

Mr. Schmelzing explained. "Nala was asking about *Raisin in the Sun*, and I was extolling the virtues of the movie."

"Actually," Ms. Snede said, "the movie is based on a play with the same name. Offhand, I don't remember who wrote it, but I do remember learning in college the title is from a famous line in a short poem called 'Harlem', but people sometimes call it 'A Dream Deferred.'"

While Amy hurriedly tried to probe Mr. Schmelzing about the upcoming test, Zoey turned to Nala. "There you go. We should get the video."

"Do you know who wrote the poem?" Nala asked as the two teachers turned to head off. Ms. Snede stopped. "I do, indeed. One of Harlem's most famous and one of my all-time favorite poets. Langston Hughes."

The teachers moved on, and the girls returned to their chatter. Nala returned to her cookie and didn't hear a word they were saying.

Riding home with her dad after school, Nala wondered if he had ever heard of Langston Hughes. She remembered their conversation from a while back about rap music when she'd pointed out she was Black, and he'd countered by saying she was half-white. The memory made her wonder if her question might be awkward. So, instead of asking about a poet – who she didn't expect he'd know – she asked, "Dad, we were talking today at lunch, and an actor named Sydney Poitier was mentioned. You ever hear of him?"

"Yeah," Dominic said, then tried to retrieve what he knew. "I know he was a famous movie actor from Grandpa and Grandma's time, maybe even sooner." Dominic suddenly realized where this might be coming from and decided to play along. "I'm pretty sure he was Black, wasn't he?"

"Yeah. That's what Mr. Schmelzing said." She embellished just a little. "He was telling us about some old movies with Black actors," adding, "After all, February is Black History Month, again." Not wanting to sound overly sarcastic, she didn't emphasize "again."

She decided she'd push on. "How about Langston Hughes?"

"Was he an actor?" Dominic suddenly remembered, "No, I think he was a poet. A Black poet? Right?"

"I'm impressed, Dad. Yes, he was a famous poet."

Dominic asked, "Is there a connection between those two? Sydney Poitier and Langston..."

He paused for just a heartbeat, making the connection to their conversation from a month ago. They'd been talking about Allan Sparks' suicide when she'd first mentioned Lang to him.

"... Hughes. Did his name make you think about your brother?" He glanced over to her.

"A little," Nala replied. "Mr. Schmelzing said Poitier starred in a movie called *A Raisin in the Sun*, and Ms. Snede, the new sophomore English teacher, said it was based on a Langston Hughes poem."

Dominic thought for a moment as he slowed down for their driveway. "*A Raisin the Sun* sounds familiar, but I don't know anything about Langston Hughes. You just taught me more Black history than I think I ever had at school."

He pulled up to the mailbox. Nala reached out to get the mail before they drove up the driveway. "If this is a famous movie, it's probably on video." He pulled into the open garage and cut the engine. "Why don't we get it? We can do a family movie night and watch it together?" The vision in his head of him and Kate with Nala between them watching the movie seemed perfect. He was already looking forward to it.

"That would be great, Dad. But Zoey and I were going to get it and watch it together."

Dominic's family movie night vision burst with a soft muffled *poof*, leaving a heart full of disappointment.

56

Ayden stopped outside the main office door and looked up and down the halls. No one in sight. Through the large windows, he could see Mr. Davvis looking over Mrs. Edmonds's shoulder at her computer. He liked that he saw them, but they weren't aware of his presence and wouldn't be until he decided to open the door. There weren't all that many things he had that kind of control over. It made him feel like a secret agent. Not being able to hear what they were saying was like watching television with the sound off. But you could still pick up on a lot of what was going on.

When Mr. D. leaned in and pointed to something on the screen, Mrs. Edmonds rolled her chair to the side and seemed to pay more attention to his profile than to whatever he was pointing at. Mr. D. suddenly stopped talking and turned his head to her. They looked at each other, but it didn't look like either of them was saying anything. This was boring. Ayden opened the door and went in.

Both adults turned to see him enter. Mr. Davvis looked a little embarrassed. He stepped away from her and greeted him. "Hello, Mr. Quant. How can I help you?" Ayden thought it was a little weird, but also kind of cool that Mr. Davvis sometimes called him and the other kids Mr. or Ms.

Mrs. Edmonds moved her chair back and said, "Ayden has an appointment. His mom called in this morning and said she'd pick him up at 1:30. You can have a seat, Ayden. Mom's not here yet."

Ayden said, "It's with Mr. Powells." He looked at Ryan. "You remember him, Mr. Davvis? From my IEP meeting?"

"I do," Ryan confirmed. "It was helpful having him there. He seemed to really know his stuff. If I remember right, you told me you liked him and thought he was helpful."

Ayden sat on one of the chairs beneath the hallway windows. "Yeah. He's okay."

"Well, have a good appointment, Ayden, and I'll see you tomorrow." Ryan walked back to his office.

After Mr. Davvis left, the only sound was the clicking of Mrs. Edmonds typing at her keyboard. She was fast. The phone rang, and Ayden listened to how friendly she sounded. She even joked with whoever she was talking to. An older kid came in while she was still on the phone. She called the girl by name, handed her something saying she was "good to go."

Mrs. Edmonds seemed to know every kid and parent. He'd never heard anyone complain that she was mean or bitchy. When she hung up, she looked at Ayden and smiled, then the phone rang again. "Stienboek High School. Mrs. Edmonds speaking. How can I help you?"

A minute later his mother was at the door, buzzing to get in. Mrs. Edmonds pushed the hidden button. Still listening, she covered the mouthpiece and said, "Hi, Anna. Ayden's all ready." She waved at them as they left. *Wow,* Ayden thought, remembering Mr. Davvis and her looking at each other. *No wonder Mr. D. likes her.*

"How are you, Ayden? Come on in." Mr. Powells let Ayden lead the way back to his office. He closed the door behind them and gestured so Ayden could take a seat on either the chair or couch. He always chose the chair. They both sat.

"How have you been since last time?" At Powells' suggestion,

Anna had agreed to double up Ayden's visit since Allan Sparks suicide – just for a couple of months. He'd assured her he didn't think Ayden was any threat to himself, but the incident was another trauma for him, and, at least initially, he'd blamed himself.

Ayden offered his usual reply. "Good."

"Good?" Powells volleyed back.

"I guess." Ayden looked toward the desk. "Yeah. Okay."

"Are you looking for this?" Powells reached behind him and handed the small, framed picture to him.

"No...yeah." Ayden reached for the strange school on a hill and the windowless houses with no doors. While looking at the image, he said, "I don't think about it, you know, about Allan, all the time anymore. Only sometimes."

"Is 'sometimes' three times a day, or every night, or..." Powells left the question open-ended.

Ayden continued looking at the picture while he talked. "Usually at night. Not so much at school because there's lots of other kids, and we're always busy. But not last night. And maybe not the night before."

The therapist smiled. "Well, I think that's progress. It's not even been a month. Do you remember when we talked about long-term sadness and about grieving? How it can take a long time before it's not there all the time. I'm wondering how often you still think you had something to do with what Allan did."

"Sometimes but not so much anymore. I still just don't get why he did it."

"That's always a tough question. But figuring it out isn't your job. Your job is to keep his memory but not all the pain and sadness you felt at first. I think you're doing a good job of that. What do you think?"

Ayden remembered a conversation with Mr. Davvis about people who own businesses, like his mom, who never give up. He couldn't recall the word he'd called them but remembered what he said about them. "I think I'm getting more of that resilience stuff."

Still studying the picture, Ayden said, "These houses don't look real. Allan could've kicked down a wall if he tried."

Powells leaned forward resting his elbows on his knees. He laced his fingers and looked down. Working with children, he knew chronological and emotional age could get out of sync. Prolonged repeated trauma, as documented in Ayden's file, often meant emotional age could lag significantly behind. In severe cases, intellectual development could also be affected. Powells was grateful there was nothing wrong with Ayden's learning or intellectual ability. In fact, the boy showed real insight at times. He raised his head and said, "I didn't know Allan, but I'm getting to know you. And I'm sure you'll be strong enough to break down any walls you need to."

"But Allan was bigger and stronger than me."

"The kind of strength you need for these kinds of walls isn't based on being big or the size of your muscles. It's about what you just mentioned. It's about resilience. The ability to keep going even when things get tough. You have more of that kind of strong than most people I know." He remained leaning in, waiting for a response.

It took a few moments, but when Ayden looked away from the picture his thinking had shifted. "That doesn't mean Allan was bad, right?"

"No, Allan wasn't bad, I didn't know him like you did. But I'm sure he wasn't bad."

"But some people are bad, right?"

"It's true some people do bad things." Powells didn't elaborate. He wanted Ayden to lead the conversation where he needed it to go.

"So," Ayden probed, "can good people sometimes do bad things?"

Powells followed. "Yes. Good people – all of us – may slip up and do a bad thing, hurt someone, even ourselves or people we care about. But just like you, most people can tell good from bad and choose the good." The therapist considered for a second before deciding to go further.

"But... some people can start to believe that doing bad things to others is a way to get what they want or to protect themselves from getting hurt. They get confused and trapped." He pointed to the picture Ayden still held. "Like in a house with no door or windows. I think that's why when you first came here, you said that picture made you think of Allan. Getting trapped like that could make anybody scared if they couldn't find a way out or didn't know how to let anyone get in. Don't you think?"

Ayden had his own question. "If a person gets trapped like that, does it make them get mean? Sometimes Allan could be mean to me and others, and he was mean when he started saying things about Lilly. That made me angry."

So not to pressure Ayden, Powells looked back at the floor when he asked the next question. "Ayden? Were you mad at Allan when he died?"

"Yeah. I wanted to punch him out. But my teacher, Mrs. Berry, told me not to let him make me do stupid things and get myself in trouble."

Powells now looked up, making sure they were seeing each other. "That was very helpful of her. It also shows how much you've matured and how you're gaining control of your own impulses. You should be very proud. Since you didn't punch Allan, that also means you won over your anger. So... maybe you're ready to not be angry at Allan anymore. You've often said he was funny. Maybe that's the part to remember, the part of him you can hang on to."

Ayden glanced at the picture and then reached it out and gave it to Powells. "At least our school has doors and windows."

William Powells smiled at the boy. "I agree one hundred percent. Thank goodness schools have doors and windows."

57

By middle school, the days of passing out small Valentine's cards to everyone in class were long gone. The pool of possible card recipients has dwindled to close friends for the girls and zero for the boys. As they enter the age of teens, a boy considering delivering a Valentine's Day card to a girl is usually aware of the nightmarish twin perils of personal rejection and public scorn by peers. This is not to say that no adolescent male is willing to tempt fate on the sly or brazen enough because of their alpha standing among his peers to do so in the public eye. A third category for males of this age contains only the few who, for one reason or another, have somehow remained naïve or obtuse of middle school peer conventions.

Ayden Quant was a hybrid mix of all these. His ADHD tended to cause him to live in the moment. It accounted for much of his impulsivity and unfiltered comments which led many – adults and peers – to accuse him of thinking social norms and rules either didn't apply to him or that he was indeed obtuse.

His unstable infancy with an addicted neglectful birth mother and an absentee father led to a tendency for doing things on the sly. Then the next eleven years living with his on-the-road and rarely-home-but-hollering-when-he-was father didn't help. Along the way, Ayden had built up enough emotional scar tissue so, that now, he didn't usually let the fear of rejection or scorn stop him once he'd set his mind to do something.

And there was the other part of him. A strong sense of loyalty first developed toward his stepmom Anna. It became his definition of love. With his autistic classmate Steven, it developed into a desire to protect. With Allan, it had become an unfathomable hodgepodge of laughter, gratefulness, betrayal, and stimulation. A few adults, Mr. Powells, Mr. Davvis, and Mrs. Berry, had begun to earn his trust and respect if not yet loyalty.

But recently another candidate had appeared. Nala Samilton. Whether it was because he thought he owed her for having got her sent home when he'd unwittingly used the N-word, or because she'd sought him out at the culvert and talked to him, or because she also seemed like she didn't quite fit in – maybe because of all of these – Ayden had decided he was going to give her a Valentine's Day card. Well, not really a Valentine's card. More of a "friend" card he'd found on the rack while his mom was getting a prescription filled. He had to ask her to pay for it since he had no money. She had asked who it was for. He'd said, "A friend."

"A girlfriend?"

"No. Not a girlfriend. Just kind of a friend - friend."

"Is it that Lilly girl in your class you've always liked."

His mother didn't know about Lilly and Allan. "NO. And I didn't *always* like her."

Anna Quant decided not to pry any further. She added the card to her purchase, warning, "Be careful."

Now the school day was almost over. He'd seen Nala at freshman lunch, but she'd been with her friends. So, he hadn't given it to her then. He couldn't decide if it was because he was chicken or because he'd have been an embarrassment to her, and she'd have been teased. He decided to call it a tie.

Only one period was left, and Nala wasn't in his ESL group. He realized he didn't know whose room she was in. After that, he'd have to get on the bus for home and there was no way he could give it to her then. He'd have lost his chance. He could only think of one solution. Instead of taking his usual route to Mrs. Berry's room, he went the long way around past the cafeteria.

Mr. Samilton's office door was open. Ayden approached and saw he was on his two-way radio talking about a bus. The other voice sounded like Mrs. Edmonds in the office. Mr. Samilton saw him standing at the door. "Got it. Thanks, Sharon. Over." He set the radio aside. "Hi, Ayden. Do you need something?"

Ayden registered that Mrs. Edmond's name was Sharon. Then he remembered that day in the office when Mr. Samilton came in after he'd used that word with Nala. He started to panic but saw the man didn't look or sound mad. He decided to take a chance. "Could I ask you a favor?"

"Sure, but make it fast, I've got to go pull a bus around front before the last bell."

Ayden walked in and handed him an envelope. "Could you give this to Nala?"

Dominic looked at both sides of the card, noticing there was no name on either.

"Okay, but I won't see her until late. She's been asked to scrimmage with the varsity basketball team tonight. They're prepping for regionals next week." He glanced at the card again. "Should I say it's from you?"

The question tapped into more panic. He considered taking the card back and running, saying he'd see her tomorrow, or he'd changed my mind, or maybe just saying no, it's not from me, it's from someone else. But that wouldn't work because he'd already taken what suddenly felt like the biggest risk of his life.

Dominic could see the boy was in a quandary. Considering it was February 14th, he assumed this was a Valentine's card. He forced himself not to smile. Instead, he offered a possible way out. "You could just put her name on the envelope, and I could say I found it on my desk."

"I already signed it," Ayden said. It had taken him all night. He'd woken several times with the conundrum on his mind before he'd finally put the name on the card. He wasn't going to chicken out now, but he added, "Could you please tell her not to tell anybody?"

Dominic got up and put the card in his coat pocket. "I'll tell her, Ayden. And don't worry. You can trust her not to tell her friends. But something you should learn right now is that sometimes girls have to talk with their mothers about... stuff. But you can trust Mrs. Samilton too."

"I guess that's okay. Thanks for the advice."

"Ayden, now you have to get to class, and I've got to get that bus warmed up."

"Sure. Okay."

Ayden left. Dominic pulled his coat on making sure the envelope was safely tucked away. He couldn't help but smile. Watching Ayden struggle with the age-old male discomfort in such situations was half painful and half comical. But the main cause for the grin was the relief of knowing he'd never have to be a teenager again.

Brave – Coward. Dominic weighed his options on his way home. Nala was getting a ride after practice with one of the varsity girls who lived about a mile away from them. Ayden's envelope was on the truck seat next to him. He had barely been out of the school lot when he'd decided it would be best if he just left the card on Nala's bed and told her it was there. He'd first considered it the cowardly way out but practical. He was hoping to escape a lot of questions about how he'd gotten the card and God knows what else. But by the time he'd reached the house, he'd realized Nala might also prefer it that way. She might be embarrassed by her dad being the intermediary and prefer the privacy of her room. He took a tiny bit of fatherly pride for having thought about it from her perspective.

58

When Nala got home from practice, she was, as always, greeted by Moses. She'd then dropped her backpack by the hall leading to the bedrooms and launched into describing everything that had happened. She explained the differences between how varsity Coach Todd ran his practices compared to Coach Shimone. He'd mostly had her on defense against the starters. She'd stole the ball a few times, turning one into a layup. When she got a chance to play offense with the B-squad, she'd scored a few times. She was most proud when Coach Todd praised how quickly she'd grasped the plays he wanted them to run to mimic what he expected to face in their first regional game.

While she talked, her mom set out the reheated stew. Nala quickly finished that and had a second bowl. When she was full and talked out, her dad nonchalantly mentioned the card. Nala picked up her bag as she hurried to her room confused, excited, worried, and about twelve other feelings.

Luckily, she'd done her homework at school. Once she opened the card, her head and thoughts went elsewhere. It was definitely middle-schoolish. A jar of peanut butter and jelly holding hands with text about friends "sticking" together if they got in a "jam." She was relieved to not see any hearts or Cupids. Ayden had even put an X over the touching hands.

She sat on her bed and monitored her feelings. She could

understand the motivation behind the card. She just wasn't sure how she felt about it. Was she Ayden's friend? She knew why finding him that night after Allan's suicide and calling his house made it easy for him to think of her as a friend. But did she do those things as a friend or just because she was worried about a classmate? She'd have certainly gone looking for Moses if he'd gone missing. She loved the dog. They'd been together for much of her life. But she and Ayden had been together a long time too, since kindergarten. That was ten years. She unequivocally didn't love Ayden. So why did she do those things? She knew she wouldn't have done them for many of her classmates. She flipped on her side, leaning on her elbow, and propping her head on her fist muttering, "This is getting me nowhere!"

So, as she often now did, she closed her eyes to concentrate and see if Langston had an opinion. On Tuesday, Ms. Snede had confirmed her linkage between her twin, who survived only in her imagination, and the famous Langston Hughes – whose face she had now memorized after looking him up. She had realized something else too. Unlike Lang, Hughes had thousands of words and thoughts already written for her to read. Since then, Nala had decided it was time for Lang to grow up. From now on, she'd conjure her brother in the guise of the older, wiser poet. Surely, he'd know and could teach her even more about what she'd need to learn and understand about herself and the rest of the world.

Unfortunately, for the time being, Langston had no opinions on the matter. She decided to list Ayden's strengths as a potential friend instead. The weaknesses were too numerous, and she didn't have all night. She was already as tired as she was after an actual basketball game. She was surprised to find his strengths, though she'd only really interacted with him over the last few months, were easy to recognize. His apology and heart-felt explanation in that whole word business, his concern for Lilly when she was going out with Allan, and his ability to have such sympathy for Allan, even though the whole class knew how Allan could manipulate him.

Then there was the conversation they'd had in the culvert when Ayden didn't come home. She had to admit the list was impressive. What it lacked in quantity, it made up for in depth. More depth than she saw with some of the friends she'd hung with most of her life.

There was the phone conversation where she'd heard his mom call him A-Lee. At the time, she'd only noted the contrast of him adding a name while she was deleting one. Now she hauled herself up and scootched her back against the headboard. The name was probably something special between him and his mom. What she knew about Ayden's father told her he probably never used it. She picked up his card again and looked at the name he'd neatly printed, A-Lee. She wondered if his writing was always this neat and legible. Did it make a difference? While she'd always thought of herself as "Nala," she now pondered if Ayden thought of himself as "A-Lee" but had never let anyone know. Except... now he'd told her.

There was a knock, and her father asked if he could come in. "Come on in, Dad."

Dominic opened the door and saw his daughter sitting there with Ayden's card in her hand. He had no urge to tease her. He wanted to go sit on her bed and talk with her. Maybe she'd share what she was thinking about the card. Instead, he just gently passed along Ayden's request.

"Honey, I wanted to wait until you read your card before telling you that Ayden asked that you not tell anyone about the card. I remember being his age and how scary it was to think that a girl might reject or ridicule you. Guys fear vulnerability more than anything. I also got the sense he wanted to protect you from getting teased for getting a card from him. I think that's why it ended up in my hands. I told him his secret was safe in your hands, that you'd never do that to him."

Nala got up and hugged him. “Thank you, Daddy. I love you.”

Dominic hadn’t anticipated that reaction. He kissed the top of her head and said, “And I love you more than anything. Good night, honey.”

When her father left, Nala again sat on her bed. But now, she found she’d made up her mind about two things. Moses was himself because that’s who dogs are. But people? Especially other kids. Her experience was they often don’t know who they are or, if they do, they’re afraid and hide it. So, anyone brave enough to share his secret identity with her was no doubt-about-it friend material. It made her wonder if she’d ever be that brave.

Her other realization was how good it made her feel that her dad knew and trusted that Ayden’s secret was safe with her.

59

By 6:40 p.m., the multi-purpose room was packed. The Stienboek High Theater had a larger capacity, but Superintendent Demian had nixed its use, saying that to be up on a stage speaking down to the audience would be a mistake likely to cost support. The JV and the varsity gyms were both in use because the boys' and girls' basketball teams were preparing for the regionals starting later in the week. Demian also requested the principals: Ryan, Barb Nickel, and the middle school principal Randy Waters, act as greeters and ushers rather than being seated at the front of the room. It emphasized the point that the three administrators were there to assist the audience obtain the information they desired.

Dominic helped Mathew Lam bring in additional chairs as the crowd continued to pack in. By the 7:00 p.m. starting time, they were very close to the 120-person room capacity. The Edenton Press had sent a reporter. The coverage would be helpful – if it wasn't a disaster. Ryan, who had never been through a referendum before, was nervous and amazed at how relaxed Demian appeared.

The superintendent stepped to the microphone and asked people to please take their seats so they could be respectful of everyone's time. After her initial welcome, introductions, and greetings, she got down to business.

She began by acknowledging they, the taxpayers, rightly were the ones empowered to decide whether the school district needed and warranted the additional requested funding. She stressed that the referendum only included what was urgently needed and no more, adding, "And while not all of you may have children currently in the school system, most of you either did or have grandchildren or neighbors who will benefit."

She spoke about the last referendum three years ago, reminding the gathering how desperately the very room they were now sitting in, as well as the classroom additions on both Edenton and Westown Elementary Schools, had been needed at the time to meet the booming influx of students. She also reminded them that because of the district's careful stewardship of their money, they'd been able to also get the roofs of both elementary buildings resurfaced at the same time.

She tactfully addressed why the district's current letter to the editor had been necessary because a previous letter had unfortunately contained incorrect information. She again reiterated that a Capital Referendum only allowed the district to borrow money to be spent on tangible infrastructure and not salaries or benefits for administrators, teachers, or other staff. Without mentioning names, she urged people to avoid misinformation that might be out there and to go to the district webpage and newsletters for accurate updates and information.

Shifting her tone, Superintendent Demian then explained the evening's format. "We're not going to stand here and just throw facts and data at you. Our goal tonight is not to sell you on the referendum. We're here so you can tell us what you want to know. We'll answer what we can without getting long-winded. If you want more details, all you need do is contact me. If I'm not available, I will get back to you."

Ryan was impressed with Liz Demian's natural ability to create an atmosphere of cooperation and respect. He thought back to Minneapolis and how, like many large organizations, information often descended from above by non-personal edicts. Superintendent

Demian would get their information out in a much more engaging manner by putting the focus on the audience and their questions rather than on the administrators. For the first time since he'd met her, Ryan realized she must have been a very good classroom teacher. He looked around to see how many of his staff were here and wondered if they'd pick up on the superintendent's modeling.

She explained the evening's questions and answers would be put on the district webpage and in a weekly District Newsletter between now and when they made their decision on April 2nd. Demian then pointed to the three principals, each of whom carried a handheld microphone to pass to each person asking a question.

School board members were scattered among the crowd. Ryan could see Thynie Marsh's profile across the room. She was seated next to her husband's cousin and fellow board member, Bobby. They were already actively whispering back and forth making Ryan wonder about their topic and intentions. He told himself not to get paranoid. This was about the referendum and not him.

Demian then introduced Dominic Samilton, the District Director of Maintenance and Transportation, and Edenton's technology guru, Robert Blake. Their areas of responsibility made up the bulk of the referendum, and their task was to explain and field questions related to how and why specific needs in their respective areas had been identified.

Superintendent Demian and the district business manager then took questions about current state funding, specifically why it was no longer sufficient. They explained the revenue cap was based on what the district spent in 1993, the year the Wisconsin legislature initiated a limit on the amount of revenue schools could raise through taxes. The goal had been to lower property taxes, but due to inflation and rising costs over the last twenty years, the result for schools was insufficient revenue to keep up with repairs let alone new expenses like computers and technology. The pair managed to never bring politics into their explanation.

In response to another question, Demian explained another issue. Both the Wisconsin open-enrollment program and the new state-wide expansion of school vouchers meant district parents could enroll their children in other schools – public or private. When that happened, Edenton would lose the student, and they'd have to also send the state's "per pupil" money to the new school. She predicted the state would continue to expand both programs and any district unable or unwilling to find other funding to keep up their facilities and offerings, especially in areas like technology, would lose students – and money – each year to richer districts that did.

"Edenton," Demian concluded, "like some other districts, was disproportionately financially hurt because back in 1993, and still today, they had been conservative and frugal with local taxpayers' money."

And so, it went on for two hours. Questions were wide-ranging: possible and likely consequences if the referendum didn't pass, what a mill rate was and how much the referendum would add to tax bills, safety and security issues, changes to bus services if a new bus was not purchased before the old one died, instructional issues related to poor technology, all were raised and answered. How a question was phrased sometimes gave an insight as to which way the voter was leaning. Ryan tried reading facial expressions after each answer to gauge if minds were being changed.

The informational meeting was scheduled to end at 9:00 p.m. At 9:15, Superintendent Demian ended the Q&A, reminding everyone there would be a second informational meeting in March and that tonight's information would be available on the website by Thursday. She was thanking them and urging all to share what they'd learned tonight with friends and neighbors when a voice from a man standing in the row in front of Thynie and Bobby Marsh shouted over her closing remarks.

"Excuse me." Then even louder, "Excuse me!" the man shouted toward the stage, then waited for the audience to turn to him. "My son is in high school here at *'Steen-bach'*. I've heard Mr. Davvis has invited the League of Women Voters into the school to tell the seniors who to vote for. Probably even to vote for this referendum. That's just not right. He should resign or be fired. We all know those women have an agenda."

The murmur in the crowd escalated, and Ryan saw the faces turning to seek him out. He raised his mic to his mouth, but Elizabeth Demian beat him to it. Her voice was angrier than he could ever imagine her getting. Her stare locked in on the man who had shouted the accusation, and her voice hushed the crowd. Ryan didn't recognize the man, but the superintendent did. "Mr. Datson!" Hearing the name, Ryan could picture the guy's son who was a junior, and therefore not even involved in the voter registration presentation.

"Mr. Datson," Superintendent Demian repeated. The crowd had quieted to hear. "If you recall, I earlier warned you and everyone else to be aware of false and misleading information. That doesn't just go for the referendum but also rumors and accusations aimed at the schools and *my* staff. I don't know where you got what you just said, but it is a distortion. Whoever told you that not only lied but..." She caught herself and reset her face and tone.

"Principal Davvis did no such thing, and he did <u>not</u> invite the League to the high school. I approved their offer to share information on registering to vote. Many of our seniors are, or will be, eighteen before the April election and therefore eligible to vote. I find it hard to believe anyone..." she paused, making it obvious she was talking about him, "...would not want them to know how to vote. Both Mr. Davvis and I will screen all materials and be there during the presentation. Any parent *of a senior*," she emphasized, "is welcome to attend or to have their son or daughter excused from the presentation. As far as the rest of your comment, I find it too despicable to comment on."

She then calmly wished the audience a safe ride home.

60

The January faculty meeting had, as always, fallen at a hectic time of the year. First-semester finals and grades needed to be completed, and second-semester classes would begin the following week. For that reason, the meeting had been kept short. They'd briefly returned to Bernadette Zowak's suggestion back in November. The Language Arts committee handed out several practical examples of content class writing.

The Social Studies teachers had met with Ryan right after the holidays and had volunteered to experiment in their classes by using the last five minutes to journal about what they'd been discussing that day. They'd ask a few students to read their thoughts at the beginning of the following day's class as a review and lead into the new work. The kids seemed to have found it useful.

Their teachers also took a few minutes each day to read a few entries. They found they were getting a baseline on the kids' writing skills while dipping their toes into the formative assessment idea Ryan had promoted back in November. Ryan and the L.A. committee considered this a major step.

Today, as the teachers settled in for the February staff meeting, last night's Community Information Meeting, and especially the outburst at the end, were forefront of everyone's mind. Ryan reviewed the reason and details for allowing the League of Women Voters to provide their short presentation and how-to instructions for registering to vote. He'd arrange the presentation for the first week of March so the seniors and their teachers would already be settled into their new semester routines. He reminded everyone that parents could opt their kids out.

He downplayed the end of the meeting outburst by saying, "The man's accusation was completely inaccurate, and, as those of you who were there know, Superintendent Demian gave everyone in attendance the accurate information. I have to admit, I was personally grateful for her doing so because my response would not have been as tactful as hers." This got a laugh. The support felt good.

Ryan took a few questions about the referendum. Some reported hearing a few positive comments outside of school, though the general mood didn't seem optimistic. Ryan agreed the results could go either way and reminded them not to get drawn into discussing it in class, even if asked. Some queries were made about the possibility of cuts or layoffs if it didn't pass. He couldn't respond with specifics but tried to assure them by saying no cuts in the short term were being contemplated. If it ever came to that, he promised to be upfront with them.

Ryan then went over some class and schedule information. Having finally finished meeting with the D and F students, he stressed his desire that they make sure any student who was in danger of failing knew what he or she needed to do to pass. He acknowledged high school students should ideally be responsible for knowing their current grade situations, adding, "But not every kid is as responsible as we would hope. If taking those few extra minutes helped even a few students get their grades up, it would be worth it." He emphasized this was especially crucial for seniors who would not have time to retake classes and might be in peril of not graduating on time.

The Social Study teachers then gave a positive update about their writing experiment. When asked, Mr. Schmelzing explained they were not grading the journals. If they did, he said, it would require significantly more time than they had. In his opinion, it could also intimidate and deter some students from stretching their thinking if they were going to be graded on the writing. It was an accurate and fair point.

Ryan thanked them for their valuable observations and acknowledged Schmelzing's point as valid, His comment was greeted with several head nods and a few smiles.

61

The Stienboek High School girls' varsity basketball team had made it to state last year, where they'd lost in the first round. That showing, plus this year's very solid season, had them ranked high in Division 3, which meant they'd gotten a bye during the Regional Quarter-Final games and went directly into the semi-finals.

Nala had been thrilled to be on the bench as the team comfortably won the Friday game by making nine of their ten free throws in the last two minutes. But the Saturday finals game was a nail-biter up until the end. In the second quarter, Nala had been subbed in when one of the girls took a hard fall and needed a break. It was the scariest three minutes and twenty seconds of Nala's basketball life. Their opponents shifted to a man-to-man defense and put their best player on Nala to intimidate her. She was a senior, close to five inches taller than Nala. She was also a step faster due to her ability to anticipate Nala's moves and she was eager to teach the young substitute a few lessons, which she promptly did by stealing Nala's dribble and starting a fast break.

Nala realized her mistake and absorbed the lesson. After that, she was able to maintain possession and move the ball. She even gained two assists. When she got doubled, she didn't panic and accurately hit her open teammate with a sharp pass as she cut to the basket.

Later, Nala was anxiously watching from the bench in the fourth quarter when inside the three-minute mark Stienboek was down by four. Coach Todd called a timeout to remind the starters they were an experienced state-ranked team and urged them to take control. He called for all-out full-court pressure and a smothering aggressive man-to-man defense. At the buzzer, Stienboek won by two.

As the two teams shook hands, the senior who had played against Nala in her brief time on the court along with another of their starters, both of whom were Black, made a point of congratulating Nala on how well she'd handled herself. They called her "Sister" and wished her luck at Sectionals. As they high-fived her, the tall senior looked over Nala's head at the rest of the Stienboek team and fans and said, "You're definitely a standout at your school, aren't you?"

That Sunday afternoon, Nala sat her dad and mom at the kitchen table. She wanted to show them something she'd like to get. Dominic joked it wasn't her birthday, but that his wasn't far off. Nala opened her laptop and turned it so they could see the screen.

22 Quick Braided Hairstyles For Black Girls

Kate kicked Dominic under the table before he could even think of a response.

Nala said, "I'm not thinking anything drastic like dreadlocks. They take several months to a year to grow. But I was hoping you'd be okay if I got one of these before our regional game on Thursday."

Kate showed interest and pointed to a couple of styles she thought would be cute but practical for her sports activities.

"What do you think, Dad?" Nala asked.

Dominic knew his daughter was concerned he might be hurt by what she was asking him to accept. He wasn't going to let that happen. "Honey," he said, running his hand over the minimal stubble on his pate, "do you really want advice from a guy with a head like this? Whatever you and your mom decide is fine with me. You're so beautiful, even if you wore your hair like mine, you'd look great."

She leaned over and kissed him on the cheek. "Thanks, Daddy."

Dominic left his daughter and wife paging through the pictures, trying to narrow it down to one or two choices. As he walked to the TV room, the knot that first tightened in his gut when he saw the headline, released. He'd told the truth. Nala would be beautiful no matter what. And, most importantly, she still called him "Daddy."

Kate Samilton had been able to book a salon in Appleton experienced in Black hairstyles that could fit her daughter in on Tuesday. She picked Nala up at school after practice at 5:30, giving them time to make it to the appointment.

On the drive, as the sky moved rapidly to evening, Nala asked, "Mom, is Dad mad at me for this?"

"Of course not, honey."

"He seemed pretty quiet about it. I expected he'd have some comments or at least some wisecracks."

"Dads always have trouble handling it when their little girls all of a sudden grow up. They want time to stop until they can adjust, which never happens. To be fair, if you were a boy, I'd probably be the same way as you turned into a man."

"Did Dad want a boy?"

"Absolutely not. He fell in love the minute you picked him?"

"What do you mean, I picked him?"

"You toddled right up to him at the agency. You were carrying a white blanket, which we still have in the attic. You two locked eyes, and you fell over on your bottom and pointed at him to help you up. He fell in love with you – we both did – from that moment."

Nala looked out the windows at the other cars before shifting her torso toward her mother. "Mom, you're telling me that I picked Dad?"

"That's the way it happened. It was love at first sight for both of you. I admit, it probably wasn't exactly a conscious decision on your part. But you pointed, and that was that."

They rode in silence for a couple of miles. Kate flicked on her turn signal as they approached College Avenue. Exiting and starting down the ramp, she couldn't see the various contortions her daughter's face was going through, trying to form the question she was about to ask.

Nala looked at her mom as she came to a stop at the light. Then she watched the cross traffic for a few seconds. "You're saying I picked white parents?"

"I'm just saying *you* did the pointing." Kate had a big grin on her face which made Nala start to smile.

"But Mom, I was a baby. I didn't know what I was doing."

"Neither did we. But you didn't give us a choice. Dad picked you up and kissed you on top of your head. I remember him laughing and saying, 'Look at this hair!' You put your arms around his neck and wouldn't let go. So, like I said you didn't give us a choice."

As Nala lay in bed that night, she reminded Langston of all the great things that had happened over the last couple of weeks. She'd been practicing with the varsity and was part of their championship run. She'd even scored some points. She recalled that the two girls had called her sister and said she "stood out" at Stienbach. She knew what they were saying, but she also knew the girls on her team seemed to accept her, and her close friends were happy for her.

She replayed for Langston what she'd learned about *A Raisin in the Sun* – how Ms. Snede had told her about the short poem called "Harlem." How she'd found and read it a hundred times. She recited it for him. All eleven lines. Then told him how she and Zoey were going to watch the video when they had time.

"Dad wanted to watch it too. He even knew who Langston Hughes was. Pretty cool, right? Best of all, he really liked my new hair."

62

Ryan Davvis sat on the bottom bleacher nearest the door. The gym was temporarily empty and silent, which was why he chose to linger a few minutes. The cavernous space allowed him the room to see beyond himself and the issues and concerns which required him to keep his attention and focus on the small details. He closed his laptop on which he'd been taking notes and checking the boxes required for the scheduled observation he was doing for one of the Physical Education teachers. He removed his reading glasses, placed them in his shirt pocket, and rubbed his eyes.

"Hey, Mr. D. I didn't know you had glasses."

Ryan leaned his elbows on his knees and even before he turned his head toward the voice, he said, "They're for reading when my eyes get tired. More importantly, Ayden, why are you in the gym?"

"I was just heading to lunch and saw you sitting here by yourself." The boy walked over and stood next to Ryan. "Besides, I'm not hungry, and I don't really want to talk to nobody."

"You, okay?" Ryan asked. "They have pizza today. You like that don't you?"

"I guess. But..." It took him a few seconds to start again. "Me and Mr. Powells been talking about Allan."

Ryan moved over a bit and tapped the bleacher twice, inviting the boy to sit. "I'm guessing you miss him?"

"That's what we were talking about. How I was mad at him, for what he did but also for how he treated people sometimes. Mr. Powells says I should try to forgive him."

Ryan said, "That can be hard sometimes." After a second, he added, "I know from experience. How's it coming?"

"I can forgive him a little but not all the way yet. Was it true Mr. Sparks blamed you?" He didn't wait for a reply. "That's stupid. He was Allan's dad. He should've stopped him."

They stared up at the high ceiling. Ayden pointed to a basketball wedged into a roof truss. Ryan acknowledged the minor dilemma with a nod and a "Hmm," thinking that was much like how he was feeling. He was about to send the boy off to eat something, but before he could, Ayden said, "I know some of the kids were mad too, but I think it was good you didn't put up Allan's picture and stuff in case other kids might start thinking about you-know-what."

"Thank you, Ayden. I appreciate the support. It sounds like you and Mr. Powells have some good talks."

"He listens good, and he asks questions that help me to think. At school, they just ask questions to see if we did the work and remember stuff until the test is over. But his questions help me figure stuff out."

Ryan had two thoughts. One was the adage: "Out of the mouths of babes." The other was the memory of Mrs. Berry sharing Ayden's theory about the advantages of robots taking over teaching. The boy seemed to have a knack for hitting on some of the essential nonsense built into life, schools, and people in general. He returned to Ayden's earlier comment.

"Where did you hear that about Mr. Sparks?"

"From my dad. But he's wrong. I told him that too. I thought, at first, it might be my fault. But Mr. Powells and Nala explained why it ain't."

Ryan was surprised. "Nala told you that?"

"Yeah. That night it happened. It made me feel better."

"That was nice of her. Are you two friends now?"

"I think so. I..." Ayden had the look of a person about to reveal something.

"Maybe." He'd obviously decided not to share after all. "See ya, Mr. Davvis."

Ayden was out the door. A new gym class would soon be arriving. Ryan picked up his laptop and the yellow pad he usually kept at hand. Taking a pen from his pocket, he printed a name. POWELLS. He underlined it and headed back to his office.

63

Dominic waved Ryan into his office. He'd been hoping to catch him with no one else around. The question he wanted to ask was uncomfortable, even a bit embarrassing.

Ryan asked, "How's the proud father doing?" He took a seat across from Dominic's desk. "I have to say, I sure wasn't expecting the girls to have it so easy last night."

The girls had won their Sectional semi-final by fifteen. It had been one of those games where the entire team was hot and couldn't miss. They'd been confident going in, but no one had expected that kind of win. Up by nineteen, Nala got to play the last five minutes and picked up her first playoff points – two buckets, including her first crossover layup, and a free throw.

"I don't know who was more excited, Nala, Kate, or me," Dominic admitted.

Ryan said, "Nala sure is taking advantage of the opportunity to play with the varsity. How are you and Kate feeling about her moving up next year?"

"Coach Todd mentioned it," Dominic said. "We all agreed to get through the tournament, and then we'll have time to talk about it."

"Well, she seems to fit in well even with the limited practice she's had with them. She looks comfortable with the other girls."

Dominic shifted in his seat. "That's what I wanted to check with you about."

"What's up?" Ryan asked. "Did something happen?"

"No. Not that I know. But I remember a while ago you said something about telling Black kids in your old school to try to fit in."

Ryan checked that he had enough time, then recounted the naïve off-handed advice he'd sometimes unthinkingly dispense to minority kids back then and how he'd come to rethink and regret it.

His concern about how the kids had been interpreting his comments made Dominic wonder the same thing about himself and Nala. By extension, it also made him consider Ryan's struggle to fit in with what he must consider the conservative small-town, rural values of Edenton. How do you fit in when you can't identify with the group? He could only imagine the stories Lisa must have told him about the place. The thought of Lisa wasn't where he wanted this conversation to go, but he was certain if she had still been alive, there was no way she and Ryan would have moved here.

Dominic said, "Well, that whole 'fitting-in thing' is kind of what I wanted to ask about. Do you know if Nala's gotten any flak for her new hairstyle? I'm just a bit concerned that others may see it as... I don't know, attention-seeking or too different. Kate would kill me if she knew I was asking this, but I thought you'd get where I was coming from. After all, right after she gets to play some with the varsity, people might think she was getting... cocky? You know all of a sudden wearing her hair like..." He couldn't think of any famous Black woman he could reference who wore her hair in braids. "You know what I mean."

"I sure hope she hasn't. I haven't heard anything. I think her hair looks great. Did she say anything?"

"No. She seems happy with it."

"But you're not?"

"I think it looks good on her. I really do. It's just different, maybe too grown-up. I'm just a little concerned it might, I don't know..."

When Dominic hesitated, Ryan filled in the gap. "Might seem uppity?"

The use of the word Nala had used in Ryan's office some months ago startled and embarrassed Dominic. He looked around for a few seconds. "Maybe. So, what does that say about me? Is that why I got upset at her when she used that word? Because in the back of my head, maybe that's what I thought she was doing. Jesus, Ryan. What kind of a father would that make me?"

Ryan leaned in. "You're a great father, and Nala knows it. And honestly," he thought back to the freshman game earlier in the year when he realized he was associating her talent with being Black, "I think your daughter has made us both face some things. How does this kind of crap get in our heads? Maybe we're like the fish in the Fox River swimming all day in toxic PCB-laced water."

Ryan now also looked around for a few seconds. "Nala makes me wish I could go back and talk with those kids in Minneapolis. I had no right to tell them to fit in. I think what I was saying was, 'Don't be too Black.' I just assumed it shouldn't be any different or harder than being Swedish or Irish or German. Eat some Irish stew, or sauerbraten, and maybe have a parade once a year but fit in, don't stick out. It doesn't work like that, does it?"

"I guess I thought it did," Dominic conceded. "Growing up here, the rules seemed easy enough to follow. But I'm scared now for Nala, the difference between being seen and unseen, fitting in or standing out, can get her hurt someday."

"You're her father. You're going to worry about her and want to do whatever you can to protect her. But hoping she stays invisible and never takes pride in who she is, is not the answer. I'm not a father, but I've been around teenagers enough to know we can't always protect them from themselves or others. I can only imagine how hard that must be as a parent."

"Kate told me the same thing a bit ago," Dominic said.

Ryan stood. "You're a lucky man, Dom. Having two remarkable women in your life."

For Dominic, the man reaching his hand out to him seemed to come into focus for the first time. He was still a guy walking a tightrope. But he wasn't just the nice guy who undoubtedly got in over his head when he married Lisa Kames. He was seeing the man Walt Hannig had wanted as his replacement.

Their clasped hands and extended arms reminded Dominic of the hourglass he had envisioned last fall. But now, they were on the same side. Whether the sands of time were falling from above or were disappearing from below his feet, he knew Ryan Davvis belonged here. He knew he'd do what he could for the man. They had more in common than just Lisa Kames.

The time had come to share what he knew of Lisa from their few months together. He owed Ryan that much. Sharon had told him that Ryan met and talked with Lisa's cousin, Toni Kames. He was sure Toni knew more than him or anyone about Lisa, but he didn't know how much more or what she might have told Ryan. There was still no guarantee as to how what he had to tell Ryan would affect the man's balancing act. But in Dominic's world, friends deserved to know the truth. Then you helped each other survive it.

64

Dominic waited expectantly. He'd only seen his former high school principal the one time at Betty's funeral since his retirement party. Walt Hannig had been a presence in Dominic's life even before ninth grade. In a small place like Edenton, everyone knew who the high school principal was long before they entered the doors of Stienboek High. It was through his brother and his friends Dominic learned that not much got past the man's attention, and, despite the man's military bearing and famously strong grip, he was fair and even friendly. Dominic's parents had assured both the boys when they became freshmen, they had nothing to fear. Compared to old Mr. John Stienboek, Walt Hannig was a teddy bear.

Dominic hadn't found the man to be a teddy bear, but he came to like and admire him. He was a hands-on principal and took a genuine interest in the students and their lives. Dominic and his friends were good students for the most part. They were involved in various school activities and, except for a few occasions, caused little trouble. As Dominic moved through his high school years, he got to know Mr. Hannig as well as any student gets to know the adult authority figures in his life.

After Dominic finished two years at Fox Valley Technical College, Walt Hannig suggested he might consider getting his school bus license and applying for a maintenance position in the growing district. Dominic took the advice and had been thankful ever since.

Now, as he waited for Ryan and Walt, he sipped his beer. It

amused him to feel like a kid who'd been invited to sit at the grown-up's table. His thoughts were interrupted by friendly shouts from the front bar area.

"Mr. Hannig!" Tammi exclaimed. "Mom, look who's here." Holly hollered from the kitchen. "Walter Hannig! What the hell?" Both daughter and mother were Stienboek graduates. Other greetings came from patrons at the bar and crowded front tables. Holly came out and hugged the old man. "You look good, Walt. You come to check up on us, or just on this handsome young fellow here?"

Dominic knew she was referring to Ryan but wondered if the enthusiasm made Ryan feel jealous. He couldn't hear everything said, but it took a long minute before Walt appeared and headed for Dominic's booth. He stood up, and the two men warmly greeted each other. In response to Walt's inquiry, Dominic assured him both Kate and Nala were doing well.

They sat, and Dominic inquired into Walt's health and about his coming trip down to Chicago to visit his nephews. Ryan arrived with a pitcher of beer and joined them. Walt caught them up on the boys, one a city cop and the other a sports journalist. Both had young girls he hadn't seen in half a year and was looking forward to spoiling.

The three of them dissected the Stienboek girls' loss last Saturday in the Sectional finals. The team, like their rivals in the semifinals, had gone cold. Their defense never wavered, but they just couldn't score. They'd lost by seven. The disappointment was compounded when the boys had lost their Sectional Semifinals only last night. The loss stung, but not as much as the girls' loss since they had a serious shot at making it back to state. Ryan told Dominic he'd filled Walt in on Nala being added to the team. For a minute they talked about her possible move as a sophomore to varsity next year.

Holly herself arrived to take their orders and check on the

other occupied tables. Being Friday, no dithering was required. All three went with the fish fry. After a bit of beer and small talk, Walt changed the topic.

Looking at Ryan he said, "So, finish your story about your attempt to commit election fraud by showing seniors how to register to vote."

Ryan said, "Like I said on the way here, the guy waited until the meeting was finishing to holler out that I should be fired for letting the League do a presentation. Thank God, Liz squashed the comments. If I'd said anything, I would have gotten myself fired. Anyhow, we did it on Monday. A total of two parents opted their kid out, and two others attended. Both thanked us afterward for getting their kid registered."

Dominic jumped in. "I didn't recognize the guy – a Mr. Datson. I asked around some and found Mrs. Datson's mother was a *Steenbach* relative of you-know-who."

Walt chuckled and took a drink. "What a family. You'd have been in what, Dom, maybe late elementary when old John Stienboek died, and the high school got renamed to honor him?" Dominic nodded.

"I'd been principal for about five years and was fully aware of the great pronunciation controversy at the time. But that naming ceremony was something. Every time a speaker mentioned John's last name and used his pronunciation, someone in the audience hollered out 'Steen-bach'." Walt chuckled and took a sip of beer.

"According to their family history and lore, they were part of the original settlers to farm around here. They were a prolific group, both clans. They had relatives up and down the Fox Valley and beyond. Still, you may be surprised to know Betty, my wife... well, her mother was from the *Steen-bach* branch. But they'd bought a farm in Southern Door County in the 1940s. That's where Betty was born in 1945, but I didn't meet her until I got home from 'Nam in '64."

Dominic was the more surprised of the two men. "You're kidding me? How did no one know that?"

"Well, probably because Betty's family was long gone from the area. When John hired me as principal in '82, Betty didn't know any direct relatives living here." He chuckled again. "Course, that didn't keep me from mentioning the distant connection during my interview. Luckily, I was smart enough to pronounce it the same as John did."

Walt took a sip of his beer and then added, "But that's not my point."

Dominic felt like he was back in high school. He waited for the man to continue.

"Ryan, since you visited at Thanksgiving and told me about the referendum and the anticipated trouble to get it passed, I've been thinking. Wondering if there was some way I might help." Walt turned to Dominic.

"Dominic, you've lived here all your life. So did your parents and grandparents. So, you maybe know this better than me. These folks have a heritage and history here, and they've never taken kindly to changes they see as coming from outsiders. The longer a family has been in this valley, the more they feel their very identity has been stripped away, and the more they've seen the river and valley get mucked up. And they're right. Hell, the Feds say it's going to be still another six or seven years to finish digging all the PCBs and other crap out of the Fox." He looked at Dominic. "Think how much development has occurred and how much open land has disappeared just in your lifetime."

"I often still feel that way," Dominic said. He tilted his head to face Ryan. "My dad used to take me hunting deer right where your building is now. I guess people always want things to change somewhere else. I didn't plan to ever tell you this, but back when you were hired, I thought Mrs. Nickels should get the job because she'd been around here a long time. Luckily, Mr. Hannig didn't ask me."

Walt topped off everyone's glass from the pitcher. "I don't know how many folks would remember this, but back in the day, John Stienboek did everything he could to keep the local schools from consolidating. But after they did, and he became superintendent, he never tried to sabotage the change. He thought he had the best chance to manage it and keep it from tearing the communities apart. He understood how people felt when they lost their local schools."

Ryan shook his head. "Damn it, Walt. Just when I think you're done mentoring me...You're saying that's where Thynie is coming from, and this Mr. Datson, and a good chunk of the district."

Walt raised his beer glass to salute the insight. "Always remember, you need to understand the other guy's truth before you can separate it from their bullshit."

Tammi appeared with their food. "You guys having fun?" She set their baskets of fish and fries down. "It's good to see you, Mr. Hannig." She then smiled at Ryan, saying. "It's always nice to see you too, Mr. Davvis, and this guy too." She put her hand on Dominic's shoulder for a moment, then pulled silverware from her apron pocket. "Mom said the next pitcher is on the house." Then she leaned in slightly, "I'm trying to convince Mom to vote for the referendum."

65

In Ryan Davvis' mind, Thynie Marsh was older and larger than she actually was. Not only was Ryan aware of this, but he also knew the cause. Thynie's obstructive and meddling ways reminded him of an overbearing aunt, his mother's older sister, who personified both traits when he was growing up. He remembered how incredulous he and his father would become at the woman's aggravating ways and mannerisms. And each time, his mom would say, "Be kind," followed by a rationale for her sister's behavior. Ryan couldn't help but think Thynie's T-Rex nickname would have suited his aunt as well.

There was another puzzle he'd been aware of since soon after his arrival. When he observed Irving and Thynie Marsh's youngest son Jacob, whether in school, quarterbacking the football team or playing forward on the basketball team, Ryan found himself thinking of Thynie as his aunt, or even grandmother, rather than his mother. It seemed incongruous, maybe even ironic, that the boy was quite popular and well-liked. Ryan assumed Jake must have been a surprise addition to the Marsh family. He was seven and nine years younger respectively than his brothers. Neither of those boys went beyond two years of post-high school education. Both now worked in the family businesses. But Jake seemed different.

He had confidence but not swagger. He was driven and excelled but wasn't cocky. He was talented but realistic. He recognized, despite his parents' bragging and ambitions for him, that he didn't possess the level of talent to play Division 1 football or basketball. He did, however, have the realistic goal and ambition of doing both at either the Oshkosh or Green Bay campus of the University of Wisconsin – each of which anchored opposite ends of the Fox River Valley. Jacob was not shy in the least, but he was respectful. His classmates liked him, and so did Ryan, who sometimes wondered if the boy had been adopted.

Ryan was glad Thynie's maddening traits had not been passed down to her youngest. Unfortunately, neither had the boy's traits seemed to have rubbed off on his mother. The contrast between Thynie and her youngest son was of puzzling interest to Ryan, but it didn't change his reality as he'd attempted to deal with the woman since coming to Stienboek. Their abrasive interactions had forced him to focus all his attention on the part of her that seemed constantly in his face and out to get him. He hadn't been able to believe she possessed any other parts. Yet, now and again, when he'd see or chat with Jake, he had to consider the possibility that maybe at least a few other parts of Thynie might exist – somewhere.

These thoughts, along with the newly gained perspective provided by Walt Hannig, were on his mind as he closed the office door behind her and offered her a seat. Slightly stocky, befitting the mother of three, she wore one of her trademark pantsuits. He sat across from her, determined not to focus on the wary animosity he felt in her company but rather on his hopeful desire to get a sense of the person Walt Hannig had described. A local iconic legend to all those whose identity and way of life were perceived to be under chronic existential threat.

"Thanks for coming, Thynie. I appreciate it."

"Well, Mr. Davvis, I have to say I was surprised by your call. After all, you've been here twenty-one months. I gave up waiting to be invited quite a while ago."

Determined not to get side-tracked, Ryan let the admonishment pass. “I owe you an apology for that. I was too used to the impersonal ways of big-city schools. But I’m learning.” Hoping to make a connection, he tossed out his first cast. “I’ve been learning more about the area. I understand your family was one of the first to farm the Fox Valley. That’s an impressive legacy. It’s helped me to appreciate your commitment to the area. I understand the original family homestead was in Westown?”

He hoped he hadn’t sounded disingenuous. He certainly had not meant to be. For a moment, Thynie’s face relaxed. Ryan saw a glimpse of the part of her that could produce a kid like Jacob. She was forty-nine, just five years older than he was. But all forty-nine years had been spent here, where everyone would have known her, and she’d have known everyone. Her history was entwined with the district. John Stienboek, with whom she shared a branch on the family tree, was Superintendent throughout her school years. He realized Walt Hannig would have been her high school principal for at least two of her four years. He regretted not considering this earlier and tapping into Walt’s memories.

Ryan could sense there was something about her that seemed to sprout from the taproot planted by those first immigrants. She was a living connection to those who had taken the Fox Valley from the indigenous clans and made it their own, only to quickly see it overwhelmed by the waves that followed them with different visions and priorities. He felt they could understand each other if she gave him a chance.

When she responded, Thynie sounded caught off guard and not quite sure where this was going. “Did you invite me here to discuss my family history?”

Ryan pressed on. “Actually, in a way, I did. I know I’m an outsider. I also know you didn’t vote to hire me. But I think that makes you the perfect person to teach me what I need to know so I can understand all sides of Edenton. I was a history teacher, Thynie. I respect the past and know how important it is to the present and future. Walt Hannig told me that Edenton's first superintendent" – Ryan avoided pronouncing the last name – "fought against consolidation, but when the change became inevitable, he led in a way that respected all sides. In my small way, I'd like to model myself after that." Ryan stopped and folded his hands together on the table and hoped she'd accept his offer of a détente.

"Why did you come here, Mr. Davvis?" It was Ryan's turn to be caught off guard. Before he could respond, Thynie continued. "I know Walt Hannig was kind of a mentor for you. And I know your late wife, Lisa Kames, introduced you two."

Hearing Lisa's name, Ryan felt his entire demeanor change, and he removed his hands from the table. The momentary glimpse of Thynie's face that hinted at being the mother of Jacob Marsh was gone.

"I'm wondering how much you know about your wife, Lisa Kames, or should I say Lisa Davvis? You were a history teacher? Okay. Then you should know how important it is that we learn from the past and that we fight like hell to make sure the evils of the past are eliminated."

Alarmed, Ryan asked, "What are you getting at, Thynie?"

"Let's just say your wife had a bit of a reputation back in high school. And a lot of people got hurt. Did you ever meet her Uncle Simon? The poor man's life was devastated when Lisa claimed some wild story about biting or some such ridiculous thing and called Family Services. He tragically died in a car accident a few years ago. Many of us think it was related. And he wasn't the only one. Your wife severely hurt the reputation of several of the boys in school, including my nephew who was foolish enough to believe her lies. So, suffice it to say, Mr. Davvis," she almost hissed his name, "that would be a part of the past we could do without around here.

"Yet, here you are. And now all of a sudden, Sharon Edmonds, *your secretary*, up and leaves her husband and starts spending time at your apartment and you two have been seen hugging around your office."

She stopped. Ryan was angry and incredulous. Yet ironically, with each hateful remark she spewed, he felt the woman's ability to intimidate him diminish.

She stood to go then added, "Oh, and one other thing. Why wasn't Natalia Samilton suspended when she attacked the Quant boy? That seems to smack of big-city reverse discrimination to me. What message does that send to the other students, Mr. Davvis?"

After Thynie Marsh had marched out of his office, Ryan kept running a phrase through his mind. *No good deed goes unpunished. No good deed goes unpunished.* For a moment he thought maybe Walt had set him up, but he immediately felt ashamed of the thought. If Walt had known about Thynie's bizarre vendetta, he would have warned him.

Ryan couldn't help asking himself – "*Is the woman nuts?*" He knew the only source for her comment about Sharon being at his place had to come from her husband, Dave. He also knew if Dave Edmonds was spreading that information, he was probably embellishing the story with his fictional accusation of an adulterous affair. He wouldn't mention this to Sharon. It would do no good and only add to her worries. But he did know who he did have to talk to.

66

William Powells suggested, "How about we take a break? I could use a cup of coffee and a few minutes to process. I suppose, considering the date, a Guinness would be more appropriate, if less professional. I'll put on a pot. If you need the washroom, there's one at the end of the hall."

Powells stepped out of his office and crossed into the small kitchen alcove. Ryan Davvis followed. "I raised a couple Guinness last night to toast St. Paddy's, so I'm good with coffee."

He kept walking toward the restroom. The therapist pulled a can of coffee from the refrigerator and filled the carafe with cold water. He had offered Ryan the option of meeting on a Sunday morning to help assure the high school principal's privacy. He'd done it before for a few particularly recognizable community members. He knew such folks often chose to drive to one of the bigger cities to assure anonymity. He had also offered to recommend someone else, but Ryan was adamant he wanted to see him.

Powells measured out the grounds and hit BREW. Leaning against the sink, he sifted through all Ryan had told him, trying to find an entry point into the story. With no other appointments, and his wife out of town visiting her mother, there were no time constraints. He'd let Ryan tell his story at his own pace, asking for only occasional clarifications. On the surface, it was a story of a man trying to deal with the sudden, violent death of his young wife. That alone would have been enough, and it might be where he'd start.

But Ryan had added so much more: the details about Lisa's affairs – and his own – the background stories from Lisa's cousin. Twice he'd mentioned a photo he kept locked away.

Ryan reappeared back at the kitchenette. "I want to thank you again for taking time out of your weekend and for the offer to recommend someone out of town. But I was much impressed with you at Ayden Quant's IEP. You made me think differently about all that happened between Lisa and me. By the way, Ayden has mentioned you more than once. Seems he finds you funny."

"Well, back at you, Ryan. The boy holds you in high regard, and for him, that's important. You want cream or sugar?"

"Black's good. Thanks."

The men recrossed the hall to Powells' office. After a few sips, Powells asked his first question. "What do you think it means to deal with the death of someone so close?"

Ryan set his coffee down. "I'd have to say acceptance."

"You mean acceptance that the person is gone?"

"Yeah. That, and you don't get a chance to reconcile the things you'd like to, or need to."

"Do you accept that Lisa is gone, is dead?"

"My hands were covered with her blood. I watched the paramedics trying to restart her heart. I scattered her ashes. Yes, I accept she's dead."

"Where did you scatter her ashes? Was there any kind of ceremony with that?"

Ryan described how he had not known what to do with them, not even known why he couldn't decide. Her estranged parents wanted no part of either Lisa or him. He described how he'd driven in tears to a park along the Mississippi and scattered the ashes. They'd made love in his car like teenagers there once. Lisa had called the river a DMZ between her old and new life.

Powells asked, "And you did everything alone? I'm sure you two had friends, colleagues, and some family members, at least on your side, who wanted to support you. Why no service or ceremony at any point?"

"I just couldn't face people at the time. That's what I told everyone."

"Why? What couldn't you face? People want to express their sorrow and shock about the tragedy; offer condolences, commiserate, tell stories, and offer support. Was that what you didn't want to face? Or was there something else?"

Ryan reached for his coffee, then decided not to. Then he picked it up, drank, and put it back. William Powells held his cup in both hands but didn't lift it to his lips. Ryan closed his eyes, either trying to hide from something or to remember it. "I didn't want any of that. I didn't deserve it."

"Why wouldn't you deserve condolences and empathy?" Powells asked.

Ryan appeared to try to answer but couldn't. Sensing he was willing but needed encouragement, Powells altered the question. "Was it that you didn't deserve condolences or empathy... or you were afraid of it?"

The answer came after a few moments of hesitation. "Both."

Respecting the trust Ryan had just placed in him, Powells waited several seconds before saying, "If you're ready, can we start with the fear? What do you think you were afraid of?"

Ryan didn't think he had an answer until a tear ran down his cheek and what he'd been feeling erupted. "That all that stuff would be too much, too confusing, or maybe too honest. What if I ended up trying to explain what had been going on, about what Lisa had done? What I had been doing? How could I explain that if we hadn't gone for ice cream, or if we had made it home safe that night, we both may have been saved?"

He stopped talking. Powells was about to ask another question when Ryan started again. "I was also afraid I'd have to stop my affair and, God help me, I didn't know if I could. To stop would mean I was again abdicating control, taking my hands off the wheel and passively letting Lisa, even in death, hold me hostage. For almost two months, I'd pretended to be understanding and supportive, but what I was, was terrified of losing her. And even more afraid of what it said about me. That thought paralyzed me. When I first discovered she was..."

When Ryan seemed stuck, Powells prompted, "Was what?"

"Was having sex with someone else." He stopped again. "Had *fucked* somebody else. My first thought was total and utter humiliation. A personal shame and mortification and fear of forever being known by all as a fool, a cuckold, a joke, a punchline. A man who couldn't satisfy his wife. Do you have any idea how that felt?"

William Powells gave the slightest shake of his head. "Tell me."

"I felt like a helpless little boy whose shorts had been pulled down for the amusement of others and had to stand there naked while they inspected and mocked me." The tear had stopped at his jawline. He wiped it away.

"Is that how you always envision your feelings about her unfaithfulness?"

Ryan took some more coffee while he considered. "No. Usually, I see myself getting kicked in the balls... Maybe that's a way of remembering I had some."

Ryan shifted in his chair and said, "Lisa validated me... as a person and a man. I didn't think I needed that, but from the moment we were introduced, and as I told you, she joked to everyone that we'd already had an affair, I felt a foot taller. But that night when I found out, I became a punctured balloon with all its air rushing out. I wanted to douse myself with gasoline and drop a match."

Powells gave Ryan a few seconds to gather himself before again gently prompting. "Go on."

"But what did I do instead?" Ryan rhetorically asked. "I acted reasonably, swallowed my pride and anger so it didn't ignite and make it worse. I believed if I didn't get angry, didn't overreact, I could rescue her, rescue me too. I held on like a drowning man to her promises: that she'd never let anyone know, that it wasn't my fault, and that her behavior was some unexplainable flaw in *her*. I had to believe it could be fixed."

Ryan paused, perhaps contemplating what he would have done if he hadn't believed it fixable, wondering if she'd still be alive if he'd left. After several moments he went on.

"I believed she loved me because I had to. I knew if I let go, my image of who I was and what I wanted to be, what she and I could be, would be ripped away from me. And then, of course, several weeks later *she* was ripped away, of all things by some anonymous fuck-head trying to prove *his* manhood by shooting at someone the police never did find."

Ryan stopped talking, surprised that no other tears had followed the first. Both men let the weight of his words settle into the silence. Knowing how draining and important Ryan's insight had been, Powells patiently waited for a signal. He didn't want to end the session without touching on the other half of Ryan's reason for isolating himself. So, when Ryan finally made eye contact, he asked, "You also said you didn't deserve empathy?"

"Why would I? Who could empathize with a guy who denied his emasculation by doing the same thing to another man?"

"You mean with the wife of the school board member? Why her?"

"Because she gave me complete control. Or so I thought at the time."

67

The disappointing losses by both the boys and girls had faded or, more accurately, been erased by more pressing concerns. The second semester was in full swing, and spring break would begin in under two weeks. Then only two days after that would be April 2nd, Election Day, and the fate of the referendum would be decided. That had been Ryan's main concern up until he had met with Thynie Marsh last Wednesday. Now, her overt hostility was top of mind. It was closely followed by, and directly connected to, his concern about receiving his contract extension. The thought of not being renewed had exploded from theoretical to very real as soon as Thynie had walked out of their meeting.

Administrators received their contract offers in early April. The wait would be tough on his blood pressure. He'd considered talking with Superintendent Demian about the threat and the contract but had opted to just inform her he'd talked with Thynie. Not wanting to appear as unable to stand up to the pressure, all he'd stoically reported was she'd made it clear she didn't think him a good fit at Stienboek and that she seemed to hold his marriage to Lisa Kames against him. Demian's reply was, "No surprise there." It hadn't been the unconditional support he'd hoped to hear.

He'd also talked with Dominic. Again, he didn't share the threats against himself but informed him that Thynie had asked why Nala hadn't been suspended when she'd hit Ayden. Dominic was more than annoyed that she had been asking about his daughter. That was last Thursday, but now, Dominic was on his way over. He'd called to say T-Rex had just left his office, and he needed to talk with Ryan.

Dominic declined anything to drink, and the two men sat at the table. He started with, "Thynie is out of her damn mind, Ryan. What all happened when you met with her?"

While waiting for Dominic to arrive, Ryan had decided he needed to trust him. If he couldn't believe the man was his friend, then he might never be able to do so with another person again. So, he explained to Dominic why he'd set up the meeting with Thynie after talking with Walt. He'd really thought he understood her point of view and wanted to let her know he respected her for it.

"It turned out, I didn't understand shit," Ryan said. "Lisa used to claim I sucked at reading women. She was right. Thynie accused Lisa of ruining her nephew's reputation. Do you know anything about the guy? She blamed her for her uncle's car crash, saying she'd hurt a lot of other people. And then..." Ryan stopped to rub his hands across his face as if he wanted to wipe the conversation from his memory. "And then, she all but accused me of being the reason Sharon left Dave. He must have told her that Sharon was spending time here. Her bottom line was that I was unfit to be principal and was ruining people's lives."

Ryan realized how good it felt to say this stuff out loud. Then for a moment, he wondered if he needed to remind Dominic this was all to be kept confidential. In frustration with himself for having any uncertainty, he shook his head to toss off the doubt.

Assuming Ryan's head shake was disbelief at Thynie's accusations, Dominic said, "I think she went off the rails last year when she again came up a vote short to become board president. Now she sees another opportunity with this election to pick up that vote. I guess she thinks discrediting you will discredit Superintendent

Demian and the board president and affect the election. I also have absolutely no trouble believing she is capable of holding you responsible for her nephew."

"What the hell happened between the nephew and Lisa?" Ryan asked.

Like Ryan, Dominic had made up his mind he'd tell Ryan the whole truth. He explained as directly as he could. "The guy was part of a group that delighted in harassing girls. Lisa was a frequent target. I don't know what you learned from her cousin, but there were some weird goings-on and rumors about the Kames family, especially the uncle. For these guys, that made it open season on her. They'd alternate between harassing and hitting on her. Then, I think it was over the summer after her freshman year, she suddenly started going out with some of them, only to start telling everybody about the guy. Saying they had tiny peckers or couldn't get it up, stuff like that. You know how easily guys get embarrassed at that age and how quick they are to mock each other to hide their own paranoia and embarrassment. Still, one by one, they fell for it."

It was hard, but Ryan had to bring something up. "Toni told me that Lisa didn't see you that way. I mean about the harassment and stuff. She said Lisa trusted you and thought you were a good guy. Walt thought you guys would get married after high school. Can I ask, what happened?"

Dominic hesitated, but only for a moment. "You got a beer?"

Ryan went to the refrigerator, took out two bottles, and brought them to the table. They each took a drink. After another, Dominic set his bottle down.

"I felt sorry for her. I knew people loved to spread rumors, especially about sex. I assumed most, if not all of it, was crap. But when I'd see and hear the taunting, it pissed me off. Back in high school, I was into weightlifting, and the farm work kept me in shape. So, I'd get in some of those guys' faces about their picking on the girls. Particularly Lisa because she seemed to catch the most shit. I had enough friends to back me. It wasn't like I was being a big hero.

"Anyhow, Lisa noticed. We'd talk some, and we just got along. I never asked her out back then. I was just nice to her. There were others too but not enough of them. Anyhow, I didn't see her much over the summer before my senior year. I was working a lot, trying to make and save money. Then after school started, just before homecoming, she asked me to the homecoming dance. I wasn't going with anyone then. A couple of my friends made a few wisecracks, but when I told them to back off, they did." Dominic stopped and took a few sips of his beer.

Ryan used the pause to finally ask his question, but it came out as a statement. "You said you had sex with her once."

Dominic set his bottle down and looked directly at Ryan. He didn't see anger or fear or jealousy, just a desire to get everything on the table. "The dance was nice. We didn't get any shit from anyone all night. It ended at midnight. I was driving her home when she said she had a key to her uncle's place, and he wouldn't be home until after the bars closed at two. She said she had something she wanted to tell me. I figured she just wanted to make out some. Of course, I did too. When we got there, she led me right into the bedroom and started to undress. I hesitated. I wanted to, and I might have, but..."

Ryan stopped him. "You *might* have?"

"I wanted to. Probably would have. But I just didn't want to see myself as being like those other guys. The thing is, I almost did. I only stopped because of my pride. That's not a very honorable reason for not taking advantage of someone, especially someone as vulnerable as Lisa at the time. So, when Dave Edmonds said I did, I told you that I had."

Dominic stopped again. He finished his beer and stared at the empty bottle before quickly finishing what he had to say. "Lisa must have assumed I was hesitating because I didn't have a condom. She said, 'You don't have to worry.' And, before I can tell her that wasn't the reason, she says… she's pregnant and starts to cry."

Ryan again scrubbed his hands across his face.

"I'm sorry, Ryan. I didn't know if Toni told you about that or not, so I had to. I don't want you to think I'm holding anything back from you." He waited for Ryan to lower his hands and respond.

"Toni didn't mention anything about Lisa being pregnant."

Dominic thought a moment and then said, "Maybe she didn't know. Lisa told me no one else knew. I believed her."

"Whose baby was it?"

"She wouldn't tell me. I was scared for her. If the rumors were true, it might be her uncle's. I didn't ask twice."

Trying to figure out what to say, Ryan asked tentatively, "Did she have…" He couldn't bring himself to say "the baby."

"I told you I'll tell you everything if you want it."

Ryan nodded. Dominic kept his word. "She got dressed. We got out of there and drove around a bit. She cried and begged me not to tell anyone. She was scared, told me she couldn't have a baby but didn't know what to do. I promised her I'd help. She was so relieved and believed me, so I had to find a way."

Dominic needed to finish the story. He didn't want to possess anything more that could hurt Ryan. "I had no idea what to do or where to find out. So, I took a chance. I knew Lisa wouldn't approve, but I felt desperate for her. I went to the only one I could think of at the time who might give me advice and not judge or insist on too many details."

Ryan shook off the numbness that had gripped him as he listened. "That must have been hard for you, and, for what it's worth, I'm grateful to you for helping her."

Dominic said, "I never told Lisa I talked to anyone. But I'm going to tell you because I think you should know."

Ryan looked at him quizzically. Dominic said, "First, finish your beer." Ryan didn't question the request. He picked up his bottle and drained it. Setting the empty down, he said, "It was Walt, wasn't it?"

"You're right... Walt was the first one that came to mind that I thought I could trust. But I was afraid as principal he might be duty-bound to get actively involved. I couldn't do that to Lisa. I needed someone ... I don't know. Ballsy." A little grin showed in Dominic's eyes.

"Dom, you're killing me here. Who the hell did you talk to?"

"Bernadette Zowak."

Ryan's mouth dropped open. "What!" Really?"

"I told her I had a friend in another school whose girlfriend *might* be pregnant and *might* need some help. To her credit, she didn't outright call me a liar. She told me to come back the next day after school. When I did, she gave me a clinic name and phone number in Waukegan, Illinois. She said, 'Tell your friend...' Mrs. Zowak stopped and looked at me in a way that made me sure she knew I was talking about Lisa. But she didn't say so. She just started again saying, 'Tell your friend she'll need to show she's eighteen, or she'll have to have parental permission.'

"I was embarrassed and just mumbled my thanks and headed quickly for the door. Before I got out, Mrs. Zowak said in that sarcastic tone of voice she uses, 'Mister Samilton. Your friend... is lucky to have a friend like you.'

"I immediately said, 'It's not me, not mine.' And she says, 'Okay. Then I assume *your friend* knows where to get an ID if needed. Make sure you have blankets and maybe a pillow in your truck for the ride home. And drive safely, for God's sake.' She never mentioned another word to me about it. Lisa had her the following year and was never the wiser."

"I don't know what to say," Ryan admitted.

"Saying nothing is probably best. Saying anything about it won't help anybody."

"How long were you two together after that? I promise that's my last question."

"I played mother hen after that. People thought we were dating, but we were just friends. The abortion was what started her volunteering to work with little kids. That May, we went to prom where I almost got suspended days before graduation for punching Dave Edmonds – this was before he was with Sharon – when he started leering at Lisa. A few days later, Lisa told me I couldn't be her protector forever and broke up with me, but she let people believe I'd broken up with her.

"We'd run into each other once in a while. But after she graduated, she moved to Green Bay. I never saw her again until that volleyball game she brought you to. I wanted to say 'Hi' to her, but her uncle was there. I couldn't face them together."

Dominic's shoulders relaxed, and he felt very tired. But it was finally all out.

"You want another beer, Dom?"

"No. Thanks. I've got to get home." He stood. "I'm sorry Ryan. I know you loved her."

"I loved her," Ryan repeated. "I still do."

68

Ryan hadn't given much thought to Superintendent Demian's call to meet in his office after lunch. With the referendum happening the following week, the superintendent had been touching base with everyone on the team. However, by the time they met, Ryan was anticipating the worst. When he entered the front office, Sharon raised her eyebrows and let him know she was waiting back in his office.

"Sorry to barge in early on you, Ryan." The superintendent was sitting on one of the blue metal chairs. She pointed to the faux suede chair on rollers he usually offered to students. His inclination was to take one of the other metal chairs but then complied with her gesture.

"I hope I didn't keep you waiting, Liz."

"Not at all. I came a few minutes early. I need to be back by 1:30 to meet with Chuck Templeton. We've got some things to discuss."

Ryan hoped one of those things wasn't to talk with the board president about posting the position for a new principal at Stienboek.

Demian slid an envelope across the table. "Thynie Marsh came to see me on Monday."

Ryan's heart accelerated. He wanted desperately to ask what it was before opening it. He'd never thought of Liz Demian as having a cruel streak. Until now. This was torture. He took out the two pages. He hoped his hands weren't visibly shaking.

"I'd like to get this signed today."

Ryan forced his eyes to focus. "Edenton Area School District" was on line one and his name was typed on the second. Already added on the appropriate lines were "Position of Principal - Stienboek High School" and the dates "July 1, 2013 - June 30, 2015."

"You look relieved," Demian said with a hint of a grin. "Mr. Templeton and I agree it would be a good idea if we have this signed before the election."

Ryan's relief was visible. "Does this have anything to do with your conversation with Thynie?"

"There are a few things we should discuss, but I'm most concerned about why she is so hell-bent against you. So, I did some homework. Thynie implied Dominic could corroborate what she was telling me. As I anticipated, he told me I should ask you. But he also said she'd come to him trying to dig up information about your wife. He informed me once upon a time back in high school they'd dated, and Thynie knew that. Dominic also said she got visibly upset when all he would tell her was Lisa was great with little kids, and he'd always respected her. He also said Thynie made some innuendos about his daughter getting special treatment and accused him of covering up that you were the reason Sharon left her husband. He filled me in on her estranged husband's threats and said the only time she's been to your place was to drop off her kids' cat, which, he added, you seem to be allergic to. Is that true?"

"Yes. That was the only time she's been there."

"I meant about you being allergic to the cat?"

Ryan smiled. "Allergy tablets take care of it. I'm sure Hamilton will be back with her kids soon enough."

Demian smiled. "Hamilton? I'm glad you took the cat and not Dominic. Hamilton Samilton would have been an awful name."

She handed Ryan a pen, and he signed and dated the offer. Demian did the same and slid it back into the envelope. "Of course, it's not legally binding until the board approves it. But even should one of the two incumbents lose – and I don't think that will happen because they both have had solid support in the past – it will put us in a better position to get it through quickly. It would certainly ruffle feathers, but, if push came to shove, we'd have time to call and post an early meeting and bring the signed contract to the current board for a vote. I expect if the rest of the board heard about Thynie's conduct, you might even pick up an additional vote."

Ryan asked, "Thank you. But why? Thynie and Bobby could use that against you down the road."

"Mrs. T. Marsh has overstepped and, if I'm honest, she's also really pissed me off. She is righteous, pompous, and loves being the center of attention. Frustrating as that can be, she does bring an important balance. Having one or two old-school thinkers on the board and faculty forces everyone to think a little deeper before sending the educational pendulum swinging wildly in another direction. But she is not going to manipulate her way to the board presidency by slander and intimidation."

Superintendent Demian slid the envelope into her coat pocket and then loosely folded her hands on the table. "Ryan, it's clear to me you have the potential Walt Hannig said you do. I also know everyone judges us based on their expectations and biases. Yet everyone's expectations are different. It can drive you crazy if you let it or if you don't have a vision of who you are and where you want to go. I'm convinced you have the vision and you're learning the rest."

Demian stood. "I'm comfortable with this, Ryan. I've done my due diligence, and I have confidence you bring things to the table we need around here. And," she slid her chair back under the table, "you may be surprised at some of the staff you've begun to influence and who have begun to trust you."

She put her coat on and extended her hand to Ryan. They shook. "One last thing. If there is, in any sense, a 'you and Sharon' – remember this is not Minneapolis. Don't do dumb things."

69

The City of Edenton was divided into five districts – some more conservative, some more liberal-minded, but all still feeling the effects of the last recession. Based on the 2010 Census, the current city population had risen to 4,109. The surrounding rural area, which comprised the rest of the Edenton Area School District including Westown, Cooper, and two other smaller municipalities, covered almost 90% of the district's land but had a population of just under 2,900 and was mostly conservative by nature. Because the typical voting trends for each area were well-known, those in favor of the referendum were not feeling particularly optimistic. Ryan remembered Superintendent Demian's comment. "No" voters were often more motivated than the "Yes" voters.

Wisconsin's unusual election laws made each municipality, rather than the county, responsible for running its own election and counting its votes. That meant the vote count was usually announced in a piecemeal fashion The polls closed at 8:00 p.m. The hope was results from the small polling places would be in by 10:00. The city vote would take longer.

Besides the school referendum – which was one of over two dozen across the state this April – the administrative team would be keeping a close eye on the school board contest. The conventional wisdom was that if the referendum was defeated, it meant turnout favored the conservative candidate. The only other contested races were for a seat on the City of Edenton Common Council and two county supervisors' seats.

Dominic and Kate had invited Ryan and Sharon over for dinner. Nala and Sharon's kids were downstairs playing a board game and watching a movie. At 8:00 p.m. when the polls closed, the unofficial numbers started to trickle in. As the adults talked, each kept one eye on the numbers from across the state as they crawled across the bottom of the muted television.

Earlier, after the kids had left the table, Sharon told the others that David had informed her he'd retained a lawyer. It was a small step forward. No one believed it would be amicable, but at least the divorce process could move forward. She also said Toni had convinced her the kids could bring Hamilton back home. They'd agreed to split the cost of having the house professionally cleaned when Sharon and the kids found a more permanent arrangement. She wanted to move into the city so the kids would have easier access to friends and events. Dominic teased her saying she'd always been a city girl at heart. He was on the verge of ribbing Ryan about saving money on allergy pills, but Ryan cut him short by moving his finger across his throat. The girls tried to pry out of them what that was about, but they resisted. His cat allergy secret would remain between him and Dominic.

A little before 9:00 p.m., the Edenton referendum and school board results began to appear. The early results showed 54% against. The 46% 'Yes' vote was, however, higher than they'd hoped. Kate brought out a bottle of wine. "Let's toast and celebrate each little victory."

By 9:30 the numbers had tanked and a negative eighteen-point gap opened up. Having been forewarned of what to expect, they encouraged each other, knowing the Edenton city vote never came in before 10:00 and usually came in two waves. As they waited, the local trio used the opportunity to learn about Ryan's life. They asked about his childhood and college life. By tacit agreement, no one asked about Ryan's life with Lisa. They knew his parents had been educators, but he surprised them by talking about his high school years on the track and golf teams. After a while, they'd almost forgotten about their vote vigil. The easy flow of information, anecdotes, and teasing would make anyone watching think they were all old friends catching up and reminiscing.

When the first batch of Edenton votes dropped at 10:35, Sharon's fifth-graders were asleep in the basement, and Nala was in her room. The gap was narrowed to seven points. Ryan breathed easier and the knot between his shoulders eased. But it wasn't clear which districts were included in this wave. They'd been hoping the first Edenton votes would at least even things up. There was good news, however. The two incumbents were now up by 5% and 7% respectively. Hopefully, that would translate into more "Yes" votes when the last batches came in. Sharon excused herself to use the restroom. As she passed, she openly put a hand on each of Ryan's shoulders and squeezed. His breathing got a bit tighter again.

It was near midnight when the final unofficial votes from Edenton were posted. While both school board incumbents won reelection rather handily, it was obvious there would be a recount on the referendum vote count. As it stood, the Edenton Area School District voters had chosen to fund the district's borrowing for maintenance and technology needs by a total of twelve votes.

As Sharon's daughter nuzzled their cat in her arms, she said, "Thank you, Mr. Davvis, for taking care of Hammy." Her brother scratched the cat's head, then turned his attention to checking out the high school principal's less-than-interesting apartment.

Sharon had her daughter settle Hamilton into his carrying box.

"Okay, you guys take Hammy to the car, and I'll be right out." She closed the door after them and turned to Ryan.

"What are you going to do with all your free time now that the recount has held up, and you don't have a roommate to take care of?"

"I think Hamilton did more for me than the other way around."

They stood awkwardly, not looking at each other, something hanging in the silence of the moment. Sharon said, "You know, Ryan, for a long time Dominic has been like a big brother to me. He told me about Thynie trapping him in his office. He was quite upset. He said she accused him of hiding something going on between me and you." She stopped and locked eyes with Ryan, then asked. "Is there?"

Ryan held her gaze. "Lisa contended any beautiful woman could make a fool out of me."

Sharon's voice carried the color of hurt. "Do you think I could do anything to make a fool of you?"

"No. I meant you're beautiful."

She smiled wider than Ryan remembered ever seeing. He said, "But I should tell you; I've been advised by my boss that Edenton is not Minneapolis. I'm under orders not to do anything dumb. I've learned Liz Demian's advice is usually worth paying attention to."

Sharon agreed. "She's right. This isn't the big city and, as you know, the things you'd prefer to remain private, never do. But," she said with a flirtatious smile and glance, "you know, by the fall, I'll be a divorcee and free to see anyone I want. Even in Edenton, that's only a minor scandal."

Now a smile crossed Ryan's face. "If I'm reading you right..." he paused, "I'd like to suggest October is a beautiful time to visit Door County."

"Hmm," Sharon said, taking something from her bag. It was wrapped. "Maybe this will help decide if you're reading me right."

She handed it to Ryan. "Thank you for taking such good care of Hamilton. See you at school."

Ryan stood still after she'd left, not wanting to dislodge any of the emotional or physical warmth he was feeling. It was part contentment and part hope, two feelings he'd thought were no longer available to him. He remained still and quiet until his curiosity demanded he look. He slid his finger under the taped seams and opened the wrapping. His laugh was as spontaneous and hearty as any he'd ever had. When he stopped, his grin remained. Maybe he was getting better at reading women. He tossed Ayden Quant's confiscated *Playboy* magazine onto the couch, thinking, maybe later on, he'd see if it contained any good articles.

70

"Congratulations on getting the referendum passed. That was a real squeaker." William Powells sat on one of the blue chairs across from Ryan. "Getting it passed must have felt good."

"You have no idea," said Ryan.

"Do you mean that in a school or personal sense?"

"Both."

"So, you had some personal stake in getting it approved?"

As Powells asked the question, and for a few seconds afterward, his head swiveled taking in all aspects of Ryan's small office. He'd suggested meeting here this time rather than at his office. Being another Sunday morning, the rest of the building was empty. Not having to chance being noticed entering or leaving Powells' clinic, Ryan was at ease as opposed to last month when his stress and anxiety had been high.

A good chunk of all that had dissolved with the election followed by Superintendent Demian's assurance that all current administrative contracts, including his, would be approved at the next board meeting. She had also privately informed Ryan that, when confronted with possible censure and an all but certain recall for her attempts to threaten and intimidate district staff, Mrs. Thynie Marsh had promised to quit harassing him. Demian had also mentioned Dominic had played a big role in her decision.

However, still shadowing Ryan's new optimistic outlook was Lisa's apparent inability to escape what had happened to her in Edenton. He continued to want to believe they'd gone for ice cream to reconcile and maybe even celebrate that she'd found a way through the past in the final hour of her life.

"I did," Ryan responded to Powells' question about personal stakes. "And as they say, 'All's well that ends well.'"

"I'm glad to hear that," Powells said, then pivoted. "Is Lisa's photograph still here, locked away somewhere?"

Ryan grinned and gave his head a slight shake. "So, that's why you suggested we meet here?"

Powells didn't answer directly. "You don't seem to have any other pictures here either. Do you keep them at home?"

"I guess I'm not much of a picture guy. I must admit, my walls at home are pretty bare too." Ryan regarded what he'd just said with interest. This was another reason Ryan liked the man. He'd be a great detective. Ryan saw the path Powells was pointing him toward and decided to again trust him and take a few steps in that direction. "I'm guessing Freud would have something to say about that."

"Undoubtedly," Powells said. "He'd probably see it as avoidance of some kind. Maybe avoidance of the past...or a desire to detach from it. On the other hand, the Eastern perspective might interpret it as acceptance of impermanence." The therapist again looked around. "Which do you think fits better? If you had to choose."

Ryan crossed his ankles. "As you know, I was born and raised *west* of the Mississippi."

"I do," Powells said with no inflection or intent other than acknowledging the fact. "You spent your entire life there. So, why did you want to move here after Lisa died? Do you know what that might have been about?" The therapist's eyes came fully to rest on Ryan.

"I knew I needed to come here from the night I scattered Lisa's ashes in the river. Or at least soon after." Ryan paused, expecting a question. When none came, he named his reasons out loud, as much for himself as Powells. "Anger and revenge." Still, no question came, so he tried reversing the words. "Revenge and anger."

When the silence reached ten seconds, rather than a question, Powells said, "Anger is understandable with all you've told me. And revenge...Well, revenge – or more specifically thinking about it – is one of the few pleasures angry people allow themselves. So, that also makes sense."

Powells' words made Ryan ask, "Pleasures?"

"Anger is experienced as pain. Something we all try to avoid or mitigate. Mentally healthy adults – *like you*, Powells emphasized – aren't planning to carry out any serious large-scale retaliation. They know it only makes the situation worse – not that a person can't cause real harm to himself or others with more targeted reprisals..."

Ryan experienced his instantaneous flash of Mrs. Rupert as a hard slap to the back of his head, but he stayed focused on Powells' explanation. He'd have to deal with that guilt and behavior another time.

"... But," Powells continued, "thinking about revenge is satisfying. It activates the part of the brain connected to reward. It feels righteous and pleasurable. At least in the short term."

It was a lot for Ryan to think about. It matched his experience. But left lots of long-term questions. "I know I came here seeking some unspecified revenge. That doesn't seem so healthy."

Powells said, "Ryan, I think you're coming to Edenton speaks to the toll of the traumas you experienced and, in particular, to what Lisa was going to share with you about her life in Edenton. It's also rational to think what she was about to tell you would have let you see that your reaction to her infidelity – what you call cowardice and fear – was equally a brave, courageous act of love. The mind is perfectly capable of holding such contradictions. It's rarely one or the other.

"But even with that, I'd venture that by the time you came here, you were after answers, not revenge. From what I hear, you've been an outstanding principal and person."

"Hear? Who have you heard from about me?"

"Ayden Quant, for one. The kid who somehow seems to be a fountain of insight." Both men nodded their heads as they thought about the boy.

"We can't oversimplify this," Powells said. "Trauma makes people question their identity, their sense of who they are, their ability to feel some control over their lives and to stay safe. There's no end to the ways people try to maintain or regain those things. It seems you're having trouble accepting how you went about it."

Ryan asked, "You're saying I should forgive and forget?"

"No," Powells said emphatically. "I'm saying accept you're human. Don't forget it or try to lock it away. Otherwise, forgiveness or forgetting doesn't have a lot of value."

Fifteen quiet seconds later Ryan's smile began. "I suppose this is why you get paid the big bucks."

"Actually, since I came here just to chat, I don't owe the business anything, so there's no charge. No wait! I take that back. I haven't had a Sophie's Burger in a long time. How about you buy us some lunch."

"You haven't seen the end of me," Ryan laughed. "I've got more issues than that."

"Don't we all?" Powells said. "But there is one I think you're ready to tackle." He pointed at the bottom desk drawer. "I think you told me it's in there. And I'm guessing she'd agree it's time you two had the conversation that didn't happen over ice cream that day. You've accepted her death. The next move is to accept her life."

71

Bernadette Zowak sat across from Ryan. "You look rather pleased with yourself, Mr. Davvis." The rest of the faculty had already departed to pack up and head home.

"Not with myself, Bernadette. With them, with all of us," Ryan said. "By my count, that was the fourth faculty meeting in a row that felt like we were getting somewhere. That's if you count the short January meeting, and I do. Maybe I'm deluding myself, but it also seems that since the election, moods, and morale are better for the first time since I've been here."

"It's the first time in the last couple of years we've had something to feel good about," Zowak said. "Where they felt some support from the public – as slim as it was. Keeping the current balance on the board was big too. A different result could have turned ugly. The talk in the lounge the next day was mostly about that. They were relieved that Thynie Marsh didn't pick up another ally. I didn't think her hand-picked candidate had a real chance anyway. Both incumbents were already fiscal conservatives, and there wasn't much in their records to run against. But I also know not to underestimate that woman. Have you heard from her? She can't be happy with the results."

Ryan grinned. "I've not heard a peep. No calls or emails. It's freed up an hour a day for me," he joked.

Zowak smiled. "She hasn't been your biggest fan, has she? On the other hand, I think she, or at least Mr. Datson, did you a big favor at the referendum meeting."

"Didn't feel like a favor," Ryan said.

"It made you one of us. Getting attacked with distorted information made you a comrade in arms of sorts. That's something you needed to earn around here, and the attack went a long way toward paying your admission fee."

"I have to admit that's good to hear."

"Now, Mr. Davvis, it didn't pay your entire dues." They shared a chuckle. "After all, you are an administrator..., and you're young and you're trying to get people who have long thought of themselves as successful independent contractors to get excited about changing their practices and to accept common standards and all that entails. That's a lot to ask, especially when experience has taught us most of these initiatives go away on their own. We're already hearing the governor and the legislature want to dump the current standards and create their own."

Ryan sat quietly and let her words sink in. Zowak gave him what teachers refer to as 'wait time', something she was not particularly well suited to. After nearly half a minute, he leaned toward the one teacher whom he'd most wanted to convince and, considering what he'd learned from Dominic, most wanted to thank. He realized now her "Yeah but" comments hadn't been about him or his ideas. They were honest challenges he needed to face and seriously consider.

He thought about Walt Hannig's comments about time and trust. He thought back to his teaching career as a broad-field social studies teacher where a primary underlying premise in all disciplines was that quick change only occurred by conquest or disaster. Buy-in, on the other hand, required respectful and thoughtful responses to all the "Yeah buts" people needed to ask.

In that half-minute Bernadette Zowak had given him, he decided a lot. If he was going to get unstuck, he had to accept what came next. If he advocated change, for himself or others, he needed to accept and trust who they were. He thought of the burning monk.

Then he thought of Lisa. Then he said, “Bernadette, I can’t thank you enough.”

While Bernadette Zowak looked at him with a touch of her famous skepticism, Ryan thought about how she’d helped Lisa, keeping her pregnancy a secret all those years ago, and that Dominic had asked him to keep it to himself. So, he added, “And I literally *cannot* tell you how much I appreciate everything, and I do mean ‘*every*’ thing, you’ve done.”

Zowak’s face turned quizzical. “Why am I getting the feeling we’re not just talking about school here, Mr. Davvis?”

Ryan smiled at her. “How about life, past, present, and future?”

Her face softened. “Past, present, and future?” Her eyes smiled. “You are very welcome, Ryan. I was glad I could help.”

72

Dominic had let go of most of the anger from his conversation with Thynie Marsh. But the accusation that his daughter received preferential treatment wasn't so easily dismissed. He still couldn't believe Thynie had used the words "reverse discrimination." He'd talked about it with Superintendent Demian. But first, he'd talked with Kate. Her first reaction was to laugh. That turned immediately to wanting to go for Thynie's throat. Kate, even more than Dominic, had felt her daughter's pain when a few of her friends had melted away. She'd been the one to notice when Nala started recognizing the uncertain looks and reactions she'd attract when they were out shopping.

She'd told Dominic she and Nala had in the past had some mother-daughter conversations on the topic over the years. The most recent was on their drive to Nala's hair appointment. Kate also let him know that since middle school, Nala had been adamant about not telling him about the incidents, saying she knew how much it would hurt him, and she didn't want him to do anything crazy, especially at school. "After you brought her home after the incident with Ayden, she told me how hurt she was at first that you didn't rip Ayden's head off but then was relieved you hadn't."

Dominic concluded that having tiptoed down this path for over six months, following the breadcrumbs of realization Nala had been leaving for him, the time had come to talk with his daughter. He was scared. What if he screwed it up? He had no idea what to say.

His anxiety was foremost on his mind as he stood outside Nala's bedroom door trying to muster the courage to knock. He thought about Ryan's regrets about telling the Black kids they should try to fit in. When he remembered his friend's wish to go back and ask them how they'd felt, he knew what to do. He tapped. "Nala, honey? Can I come in? I have something important to ask you."

She opened the door for him. "What's up, Dad?"

"Do you have a little time to talk? I don't want to interrupt your homework or if you're busy..."

"No, it's fine. I was going to call Zoey but just to talk. Nothing urgent."

Dominic looked around, feeling awkward and not sure where to sit. Nala noticed and said, "I'll take the beanbag. You can have the chair or bed. Are you okay, Dad?"

"Yeah, honey. I'm fine. Or at least I'm getting better, I think."

"Daddy, you're scaring me. What are you talking about? Are you sick?"

"No. I'm sorry. I've just been doing a lot of thinking about things, about me and you, about things I should have thought about a long time ago but was too scared. I just want to ask you a question, but I'm not sure how, or exactly what to ask."

"Daddy, you're completely losing me."

His daughter's words clicked his thoughts into place. "That's one question I have. Am I losing you? You've been changing so much...I mean you've been growing up and, of course, that means you're changing..."

Nala tried to save him. "Dad, Mom already talked with me about puberty and sex and that stuff already."

Dominic blurted, "That's not what I mean. God no."

Nala gave him one of the looks she saved for his worst lame jokes.

"Honey, it just seems like this year you've been thinking a lot about who you are, who you want to be...and you've been trying to share that with me, and I haven't been listening very good." Dominic looked at his daughter, maybe harder and deeper than he'd done since she was a baby.

"Do you remember last fall in the truck, when you told me you were Black?" Nala crossed her arms across her chest and nodded.

"You showed me your hands, wanting me to understand you were someone even before Mom and me found you. I think that's what you wanted me to get. But I didn't get it. I didn't help you. Instead of asking what you meant, I said something stupid like you were also half-white, and I'd love you if you were purple. That must have sounded like I was saying that being half white or purple was better than Black. I'm sorry for that."

Nala uncrossed her arms. "That's okay, Daddy."

"It's not. I think I was trying to protect you, or more likely maybe myself, because I'm scared of how hard that might become. Instead of telling you how *I saw you* or thought you should be, I should have asked you how *you* see you. I should have been listening not talking. I'm sorry. And I'm ready to listen. I couldn't bear to lose you."

He moved from the chair and sat on the floor, leaning against the wall by his daughter. When he settled, Nala said, "You know something funny? Or at least now it seems funny. The first person to ask me how I saw myself, what I was feeling about being Black, was Ayden. But I sure wasn't ready to listen either. I tried to knock his head off."

They looked at each other. She scooted over so he could sit with her on the beanbag. The added weight shifted the stuffing bringing them closer together. Dominic asked, "Has he sent you any more cards?"

"You know Dad, I was wrong about him. There's a lot more to that kid than I saw or knew."

"You got all that from his card?"

"Yes and no. The card was as lame as some of your jokes."

"Ouch!" Dominic shifted his shoulder to bump Nala's. "You're going to hurt my feelings."

Nala bumped him back. "It was peanut butter and jelly saying they should stick together."

"Okay, I admit that is a bit lame," Dominic said.

"But," Nala said, "it was so sweet. I told him that the next day and promised I'd keep the card a secret. I also told him I didn't care if other kids knew."

Dominic put his arm around his daughter. He played his fingers through her braids. "I'm so proud to be your father." He kissed her hair.

"Mom told me you did that before you adopted me."

"Did what?"

"Kissed my hair."

"I did."

"Would you do it again?"

"In a heartbeat," and he did.

"I mean adopt me?"

Dominic shifted putting his nose against hers. Their faces blended into one. "In *less* than a heartbeat."

Nala leaned her head on her dad's shoulder. "Do you think you would have adopted me if Lang was with me... if he hadn't died? Would that have caused you and Mom to adopt some other little girl?"

Dominic's response came as naturally as his next breath. "I know Mom and I would never have split you two up. We hadn't ever talked about two kids. But I know for sure after you'd wobbled over to us, and I picked you up, I wasn't going to put you down. We would have adopted you both. If we didn't that would have been the biggest mistake of our lives." He sat, only aware of his daughter's head on his shoulder, always wanting it to be there for her.

"Do you still think about your brother?" he asked. "I remember being surprised when you wondered about Allan Sparks meeting him in heaven."

Nala lifted her head. She leaned forward and watched her fingers fidget with each other. "Would it sound crazy, Dad, if I said I sometimes pretended to talk with him?"

Dominic softly ran his fingernails back and forth, left-right, up-down on Nala's back. "No, honey. It's not crazy. I think everyone sometimes talks to someone they miss. I think it's the brain's way of keeping them near, of sorting through things. Can I ask... is it easier to talk with Lang sometimes than with Mom or me?"

"I call him Langston now that we're older and after I learned about Langston Hughes."

"The poet you asked me about? The *Raisin in the Sun*, guy?"

"Yeah." Nala's face lit up and she turned to look at his face. "Daddy, it made me feel so good you knew about him. I don't know why, but it just did."

"Well, I must have heard something about him in school sometime. Though there wasn't a Black History week or month back then. Some teacher must have read one of his poems, I guess. Anyhow, I'm very glad it stuck in my noggin so I could make you feel good." He paused slightly. "What do you talk with Langston about?"

"Just about being Black," she said.

"Well, that makes sense. I sure wouldn't be any good talking about that."

Nala's face turned thoughtful. "You don't have to talk about it, Daddy. Listening is enough. Do you remember, in *The Lion King*, how Nala was there for Simba when he finally came back after running away?"

"How could I forget? We must have watched it a hundred times. I miss those days."

"Well, that's you, and that's Mom. I know you'll always be here for me because I'm your daughter. And I'll always be here for you because I know that, even if I was purple, you'd love me, and I love you. So, don't be scared anymore. No matter who else I am or become, I'll always be Nala Samilton."

Nala brushed a tear from beneath her father's eye. "I love you, Daddy." She kissed his cheek and hopped off the beanbag. "I promised I'd call Zoey before bed. But first, can you do me one favor?"

"Of course," he said, rolling to get up off the bag and realizing he wasn't getting any younger.

Nala asked, "Could we get the Sidney Poitier, *Raisin in the Sun* video this weekend and watch it together?"

"Are you sure? I thought you wanted to watch it with Zoey?"

"I changed my mind."

"Nala. Nothing would give me more pleasure. I'll call and put it on hold." He kissed her head. "Good night, Nala. I love you."

He closed the door behind him, realizing how much his daughter had taught him about holding and working through the conflicting and seemingly opposite things that live in our hearts at the same time. There was a feeling of wonder in it. He whispered, "Thank you," to his daughter, both the Nala and the Samilton parts of her, for sharing it with him.

But he also knew there was useful, practical knowledge to be taken from what she'd taught him. That was his area of strength. That was what he'd now know how to use to support her on her journey. He walked toward the living room to be with Kate. He stopped for a glass of water. He held it up to the light and decided half-full may just be the perfect amount. It wasn't up to him to decide if it needed to be topped off or drained.

73

Shortly after arriving in Edenton nearly two years ago, Ryan had decided to read some John Steinbeck novels. Earlier on their first visit before they'd married, Lisa had pointed out the high school's odd spelling of the name, explaining that although pronounced the same, the John Stienboek for whom the school was named was not the famous John Steinbeck. Until then, Ryan had assumed the school was named for the author, as did his friends and parents back home when he told them where he'd been hired.

Ryan was a reader but tended to biographies and histories. Lisa had been the fiction reader. She eclectically jumped from mysteries to romance, from light summer reads to literary works, rapidly devouring them almost as if she were hunting for something. She'd read Steinbeck, saying she'd taken great perverse pleasure in reading the fiction created by the man for whom her school was NOT named.

Ryan remembered *Of Mice and Men* from back in high school, or maybe it was early college. He'd never forgotten the poignant, tragic friendship between the two characters, Lenny and George. He began his quest by rereading it. Being short, he soon moved on to Steinbeck's most celebrated work, *The Grapes of Wrath.* Having taught units on the Depression and Dust Bowl era, he found the mix of characters and history well-written and interesting.

Last July, he'd read *East of Eden*. He'd read it slowly, rationing out the pages to make it last. On one hand, the slow-paced multi-generational scope of the book had been a balm against the insistent immediacy of his external and internal worlds. The characters, and the way the author pitted their natures and identities against themselves and each other, felt truer and more intimate than most histories or biographies he'd ever read.

However, on the other hand, – and Ryan knew this at the time – reading and rereading the scenes describing the relationship between Adam Trask and Cathy Ames was his version of the self-inflicted razor cuts some teens used to distract themselves from the perpetual psychological pain consuming them. Now, ten months later, alone in his office and the late April setting sun still playing in his window, Ryan found those scenes a good place to start the conversation.

He inserted the key and turned it. Working his hand down to the bottom of the drawer, he felt the frame. He hesitated, listening to assure himself the office was empty before disinterring the photo from its exile and gently placing it on his desk facing him. He rolled his chair back to a respectful and safe distance.

"Do you remember, Lisa… the scene when Adam locked Cathy in the bedroom to keep her from leaving him? She goes nuts for a bit, and then she convinces him to open the door by swearing she's come to her senses and loves him and of course, she'll stay. Do you remember that? When he unlocks the door, she shoots him.

"That's how it felt. For a long time. I think, in a mixed-up way, we lived that scene. You said you'd figured it out. Would finally explain it all to me, called for a celebration, for ice cream. Of course, I opened the door. Just like Adam did. Like him, I so much needed to believe you, to hear you say you were going to stay, and things were going to turn around, and we could be…I don't know, our real selves again?

"Of course, that's where it went off-script because you got shot

instead of me. In the book, it takes Adam a long time to recover, but with help, he eventually learns and accepts who Cathy is, and she loses her power over him."

Ryan stopped to examine what he'd just said to see if his version felt like the truth. More than anything, he needed it to be true if it was going to be of any help. When he decided it felt right and didn't hold hints of blame or anger, he slid his chair a little closer so he could see Lisa's face as clearly as he had that day he'd closed her eyes.

"Do you also remember how Steinbeck included details about the major characters?" He focused intently on her face until he imagined she'd nodded in agreement.

"All that slow, detailed background let us understand why they behaved the way they did. But for some reason, Steinbeck didn't do that for Cathy. I've thought about that ever since I finished the book. I mean, she's at the center of so much of Adam's behavior... and then his sons. Was I the only one who wanted to know what made Cathy, Cathy?

"Of course, you know that's why I'm here. I lacked the courage and imagination to accept without knowing and understanding. I had to know what Steinbeck never gave us. I needed the detailed background, or I wouldn't find or give forgiveness – wouldn't get to where that part of you lost its power over me. And like Adam Trask, I needed to relearn to accept and trust others before I could accept and forgive myself."

Ryan stood and gently picked up the photograph of his wife and kissed it. With his foot, he closed the bottom drawer where it had lain face down for all this time. He dropped the key on his desk. There was no further need to lock the drawer.

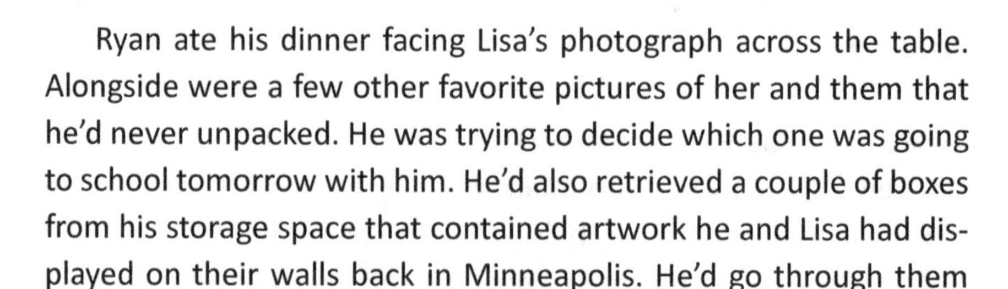

Ryan ate his dinner facing Lisa's photograph across the table. Alongside were a few other favorite pictures of her and them that he'd never unpacked. He was trying to decide which one was going to school tomorrow with him. He'd also retrieved a couple of boxes from his storage space that contained artwork he and Lisa had displayed on their walls back in Minneapolis. He'd go through them this weekend and hang up a few around the apartment.

His plate was empty. He stretched his feet out and again focused on the image he'd been hiding from for too long.

Brown, highlighted shoulder-length hair combed but windblown. One fashionable black boot casually resting on the opposite knee, ever-so-slightly inclined in a high-backed booth in the ice cream parlor on the edge of the University of Minnesota campus. When first dating, it had been their favorite hang-out on Saturdays after an afternoon of first sex and eventually lovemaking. It was only a couple of blocks from his apartment back then, a few miles from the high school where he had taught and then became an assistant principal.

Lisa's deep red blouse – top button open, highlighting a gold choker against summer tan – and snug jeans emphasized her allure and body and tweaked Ryan's pain and passion. Her sunglasses lay beside her, next to her open bag out of which stuck the cell phone that for so long had haunted him.

Where is that phone? He knew it was here, somewhere in his new life. He'd just been through the basement storage space. He couldn't remember seeing anything labeled to suggest it held the phone. He recalled a box of miscellaneous electronic detritus, much of it obsolete, in the back corner of his closet.

His focus went back to the photo, to her hair and sunglasses, the bag, her clothing, and posture. Each was a striking contrast against the rigid straight whiteness of the wooden enclosure where she sat. It was what made him take the photo. But her eyes were what now made him sit up and lean in closer. Had he forgotten? As he'd snapped the picture, they'd moved from him and the camera toward the phone that had just buzzed, signaling an incoming text.

When she saw the message, her eyes, her entire face, flashed anger. But only for a brief second before a sense of confidence and self-assurance seemed to shine from within. In that moment, Ryan now recalled thinking she was more beautiful than he could ever remember.

She smiled at him and said, "Love, will you please order the sundaes? It will only take a minute to handle this. Then we can talk."

He'd gotten in line to order very aware she'd called him "Love" for the first time in months. She'd slid out of the booth and stepped through the door outside. He'd assumed she was going to "handle this" by calling the person. That was when he, and everyone else, heard three loud pops and screeching tires, and he raced out the door after her.

The remembered sounds of her phone buzzing, the gunshots, screams, and sirens took a full minute to fade back into the past. He got up and put his plate and silverware in the sink and decided to check that electronics box. Digging it out, he sat on the bed, their bed. Tangled among what seemed a lifetime of cords, chargers, and adaptors, he found her phone. He rummaged for a charger that fit and plugged it into his nightstand to charge.

After an hour of restless channel surfing, Ryan brushed his teeth and crawled into bed. For a few minutes he sat, eyes closed, taking deep breaths to calm himself until he was ready. Lifting the phone he found, like himself, it had enough life pumped back into it to allow him to check her text messages.

Douglas Rupert

You can't just walk away. Need you soon! When?

Lisa Davvis

Never! Having ice cream with the only Love I need.
Don't contact again! Or wife and school board will learn all.

74

"Come on, Quant. You used to be the fastest kid on the playground when we were kids. We told Coach about you, and he said we should ask you. You'd be good. We need a sprinter and some new blood on the relay."

Ayden found the offer hard to balance against his father's voice telling him he sucked in sports. There was also his fear of being set up, the butt of a joke. The hard lessons learned from his friendship with Allan Sparks had deep roots. He harbored no doubt about being fast. He'd always been quick and agile. Knowing his dad was on the road helped him decide. "Let me talk to my mom about getting picked up and stuff."

"Okay but tell her we need you." The two juniors walked off toward class, and Ayden got in the freshman lunch line. Tacos, sliced pears, and chocolate milk. He stood with his tray looking around until he spotted Steven and a couple of other guys.

He sat opposite them and decided not to mention the track discussion. The guys were talking video games and the Brewers' early season win streak when Nala and Zoey joined some other girls sitting on the other half of the long table. Zoey interrupted the boys by asking, "Hey Ayden. What did those older guys want?"

His friends stopped talking to hear the answer. "Nothing."

Nala said, "We could hear they wanted you to do something."

He didn't like being put on the spot or being spied on. He knew Zoey kind of kept watch over him in science class and wasn't just being nosy. Nala, too, had become much friendlier since that night at the culvert. She'd thanked him for the "nice card" and said they could be friends. They'd talked some on the bus sometimes. She'd even encouraged him to take a chance and ask Lilly to the movies or something. He was still working up to that, but he'd come to accept he could trust these two girls. They wouldn't set him up.

"They wanted me to join the track team," Ayden admitted.

Steven jumped in enthusiastically. "You should do it, dude. You're probably the fastest guy in school." Nala and Zoey encouraged him too, all the while a couple of their friends looked at them like they were nuts talking to these boys.

Ayden said, "I don't know. I gotta check about rides and stuff. Anyhow, it's probably a joke. I'm just a freshman."

Zoey pointed out that Nala had played with the varsity in the playoffs and would probably be on the team next year.

"I guess," Ayden said, sticking a taco in his mouth so he wouldn't have to talk anymore. When he looked up, Nala was staring at him. He stopped chewing, so he could hear over the crunching in his mouth if she said something. But she didn't.

The girls left, but the boys hung out until the bell rang. When Ayden got to his locker, Nala was waiting. "Look, Ayden," she said, coming close to putting her hand on her hip like her mom sometimes did. "You can't be scared to try or to let people see how fast you are. I almost didn't join the varsity." She paused. "Someday...maybe... I'll tell you why, but for now, I just want you to know Zoey and I think you should try. If it doesn't work out, or you get in a jam..." She saw he didn't get the reference so she added, "Remember? Your card? Peanut butter and jelly." Ayden smiled. Nala rolled her eyes and hurried to her class.

"I like your braids," Ayden hollered after her.

When Ayden got to ESL last period, he accosted Mrs. Berry as she, as usual, stood by her door. "I gotta see Mr. Davvis right away.

Can I? Please. I've got all my work done, even all the math. I can show you. And I understand it all. Please?"

"Ayden, what do you need to see Mr. Davvis about in such a hurry? You can't just barge in on him."

"It's about the track team. Some guys said the coach wants me to try out. I gotta talk to him before I ask my mom. Please?"

"What guys?" Mrs. Berry asked.

"Some track guys. They're juniors and know I'm fast."

"Come in and set out your math for me to check. I'll call and see if Mr. Davvis is in his office."

Sharon Edmonds smiled at Ayden and told him he could go on back to Mr. Davvis' office. He stood at his principal's doorway, feeling excited but not nervous. Ayden realized it was the opposite of how he usually felt when he talked with his dad. He watched Mr. Davvis rapidly typing for several seconds before he looked up and saw him.

"Mr. Quant. Come on in. Mrs. Berry said you wanted to talk to me about the track team. What's up?"

The boy walked in, taking his usual seat in the swivel chair at the table. Ryan had assumed Ayden would just ask a quick question while standing. But when the boy came in and sat, Ryan glanced at the email he was writing, deciding it would have to wait. He moved to one of the blue chairs. Ayden's hands were on the edges of the table. Ryan anticipated the boy would begin to push and pull to swivel the chair. "So, what's up about track?"

Ayden removed his hands from the table. He sat erect, putting his hands under his thighs and then leaning forward toward Ryan. "She likes you, doesn't she?"

"What are you talking about, Ayden? Mrs. Berry?"

"No," Ayden tilted his head in the direction of the front office. "Her. Mrs. Edmonds. I saw her looking at you when you were up by her one day when I was coming to the office. She looked like she liked you."

A couple of weeks ago, Ryan knew the boy's comments would have set off alarm bells. He was pleased that now they only confused him. "You saw Mrs. Edmonds look at me and decided she liked me? Ayden, we work together. We're friends. I like her too. I like all the people I work with. Besides, Mrs. Edmonds smiles at everybody."

"Yeah, I know. She even smiled at me. But I know she likes you because she looked at you that time like ..." He paused.

Ryan knew he should just move the conversation to whatever Ayden had come to ask about the track team. But as had happened at other times, he found himself curious and intrigued by what might come out of the boy's mouth. Fact or fiction, it often made him ponder. So, instead, he found himself asking, "Like what?"

"Like – you gotta promise not to tell..."

Ryan decided the odds of Ayden saying something he couldn't keep secret were minuscule, so he nodded his head.

"Like when I sometimes see Lilly when she's doing her work in class."

"Lilly McKnight?" Ryan clarified.

"Nala says I should ask her out."

Ryan had to smile, but he decided it was time to talk track. "Ayden, you wanted to ask me about track? What was on your mind?"

"Do you think I should... you know, ask her out? I mean, I think she likes me. How am I supposed to know?"

"Believe me, Ayden, I'm *really* not the best person to answer that question. Why don't you ask your mother?"

"What if she says yes?" Ayden persisted.

Ryan smiled. "Ayden, if she says yes, then you go out. If you like each other, maybe you'll go out again until you each learn what the other person is like. And if it doesn't work out, then you have to accept that and be grateful for the time you had together and move on."

Ayden thought for a few seconds before nodding and saying, "I guess. Mom said I should be careful."

"That's probably good advice too."

That apparently was enough information because Ayden moved on and asked about joining the track team. Ryan explained and answered his questions. He gave him a parental permission form and told him to have his mother call if she had questions. He checked Ayden's current grades and explained he had to keep them up and said that he was confident Ayden would do that.

Ayden thanked him and was about to head back to Mrs. Berry's room when he stopped and turned. "One more thing, Mr. Davvis."

Ryan had moved back to finish his email. He wanted to sigh but didn't. "What is it, Ayden?"

"You remember the tee shirt with the saying that got me in trouble?"

Ryan said, "Ayden we can talk about that another time. You've got to get back to class before dismissal, and I've got to finish my work."

"Okay, but I just have to tell you I kind of lied about that. The book, and using the famous sayings, *was* my idea, but that shirt... my dad made that one and gave it to me. I'm sorry I lied about it." He again turned to leave.

Ryan said, "Ayden, thank you for telling me." He considered and then reconsidered the thought that came to him before deciding to go with his gut feeling. "Do you remember the quote that was on that shirt?"

"Yeah," Ayen said.

Ryan was relieved he wouldn't have to remind the boy. "Well, I want you to know that I am very glad *you* were the quickest one."

Ayden slowly reread the quote back to himself in his mind. When he was done, his smile spread from his eyes to his lips and then his entire countenance. Ayden Quant's smile reminded Ryan, for the first time in a very long time, why he had become a teacher and a principal.

"Thanks, Mr. D."

"No...Thank you, Ayden."

The boy was still smiling when he said goodbye to Mrs. Edmonds, and it was still there when he got back to Mrs. Berry's room. The boy's smile made both women glad they worked at John Stienboek High School.

danpowerswrites.com

ACKNOWLEDGMENTS

There are many I need and wish to thank for getting me to the finish line with *Stienboek*. Often their kind act of asking about the book kept me motivated and encouraged. To all of you, I offer my gratitude.

Others graciously shared their experience and knowledge so that I could make *Stienboek* as accurate and realistic as a work of fiction can be. Thank you.

Ann Smejkal, Steve Bousley, Dan Viste,
Randy Watermolen, Brenda Shimon

Over the long course of writing a novel, there are those without whom an author would not be able to create and write to whatever ability he or she possesses. These generous folks read, critiqued, edited, and encouraged me along the way. They freely offered their time, thoughts, advice, and friendship. Their efforts gave me the all-important gift of confidence to try.

Thomas Davis, Sally Collins, Linda Thompson
Jim Black, Joan Mosgaller, Scott Powers
David Natwick, Ann Heyse, Terie Johnson,
Robert Davies, Marge Grutzmacher

Printed in the USA
CPSIA information can be obtained
at www.ICGtesting.com
JSHW081718200924
70063JS00003B/7